G000123472

HUNTER SHEA

FAITHLESS

This is a **FLAME TREE PRESS** book

Text copyright © 2021 Hunter Shea

FLAME TREE PRESS
6 Melbray Mews, London, SW6 3NS, UK
flametreepress.com

US sales, distribution and warehouse:
Simon & Schuster
simonandschuster.biz

UK distribution and warehouse:
Marston Book Services Ltd
marston.co.uk

Thanks to the Flame Tree Press team, including:
Taylor Bentley, Frances Bodiam, Federica Ciaravella, Don D'Auria,
Chris Herbert, Josie Karani, Molly Rosevear, Mike Spender,
Cat Taylor, Maria Tissot, Nick Wells, Gillian Whitaker.

The cover is created by Flame Tree Studio with
thanks to Nik Keevil and Shutterstock.com.
The font families used are Avenir and Bembo.

Flame Tree Press is an imprint of Flame Tree Publishing Ltd
flametreepublishing.com

A copy of the CIP data for this book is available from the British Library
and the Library of Congress.

HB ISBN: 978-1-78758-623-9
US PB ISBN: 978-1-78758-621-5
ebook ISBN: 978-1-78758-624-6

Printed and bound in Great Britain by Clays Ltd, Elcograf S.p.A.

HUNTER SHEA

FAITHLESS

FLAME TREE PRESS
London & New York

For John Wilson and Anthony Ventarola.
Brothers for life.

CHAPTER ONE

Father Raul Figeuroa hated driving in the rain. He'd been a late bloomer when it came to driving because his family had been too poor to afford a car. Not even attempting to get a license until he'd graduated college, Raul failed his road test three times before someone took pity and gave him a barely passing grade. Parallel parking was still a mystery to him these ten-plus years later and adverse road conditions gave him palpitations.

Jesus, I wish you could take the wheel.

His wipers could barely keep the windshield clear as the downpour mired his vision, great whorls of rain distorting the road and cars around him. They were on the highest setting, their hyper *whump-whump* both hypnotic and alarming. Any moment, he expected them to simply fly off the wiper bar. Headlights and brake lights wavered, the double yellow line in the road more a theory than verifiable fact.

He should just pull over and wait it out. How long could it possibly come down like this? This wasn't the time of Noah. The deluge would fall far short of forty days and forty nights. The way the storms had been rolling in and out lately, it would more likely be forty minutes, tops.

The rosary beads he'd wrapped around his rearview mirror clacked together when he hit an unseen pothole. The wheel worked against him, wanting to turn the car into a sharp right. The priest tightened his grip and forced the car to remain straight.

There was a flash of twin red lights several car lengths ahead of him. Father Figeuroa tapped the brakes, resisting the impulse to mash the pedal down. The last thing he wanted was a spinout.

His rear tires slid a bit to the left, but the car mercifully corrected itself. What he hadn't seen was the glowing red orb of the stoplight overhead. He managed to settle the car to a stop and said a quick Hail Mary under his breath.

"Hail Mary, full of grace, the Lord is with thee. Blessed art thou amongst women, and blessed is the fruit of thy womb, Jesus. Holy Mary, Mother of God, pray for us sinners, now and at the hour of our death. Amen." He cast his eyes to the wet sky. "I really could use a break in the rain. Hate to say it, but this weather sucks."

After that, he checked his map on his phone. Still six and a half miles to go. He'd needed the map to find his way around a traffic jam a few miles back. He'd kept it on to alert him to anything that might further delay his drive home. Bella, his wife, said she was going to make his favorite tonight – meatloaf and garlic-and-rosemary mashed potatoes with a side of parmesan green beans. She hinted at making biscuits from scratch. His mouth watered at the thought.

Staring at the glowing map, wishing he could teleport home, he missed seeing the light turn green. The bellowing horns behind him made his head snap up, hands tightening on the wheel.

"For Pete's sake," he said, eyeing the cars in his rearview mirror. "Hold your fucking horses."

People were always shocked when they heard him curse, forgetting that he was a man as much as an Episcopalian man of the cloth. In fact, when his kids weren't around, he could, when he was in an exceptionally good or bad mood, sound more like a longshoreman than a pastor. It wasn't as if he had a squeaky-clean history. He'd done as Billy Joel had once sung (Billy being a favorite of his grandmother's) – he'd laughed with the sinners. Now he cried with the saints.

Well, Lizzy and Abel weren't in the back seat now, and he was most certainly in a bad mood. The reins were off.

He hit the gas and gave the car behind him the finger. Not that they could see it in the dark and rain, but it made him feel better. If the rain hadn't been pissing down, he would have unrolled his window and lifted his arm out so the drivers behind him couldn't miss how he felt about their honking. It never failed to amuse him when someone whipped into road rage by something as simple as a raised middle finger would stop dead in their tracks the second they saw his collar.

Maybe he used his collar as an excuse to exercise his own road rage without fear of repercussion. So be it. Sooner or later, he'd come across someone who didn't give a whit and then, maybe then, he'd learn his lesson.

Rain thumped the roof of the car with greater intensity. How was that possible?

Father Figueroa's heartbeat accelerated as if it were in tandem with the steady patter of the rain on his used Outback. He swallowed dryly, realizing he'd forgotten to bring a water bottle with him for the trip. His mouth felt tacky and his stomach cramped.

You'll be home before you know it. Just take a deep breath.

He needed something to ease his mind. Another Hail Mary or an Our Father wasn't going to cut it.

"Call Bella Babe," he said aloud so the Bluetooth would dial his wife. She was most likely busy in the kitchen, but she would stop what she was doing for him. She knew more than anyone how much he despised rainy drives. The phone rang three times before she picked up. He could hear the TV on in the background, SpongeBob SquarePants cackling like the happy lunatic he was.

"You okay?" she said immediately.

"Just peachy," he replied.

"I can barely hear you over the rain."

"Hence my call."

"My poor baby. Why don't you pull over?"

Father Figueroa squinted, trying to make out if there was anywhere to stop on the side of the road. He didn't see anything remotely inviting. "I'll just have to tough it out. I'm not that far away." It sure felt it, though.

"I wish I could be there with you."

"You are...in a way. I just wanted to hear your voice. What are you up to?"

He heard her take a sip of something. He could picture her holding her favorite wineglass by the stem. She loved to have a glass or two of merlot when she cooked. "Just sautéing the green beans. Everything else is ready and keeping warm."

"By any chance, are there warm biscuits?"

Bella giggled. "You'll have to get here to find out."

That was a yes. She wouldn't get his hopes up just to let him down. He loved her biscuits more than just about anything in the world.

A car whizzed by his left, startling him. He nearly lost control of the wheel. "Shit!"

"Raul, what happened?"

"Am I on speakerphone?" His heart thumped in the middle of his throat. His spine felt as if it had been flash frozen in liquid nitrogen.

"No."

"Some asshat is driving like a maniac. He's zigzagging between the cars and has to be going at least thirty miles an hour over the speed limit. He's going to get someone killed, if not himself. And I'm not in the mood to give someone unction."

"Just stay calm. You're fine."

He took a deep breath. The windshield wipers battled the lashing downpour. Thoughts of the overtaxed wiper motor burning out while he was in the middle of the road made his stomach acids curdle. Fresh-baked biscuits no longer sounded so delicious.

"I know, I know," he said through clenched teeth.

Bella laughed softly. "You're such a drama queen. There are old people with cataracts driving right now who are calmer than you."

"Very funny." He knew she wasn't making fun of him. Bella was an expert at quelling his anxiety, even if it came to making light of the situation with just the right turn of phrase. "They don't care because they can't see anyway. It's just another night for them."

"Next time you get called to St. Luke's for a prayer meeting, I'll drive," Bella said. "Especially if there's rain in the forecast."

St. Luke's wasn't even his parish. It was three towns away and their current priest, Jim McMahon, was in the hospital after his appendix had burst. He'd gone septic and barely pulled through. The doctors expected him to be in the hospital for another two to three weeks. When they'd asked Raul to help cover some of the church's activities, he was quick to jump in. Jim was a friend and Raul would do whatever he could to keep things status quo until he was well enough to return to his regular duties.

"What are the kids up to?" he asked Bella to help take his mind off things.

"Abel got an A on his English essay."

Abel shouted from the other room, "Ms. Palmer posted it on the board outside class."

Raul had helped him with the essay on Harriet Tubman. Abel had worked hard on it and deserved the A. Getting an essay tacked to the brag board in the hallway was the highest praise a fourth-grader could receive.

"Way to go, buddy," Raul said, hoping he was loud enough to be heard.

"Now you're on speakerphone," Bella said. "Lizzy, why don't you tell Daddy what happened in school today?"

Lizzy, their precocious second-grader, wasn't as enthusiastic about school as her older brother. She faked being sick often so she could stay home or get sent home. She and Bella were attached at the hip and three years of school had barely put a dent in the invisible cord that bound them to one another.

"I fell on the playground and cut my knee," Lizzy said over the nasally sound of Squidward yelling at SpongeBob.

Raul slowed down for another red light. He'd caught every red light on the drive. Not a single green light to be found. "I'm so sorry. Is your knee all right?"

"I went to the school nurse and she cleaned it and put a bandage on it. The cleaning part hurt. But guess what?"

"What?" Some of the tension bled away as he talked to his little angel.

"I told the nurse I wanted to go back to class and not home."

"Wow. What a big girl. I'm so proud of you." Those weren't just words. He was proud and impressed. An accident would normally be followed by wailing for her mommy.

"Mrs. Kendicott even gave me a sticker. I'll show you when you get home."

"I can't wait to see it."

"Mommy and Daddy are so proud of you both," Bella said.

Raul was about to add to the praise when a car going in the opposite direction hit a deep puddle of rainwater, sending an explosive wave over the divider. He drove right into it. Gallons of water slammed into the windshield with a sickening *whump*. Raul couldn't see a thing.

"Oh crap!" he shouted.

Driving blind for a second or two, he had to hit the brakes just in case the car ahead of him was slowing down for a light. His eyes flicked to the rearview mirror and the incoming white lights of the car behind him.

"Raul?" Bella's worried voice filled the car.

The wipers did their magic and he could mercifully see in front of him again. He toed the gas pedal to keep from getting rammed from behind. Raul's eyes flicked to the rearview mirror. He didn't see the virtual lake in front of him. Other cars were skirting around it. He plowed right through it. Water exploded from beneath the chassis and washed over the hood and windshield.

As soon as he got to the other side of the pool of water, his car sputtered and died. The Subaru rocked from side to side as cars sped past him. The Bluetooth cut out and Raul had to put his phone on speaker.

"The car just died," he said.

"What? How?"

What he wanted to do was punch the dashboard. Instead, he keyed the ignition. Nothing. Not a single sound. "I drove through a puddle in the road that came up to the car's doors. I think I flooded the engine."

"The news just gave a warning about flash floods."

"Well, I can confirm it."

He turned the key again. The dashboard lights flickered.

"Do you want me to call Triple A?" Bella asked.

Raul tapped the back of his head against the headrest with his eyes closed. How could he have been so stupid? He should have been paying more attention to what was in front of him. If he hadn't been so wound up and freaked out, he might have avoided it. When he was a young wildling on the streets, he'd been utterly fearless. Then again, he'd had nothing to lose and the shield of invincibility known as youth. Teen Raul would slap adult Raul silly for acting like such a wuss.

"I'll wait a bit. Let everything dry out and try again." Unless the water got sucked up through his tailpipe. Then the car might be dead for good. That was going to be a problem. It wasn't as if the coffers were overflowing. Their savings account needed a miracle of its own.

"At least let me call Bill to come and meet you. If the car won't start, he can drive you home while the car gets a tow."

Bill Samson was the church's Mr. Fix It. He was a retired cop who was also an experienced carpenter. The man was made of iron and seemingly never slept. He spent more time keeping the church, parish house, and grounds in pristine shape than his own home. A distress call from Bella would have him running out the door.

"No, let Bill stay home and dry. He just did all that work in the basement the past few days. Besides, the Yankees are playing now. I'm sure he's had a beer or two."

Not that two beers would put a dent in the older man's system. Raul had watched him drink a twelve-pack at their spring parish picnic and still win at horseshoes and lead the clean-up crew.

Bella was quiet. SpongeBob was replaced by a commercial for a new video game. Abel chatted with Lizzy. Raul couldn't make out what they were saying, but he could tell they were getting along. That wasn't always the case, especially when he was running late and they were getting hangry.

Water splashed against the side windows when a car passed too close for comfort. He wondered if he should wait outside, just to be safe. The downside was that he would be soaked to his underwear in seconds and he'd have to tuck his phone away to keep it from getting ruined. That meant he wouldn't be able to eavesdrop on the comforting sounds of his family. Heaven on earth was wherever Bella and the children were at that moment. He felt as far from heaven now as Judas must have felt when he betrayed Jesus.

"So, tell me more about those biscuits," he said. His hand was on the door handle. Another plume of water dashed against the car. Better to be safe than hurt or worse and never be with his family.

"You have a one-track mind. I never confirmed there would be biscuits. Though they might be hard as rocks – if they have indeed been baked – by the time you get home."

Rain drummed on the roof of the car. "Look," Raul said, "I think I have to leave the car for now. Between the crazy drivers, dark, and rain, I'm a sitting duck in here. I'll call you when I get back in and try to start it again."

"Good idea. We want you in one piece, you know. Do you have an umbrella?"

"Of course not. I left it in the foyer closet."

"For someone who spends a lot of time thinking about and preparing for the afterlife, you don't plan that far ahead in this one." From the slight echo, it sounded as if she were chuckling into her wineglass.

"You're a riot tonight," he replied, smiling, wishing he had a glass of his own and was close enough to smell the sweet wine on Bella's breath.

"I have my—"

The sound of breaking glass filled the Subaru.

"Bella? What broke?"

Lizzy and Abel screamed.

"It's okay. It's okay," Bella said. Her voice sounded distant. She must have dropped the phone and run to the living room.

"Bella!" Raul couldn't imagine what had crashed to make such a racket. He prayed no one was hurt.

As Bella was consoling the children, something hammered at – what? – the door, the walls? Every hair on Raul's arms stood on end. He shouted Bella's name over and over, hoping she'd hear him and pick up. What was going on in his home?

Wood shattered and there was a rush of heavy footsteps.

Bella yelled, "No!"

Lizzy shrieked, "Mommy! Mommy!"

Abel shouted, "Who are they?"

They? Who had just come literally crashing into Raul's house?

"Run! Bella, take the kids and run!" he implored at the top of his lungs.

Bella started to scream something, but it was stopped in an instant, as if someone had clamped a hand over her mouth. Lizzy howled in absolute terror. Whoever was in the house wasn't speaking, not even so much as making a grunt. But Raul heard them stomping on the hardwood floors with sickening clarity. It was the staccato of thick-soled work boots on bare wood.

"Don't you dare touch them!" Bella suddenly blurted. It was instantly followed by what sounded like a fist hitting into flesh.

Raul's world started to slip out from under his feet. He had to grab the steering wheel to ground himself. He looked down at the illuminated map. Just a little over five miles between here and his house.

He left the keys in the car and slipped out into the rain, running home. Raul ran right into traffic, heedless of the cars coming his way. Somehow, he made it to the shoulder and scrambled up the slight mossy incline. He jumped over a row of bushes and landed on a residential street. Now on the sidewalk, he ran as fast as he could, crying out for his wife and children.

All he got in return was their peals of terror through the phone's tiny speaker.

There was no way he was going to make it without his heart bursting.

A sobbing Bella cried, "Please, not my babies!"

"Mom!" Abel yelped.

Bella screamed. There was an odd sound Raul couldn't place. Next, he heard wet choking and Lizzy crying, "Abel! Abel!"

Raul sprinted, his dress shoes clapping the wet pavement. His legs and chest already burned. It had been a long time since he'd taken a slow jog, much less sprinted.

What's happening to my family? Please, dear God, make it stop!

Bella shouted something incoherent yet full of pain and despair. What followed was a series of a high-pitched yowls from his daughter, and then there was silence.

"Bella? Lizzy? Abel?"

The other end of the line had gone eerily silent. It was as if the people in his house, savaging his family, had simply disappeared.

Father Raul Figeuroa found it hard to see as he ran. Tears blurred his vision and his chest hurt. It felt as if someone were driving a knife into the center of his breastbone.

No matter. He kept running, praying to God that his family would be alive when he arrived home.

CHAPTER TWO

The rain went from a downpour to a trickle, and then to a light mist. It had stopped completely by the time Raul was a block from his street. His legs and lungs had not worked their best, his palpitating heart not making the sprint any easier. It had taken him far longer than he'd wanted.

He saw the red-and-white strobe of emergency lights playing against the row of houses as he turned the corner. The narrow street was clogged with patrol cars and people. Their dark shapes loitered about, pressing close to Raul's home.

In that moment, his knees nearly collapsed.

What saved him from falling on his face was a jolt of adrenaline that gave him a final push to join the throng of onlookers. As he tried to press his way through, a woman tapped his shoulder and said, "Father Figeuroa, what happened?"

Speech was beyond his capability at the moment. He brushed past her, wedging himself between two large men. They were brothers who lived across the street. One of them barked, "Hey, calm the hell down." His face, full of anger at first, softened when he saw it was Raul. "Is your family in there?" he asked.

Raul wanted to say yes, wanted to at least nod. His brain misfired, unable to respond. But his eyes shimmered with tears and terror.

The man – George was his name, yes, George – slapped his brother, Eugene, on the arm and said, "We gotta get him through."

George took hold of Raul's arm and pulled him along. The mountainous men barreled through the crowd with ease. Raul remembered they had both played football in college, only adding more girth as they got older. When they came to the pair of police officers facing the crowd, keeping them back as best they could, Eugene said, "That's Father Figeuroa's house." He nodded at Raul.

"I'm sorry, we can't allow anyone inside."

Raul's tongue unstuck from the roof of his mouth. "My…my… family," he sputtered.

The cop flashed him a look of pity. "It's better you don't go in there."

"I need to see them."

It's better you don't go in there. That single sentence was enough to shatter Raul's soul.

He attempted to push past the cop. The man put his arm out and kept Raul from proceeding. "Sir, it's important you stay right here. I'll call my sergeant."

George bristled. "He's not *sir*. It's *Father*. And you have to let him through."

The other officer, sensing something was up, moved closer.

Raul stared at his open door, his mind imagining a host of horrors waiting for him inside.

"Bella!" he shouted, hoping with all his heart she was alive and could hear him. Any second, she would come rushing out to him, Abel and Lizzy right behind her. "Bella!"

A man in a suit came out of the house, his face drawn and pale. He looked into the night sky, taking deep breaths.

"That's it," George said. He and Eugene towered over the cops, bumping them with their chests. The police made a vain attempt to shove the brothers back. George nearly nudged one of the cops onto his ass. The man staggered back, hand flailing for his gun and coming up short. He stumbled until his back hit the chest-high shrubs that Raul had planted years ago as a living privacy fence.

George turned and said to Raul, "Go. Go!"

Raul didn't realize he was running until he hit the top of the stairs. The man in the suit saw him and said, "It's too late for last rites, Father. You don't want to go in there. Trust me." He touched the badge that hung around his neck as if he were rubbing a talisman that could make it all go away.

Everything went numb. Someone bumped into Raul as they made their way out of his house. He didn't feel it, only sensed a shifting of his vision as he turned slightly. Walking into the house was akin to floating on air, pulled by an unseen current.

Looking down, he saw an array of muddy footprints. They were wide treads. Nothing like what his wife and children would leave behind if they tromped through the house.

The smell hit him first. He'd once been called to a horrific car accident where a delivery truck had struck a car of teenagers on their way to school. The truck had folded the car in half, trapping the students — three boys and two girls. The truck driver hadn't been wearing his seat belt and his head was embedded in the cracked windshield. He'd miraculously not only remained conscious, but lucid, asking for a priest. The accident had happened just a couple of blocks from the church, and a neighbor had hurried to get Raul.

What he thought of now was not that surreal conversation he'd had with the truck driver who knew he was going to die. It was the overwhelming stench of blood and exposed organs that came from the car of teens, all five of them having burst open from the impact. That fetor had haunted him for years. He'd asked the Lord to spare him from ever experiencing anything like it for the rest of his days.

This moment was proof that God hadn't heeded his plea.

Blood was everywhere.

The blood of his family.

Lizzy was facedown on the floor, her pale, thin arms outstretched as if she had tried to crawl out of the room, out of the house for help. Her white shirt, the one she loved with galloping ponies on the front and back, was now crimson and ragged from stab wounds. Raul felt the burn of bile when his eyes lit upon the hole in the back of her skull. A twisted section of brain peeked out of the gap where no gap should be. Ever.

Someone was snapping pictures of his daughter, the flash stinging his eyes.

Raul sagged against the doorway. It felt as if he'd been deboned and rendered mute. All he could do was let the house prop him up and view the destruction of his family, of his life.

Abel was on the couch with his head tilted back, revealing the ragged slit in his throat. His blood splatter reached the ceiling. The final moments of pain and horror were still there in his graying eyes.

And, finally, there was Bella. It looked as if her body had been staged by her murderers. Her arms were outstretched, her legs crossed over one another. Her shirt had been pulled up to just below her breasts. Raul saw the massive wound in her side. A lacerated pink organ had slid halfway from the wound. Her head was ringed with holes, a penumbra of blood beneath her.

"What do you think?" a plainclothes cop said to another, staring down at Bella's body. "Ice pick?"

He must have been referring to the pits in her skull.

The other officer leaned forward, careful not to step in her blood. Raul wondered if it was still warm. "Maybe a drill? It's hard to tell."

"Hey, who are you?" someone said to Raul.

Raul looked away from Bella to the man. In answer to his question, Raul vomited, his body unleashing what felt like everything he'd ever ingested until the world went mercifully black.

CHAPTER THREE

Detective Sam Zelinski had been the lead on what the news had coined the Parish House Murders. Christ Church was suddenly the most talked about church in the country.

Over the past four weeks, in between burying his family and being hounded by reporters outside his house, on his phone, and online, Raul had spoken to Detective Zelinski daily. The cop was middle-aged with a rugged build and impossibly sad eyes. Those eyes had taken Raul aback at first. How could a man who worked homicide have eyes like that? They should have been hardened, maybe world-weary, but not twin pools of melancholy.

Contrary to his look, the detective was a bulldog. He was, if nothing else, painstakingly thorough. He and his team had interviewed everyone in the parish, past and present, their neighbors and family. The parish house and church had been swarmed by forensics like ants marching to a picnic.

With no living witnesses, they had very little to go on. The news coverage, while ghoulish and intrusive, at least kept the story alive for a couple of weeks, constantly mentioning the tip line for anyone who might have even the smallest shred of information.

Four weeks of tips but nothing to show for it.

Speculation about who the killers might be ran the gamut, from a home invasion gone bad, to disgruntled parishioners and even a potential serial killer. The wife of a Lutheran pastor had been killed in a mall parking lot a year earlier about sixty miles away. It was a stretch, linking the two, but then again, everything seemed both impossible and possible.

There were nights after speaking with Detective Zelinski when Raul wondered if it were possible that his family had been murdered by ghosts. Other than the boot prints, there was no physical evidence. There wasn't a single fingerprint, hair, or fiber left behind. The boots were determined to be a common type of work boot. Millions were sold every year.

Raul had been asked many times over if he remembered hearing anyone say something when the killers broke into the house. Thinking back to that last phone call was like asking him to ram a sword through his heart. All he heard in his head were the cries of his wife and children as they were slaughtered.

The city waited with bated breath for another, similar, senseless attack, but blessedly, none came.

For some reason, Raul's family had been targeted.

But by whom?

And why?

Raul talked in great length about his checkered past, a youth gone wild, but that was ages ago and nothing he had done could lead to this kind of total, cold vengeance. Nonetheless, the detective looked into people from Raul's childhood. Not surprisingly, many of the guys he ran with were either dead or incarcerated. Besides, who would hold such a grudge over a stolen radio or graffiti that it would build to a payback that included butchering a defenseless woman and her young children?

Nothing made sense.

Four weeks of questions with no answers.

Raul didn't need to be told that the trail had grown colder than the grave itself.

That didn't stop the detective from implying it as artfully as he could. Raul stared at a bowl of uneaten soup. He held the phone to his ear, words failing him, as they often had recently.

"That doesn't mean we're going to stop looking. Not a chance," Detective Zelinski said. "I'd move a mountain with a teaspoon to find the subhumans that did this to you and your family."

Raul pictured his sad eyes. "I know you would."

"How have you been today?"

The detective always asked him that. Raul knew it wasn't just words.

"Numb. Always numb."

"We'll find them. Sooner or later, someone's going to say something they shouldn't. When they do, I'm going to come down on them so hard they'll wish they'd never been born."

Raul dipped his spoon in the soup and made slow figure eights, the tip of the spoon scraping the bottom of the ceramic bowl. "Look, you...you don't have to call me every day. When you do, for a moment, I get my hopes up. It's getting too hard, you know?"

"I understand. And I'm sorry."

"Please, don't apologize. It's not your fault. I'm just, well, I don't know." Raul sighed. "I don't know much about anything anymore."

"You know you can call me anytime."

"I do."

"Okay. I'm going to call you around this time next week, just to check in on you. That way you're prepared. If I call before then, it's because something important came up. Hopefully something that doesn't let you down."

"Thank you."

"Take care of yourself, Father Figeuroa."

Raul hung up without saying goodbye.

He heard the soft chanting of prayers in the church, their voices echoing in the narrow alley between the church and the parish house. Every night at seven o'clock, twenty or more parishioners came to pray for the souls of Bella, Abel, and Lizzy. They prayed for their eternal peace in the next world and justice in this one. They were led by Father Abernathy, who had assumed Raul's duties temporarily. The poor man had to drive thirty miles each day, but he never once complained.

Not that Raul would have heard him if he did. For the most part, Raul stayed in the house. A special cleaning company had come to remove the bloodstains, and Bill Samson had swapped out the furniture and painted. But no matter what anyone did, Raul couldn't go downstairs without seeing everything as it was that night.

So, he stayed upstairs, avoiding the curious, the well-wishers, the media, everyone. Each night he slept in a different bed, wanting to be as close to his family as he could. In Lizzy's bed, he clutched her stuffed sloth, Clover, that she'd loved and hugged until the poor thing was threadbare. In Abel's, he settled into the superhero sheets and called up memories of them reading comic books together, his son gravitating to titles that were related to the latest movie that he just had to see. Abel had a matching sloth, Henry, that watched Raul fitfully sleep from its spot on the nightstand.

In his own bedroom, Raul slept on Bella's side, inhaling the lingering scent of her, though it was fading fast.

No matter what bed he slept in, there were bitter tears and maybe some sleep, but never much.

Raul haunted the parish house like the specters that had stolen his family.

Most nights, he prayed his heart would stop in his sleep.

CHAPTER FOUR

"Are you sure you're making the right decision?" Valentina Diaz asked. Her eyes were red-rimmed and watery. She dabbed at the corners with a delicate handkerchief. Her graying hair was bunched up in the usual bun. She'd been a librarian until a year ago and still looked straight from central casting.

"Enough, Val," her husband, Eduardo, said, resting his beefy hand on her shoulder. His knuckles were swollen and misshapen, a retirement gift from spending too many years as a plumber. The skin around them was ashy and cracked. His wife had been hounding him for years to use lotion to heal his dry skin, but he'd simply wave her off and say that stuff was for ladies. "Raul needs time. We all do."

Raul sat opposite them in the straight-backed rocker that Bella preferred whenever they came to visit her parents. It was as uncomfortable as ever, yet knowing she'd occupied this very space innumerable times in the past gave him a small measure of comfort and pain. His coffee sat untouched on the saucer on his lap. He stared past Valentina's shoulder, through the big double windows and at the birdfeeder in the front yard. A squirrel sat atop the feeder, swatting at a sparrow every time it came to partake. It seemed like off behavior for a squirrel. Didn't they typically scurry away, tails twitching and making those strange, scratchy chirps of agitation?

The sparrow pulled away, circled overhead, and made another attempt at the feeder. The squirrel stood on its hind legs, a mini King Kong atop the Empire State Building, defending its territory. Raul didn't remember much about his father. He had passed away when Raul was only seven. The one thing that stuck was the man's love of the original *King Kong*. He used to play the soundtrack over and over, the vinyl worn until it was riddled with audible pops and skips.

He'd say, "Listen, *hijo*. This is the part where the villagers are dancing to call on Kong."

As a kid, Raul could have cared less about some weird village music. He would have forgotten even that of his father, if not for the day he unpacked his parents' belongings that had been stored in his grandmother's attic. In the box for his father was all his *King Kong* memorabilia, including a book on the making of the movie and a plastic Kong. Touching the plastic figure was like being whisked back in time. The tactile memory led to images of them watching the movie and Raul playing with the Kong figure, making him climb up the drapes or an open door.

His mother's box, small as it was, brought no memories. She had passed away giving birth to him. Raul always wondered if he was wrong for not feeling guilt about being responsible for his mother's demise. It seemed like a natural way to feel, and his inability to make that connection made him somehow unnatural, calloused even, at least in his own eyes. The human mind was an intricate machine, though, and perhaps that guilt was locked away somewhere, ready to be unleashed when he least expected it.

Now would be that time, though he didn't think his grief would allow room for anything else...ever.

"Raul, honey, are you okay?" Valentina reached across the divide and placed her warm, tender hand on his thigh.

He blinked hard and brought his attention back to his in-laws. They had been like parents to him from the very first time they met, on that night Raul took Bella out on their third date. He thought it was only proper he should meet her parents, despite her protestations. At the time, he felt their glowing approval had been a result of his having told them he was studying to be a priest. Valentina and Eduardo had both insisted that wasn't the case. According to his mother-in-law, it was that he had an aura of goodness about him. She knew Raul would always take good care of her daughter.

It had never occurred to him that he wouldn't be able to fulfill Valentina's vision of her daughter's future.

Raul took a deep, tremulous breath. When he tried to lift the coffee cup to his lips, the trembling in his hand incited a small tidal wave that washed over the edge and onto the saucer. He abandoned all hope of getting it to his lips. Her looked into his mother-in-law's sad eyes and said, "No, Mom, I'm not okay."

A tear spilled down her cheek. "I know. I know. None of us are. I can't remember the last time I slept for more than two hours straight."

Eduardo was always, to Raul and everyone who knew him, a man of steel. Since the death of Bella and the children, he'd lost a good portion of his muscle mass. For probably the first time in his life, he looked frail, if not entirely in body, definitely in mind and soul. One look at his eyes and their inward gaze was all it took. "Sometimes, I need to pray to fall asleep. Just keep on repeating the twenty-third Psalm until my mind sorta wanders. But it never lasts long." When he caught Raul's eye, he looked down at his feet and mumbled, "I'm sorry."

Seeing Eduardo humbled, apologizing, pulled Raul back into the room, back to this moment with the two people he loved most left in this world. "You have nothing to be sorry about. If praying gives you comfort, pray."

The big man gave a solemn nod. Valentina eyed the rosary on the couch cushion, resting between her and her husband. They needed their faith now more than ever. They needed Raul to guide them through this hell on earth. He wished he could help them.

But prayer brought him nothing. He'd prayed nonstop during the sprint to his house that night. God hadn't given a damn. This couldn't have been part of his grand plan. In the hazy days following the funerals for Bella, Abel, and Lizzy, Raul came to realize that all the platitudes he'd given his parishioners, especially in times when bad things happened to good people, had been nothing but saccharine drivel. It was so easy to assure someone that God had a special plan when they lost a loved one too early. It was something else entirely when it was *your* loved ones who'd been taken too soon.

Having a priest in the fold had been a cause for joy in Bella's entire family. They made Raul feel proud of himself every time he saw the look in their eyes when he spoke of God and heaven to them. Growing up without parents and with a single grandmother who hadn't been well herself, he'd spent too much time on the streets, running around without a care in the world. He'd been very *un-priestly* back then. The closest he came to God was listening to his grandmother weep while she prayed that he would be saved from his poor decisions. Raul was destined for prison, if he wasn't taken out by drugs or driving stolen cars like a maniac or being killed by a fellow miscreant. When he'd decided to change his life after *the incident,* he being the only survivor of a vicious drive-by, funneling his energies toward priesthood had been a shock even to him. Many times, he'd wondered if he'd been just fooling himself. Playacting to cover up a misspent youth.

Those doubts always melted away when he was around Bella's loving extended family.

Now they had lost their only child. Their only grandchildren. And the priest who gave them strength.

Raul looked into the coffee cup. Could they smell the alcohol on his breath? Was it true you couldn't smell vodka? That's what he and his buddies used to tell each other as they took pulls on a bottle of pilfered Popov before the first bell rang for class. They had never been caught, though that might have been due to the fact they sat in the back of the classroom. Their teachers kept a wide berth, reticent to get in their crosshairs.

He'd been drinking heavily since the funerals. He'd even gone through the Communion wine, cheap and bitter as it was. His days started with beer in the late morning and went downhill to hard alcohol as the sun raced to the west. Even all that booze couldn't give him peace at night. Raul woke up several times a night, plagued by his imaginings of what those last horrid moments must have been like for his family. In his nightmares, he was one with their fear, felt the knife puncture their flesh, smelled the release of their blood

What sent him catapulting to the world of sleeplessness was the pulse-pounding knowledge that he hadn't been there to protect them. In every way, he had failed them. Because of that, they had died terrified and without the protection of their husband and father.

So, he drank. He couldn't remember how many consecutive days he'd gone on his bender. It had to be at least two months. It seemed like years. He felt tired all the time. And weak. And nauseated.

Valentina, his dear, sweet mother-in-law, said, "How long do you think your sabbatical will be?"

"It's not a sabbatical," Raul replied. He would have been frustrated explaining this to her for the umpteenth time, but he just didn't have the strength. "I won't be going back."

"There's always hope you will."

He rubbed his eyes, weariness settled so deep in his bones it would be a miracle if he could extricate himself from Bella's favorite chair. "I honestly don't think so. Look, I know how important this is to you. To be honest, right now, I can't see myself ever leading a parish, much less saying Mass. It's just...it's just...."

What it was, was too difficult to express, in words at least. His life, and to think of it, his afterlife, had been pulled out from under him. Now, the best he could hope for was zero afterlife. Sweet darkness and oblivion were the only things he dared wish to meet him at his end. That made more sense than this.

"We understand," Eduardo said, though it was apparent Valentina didn't share his conviction. "I only hope you'll call us from time to time. We'll worry about you, especially being hours away and alone."

"And we love you," Valentina interjected, plucking the rosary beads from the couch and clutching them to her chest. "You're our son, from now until the end of days. Don't you forget that. You'll always have us."

Raul knew this would be difficult, which is why he'd downed several glasses of vodka before coming over. Part of him wanted to break down the dam of his sorrow and fall to his knees, crying all the tears he normally reserved for when he was alone. He'd throw himself into Valentina's lap and wait for Eduardo's strong and comforting hand to grab hold of him. They would give him the solace and protection he needed so desperately.

All he managed was a mumbled, "Thank you."

"Are you getting any help moving to your aunt's farm?" Eduardo asked.

Shaking his head, Raul wiped his mouth with the back of his hand and replied, "Not much to bring. Her furniture is still there. I just have a few suitcases and boxes. It'll all fit in the car."

His wife's and children's clothes and toys, scrapbooks, and anything else that had belonged to them was in a storage unit. The house and all the furniture belonged to the church, so at least he didn't have to worry about selling it. The next pastor would have to settle for living in a murder house.

"We could come with you," Valentina said. "Just to help you settle in for a couple of days."

Raul reached out to take her hand. His own trembled. He needed a drink. "I'll be fine. I just need this time to be alone. I'll call you when I get there, let you know I made it in one piece."

"You do that, son," Eduardo said.

"You know Bella and the kids will be with you," Valentina just had to add. She meant well. There was no sense getting angry.

He should have said, "Yes." Instead, he gripped the arms of the chair, tilted forward, and let the momentum get him to his feet. The room spun for a second and snapped back into place.

Valentina wrapped him up in a hug. She smelled like bath powder. He felt her sob against his chest. Eduardo clapped him heavily on the shoulder. "Take care of yourself." The look he gave Raul said he knew exactly what was going on. He might as well have said, "Quit the drinking and get your head out of your ass."

Raul left his in-laws' house and slowly made his way to his car. They watched him from the window. He could feel their eyes on his back.

One step. Two step. One step. Two step.

The last thing he wanted was for them to see him weaving. Concentrating on walking somehow made it even more difficult. He looked like a drunk trying not to look drunk. He settled behind the wheel of his Subaru, started it up, and pulled away. Only when he was out of their sight did he dare open the glove compartment, fishing around until he found the tiny bottle of vodka. It was good for two belts, which was all he needed for the drive to his house for the last time.

* * *

Ever since *the* night, sleep had been something to dread. He could still smell the spilled blood of his family. Hear their helpless cries. See their savaged bodies. Switching rooms and beds each night had become, in his mind, more than he deserved. The small measure of comfort it brought was far too good for him.

Certainty that the police would never find the killers, never be able to answer why, only added to the pressure in his skull that afforded him no peace.

For a few nights, he'd slept in his car. Waking up stiff as a board was good suffering that he felt he deserved. But the reclining seats were still too cushioned for his needs.

Lately, he'd taken to sleeping in the hard, unyielding pews in Christ Church. Now, that was pain. Getting up from a pew, crippled and hungover, was just what he felt he needed. It was impossible to get comfortable, which brought its own relief. He was unable to sleep for more than an hour straight; the pain jolted him from his dreams, or nightmares, to be more precise. His mind was a dangerous place to be. A sturdy pew was a good way to keep him out of it.

Christ Church was a modest building erected just after the Second World War. The red-brick structure used to remind Lizzy of the house the smart little pig built. It contained just ten pews on the left side of the aisle and a matching ten on the right. He'd seen pictures of a packed house back in the day, the black-and-white photos a doorway into a better time, before the world had become heavily secularized. It didn't take much to fill the seats. A hundred well-dressed asses bunched together would do the trick.

Now, he was lucky to get half that on a good Sunday. Sure, it was standing room only on Palm Sunday, Christmas Eve, Christmas Day, Ash Wednesday, and Easter. He used to wonder if people thought they were tricking God by only showing up for the big five. Did they think God only did roll call on the holiest days? Was God too busy watching football to peek in at the church? Raul bet if there was a God, he would be a Packers fan. He could see the Lord wearing a foam cheesehead hat instead of his glowing halo.

At the moment, all Raul was seeing was double. His pillow and blanket were crammed against the end of the pew. A bottle of vodka was set between his thighs. Leaning against the top of the pew in front of him, he squinted, trying to get the two crucifixes over the altar to combine into one. A wounded and dying Jesus shimmied and wiggled as Raul's focus wavered.

"If going to church was so damn important, you could have made those phonies pay. Smite them at will. Make the rest crap themselves and come running to you. That's what I would have done if I were you."

His voice echoed in the tiny church.

"But I know why you didn't. It's not because you ignored them. Or were too busy." He pointed a finger and grimaced. "It's because you're just...not...there." He took a pull from the vodka bottle. "And you never were. Talk about faith. I have full faith that you're a fucking lie."

Raul tipped the bottle back, finishing the booze. He wanted to break that bottle across Jesus's woe-is-me face. He threw the bottle with what he thought was the aim and precision of Pedro Martinez in his prime. The bottle hit the back of the pew three rows forward, bounced onto the floor, and smashed to pieces.

The back of his head thunked against the pew as he collapsed. His foot shot out and got trapped under the kneeler, making it impossible to get into a proper sitting position in his current inebriated state.

If Bella could see him now, all tangled in the pew, she'd laugh at first, then help him to the house and put him to bed, but not before making him drink a bottle of water and taking two Motrin so he wouldn't wake up with a banging hangover. Most wives would throw in a few jabs about getting piss drunk, leaving their stumbling husband to his own devices. Not Bella. She was always so nurturing. He used to tell people with great pride and surety that his wife was the best mother a child could ask for. Lizzy and Abel adored her.

And Raul adored them all.

"Why did you leave me?" he cried out. A bubble of sorrow burst in his chest and he wept. He cried himself to sleep, his body twisted and exhausted.

★ ★ ★

When Raul woke, he smelled urine. Bleary-eyed and his hip howling in pain, he struggled to sit upright and had to use both hands to extricate his foot from its odd angle under the kneeler. The back of his hand grazed something cold and wet.

"Well, that's a first," he said, staring at his wet crotch.

The morning sun was just beginning to kiss the stained-glass windows, projecting a kaleidoscope of color onto the polished floor around the altar.

"Gaaaahh!"

The mother of all leg cramps had him flailing for his thigh. The sudden onset of pain made his guts roil. The last thing he needed was to add vodka-infused vomit to his piss. He might have been departing Christ Church today forever, but there was no way he could leave this for Bill Samson to clean. If he could get the cramp to go away and stop the world from spinning, he'd grab the mop and bucket and erase any sign of his presence.

Standing. Standing will ease the cramp, he thought.

It took a monumental effort to extricate his ass from the pew. He was right, though. The muscles in his leg were already starting to loosen. That's when he saw the shattered bottle. If he could go back in time, he would strangle drunk Raul from the night before. Now he could add a broom and dustpan to the things he needed before he locked up.

He had just gathered his strength and sensibilities when he heard footsteps.

"You really tied one on."

Bill Samson emerged from the narthex with a can of polish in one hand and dust rag in the other. His bald head was covered with his trademark tweed flat cap and he had donned a gray tracksuit for his morning cleanup.

Raul groaned but not loud enough for Bill to hear. His cheeks burned with shame. "This mess is mine to clean up," he said. His throat was raw. He must have been snoring hard last night.

"By the look of you, you'd only add to it if you tried," Bill said, ambling down the aisle with his bowlegs and a slight limp, courtesy of a thief stabbing him in the hip with a knife decades earlier. As Bill told it, he hadn't felt it at the time and had chased the criminal four more blocks before tackling the son of a bitch and giving the man's dentist plenty to work on. It wasn't until he got up and saw the blood that he'd realized the punk had stabbed him. "I've cleaned up worse. When I was a rookie, part of the hazing that first year was cleaning the drunk tank on Sunday mornings. This is like a breath of mountain air compared to that mess."

Raul took a step and had to grip the pews on either side to steady himself. "You may be right, Bill. I'm really sorry."

Bill took him by the upper arm with a grip of iron and helped him to the aisle. "Don't you apologize, Father."

"I'm not a priest anymore." Raul's temples throbbed.

"You know how you always have to call a president Mr. President? Same applies to you, at least with me. You don't like it? Too bad. You're the best this parish ever had. I hear the next fella is one of those neurotics. Maybe a little too green around the gills."

They walked to the back of the church, leaving Raul's indiscretions behind.

"Father Gilmore is a really nice guy," Raul said. He'd been meeting with the young man twice a week for the past three weeks, readying everything to hand over the keys to the small kingdom. Raul had made sure to stay sober for the first week. The poor kid had had to deal with a less than coherent Raul for the past two. He liked Father Gilmore. He was young and full of faith and vigor, kind of the way Raul had been at the start. Raul's one good deed, call it a need to keep some semblance of good karma, was not to besmirch the faith and special position in the church the man was taking. In a way, he envied the priest's blind devotion and wished he could turn back the clock to recapture his own, with the added benefit of bringing his wife and children back to him.

"They say he has panic attacks during his sermons," Bill said, practically carrying Raul out the wide double doors. The crisp morning air was a needed slap to the face.

"I have heard that."

Father Gilmore was like an excitable puppy with a nervous condition. The parishioners would take care of him. Most of them were lonely older women who would look after him like a son or grandson. One thing would happen for sure – he would add some pounds to his slender frame. Those ladies liked to feed the father. Raul's own paunch had only gotten under control thanks to Bella's constant vigilance. Not every crumb of pound cake or gooey slice of lasagna had to be eaten. Bella made sure to take most of it to the soup kitchen.

Sooner or later, Gilmore would grow comfortable with public speaking, once he learned there was nothing to be frightened about. There were plenty of priests who would rather have cut off both arms and legs than get behind that pulpit on Sundays when they first started out.

Bill chuckled as they made their way down the stairs. "They say his cheeks puff out like a fish and his eyes bulge when it hits. That will sure be a sight."

"He'll have you to give him pep talks."

"Or a kick in the ass. Sometimes that works better."

Bill led Raul into the house and deposited him in a kitchen chair. He went to the refrigerator and said, "Ah, this will do just fine." He popped the tops on two cans of beer.

Raul covered his mouth with his fist. "I can't possibly." He stank of piss and the vodka sweating out of his pores. All he wanted to do was crawl into the shower with his clothes on and blast himself with scalding-hot water.

"Sure you can. Here, take a swig."

The icy can felt good in his hand. "There's no way I could drink two."

"Who says they're both for you? You're not the only one who tied one on last night. I met up with my old staff sergeant last night down at Woody's. Did you ever hear of this drink the kids all love? It's called Fireball."

Raul took a reluctant sip. His dehydrated body reacted instinctively, sucking down half the beer before he could pull it away from his lips. "Yeah, I have. Bella's younger cousins brought it to the last Christmas Eve party."

"Shit tastes like cinnamon. The pretty bartender kept bringing us free shots. I think she liked the idea of a couple of geezers getting drunk on kid stuff. There's so much sugar in that crap, I thought my head was going to crack open when I woke up. Some hair of the dog is most definitely in need."

Raul took another sip and surprised himself by finishing the can. "I thought that was something drunks said to justify picking up where they left off."

Bill chugged his beer and crushed the can. He'd told Raul years ago he thought recycling was a scam. "You feel better, don't you?"

Raul had to admit, his hangover had abated some. He nodded.

"Never doubt a cop, especially when it comes to our dear friend, Al Cohol." Bill took the empty can from Raul and chucked it in the garbage pail under the sink. The counters and shelves were bare. Raul had donated Bella's prized KitchenAid to Dolores Rearden, one of his parishioners who loved to bake. When it came time to raise money with a bake sale, Dolores could crank out brownies, cookies, and cupcakes like a machine. Raul looked at the empty spot where the heavy KitchenAid had resided, remembering the joy on Bella's face when he'd brought it home. She'd used it so often, the original motor had burned out. Thankfully, it had been under warranty and a replacement arrived on their doorstep two weeks later. He could taste her snickerdoodles, hot from the oven, he and the kids jockeying to see who would get the first one. Of course, he always deferred to the kids, taking more delight in their joy than his own.

"It's everywhere," Bill said.

Raul had forgotten he wasn't alone in the house. "Huh?"

Bill shook his head. "I meant, *they're* everywhere. In the house. In the church. I understand what you're going through and why you're doing what you're doing."

Biting back tears, Raul said, "You can't know how it is."

"Not personally, no. But I worked homicide for seven years. Some families, those left behind, the survivors who felt more like the abandoned, I kept up with them over the years. I may not have felt their exact pain, but I'd been around it enough to get at least a kind of secondary anguish that goes beyond empathy. I can't tell you this will get easier. It might, it might not. I've seen it go both ways. No matter what, you'll always miss them. And you'll always ask why."

Raul bent forward and put his head in his hands. Sweat dotted his hairline. "The *why* is eating me alive. It was so...so *goddamn* senseless. Who were they? Why did they choose my family? Why wasn't I there?"

He felt the weight of Bill's hand on his back.

"I don't know the answers. I've been checking in with folks I know who are still on the force. They're working hard to find the sons of bitches who...." Raul heard the dry click in Bill's throat. "They'll get them."

The case was colder than a well-digger's ass. There was nothing to go on. Just a smattering of boot prints that pointed to at least four assailants. Four monsters in Raul's home. It took four murderous cowards to snuff out the lives of a small woman and two children. If Raul were given the chance to meet them, he would not give them forgiveness. Turning the other cheek was for the weak. The only shred of solace he had each night were those moments spent contemplating the horrible things he would do to the men who took his family away. Some of the images would have made Jeffrey Dahmer blush.

Raul and Bill endured an awkward silence before Raul marshaled enough energy to get up. He waved Bill off when he leaned forward to take his arm. "I'm fine. Much better than when you found me. Thank you. I'll have to remember that for the future."

"You need any help loading the car?"

"Nah. Just a suitcase left. The rest is in the back. I'm gonna take a shower and shake the last cobwebs off before hitting the road."

Bill's eyebrow shot up. "Thought you said you were leaving around three?"

"That's what I told everyone so I could sneak out early. I'm not really in the mood for goodbyes."

Bill studied him for a moment with his hard yet sad eyes. "I hear you. If Gabriele and Frannie got ahold of you, your rubber wouldn't hit the road until nightfall. Don't worry about locking up. I've got it."

Raul took a few steps into the living room and turned. "Thanks again. For everything."

"Just doing my job. And I won't say goodbye. How about, see you later?"

"That sounds good."

Except Raul was pretty sure this was goodbye.

CHAPTER FIVE

The highway was remarkably empty, even for a Sunday. Good. Raul didn't know if his nerves could handle traffic. He'd set the cruise control for sixty-two, seven miles an hour above the speed limit, which was just enough to not get pulled over by a bored trooper.

The bag of Funyons on the passenger seat crinkled when he stuffed his hand inside, searching for the last couple of fried puffs of pseudo-onion flavor. He chewed with his mouth open, a pet peeve of Bella's, but she wasn't around to tell him to shut it. The snack was a favorite of Abel and Lizzy's, and each open-mouthed chew made him miss his family more.

On the seat next to him were their stuffed sloths, Clover and Henry. One lay slumped over the other, its plastic eyes fixed on the glove compartment. Raul hadn't been able to pack them away. He'd already packed his children in small coffins. The sloths would never be crammed into a dark box.

Passing over into New York a half hour back, he'd found an oldies rock station, or at least what passed for oldies now. It was hard for him to think of Metallica and Guns N' Roses as classic rock. When he was a teen, he had Metallica's *Master of Puppets* poster on the wall right by his work desk. He'd missed out on the Eighties metal scene, but something about the raw, visceral nature of the music had appealed to him. While his friends were gravitating to grunge rock, he was banging his head.

It had been a long time since he'd lost himself in the music of his youth. The past ten years had been dominated by cartoon themes and saccharine kids' pop. He used to complain to Bella, asking her if they could possibly train Lizzy to listen to Vixen over Selena Gomez and Abel to give up Taylor Swift for Tesla. She'd laugh and tell him there would come a day when he would miss his children's musical obsessions.

She was right. As always.

The farther he drove up I-87, the worse the reception. Passing exit seventeen, he lost the classic rock station for good. He checked the clock on the dashboard and estimated he had about two and a half hours to go. More than enough time to stop for some groceries and liquor, and still get to the old farmhouse with plenty of light left in the day. He hoped the electricity had been turned on. He'd contacted the utility company last week and was less than enthused about the competence of the rep who took his call.

Raul's Aunt Ida had passed away last summer, a lifetime bachelorette who had inherited the house from her parents. He'd spent five summers with Ida, each visit preceded by his antics wearing his grandmother out to the point where she had to ship him off to the Adirondacks. Oh, she didn't tell him that was the reason, but at fourteen, he was smart enough to know. The following year, he made sure to act up a little more toward late spring so he could get a return trip, which he did. Ida doted on him and let him run free. He spent days swimming in ponds, throwing an axe into trees, and riding Ida's mare, Betty.

Old Betty had long passed. The barn had collapsed, and the remains had been carted away. Now Ida was gone. So were his and Bella's plans to tackle the DIY repairs and make it a summer retreat for their family. He had no idea what he was going to find when he got there. The lawyer told him all of Ida's furniture was still in the house and the estate left some money aside for the annual taxes, which were miniscule, and general upkeep, like making sure the pipes didn't explode in winter and the roof didn't blow away in spring.

Raul suspected Ida was a lesbian with the misfortune of being born at a time when coming out was not something a proper woman would do. She had a passel of lady friends and there were pictures of her and her best friend, Charlene, all throughout the house. Charlene had died of cancer in her forties and Raul suspected Ida lived the rest of her life heartbroken.

At least he was moving into a house whose walls knew full well how to care for a shattered tenant. He wouldn't be as much fun as Ida, who, despite losing her love, was a spitfire who drank Piels beer, smoked cigars on the front porch, and played a mean game of poker. She also taught him how to shoot a rifle, using a tattered scarecrow she'd found in the barn as a target.

He wondered what she'd think if she could see him now and know his plan.

"Let's hash it out over some Piels," she'd say, doing her damnedest to change his mind.

Piels. He wasn't sure they even made that brand anymore.

Raul wanted a drink.

He had a warm twelve-pack of Budweiser in the trunk. The next exit was over twenty miles away. This stretch of 87 was not rife with options. He pulled over onto the shoulder and rummaged around the back until he found the beer. He poured a can into a coffee travel mug that had been in the cup holder for longer than he could remember. After stashing a couple more cans under his seat, he eased back onto the highway.

The first sip was less than appetizing. "Piss-warm beer in a dirty mug. Christ, what was in this before?" Raul wasn't a coffee drinker, so he suspected the last liquid he'd put in there had been one of those fruity energy drinks.

By the fourth beer, he'd grown accustomed to the horrid flavor. He poured another and tossed the can into the back of the Subaru. How many times had he warned his parishioners about the dangers of drinking and driving? It was easy to cast judgment when your life was close to perfect.

His cell phone buzzed. Raul gave the lit screen a quick look. Detective Zelinski was calling. He let it go to voicemail. Thirty seconds later, there was a sharp beep alerting him to a text.

Just checking in to see how you are. Good luck with your move. I'll keep in touch.

Good luck with your move.

Raul wanted to throw the phone out the window. Zelinski meant well. He had from the start. But if he couldn't do the one thing Raul needed most from him, the rest was pointless. A burp of acid and a sudden craving for vodka had Raul's mind wandering until his tires sped over the cut grooves in the highway's shoulder.

The sun was peeking out from behind some slate-gray clouds

by the time he officially entered the Adirondacks. The town of Morrisburgh was a flat, dry spit of land west of the much bigger Glens Falls (the place Rachael Ray was born, as Bella would always remind him) and north of the horse racing mecca, Saratoga. There were no fun water sports like in Lake George, attractions, or even something of historical note in Morrisburgh. Population less than a hundred currently, it was simply there, a collection of farms with an actual general store and an abundance of peace and quiet. If a tourist ever ended up in Morrisburgh, it was because they'd made a wrong turn.

It had to have been at least fifteen years since he'd last been up here. As he drove through the town's sole stoplight, with nothing but green fields on either side, it looked like nothing much had changed. If a pair of McDonald's golden arches appeared out of the vegetation, he thought he might have a heart attack.

No one was out and about, not that there was much to do. It was Sunday and he suspected the faithful had gone to church over in Glens Falls and were at home having supper or just relaxing. The general store was still there, except it was closed. Raul slowed down to read the sign on the door. There were carefully stacked items in the window, from home cleaning products to cans of soup and tools. At least it was still in business. He'd hoped to do some shopping there in the coming days, get at least a few supplies and drink in some nostalgia. For today, the plan was to check on the house, then slip over to Glens Falls and find a supermarket. He needed to empty the car in order to pack it with groceries anyway.

Everyone in Morrisburgh was a farmer, except for Aunt Ida. She'd sold the farmland to her neighbor ages ago, having no interest in tilling and toiling with the earth. Raul had always wondered what Ida did to make money. He'd never seen her work. And she didn't seem like the type to live off the government. In his youth, his curiosity was overwhelmed by the freedom of being in the country. It was too bad she wasn't around to ask. There were so many things he'd love to talk to her about now as an adult, preferably over some cold Piels.

Then again, if she were still here, he wouldn't be making this journey, his car packed for the duration.

"Well, look at that."

The mailbox was still there on the side of the road. 'FIGEUROA' was barely visible, the paint worn by the sun and time. The flag that would be raised to alert Ida that she had mail was missing. The property itself was hidden behind a tall row of thick evergreens. He used to lose a lot of tennis balls within that mass of trees. He wondered if they were still there nestled in the darkness, the yellow fuzz long gone.

He turned into the narrow drive, the only way in or out from the road. The gravel popped under his tires. Ida's house was set just about fifty yards back. The old place looked remarkably well kept. Raul remembered the lawyer telling him that Ida had had the exterior painted the year before. The bright yellow house looked like it should be surrounded by singing birds, fresh, brightly colored flowers bursting from planters, and wind chimes tinkling in a soft breeze.

There weren't wind chimes or flowers. But there was the porch swing Ida used to sit on and read the paper, or at night tune in to talk radio, the transistor radio set on her lap.

"It's nice."

"I told you it would be," Raul said, and then immediately realized that Bella was not sitting beside him, marveling at the house. His heart raced. He'd heard her with his ears, not in his head.

Hadn't he?

Raul had to steady himself for a moment. The windows were shut and there was no one around who could have sounded like his dead wife. He looked into the back seat, knowing full well no one was there.

The empty coffee mug. Had he poisoned himself? Who knew what kind of bacteria had been growing inside. No. That was ridiculous. Even if it were toxic, it would take some time to affect his mind, if ever. He'd be sick to his stomach first.

Suddenly, he was frightened to be in the car. He unbuckled his seat belt and threw the door open. He was overwhelmed by the scent of cut grass and clean mountain air. It had an instant soothing effect on him. Raul leaned against the car and took in the house, waiting for his heart to settle down before heading inside.

Stress. All that stress is coming back to haunt me. Not Bella. Just gotta get this shit inside and go to the store. Self-medicate with vodka. That'll do it.

He grabbed a backpack loaded with books and clomped up the warped steps. The knothole was still there on the next-to-last step. When he was a kid, Raul used to put his eye to the hole to see what lurked in the darkness. Of course, it was too dim to see anything, but that didn't stop his imagination from populating the cramped space with all sorts of strangeness and wonder. In the daytime, he thought it would be cool if some bizarre creature called it home. He conjured all kinds of cryptid fantasies, gaining world acclaim as the first person to ever capture said beast alive. At night, however, when the old wood house settled in the cooling gloom and the real critters of the dark called out, thoughts of an unknown animal hunkered down under the porch were not so thrilling.

The screen door opened with its typical rusted screech. It took some time to find the keys in his jacket pocket. Taking a quick glance back at the car, he slipped the key into the lock, opened the door, and hurried inside.

Ida's scent, a combination of the musk perfume she wore and her baking – because she always had something in the oven – was so strong, he would swear she was still living in the house, whipping up sourdough bread and jam star cookies. When he'd first heard of her passing, he'd felt sorrow, but not a deep pang of loss. After all, they hadn't seen each other in quite some time, exchanging Christmas and birthday cards and the occasional call. Ida had lived alone for so long, she hadn't been the type to work hard at maintaining contact with others. And that was just fine. It was Ida and there was no changing her ways.

Raul instantly wished he'd forced himself to stay in closer contact with his aunt.

Here, now that he was wrapped in the lingering essence of the woman who had become intertwined with his summers, those first tears ran down his face. The lumpen shapes of her furniture were in the same places he remembered them to be. The floorboards crackled when he walked to what she called her TV chair, a stuffed find at a flea market. Plucking the sheet with his fingertips, he pulled it back to reveal her worn and ratty throne. The seat cushion still held the shape of her body. If he were to rekindle his youthful fantasies, he could imagine her ghost sitting there, staring at him, the weight of his missing her pressing into the used hunk of furniture.

Raul knelt down, the way he'd huddle at her feet, and let his hands graze over the knotty fabric.

"I'm so sorry, Aunt Ida," he said between soft whimpers. "I should have come to see you more often. I'd like to use getting ordained, starting and raising a family, and watching over a parish as an excuse, but it would be a poor one. I should have made more time for you."

He'd been told she had died in her sleep upstairs in her bed. There was no way he could go in that room today. In fact, he wasn't sure he could even look inside it.

After resting his backpack against her chair, he went back to the car and began to unload his scant belongings. His old bedroom was in the back of the first floor, just off the kitchen. He dumped everything on the single bed. Dust swirled in the rays of fading sunlight.

Walking through the kitchen for the last load, he tried the faucet. The pipes made a long, loud belch, rattled a bit, and finally spit out a wad of brownish water. He let it run for a minute until the water was cold and clear. Next, he flicked on the overhead light. A bulb sprang to life and popped.

At least there's electricity, he thought, adding light bulbs to his shopping list.

Every time he went past Ida's chair, he had to stop for a moment and look at it, as if waiting to see her magically appear. He sat Clover and Henry in her chair. "You take care of the kids for me, Ida." He ran his thumb over Clover's downy fur and bit back a sob.

Once the car was empty – and he'd tossed his empty beer cans in the metal bin in the kitchen – he set out for Glens Falls to get what he needed to begin his life of solitude.

★ ★ ★

An hour and a half later, the shelves were no longer bare. Night had fallen and the outside noises of spring in the country were anything but silent. Raul rocked gently on the porch swing. The crickets always sounded like they had been irradiated and grown to sci-fi movie proportions out here in the country. Raul nursed a cold can of beer. He'd kept the lights off, blending in with the cool spring darkness. A deer cried somewhere back in the trees. The sounds deer made used to scare the life out of him when he first came to Ida's. The first time it had happened, he'd sprinted to Ida's bedroom, swearing he heard a lady screaming.

Ida had chuckled and patted the mattress for him to sit beside her.

"In a way, you're right," she'd said.

Raul's eyes bulged. "Should we call the police?"

She took his hand in hers and gave it a gentle squeeze. Her hands were powerful from years of kneading dough. "That's a lady deer, I suspect."

"Deer don't sound like that," he'd insisted.

"Oh, and what makes you say that?"

"I don't know. I mean, how can an animal sound like a person?"

"Better yet, how can a person sound like an animal?"

"What?"

"We're a lot closer than we think, especially when we're scared. Or lonely. Or even angry. I don't speak deer, but I heard it too, and it sounded kind of scared to me. Maybe that old deer stumbled upon a coyote. Or could be she just stepped on something that made a strange noise and gave her a good jolt of the willies. Either way, it's nothing for you to be frightened of. I know it sounds strange, but it's just nature talking."

Raul still hadn't been sure he believed her, but something about the calm in her eyes had settled him down. The next night, she'd taken him onto the porch so they could, in her words, eavesdrop on 'nature conversatin'.

He'd forgotten how much he loved to just sit back and let the world talk to him. It was impossible to do back home, what with all the distractions that had been slicing off every last shred of silence to be had. All that noise gave birth to a monster of neurosis.

"Here's to you, Ida," he said to the night, raising his beer. "Thank you for teaching me how to live."

The porch swing rocked when he got up.

"And thank you for leaving me a place to die."

CHAPTER SIX

Sleep had not come easy. Bella used to keep the television on all night. It had taken Raul some time to adjust, especially when movies and commercials bled into his dreams in distorted ways or there was sudden machine-gun fire if Bella had fallen asleep during a war movie.

The cable company wasn't scheduled to come out and hook everything up for another couple of days. So last night, there had been no irritating commercials, no screaming soldiers, no flickering lights. It should have made for ideal sleep conditions, but it only reminded Raul of everything he'd lost. What he wouldn't give to have Lizzy or Abel come barreling into the room because they'd had a nightmare. Or to find Bella snoring softly beside him with the remote clutched so tightly in her hand, he couldn't pry it out to turn off the television.

A little bleary-eyed, he shuffled into the kitchen and made scrambled eggs and toast. He'd hoped to listen to a podcast on his phone, but reception was laughable without Wi-Fi. Eating in silence while standing over the sink, Raul gazed out the window at the rolling waves of grass. Ida's property still had a few acres left after selling most of the farmland. He figured the grass would get up to his hips soon if nothing was done about it.

Grass cutting was not in his plans.

After getting dressed, he spent the rest of the morning removing the white sheets from the furniture, balling them up and tossing them in the laundry room. He wasn't sure whether he would wash them or just throw them out.

"That has to go."

He gazed at the crucifix on the wall behind the couch with his hands on his hips. He'd bought it for Ida for her birthday when he was in seminary. She'd been so taken with his decision to become a priest. The woman who wouldn't so much as drive past a church, much less step inside one on a Sunday, had suddenly found God herself. She hadn't been over the top about it, but his calling had brought prayer into her life, and she'd even read the Bible from cover to cover. He pulled the crucifix from the wall and dumped it in a plastic trash bag. It wasn't a part of Ida, or his memory of Ida. It was more a part of himself that he wanted to wipe away.

A dozen copies of *Reader's Digest* were on the coffee table, a few with dog-eared pages and spines cracked to the point of breaking. Ida hadn't been much of a reader, but she loved her *Digest*. That and the occasional soap opera rag. He didn't see any around and assumed she had moved on to other entertainment. Most likely court shows. Did they make magazines for Court TV fans?

With a reward for a hard day's work in mind, Raul set about cleaning the living room, dining room, and kitchen. He had to go downstairs for a bucket. The cramped cellar was as musty as ever. There were a lot more boxes and crates than the last time he'd been down there. Rusty tools lay about a workbench, most of the pegs on the wall empty. Knowing Ida, she'd let her friends and neighbors take what they wanted with no set time to bring them back.

He found a steel bucket with a dent on one side.

"Did Ida try to make an extra point with you?"

Bending down to extricate the bucket from a tangle of rotting wood and chicken wire, he spotted Ida's transistor radio hanging from a hook under the workbench. It was a little bigger than the palm of his hand and had a black strap on one corner. He thumbed the tiny wheel on the side of the radio and was greeted by static. After a few adjustments with the tuning dial, he zeroed in on an AM station. A voice he'd never heard before was talking about the upcoming spring swap.

"I'll be damned."

Ida must have splurged for the good batteries, not the no-name brands that died quicker than a shooting star passing overhead.

He carried the bucket and radio upstairs, and filled the former with hot water while fiddling with the latter until he came upon a station that played music instead of featuring talking heads. It was an old song and the reception faded in and out. He assumed all crooners were Frank Sinatra, his musical education beyond old heavy metal dearly lacking. No matter who was singing, it was good company while he polished furniture and scrubbed the floors with a massive sponge while on his hands and knees.

By the time he got to the dining room, his knees were killing him. He pressed on, ignoring the pain, occasionally mirthlessly singing quick bursts of lyrics when a familiar song played. He found himself sponging his sweat along with the soapy water. The smell of pine and bleach was dizzying.

"Better open you up." He paused to open all of the windows before the chemical haze had him puking or passing out.

Raul went out back to get some fresh air and clear his head. It was a picture-perfect day and here he was cleaning an old house just so he could shut himself inside. It didn't make much sense, but nothing did anymore. He craved a cigarette for the first time since he'd quit that fall after graduating college. Bella had begged him to kick the habit because she wanted him around to see his kids and grandkids and their kids.

"Shoulda never stopped."

Staring off into the distance, he jumped when something brushed against his leg.

A gray-and-white Maine coon cat as big as a small dog looked up at him as if he were a sissy for being spooked by a little leg rub. The green-eyed feline sported a thick coat of fur with a fat tail that swished back and forth. It looked like a smaller cousin to a snow leopard.

The cat meowed, pulled the door open with its paw, and sauntered inside.

"Where the hell do you think you're going?"

Raul didn't remember Ida having any pets. Then again, it had been a long time between visits, and she must have gotten awful lonely out here. The cat definitely seemed right at home. It patrolled the kitchen, rubbing against the legs of the table and chairs. After a while, it lay down in front of the refrigerator.

The last thing Raul wanted to be was responsible for a living creature. He opened the kitchen door wide and stomped his foot on the linoleum floor. "Go on! Get! Ida's not here anymore and it looks like you've done pretty good all by yourself."

The cat looked at him sleepily, then licked its paws.

"I'm not feeding you, so you might as well go find food somewhere else."

There was no way he was going to try to pick it up. First, it looked like it weighed enough for him to throw his back out. Second, what if it had rabies or just didn't like to be touched by strangers? Cat scratch fever was not in his plans for tonight.

"You don't want to go?"

It closed its eyes and rested its head on its clean paws.

"All right then."

Raul walked to the living room and found the vacuum in the coat closet. He rolled it back into the kitchen and plugged it in. The cat opened one eye, curious about this new development.

"I'll make it easy for you." Raul propped the back door open with a brick that had come loose from the patio area. "Last chance to go of your own free will."

The cat's ears perked up, but that was about it.

"Suit yourself."

Raul pressed the on button. The vacuum roared to life just a foot from the intruding cat. Its tail puffed up to twice its size and the cat bolted out the back door as if the Devil and the IRS were on its ass. Raul couldn't help but laugh.

It was the first time he'd laughed in months. And it was at the expense of a defenseless animal.

Quick to shut the door before the cat tried to make it back inside, Raul cut off the vacuum and went back to work.

"Stupid cat."

By the time he was done, the house might not have gleamed, but it did smell fresh and clean. There was still the upstairs to contend with, which included Ida's bedroom and bathroom, a guest room that had been mothballed when he was a kid, and a third bedroom that she called her thinking room. It used to contain a chair and shelves of old books she'd rescued from library sales. Ida was big on her quiet time and reflection. What she thought about was no one's business but her own. The woman loved to read and that was her preferred corner of comfort.

Back when he was a kid, Ida gave him free rein to go anywhere he wanted. Except the second floor. That was by permission only. She'd say, "Every woman needs her sanctuary. I'm lucky enough to have a whole floor to myself. There's no big secrets up there, so don't go getting overly curious. You can come up, but only when I tell you. We have a deal?"

"Deal," he'd said, a fever of inquisitiveness burning through him. She must have sensed it, because she took him by the hand at that very moment and walked him into her special domain. She'd been right; there was nothing to pique the interest of a young boy, other than her vast collection of porcelain pigs in her bedroom. When he asked her why she was so interested in them, she'd simply replied, "I just like them. They make me smile."

He leaned against the kitchen counter and looked at the ceiling, picturing in his mind the work that would need to be done up there.

Or, he could just choose to leave it as is. He didn't need the space. Everything was right here on the ground floor. Besides, poor Ida wasn't here to give him the thumbs-up to go there anyway. Either out of laziness, loyalty, or a combination of both, he would honor her wishes.

"Time for my reward."

He caught himself talking aloud in the mirror tacked to the wall beside the refrigerator. He'd been doing that a lot lately.

"Fuck it," he said to his reflection. "No one around to care what I'm doing."

He opened the freezer door and contemplated whether to heat up a frozen pizza or microwave a meatloaf dinner. After he'd worked so hard without a break, both were more appetizing than they should have been. The meatloaf won on account it would cook quicker. He also took out the bottle of vodka he'd put in there the night before.

The cold vodka hit him like a magic elixir. Even though he'd worked his ass off, he hadn't put a dent in the tension that had wound him up tighter than a golf ball these past months. In the beginning, he'd tried going back to running, but that just gave him time with his thoughts, which was not a good thing at all. Then there was the rabbit hole of internet porn, something totally new for him. It's not as if Bella ever would have allowed such a thing in her house. No amount of video sex could release enough endorphins to calm his mind.

But vodka was another story. It not only relaxed him, it dulled his brain. If he did it right, he could even forget who and where he was by the end of the day. If he happened upon a genie in a bottle down in Ida's basement, that's exactly what he'd wish for — peace and oblivion.

He downed a quarter of the bottle while the meatloaf cooked. A stab of brain freeze made him stop and take a breath. The microwave dinged. He pulled back the plastic cover. The aroma coming off the frozen dinner brought to mind a chemistry set more than home cooking. Raul's stomach grumbled anyway. He ate it while it was still in the microwave. When that was done, the edge of his hunger slightly dulled, he tossed the rock-hard pizza in the oven.

"Twenty minutes on four hundred degrees," he said, reading the box. Considering he'd forgotten to preheat the oven, he estimated thirty minutes instead. More than enough time to sit on the couch and work on that bottle of vodka.

The radio had stopped at some point when he was trying to evict the cat. Raul turned the radio off and back on again, but the batteries had finally given up the ghost. He drank his vodka in the silent, piney house, waiting for a meal fit for no one with discerning taste buds.

His head starting to swoon and his feet feeling as if they were losing their grip with the ground, Raul went to his old bedroom and dug through one of his bags. The muffled rattle told him he'd picked the right bag. Two amber pill bottles were pulled out of the mess of socks and underwear he'd unceremoniously stuffed inside.

The Wellbutrin had been prescribed by his doctor to help with his depression. Raul hadn't needed to see a shrink to discover the source of his emotional despair. Having his family's murder plastered all over the news for a week gave him a free pass straight to pharmaceutical land.

The other was Ativan, which he was told he could take for

moments when his grief or anxiety felt like it was getting to be too much. That translated to 'take one every waking minute of every day'. Doctor Lynd had been very clear with him that he was to avoid drinking alcohol while taking these drugs. Raul had obeyed his orders and followed the scrip for a few days. To tell the truth, they got him a little fuzzy but didn't come close to getting him to where he wanted to be, which is where the drinking came in.

Now, even that didn't seem like enough.

"Like peanut butter and jelly," he said, shaking a pill out of each bottle. He washed them down with the warming vodka, exhaling loudly. He'd been no stranger to pills and booze when he was a teen. Back then, he was young and invincible and knew all there was to know. After seminary and marriage, fathering children who depended on him, he'd become cautious, aware of his limitations, and very fragile. Now, nothing much mattered, least of all his health.

He was going to ride the booze and pills train to the last stop. It didn't need to be an express. The local would do. Time spent on the rolling nightmare was time spent repenting for his cardinal sin of not saving his family.

The pizza should have been ready by now. Raul opened the oven door, saw the cheese bubbling, pulled the pan out, and rested it atop the stove. He couldn't find a pizza cutter anywhere (had Ida ever even tried pizza? – he couldn't recall) and settled for a butcher knife.

He sat down and eyed the sizzling pizza. The first bite singed the roof of his mouth. He cursed and threw the slice onto the plate. It hit hard enough to bounce off the table and land facedown on the clean floor. "Fuck, fuck, fuck!"

Another swig of vodka to kill the pain.

And another to kill time, waiting for the pizza to cool. He stared at the fallen pizza in disgust, although he suspected it was with himself.

When the Ativan kicked in, he had to grip the edge of the table to keep everything in focus and prevent himself from sliding sideways off his chair. The booze and drugs skinny-dipped together in his system and it was wonderful.

Raul chewed on a cooler slice, resisting the pull of sudden exhaustion.

I really should pick that pizza up off the floor, he thought.

He felt his heartbeat slowing down. Or at least that's how he perceived it.

"Doc was right," he said, his distorted reflection in the vodka bottle matching the way he felt.

Was he dying?

He'd once counseled a former parishioner whose wife had taken the wrong combination of medicine by accident. Albert Braxton, a man with an impossibly long face and perpetually moist lips, had come home to find Tabitha, the woman who made the best potato salad on earth anytime there was a special church function, dead on the kitchen floor. She had still been wearing her pajamas because she'd been home sick with the flu. Her pharmacist had neglected to tell her about the potentially fatal interactions with her new and old medications. Raul remembered wondering if she hadn't done it on purpose. It seemed hard to overdose simply by accident. She'd been an important member of the parish for three years, but he'd learned that you could never truly know someone. Just look at the number of serial killers whose neighbors swore they were quiet, affable, or just a regular guy who volunteered for the Boy Scouts or was a lector in the church.

Now, he saw that maybe he was wrong to think that way.

Because this definitely felt like the universe had bided its time to make him pay for his doubt.

The joke was on the universe.

Raul didn't give a shit.

In fact, if this was what death was like, he wondered why he hadn't done this sooner.

★ ★ ★

Something's scratching in the walls!

That was Raul's first thought as he awoke with a start. The side of his face felt strange. He went to touch his cheek and instead came upon cold pizza crust. The pizza peeled wetly from his oily skin.

Silence.

He must have dreamt about the scratching.

Outside was dark.

"Passed out in my pizza. You're a real fucking winner, Raul."

The muscles in his back ached from sleeping bent forward. His ass tingled with pins and needles.

So, he hadn't died. Where was the vodka bottle? He turned on the little fluorescent light under one of the cabinets and looked around the room. He found the bottle on its side, resting against the opposite wall. The glowing display on his phone informed him he'd been passed out for a little over four hours.

"Ungh, your mother," he grumbled as he stretched. It felt as if every muscle had cramped at once. Worse yet was the banging headache that came from out of nowhere. He pinched the bridge of his nose as if it would hold the agony at bay. Fat chance of that.

Scritch, scratch, scratch.

There it was again. Though this time, now that he wasn't drooling on his pizza in a narcotized haze, he knew exactly where it was coming from.

"What do you want?" he barked at the coon cat as he opened the door. It sat on its haunches and looked up at him with a *Who, me?* face.

"You're not coming in."

Raul slammed the door. Big mistake. The loud bang was like a hammer blow to his head. He winced, which only made the throbbing worse.

The cat went back to scratching and now yowling. It scratched and scratched until Raul wondered which would come first – the relentless sound sending him to an asylum or the cat's paws wearing down to nothing.

Knowing he'd been defeated by a goddamn stray cat, he seized the plate of hardened pizza slices, threw the door open, surprising the cat so much it jumped backward, and tossed the pizza onto the ground. He shut the screen door before the cat could regain its courage and try to scurry inside. It cautiously approached the nearest slice and leaned forward to give it a sniff. Then a quick lick. Deciding it liked the taste, the cat got to chewing in earnest.

"Great. Now I'll never get rid of you."

A brief burst of laughter, a child's stifled chuckle, came from somewhere behind him. The flesh on the back of his neck prickled.

Raul spun on his heels, staring into the dining and living rooms, his eyes unable to penetrate the darkness. "Who's there?"

He paused to listen for the telltale sounds of someone hiding in his house. The nearest light was in the dining room, the switch on the wall about twenty feet away. It might as well have been on another planet.

"Hey, I know you're in here!"

But did he?

Why would a child be in his dark house? It was late for kids to be out and about. Didn't dark houses scare kids anyway? He knew Lizzy and Abel would never dream of going into such a place. He was barely able to get them to turn the light off in a room they were leaving.

It couldn't have been the cat, because the sound definitely came from the front of the house and the cat, as he could see, was still munching on the pizza.

His phone had a light. He took it from his back pocket and had to fumble around a bit to get it to work. The harsh shaft of white light chased a swath of darkness in the dining room into the corners, creating strange, elongated shapes on the walls that danced and twisted when he swung the phone around.

There was nothing there.

If someone was in the living room, they could see exactly where he was, and for the moment, he couldn't see them. That gave them the advantage.

One thing that childlike laugh had done was sober him up. His headache was still knifing through the center of his head, but the pain was keeping him focused.

Wanting to regain the upper hand, he ran into the living room and reached up to pull the chain on the ceiling light. The room came to life just as his shin cracked against the corner of a side table. Raul went sprawling. His hand hit the floor and the phone went skittering under the couch. Feeling exceedingly vulnerable, he flipped onto his back and jumped to his feet, wildly looking around the room.

The front door was closed. He rushed to it and grabbed the knob. Locked.

No one was in there. If someone had been, he'd hear them scampering to hide or flee the house.

He'd been all alone in the house when he heard the brief laugh.

All alone.

CHAPTER SEVEN

Raul hadn't been sleeping well. Passing out just fine. But that kind of unconsciousness did not constitute honest sleep.

The sound of the kid's laughter from a few nights ago was still freaking him out. First, he heard Bella in the car, and now what could have been Lizzy or Abel having a giggle in the pitch-black living room. Thinking about it now, back at the parish house, his former home, he'd heard his family from time to time, clear as day, but it was always in those moments before falling asleep or waking up. It was easy to imagine they were still alive when he was in that semi-limbo zone.

He thought that when he ditched his belief in God and an afterlife, the mere idea of ghosts (holy or not) would seem even sillier than it had before.

What he chose to cling to was that the only haunted thing was his mind. That was something tangible he could believe in. Or was it some form of self-preservation comfort, his brain pressing the play button on recordings of better times? Frightening or strange as it might seem, he could live with it.

He just couldn't sleep with it.

The cable guy was outside drilling a hole in the house so he could wire it up. Ida's television was a relic that, from what Raul could tell, didn't have the inputs for cable or modern external components like Blu-ray players or game systems. Good thing he'd brought his own. He needed something to break up the ever-present silence. He would have gotten replacement batteries for the transistor radio, but by the early afternoons he found himself too drunk to drive.

"You need a drink or something?" Raul said when he went out to the porch.

The cable installer was a young guy with an Abe Lincoln beard and one of those ear piercings that stretched your lobe until a poodle could jump through it. He came down from the ladder and wiped the sweat from his forehead with the back of his forearm. It was a hot day for late spring, feeling more like midsummer.

"You have water?"

"As long as you don't mind it from the tap."

"Why would I mind?"

The kid went back to the van and Raul went inside to get him a glass of water. He had to remind himself he was in a different place, with people who had a sharper perspective on things. He could see people dying of dehydration if there was a shortage of bottled water in the city.

Raul took a quick pull from the vodka bottle in his freezer before getting some ice for the water. It was only ten in the morning, but Bill had been so right about the hair of the dog.

"Here you go," Raul said, handing the cable guy the glass. The kid drank it in one long chug.

"Thanks. Wasn't expecting it to be this hot already. Jeez, I'm not ready for this."

"I didn't even have a clue what the weather was going to be. No TV, radio or Wi-Fi."

"Man, that would drive me crazy. Especially out here."

If he only knew how right he was. "It hasn't been fun, I'll tell you that."

"Well, I just have to run this line into the living room, hook up your box and router, and you'll be plugged back into the world. Should take a half hour tops."

"Works for me. If you need me, I'll be out back."

The kid eyed the paperback books Raul had left on the porch swing. On the top was *On the Beach* by Nevil Shute, the nuclear end-of-the-world downer that he'd wanted to read when he was in college but had very little room for recreational reading. It was as downright depressing as he'd expected. "They made us read that one in school. It could have been so much better. I don't think people will take the end of the world that, I don't know, casually. Everyone seemed so calm. Truth is, you tell the population they have thirty days to live, it's gonna be hell on earth."

Raul picked up the used paperback and crammed it into his

back pocket. "You're absolutely right. Guess it's all just a fantasy. Sometimes we like to think we're better than we actually are."

"*A Clockwork Orange* is so much better, as long as you can figure out the made-up language. Did you know there's a killer movie version? Just crazy."

"Really? I'll have to check it out." Raul wasn't one to make younger people feel dumb just because they discovered the past at a later date than he had. He was tempted to tell him there was also a movie adaptation of *On the Beach* but let it pass.

Before the kid went back to work, he chewed on an ice cube and then asked, "You live alone here?"

"Well, there is this cat that refuses to go away." Said cat had irritated him nightly until he threw some food out the back door every night.

"Cool," the kid said, bobbing his head. He inserted his earbuds and got back on the ladder.

Cool.

That was the last thing Raul would consider his new living situation. He went out back with a can of beer and his book and read about a nuclear fog making its way Down Under. The drone of insects basking in the unseasonable heat buzzed in the background. At one point, he looked up from his book to find the cat staring at him from its spot under the rotted picnic table that had been squatting in the same spot for as long as Raul could remember.

"It's a little early for you."

The cat yawned. Damn, he had big teeth. Or she had big teeth. Raul wasn't ever going to check to be sure.

When Raul finished the first can of beer, he crushed it and tossed it onto the cracked cement patio with a clatter. Same with the next and the one after that until he was building a considerable pile of empties and a pleasant buzz.

By eleven the cable was installed. Raul tipped the kid and waved goodbye to the cat. He went inside and settled on the couch – a couch that still smelled like Ida even though he'd sprayed it with fabric deodorizer and vacuumed the cushions with a brush attachment on the hose. With a press of the remote, the oppressive silence of the house was vanquished. He went up and down the dial, just to see what channels he had, mentally earmarking ones to go back to because they were showing movies that piqued his interest.

Settling on a horror movie from the early Nineties that'd he'd seen once on VHS back in the day, he took an Ativan with his beer and settled in for a lost afternoon.

★ ★ ★

By the fourth movie in a row, his head was wrapped in a dull fog. He'd fallen asleep several times, waking up once to a woman getting a drill to the head. It was jarring to say the least. He picked up the can of beer from the coffee table and tipped it back, lapping up the remaining warm suds. It was getting dark outside and he should have been hungry, but he wasn't. The beer had bloated his belly. That didn't mean there wasn't room for one more.

With a slow shuffle to the refrigerator, he counted the cases of beer he'd bought his first day here. "And then there were five." It was cheap, just right for his budget. No specialty double IPAs with a price tag equal to a four-course meal at a fancy restaurant for him. He'd been surprised they still made Genesee. Even when he was a kid, it was the beer the older kids talked about swiping from their parents' fridges so they could chug them in the woods. By the time Raul was rebelling and sneaking beers, Genesee had become the stuff of legend.

The lager was low on alcohol content, but quantity made up for it. He bent down to get a fresh can from the bottom of the refrigerator when he heard Bella call his name.

"Raul?"

The beer slipped from his hand and he staggered into the wall.

Again, he heard, *"Raul?"*

His eyes slowly fell to the louvered grate in the kitchen floor.

It was coming from the basement.

No. Bella was not in the basement. She was in a box under six feet of earth at Christ Church Cemetery. Lizzy was to her left and Abel to her right. When Raul's time came, he would be laid to rest next to his daughter.

Raul smacked his forehead with his palm. "Shake it off, man. Wake the fuck up."

He stared at the tarnished grate and thought he heard something. Was something moving down there?

His mouth dry as cotton and heart whamming in his ears, he inched down to his hands and knees. Crawling several feet with the speed of a wounded tortoise, he strained so hard to listen to what was going on in the basement that he forgot to breathe. His body took over, consuming a great breath that he felt was much too loud.

Why would that matter? Whoever is down there knows I'm here. She knows my name. And she IS NOT BELLA!

Hovering over the grate, he turned his head to the side and oh-so-slowly lowered his ear to the ground. The heady stench of mildew wafted through the slats.

He held his breath and listened.

The basement had gone silent. There wasn't even the hint of a wisp of air passing through the old window frames above and behind him.

Raul felt exposed, hunched over like this, unable to see if someone, or something, was standing over him.

Why would there be? he thought. *It's coming from down there, not up here.*

Fear and booze and the antidepressant were wreaking havoc with his thought processes. He could add sleep deprivation to the mix as well. He was hearing things because that's what happened when you ingested substances that fucked with your mind.

But still.

He couldn't quite pull away.

His knees ached and he could feel the metal slats digging impressions into his flesh. This was crazy, part of a continuing deterioration of his mind, yet his body refused to get up.

The old Raul would have offered a prayer to God, asking for his strength and guidance.

Instead, he lifted his head and stared into the grate as if it were possible to see down into it, cutting through the oppressive gloom.

"Hello?"

His voice made a slight echo as it whispered through the vent.

The one-word reply of *"Yes"* had him scrabbling backward to get away from the grate.

"That's enough," he said, grabbing the mop he'd left resting against the wall. Should he make a bull's rush into the basement, the way he had the living room a few nights ago?

With those rickety stairs, he'd end up getting hurt or worse. That wasn't in the plan. Not yet.

Raul yanked the basement door open, reaching for the light switch on the wall. Mercifully, the light turned on downstairs and the bulb didn't burn out.

The stairs cracked like small-caliber gunshots with each step. Raul kept pausing, waiting to hear someone shifting their feet to get a better hiding spot. There were plenty down there amid the towers of boxes and metal shelves crammed with several generations' worth of junk.

With the mop cocked behind his shoulder like a bat, he touched down on the dirty, bare floor.

"There's nowhere to go this time. You want to keep messing with me? Huh? Do it to my face."

He thought he heard movement behind him. Raul swung the mop and connected with the top box on a stack. The side ripped open like a piñata, spilling out old *Time* magazines. There was a loud yelp that unmoored him until he realized it came from him.

It took a few moments to steady his nerves. Here he was in a creepy basement, hunting for someone who was imitating his wife, and all he had to see by was a forty-watt bulb in the ceiling.

"This is crazy."

A huge flashlight sat on its side on the workbench. He thumbed the switch and was taken aback by the amount of light it gave off. It helped him find the rust-flaked machete crammed between two boxes.

Did he want to be carrying a machete? He could kill someone with this thing, if not from the initial wound, certainly the ensuing infection. Of course, just holding it gave him more of a boost of bravado than the mop.

The machete it was.

Thanks to the flashlight, there were no dark corners in its path.

It sliced through the pitch like a light saber, only without the cool sound effects. Raul used to pretend he was Luke Skywalker, battling Darth Vader with his light saber, making the humming and whooshing noises with his mouth as he swung his Wiffle ball bat around his grandmother's house.

This was not make believe and he was certainly no Jedi knight. He was a frightened, slightly inebriated, shattered fallen priest who had been hearing voices and was now wandering around a cellar, presumably with someone who took great joy in making him shit himself.

Who in the hell could it be and why? Only two people knew he was moving here and they loved and respected him. Some local hick couldn't possibly have found out he was coming. It wasn't as if he took an ad out in the *Morrisburgh Gazette*, not that the town even warranted a newspaper.

The grit on the floor scraped under his shoes with every step, helping whoever was down there know his exact location at all times. He was tempted to take his shoes off, but that would only result in his stepping on a rusty nail or whatever other corroded bits of metal were lying about.

As far as farmhouse cellars went, it wasn't all that large. Or maybe it was and simply seemed smaller because of all the crap packed within it. It only took Raul a few minutes to fully explore all of its nooks and crannies. He wasn't sure if he should be relieved or even more concerned that no one was lurking in the shadows.

At least no one living, he thought.

"There's no such thing as ghosts," he announced to the empty cellar. He wasn't sure its only living occupant still believed it.

CHAPTER EIGHT

The next three days had passed without any voices from the cellar or otherwise. Or maybe there had been someone calling Raul's name and he was simply not coherent enough to hear it.

That night in the basement had started a wicked three-day bender filled with beer, vodka, pills, and a constant parade of movies. He'd found a streaming channel that specialized in horror movies, paid the nominal monthly fee and dove straight in. Back when he was a wayward child, heavy metal and horror went hand in hand. His poor grandmother had tried to steer him toward more highbrow entertainment, but as with any youth, if you were told something was bad for you, that only made you want it more. They had a video store a few blocks away, a place called MOVIE NITE, and he was in there every Friday, renting the two-tape maximum, all of them horror movies with lurid covers that were almost always superior to the film within. He and his friends saw things they maybe shouldn't have seen – movies like *Snuff*, *Faces of Death*, *The Last House on the Left*, and *I Spit on Your Grave*. His grandmother would plead with him to stop watching those awful movies that were the products of the Devil, but what the hell did she know? She was old and liked black-and-white movies that were as boring as math homework.

Of course, once he'd entered the seminary, all of that changed. In fact, he'd given a few sermons over the years preaching against dark rock music and scary movies. He let his parishioners know he spoke from experience, how God had saved him from an unsavory life of sex, drugs, alcohol, and video blood.

Fucking hypocrite, he thought now, flicking a potato chip off his chest. He guzzled a warm beer (it had been cold before he'd passed out for a spell) while watching *Dead Alive*, the New Zealand zombie horror/comedy by the guy who went on to direct all those *Lord of the Rings* movies. At the moment, the movie's hero was using a lawn mower to chop the vicious infected into mulch. The amount of gore was staggering. Raul was seventeen again, complete with righteous anger at the world.

The scratching at the back door pulled his attention from the onscreen carnage.

"Go away!"

That damn cat had been coming around more and more, always making a racket to be let inside. The last couple of times Raul had tossed some food out the door, the cat had ignored it, instead meowing nonstop until it got tired and slunk back into the woods.

Raul checked his phone. It was only one in the afternoon. Way too early for supper.

Scratchscratchscratchscratchscratch.

"Fuck off!"

He crumpled the can and threw it, coming up well short of the back door. It clattered under the dining room table.

Turning up the volume was no match for the cat's desperation to get his attention. The damn thing was like one of those relentless zombies pounding to get inside for fresh brains.

After pausing the movie, Raul had to rock back and forth a few times to build momentum so he could extricate himself from the couch. He got a whiff of body odor that made his nose crinkle. He plodded to the back door, the cat increasing its scratching as it sensed he was near.

He pulled the door open and shouted, "What the hell is wrong with you?"

The cat didn't so much as flinch.

He opened the screen door a crack. The cat stuck its paw inside and pulled the door open wide enough for it to slip its bulky body through. Raul watched it pad across the kitchen and into the living room, where it settled on one end of the couch. It looked at him as if to say, *Well, aren't we going to hang out?*

Raul rubbed his hand across his face and sighed. "I give up. Do whatever you want."

He got a beer from the fridge and plopped down on the couch. The cat studied him for a moment, then turned away and settled its head on its paws, eyes on the television. It purred like an outboard motor.

"I hope you like blood and guts," Raul said. The cat flicked its tail. "Of course you do. I'll bet that's what you ate when I wasn't around." Raul had never had a pet because of Bella's allergies. The hardest part was that they hadn't allowed Lizzy or Abel to have one either. That had been the cause of quite a few tears over the years. He remembered Abel begging for a hamster one night, going so far as to draw up a presentation on colored construction paper about how amazing a pet owner he'd be, complete with an outline of his daily and weekly duties in service to a hamster.

Bella was the one who had wept that night.

"I feel terrible," she'd said, sniffling. "Our kids are the only ones in the class who don't have a pet."

They had been lying in bed, open books draped across their laps. Raul pulled her close. "We can get them one of those betta fish."

"They want something to hold. Something to love. A fish isn't the same. Maybe we should just get the hamster."

"And have you sneezing all day and night? Or worse, in a fog from those allergy pills? He'll get over it. Tomorrow, he'll be asking for a motorized skateboard. You'll see."

She dabbed her eyes with a tissue. "They hate me."

Raul kissed the top of her head, staring at this incredibly beautiful woman who was so strong, the general of the family who kept the Figueroa army marching, but could also be as fragile as spun sugar. He loved her more in that moment of vulnerability than ever. "They love you to Saturn and back, honey. Sure, they have their moments, but all the love you've poured into them, it's like cement, you know? It binds them to you. To us. Motherhood has never come more naturally to a woman. God gave you a gift and you've never once squandered it."

She smiled. "He gave *us* two gifts."

"The best gifts anyone could ever ask for."

Moments later, they were kissing, their nightclothes on the floor, bodies entwined beneath the sheets, both of them hoping the kids stayed in their rooms for just a little bit.

The memory was like a hand, squeezing Raul's heart. Breathing felt like a chore, a chore he no longer wanted.

He'd come here to die.

And as bad as he felt at the moment, his mind and body both knew this wasn't the time. It was just another in a long line of painful interludes that left him breathless.

His attention was so fixed inward, he didn't detect the cat getting up and walking across the couch until it rested its considerable girth on his lap.

Raul wiped the tears from his eyes and looked down at the cat. The front half of its body was draped across his legs as if this were something they did, man and cat, every day. He thought of the ticks and fleas that must be crawling within all that fur.

He was about to shoo it off his lap when a thought hit him.

"Did you hang out like this with Ida?"

The cat responded with a continuous purr.

For a woman raised on a farm, he didn't remember Ida having a great fondness for animals, except the horse. Had she fed a stray cat for a spell that one summer? Raul couldn't remember. He did recall her saying that dogs were like men, preoccupied with gazing at their balls, eating, and doing the thing that male and female dogs will do when the mood hits them just right.

That was dogs.

This cat seemed to know the house too well. It was awfully comfortable here on the couch, with him. Ida must have taken it in. Was it always an outdoor cat who just popped in for a visit each day? Or had it been Ida's indoor cat, forced to fend for itself after she'd passed?

Without thinking, Raul stroked the cat's fur. It was remarkably soft. The cat purred louder, the motor in its chest firing on all cylinders. Raul un-paused the movie and he and the cat watched the rest of *Dead Alive*. When it was over, the coon cat turned and looked up at him. Its eyes were glassy, looking as if it were crying.

He stroked the fur under its chin.

"I know. It sucks to miss someone you love." Raul let out a mirthless laugh. "I used to make grief sound so poetic. I have hours of sermons dedicated to it. But you know what? It all comes down to, *it simply sucks*. Some days, it *fucking sucks* more than others. You wish Ida were here instead of me? I miss her too. I miss all of them."

The sob that tore through him came on in a flash.

Raul held on to the cat while he wept, its fur absorbing each and every tear.

★ ★ ★

Two days later, his cell phone started ringing. Raul would look at the incoming number and swipe it to voicemail. The last person he'd spoken to was his mother-in-law the day after he'd arrived at the house. And that was a two-minute conversation to let her know he was safe and sound.

Bill Samson had called, probably to check up on him. Raul wasn't in the mood to talk. His mouth was drier than dirt, and it felt like a giant was stepping on his head, applying just a little more pressure with each passing second. He wasn't sure he could even form words at the moment.

Sometime in the night, he must have opened the window. The temperature had dropped this morning and his room was freezing. He didn't even remember getting into the bedroom. Last thing he knew, he was watching an old Vincent Price movie and finishing the last of his beer.

Lifting the sheet off his shivering body so he could take a piss, he was startled by the clanging of empty beer cans falling to the floor.

"Why the hell did I bring them to bed?" he mused.

He was losing days and nights to the numbing stupor he'd gathered around him. It didn't bother him one bit, though there were moments like this that made him curious. It was as if he were living with another person, a man who skulked around his house when Raul was asleep, doing strange things just to confound him when he came to. Like finding his pants hanging off the blade of the ceiling fan the other day. Or empty vodka bottles duct-taped together from end to end like a glass bat. He'd spent the better part of an hour searching for the roll of duct tape and came up empty.

The coon cat was sitting on the radiator in the bathroom. It regarded him with a feline look of disgust. "At least I don't lick my own asshole," he said to the cat. It jumped off the radiator and ambled away. Dealing with hangovers was not its forte.

Raul flipped the toilet lid open with his toe and almost lost his balance. He might or might not have gotten the stream in the bowl. It was hard to tell at the moment because a spike of pain in the center of his head had forced his eyes closed.

The kitchen was a mess. He'd been existing on boxed mac and cheese and Steak-umm sandwiches. His blood pressure and cholesterol were most definitely on the rise. Salt and fat did not a healthy body make.

Fuck it, he thought, staring at the collection of pots and dishes in the sink. A discarded Steak-umm box was on the floor, about seven feet from the garbage pail. He lifted his foot to peel off a clear cheese wrapper.

Bella would be furious with him.

Lizzy and Abel, well, if they could see him, he knew they'd be scared. Just the quick glimpse he caught of himself in the mirror made him wince. He hadn't shaved in over a week and his stubble was growing in unevenly. No biggie, he'd never been a beard guy. What was troubling was how much of that stubble was suddenly gray. His eyes were a mess. Black bags hung underneath them like curtains, the whites of his eyes predominantly red.

Plain and simple, he looked – and smelled – like shit. And it didn't matter a whit. Bella and the kids could not see him, so there was nothing to feel shameful about. This was his choice.

He opened the fridge and found it empty save for some ketchup, half a stick of butter, a jar of pickles and an empty carton of milk. In the freezer was his last bottle of vodka, with maybe a quarter left. He unscrewed the cap, took a long pull, and put it back next to the empty ice tray.

As much as he hated to admit it, he had to get his ass together and go out for supplies. He wasn't sure what day it was or how long he'd been living like this. Every day, every moment, blended into the next. The only thing he could count on was the cat nudging him for food around five every afternoon. It no longer went outside. Just disappeared within the house for hours at a time until it got bored and decided to find him on the couch to pester. Raul knew it was upstairs those times, but he'd kept to his vow and left Ida's ghost to her private space.

Getting dressed was not easy. Even his skin hurt today. Dehydration had set his nerves on fire. He brushed his teeth and put a baseball cap on his unwashed hair. It had been months since his last haircut. He was devolving back to his long-haired college days. He misted the air with a can of men's body spray and walked through it, hoping it would dull his funk.

"Clean this place up while I'm gone," he said to the cat before he closed the door. The coon cat was on the floor, basking in a ray of sunlight. It gave him a tail flick as either a confirmation or the cat version of flipping him the bird.

The sun was blinding. Raul couldn't find his sunglasses. The car turned on, but not without some prodding. The trusty beater wasn't used to being neglected for this long.

It was immediately apparent that driving all the way to Glens Falls was out of the question. Between the sun and his headache, his skull was going to explode. He needed to add aspirin or anything remotely like it to his list. He crossed his fingers, hoping the general store was open.

He stopped the Subaru right in front of the store. There was a 'We're Open, Come On In' sign in the door. A bell chimed overhead when Raul entered.

"What can I do for you?" the old man behind the counter said. He was working on a crossword puzzle and had a pencil behind one ear and a pen in his hand. His bald head was dotted with brown spots and he had a bushy white mustache.

"Just picking up a few things," Raul said, his eyes scanning the four mini-aisles of shelves and back rack of cold cases. There was a little bit of just about everything in the store, including bait in a cooler that was perched on a stool by the register. Everything looked exactly the way Raul remembered it. The tin of sardines might have been the same tin he'd spotted the first time he went shopping with his aunt.

The ancient shopkeeper must be Sully. Wow, he'd really been beaten with the old age cane. Unless the man was Sully's father.

It didn't matter. Raul needed to get his stuff and get home.

He picked up a hand basket and filled it with a loaf of bread, off-brand mac and cheese, and two cans of chicken salad, as well as some soup and a bottle of aspirin. Milk and butter from the cold case were needed, as well as a tub of French onion dip. The general store had a box of Bavarian pretzels, and nothing went better with them.

"You have any beer?" he asked the man as he put his food on the counter.

"Yep. I've got PBR and Keystone Light in the back. What do ya need a six of?"

"I'll take a couple of cases of PBR." Raul hadn't had Pabst Blue Ribbon since he was in high school. He hoped they'd improved the taste over the ensuing years.

"Two cases? Having a party?" The old man grinned.

"Something like that."

"Let me go get it."

Glancing out the store window, Raul saw a frail older woman with hair so long it went to the small of her back, walking alongside a giant of a younger man. He must be a day nurse or some kind of caretaker. *Or a pro wrestler who got lost in Morrisburgh on the way to a match and wanted to do a solid for an old soul in need*, he thought, chuckling to himself. Raul's eyes met the old woman's for a moment before she turned away, her trembling hand gripping the man's meaty forearm. They must have been walking too slow for the man's taste, because he scooped her up and carried her away like a groom ushering his bride over the threshold.

Raul was shocked to watch the rail-thin proprietor return from the back of the store hauling both cases in his stick-arms. He set them carefully on the counter. "Anything else?"

Did that guy just abduct that poor old lady?

"One second," Raul said. He rushed to the front door, opened it, and looked outside. The odd pair were gone.

"Weird."

Not your problem. You have enough of your own shit to worry about. Forgot how strange the people up here can be. Best to steer clear of them as much as you can.

He went back to the counter and asked, "You wouldn't happen to sell any vodka, would you?" Despite the chill in the air, Raul felt himself starting to sweat. He had to go home and lie down. And tuck into the PBR.

"No, no hard alcohol. If I did, I'd ask if I could come to your party." He used his pencil to write down the price of each item on a brown paper bag, adding it all up and circling the total. When he looked up at Raul to tell him he owed fifty-eight forty-seven, his eyes widened. "I knew it."

Raul checked his wallet for cash. "Knew what?"

"You're Ida's nephew. Ronnie. No, not Ronnie. Ralph?"

"Raul."

The man slapped his hand on the counter. He might as well have punched Raul in the temple. "Yes. Raul. Your face was so familiar, but you're all grown up now. I remember when you used to come in here to buy your aunt's smokes and a grape ice pop for yourself."

Grape ice pops. Raul had forgotten all about that. Which meant this man was the actual Sully.

Raul tried to smile, be friendly. "Yeah, that's right. That was a hot walk from my aunt's to here."

Sully grew somber. "I'm so sorry for your loss. Ida was a good woman. She talked about you all the time. Said you even became a priest and got yourself a family. Boy, was she proud. It's going to be strange calling you Father. I'd heard someone was living at her place. You bring the family here for a little vacation?"

The words came before Raul could stop himself. "They were killed."

Sully looked dumfounded.

"And please don't call me Father. I'm...I'm not a priest anymore."

The old man dropped his pencil and gripped the counter, as if to keep himself from falling. "Ah, jeez son, I didn't know. I can't imagine."

Raul shook his head. He hadn't meant to drop a bomb on Sully. "Luckily, very few can. We're a pretty exclusive club. The entrance fee is too high." He felt tears coming on. Raul bit the inside of his cheek and looked down at the floor. He was not going to break down in front of old man Sully.

Sully packed his food in the bag. "No charge, son. I'm so

damn sorry."

Taking a deep breath, Raul said, "Please. Let me pay."

"Your money's no good here. I'll find you some vodka. Have it here for you for next time."

"Th-thanks. Look, I didn't mean to sound so crass. I just don't have much control over my emotions at the moment."

"You got nothing to apologize for. I lost my wife five years back and it nearly took me with her. And this is after being together sixty years, when it's only natural that one outlives the other. If she had been taken from me when we were your age, and our kids, well, I just don't know."

Raul picked up the bag. "Yeah. Me neither."

★ ★ ★

Back home, he didn't wait for the PBR to get cold before tearing into the case. It would have been nice to have a Piels just to feel a little closer to Aunt Ida. Pabst Blue Ribbon was close enough.

He drank the first two while putting his meager groceries away, and stuffed six cans in the freezer. The empties were tossed out back, clinking into the existing pile. He wasn't sure why he'd chosen that spot to discard his cans. It just was. The Other Raul must have started it and he was just following suit.

The Other Raul had been born the first night he'd blacked out on pills and vodka back when he was still living in his house. He'd apparently made a huge feast of every canned food in the cupboards, spooned it all into one bowl and had left the mess on the kitchen table, untouched. Other Raul also liked to leave windows wide open on cold nights and break things at random.

He swallowed three aspirin and warmed up a can of soup. His stomach was able to handle half the minestrone soup. The rest was poured back into the can and stored on the top shelf in the refrigerator.

The headache went back from whence it came as he worked on tomorrow's hangover. He took his position on the couch. The cat scampered down the stairs and hopped onto the other end of the couch.

Raul had to get up often to replenish his beer supply. Talking with Sully had somehow made things even worse. The pity that was in his old, rheumy blue eyes!

"I don't want your pity," Raul grumbled. The cat looked over at him. "In fact, I don't *want* anyone."

He was drunker than Hemingway in a Cuban bar by noon.

So drunk, he didn't care that there were footsteps above him, as if small feet were running about. Instead of cowering in fear or once again running to face a strange noise in Ida's house, he cranked the volume up on the TV to drown them out.

CHAPTER NINE

Raul's phone had been ringing so much lately, he let the charge run out so he didn't have to see who he was ignoring. People back home were starting to worry about him. It was yet another layer of guilt coating his soul. He could take it. Nothing trumped being AWOL and whining about driving in the rain while your family was being murdered, crying out for you.

He'd failed his family. He'd failed his parish. Why stop there?

Meow.

The cat tapped his arm with its paw, vying for his attention. A movie he'd seen a dozen times flickered on the screen. Raul had barely been paying attention. The cable connection had come loose from the television half an hour ago and he'd yet to manage to get his ass off the couch and tighten it so the image could stabilize itself.

"What do you want now? It's not time to eat."

Eat. He couldn't remember the last time he'd eaten. Or what day it was. Or even if it was the morning or the afternoon. He did know it was daytime, thanks to the sunlight coming through the windows.

"Rise and shine, nephew o' mine," Ida used to announce while she stood over his bed. He never minded her waking him up, because it also meant she had baked something delicious for breakfast and she wanted his ass in gear so he could eat it when it was at its best. Fresh bread that steamed when you cut it alongside farm-fresh eggs and bacon was as close to heaven as Raul thought he'd ever get. That is, until dinner that night with country fried steak and hot biscuits with a homemade pecan pie waiting for dessert.

The cat nudged his arm so it could slip its fuzzy head under it. It closed its eyes seconds after settling in.

"Oh, we're cuddling now, are we?"

He wanted to sound miffed, but he was too tired, way too hungover, to dredge up anything short of a flatline of emotion.

On the screen, Rory Calhoun signed a pair of swingers in to his roadside motel. One of them was munching on a stick of Farmer Vincent's beef jerky. Raul knew the jerky was made from people and that pretty soon that kinky couple would be knocked out and buried up to their necks in the hidden human farm, fattened up until it was time for the slaughterhouse. It was not five-star entertainment, but it gave him comfort. The first time he'd seen *Motel Hell* was in his grandmother's basement with his friend Felix. The VHS copy they'd bought at the flea market was used and required a lot of tracking adjustments. They drank stolen beers and ate Jiffy Pop popcorn and howled when Calhoun donned the giant pig mask and wielded a chainsaw.

Years later, Felix had been more shocked than anyone when Raul had told him he'd found his calling and would be entering the seminary. They had gotten into their share of trouble over the years, seeing themselves maybe running a stolen car ring someday and making enough money to disappear down in South America — someplace warm and cheap with hot chicks and sandy beaches.

He'd heard Felix had died from an overdose four years ago, his body found in an alley in Baltimore. Rumors like that had a fifty-fifty shot of being factual. No matter. Raul had turned to God to heal the pain in his heart, praying for his childhood friend's soul day and night for weeks, wishing there was something he could have done to save him from the life he'd chosen, but knowing that every man had to find their own path.

When Raul first thought of coming here, it was with the intention to separate himself from the world and let his grief finally stop his heart. For weeks, it hadn't been pumping correctly, or so he thought. Each time he conjured images of his family, a heaviness would fall down upon his chest, his heart skipping beats, or sometimes, when he'd just about pass out from crying, feel as if it were seconds away from stopping. His anguish hadn't lessened one iota since. There was no break for his overtaxed ticker. There was no way it could continue on this way and still function. Raul would aid it along by doing all the wrong things.

Except that was no longer enough. If he simply drank himself to death, would three months be enough pain and suffering to atone for not being there for his family in their final moments?

"No, it won't," he said to the cat. "I'll have to drag this out until I feel I've paid the price. You'll have to wait a while before you chow down on me."

Ever since taking in the coon cat, he'd had visions of dying on his couch, the animal waiting a couple of days until the sweet stench of rot and lack of food had it nibbling on his decaying flesh. The cat was so big, he had no doubt it could finish him, though it might take some time.

"I'm not dying just yet," he said, his tongue thick as wet cardboard. "And I have to give you a name. How does Bruiser sound?"

The cat stayed sleeping, though its tail lazily slapped the cushion.

"You look like a Bruiser, even if you're a girl. You're going to have to help me pace myself. See how long we can hold it together. To that end, I think I better put something in my stomach."

Moving Bruiser's considerable weight aside was no simple feat. Before he went to the kitchen, he patted Clover and Henry on their fuzzy heads. Then he made a box of mac and cheese because it was the closest thing he had to breakfast food. At least there was milk in it. Bruiser came waltzing in just as he was spooning some into a bowl.

"You'll have to wait until it cools down."

Raul guzzled a glass of cold tap water and spooned the gooey pasta. That first bite activated his dormant hunger. Even though it burned the roof of his mouth, he couldn't stop shoveling it in. He went for seconds, saving some for the cat.

Thump!

Something hit the floor just over his head.

He froze with the spoon halfway to his mouth.

Here we go again.

He'd yet to go upstairs, but Bruiser had been making daily sojourns up there. The cat surely had set things on the precipice of counters and desktops. A breeze might have come in through the warped window frames and given something the gentle nudge it needed.

Except that wasn't the first strange sound that had been coming from upstairs the past week, though it had quieted down some these last few days. Most times, it was at night and Raul was pretty wasted, inebriation winning over fear by a country mile. He hadn't been giving himself time to mull things over the next day, opting to dive right back into the drunk end of the pool as quickly as possible.

He waited.

Bruiser looked at him as if to say, *You heard that too?*

After a couple of minutes had passed, Raul felt a burn in the muscles of his arm and realized he was still holding the spoon. He dropped the cooled macaroni back into his bowl.

"Okay, time for yours."

He got up, found a bowl, and emptied what was in the pot into it for the cat. Bruiser stood on his hind legs, stretching up until his massive paws were on the counter. "Hold your horses, it's coming."

Thump-thump!

It sounded as if someone had dropped two baseballs onto the floor. Raul and the cat both turned their heads toward the ceiling. There was a long jagged crack running from one end of the ceiling to the other, some of the plaster peeling off. Raul knew he'd been watching too many horror movies when he imagined a cold, calculating eye peering at him from within the jagged fissure.

"You don't happen to have a friend hidden away upstairs, do you? Like a little sidepiece the feral missus doesn't know about?" His attempt at lightening the mood failed. He suddenly felt like a child afraid of the creature in his closet.

Which was ridiculous. It was a bright spring day. Birds were chirping right outside the window. He'd been keeping the doors locked tight and there was no such thing as ghosts or an afterlife so it was just a bunch of junk falling off a shelf or maybe Ida's rickety old bookcase (if she hadn't thrown it away).

Raul shook his head, clearing the spinning webs of fear from his brain.

"This is ridiculous. Here, have at it."

Bruiser dove his head into the bowl of mac and cheese the instant it touched the floor. Raul busied himself by cleaning the dishes, casting wary glances at the ceiling every now and again. He filled the sink, added dish soap, and let the cheese-encrusted pot soak for a bit. Uncomfortable with the silence of the house, he turned up the volume on the TV so it could be heard in the kitchen. He found a rerun of a sitcom. The laugh track was just what he needed.

The cat was done with its meal and decided the best place to have a lie-down was at his feet while he scrubbed out the pot. A couple of times he almost tripped over the lounging beast, but bit his tongue before lashing out.

At least Bruiser wanted to be near him.

When he finished, the sitcom had gone to commercial. The announcer was calling for anyone who had a settlement from a lawsuit who wanted access to their money now. Raul stepped over the sleeping cat, anxious to get a little bit of fresh air. The simple act of washing dishes had cleared his mind.

He had his hand on the doorknob to the back door when a woman's sigh stopped him in his tracks.

A voice from behind him said, *"I can see you."*

His flesh prickled and his balls shot up into his abdomen.

Raul jerked the door open and ran outside. His foot scattered empty beer cans all over the yard. He ran into the wild grass, never once looking back.

CHAPTER TEN

This was not good. The last thing Raul needed in his life was more uncertainty.

He sat on the picnic bench, staring at the back of the house. Bruiser was on the other side of the screen door, looking at him. Their roles had been reversed and Raul didn't care. The cat could have the place.

After hearing that voice – *Bella's* voice, of that there was no doubt – he'd sprinted like his ass was on fire, running until the stitch in his side was too much to bear. It was a slow walk back to the house, but he was not going inside. Not right now. He needed time to think. The last time he'd run this hard was *to* Bella. Now, for some reason, he was running *from* her.

His heart had been tapping a ragged beat, even well after he'd gotten his wind back. Inside his pocket were a couple of his pills that he'd planned to take that night. He'd never mastered the art of dry swallowing pills. Cool, clear water waited for him in the kitchen.

Not on your fucking life.

He picked up the beer cans littering the ground, swishing them around to listen for any remnants. When he found one, he popped the pills into his mouth and tipped the can back. The beer was hot from baking in the sun and tasted like it was mixed with old rainwater. He threw the can away in repulsion. Hand over his mouth, he willed himself not to throw up.

Maybe the pills could dull things enough for him to go back inside. Though, if he heard Bella's voice again, all bets were off the table.

As much as he wanted to hear his wife and children again, this was not the way he wished it to go down.

Could they really still consciously exist, their spirits or ghosts following him here? What did they want? To talk to him? To scare him? To get him to rekindle his faith?

"No, no, no, no, no." Raul tapped the side of his head with the heel of his hand with each iteration.

They were gone. Those sick-fuck murdering animals had ripped them from this world. There were no second chances, no going back.

Then what in the unholy hell was in the house?

Raul burped up the rancid beer.

"It's you," he said.

That was the only thing it could be. He was imagining his wife's voice, his children's footsteps and laughter. It was a kind of wish fulfillment, to have them back in his life, except his subconscious was imposing its will on his conscious without an invitation.

He smoothed his sweaty hair back and exhaled.

Cooped up in the house, wallowing in grief and alcohol and pills, it was a miracle he wasn't seeing things as well.

"Back up, Bruiser."

The cat actually listened to him, allowing him enough room to open the door and step inside.

"What's that smell?"

It was him. The funk of his miserable isolation that he'd gone nose-blind to until he'd had an hour to recover in the clean air.

"You wanna watch some TV?" he asked Bruiser. The coon cat flopped onto the kitchen floor. "Suit yourself."

His head spun for just a second, his body's way of letting him know it was processing quite nicely the pills he'd taken. A nap was most certainly in his very near future.

Crashing onto the couch, he pulled the remote from under his thigh and searched for something to fall asleep to.

"You heard that before, right?" he asked Clover and Henry, the stuffed sloths. When they didn't answer (and if they did, he would haul ass all the way to Canada), he scooted across the couch to the chair where they sat and scooped them into his arms.

He couldn't believe just an hour ago, he was running out of Ida's house like that family in *The Amityville Horror*. At least the dad in that movie had gone back for the dog. Not Raul. He'd left Bruiser to save himself.

Must have looked like a horse's ass. Good to know there's no one around to have seen me. One of the advantages of living in the sticks.

His eyelids felt heavier and heavier. Exhaustion from all that running and the meds were pulling him under fast. He settled his head on a throw pillow, staring at the TV but barely paying attention.

It was all in my head, he reassured himself.

All in my head.

But as he drifted off to sleep, a single thought plagued his dreams.

If it was all in his head, how come the cat was reacting to the sounds as well?

★ ★ ★

The volume on the television was what woke him up.

Goddamn networks. Why do they crank up the volume for their inane commercials?

He reached over to the coffee table, his hand slapping the surface in search of the remote. Ida's stack of *Reader's Digest* magazines went scattering. Now he had to open his eyes and search for the remote. That meant nap time was officially over.

Where was it?

It definitely wasn't on the table where he normally kept it.

But today wasn't a normal day.

He got up and checked the couch cushions, wondering if it had fallen between them while he slept.

No dice.

Getting on his hands and knees, he scoured under the coffee table and couch. Maybe the cat had swatted it somewhere. Although, to be honest, he hadn't seen Bruiser play with anything so far. He seemed content to eat, sleep, and shit in the plastic tub Raul had found down in the basement and set in the bathroom between the toilet and the sink. He'd been lining it with the pages from old magazines. Much cheaper than litter. Still, Bruiser was a cat, and cats liked to knock around whatever they got their paws on.

As he crawled around the living room, Raul's anger bubbled and boiled, the blaring commercial about home-delivered catheters sending him over the edge.

"Where the fuck did you put it, Bruiser?" he shouted.

The cat was nowhere to be seen.

He got up because his knees were starting to hurt. His frustration mounted when he felt around the television, searching for a button to lower the volume. Damn thing was completely dependent on the remote. Who designed such a thing?

A quick tug on the power cord silenced the commercial.

"Bruiser?"

As if the cat would come running. He probably had no idea Bruiser was its new name, and it wasn't as if cats cared a whit about what people said.

Raul searched the entire downstairs and found nothing but dust on the floor. How could the remote just disappear? Bruiser was big, but he couldn't see the cat putting the remote in his mouth and taking it with him to wherever he'd gone.

Fuck.

This was as good a reason as any to grab a beer. Leaning against the refrigerator, he drank half the can.

Now what?

Silence in the big old house was not his friend. He needed that television. Where would he find a replacement remote? Did Glens Falls have an electronics store? Or had online stores wiped them out?

As he finished his beer, the ticking of the kitchen clock the only sound in the house, he suddenly remembered his revelation before he'd fallen asleep.

"It's not just me."

The back of his scalp prickled. Even the softest whisper would be heard in the house now.

He eyed the back door. Sure, he could go running again, but what would that get him? Temporary relief was just that, temporary. And what would he be running from now? A quiet, empty house?

No running. That would be ridiculous. Not this time. Or at least not now.

More drinking. Yes, that's what was needed.

And not beer. That took too long. He needed to get smashed fast. He opened the freezer door and reached for the vodka.

The remote was on top of the ice cube tray.

CHAPTER ELEVEN

Two mornings later, Raul pulled his shirt over his head and was so offended by the smell as the fabric whisked past his nose that he considered throwing it in the garbage. He'd made it to his old room the night before, keeping the lights blazing. The TV warbled in the living room. This time, it was an overly loud infomercial about a deep fryer. Of all the stations to be stuck with, it had to be one where the programming was more infomercials than shows or movies. At least they had shown *Full Metal Jacket* last night, minus the swearing. It kind of took some of the impact away, though this version would have been just what he would have approved of three months ago.

Being in the freezer had killed the remote, stranding Raul on this wasteland of a station to watch. What happened to the days when cable boxes had buttons?

Time for a shower. Bruiser slept at the foot of the bed, opening one curious eye as Raul stripped and padded to the bathroom.

"Did you just crinkle your nose at me?"

Bruiser turned away.

"Fair enough. I admit, I'm putrid."

Sweating out alcohol and bad food and not showering for days made for one heady funk. Before he started it all over again, the least he could do was clean himself.

Things had been disappearing with regularity. First it was the remote, then the issue of *Reader's Digest* he'd been perusing one afternoon, followed by the knife and fork he'd left in the kitchen sink and his house keys that had been on the key hook beside the front door. So far, he'd only found the remote and house keys. The keys had somehow made it inside one of the kitchen cabinets.

Now, with the booze and pills, it was very probable that he'd been misplacing things in his stupor. That made logical sense. The Other Raul seemed to like his own hijinks.

So why couldn't he shake the feeling that he was not the culprit?

Raul stepped into the shower, savoring the scalding water as it burned away layers of filth.

"You've got to be kidding me."

His bar of Irish Spring soap, the one he'd opened from a new pack just a week ago, wasn't in the soap dish. Nor was it on the tub floor. Or the little caddy that held his shampoo. He washed up with the shampoo, yanking the shower curtain aside several times when he felt that someone...or something...was in the room with him.

I'm losing my fucking mind along with everything else in the house.

He dressed and went out to the front porch with a book, uncomfortable with staying in the house. Bruiser was on the windowsill, looking out the living room window and into the front yard.

"You want to come out?"

The cat blinked. Raul opened the door. Bruiser didn't move.

"At least you like it in there."

Settling onto the porch swing, Raul opened the cover to *Catch-22*, another classic he'd never gotten around to. Maybe a little wartime reading would take his mind off of what was happening in the house...and in his head.

The sun played peekaboo between the low-lying clouds as they scudded across a pale blue sky. There was just a hint of a breeze, a perfect day to get out and dry out.

No booze today.

It was antithetical to his entire plan, but he had to know who or what was behind the strange happenings in Ida's house. The word *ghosts* kept popping into his head and he didn't like it one bit. Well, the only way to shut that part of his brain up was to keep his shit together for a day or two and get to the bottom of things. The book shook in his hands and his stomach cramped. Sobriety was not going to come easy.

He had to just shut up and read. Go away for a while.

The only problem with going away was that you always had to come back at some point. He turned his head to look into the house. What else was missing or hidden someplace it wasn't meant to be?

Just fucking read.

No matter how hard he tried, he couldn't get past the second page. If he wasn't racking his brain for a reason behind the goings-on in the house, he was thinking about Bella, Lizzy, and Abel; alternating between fear, confusion, and grief so deep he could fall into it and never see the light of day again exhausted him.

Raul wanted his family. A day like today, Bella would have been nestled next to him on the porch swing. She'd smell of her cherry blossom shower gel, a steaming mug of coffee in her hands. He'd talk to her about his ideas for his next sermon and she'd tell him not to bore everyone. She was his harshest critic, but she was always right. Oftentimes, he wondered if she should have been the one behind that pulpit. Naturally shy and reserved, she spent a lot of time observing others and knew what needed to be said to connect with people, even if she had a difficult time of it herself.

Lizzy should be running around with her net and plexiglass carrier, searching for bugs. The girl loved all things with wings and multiple legs. Nature hadn't made a bug she wouldn't pick right up and let travel up her arm. Even those nasty silverfish that would make Raul jump when he spotted them in the shower were a cause for Lizzy's fearless curiosity. She'd been begging for them to get her a pet tarantula. Raul and Bella had put their foot down on that one. If Lizzy were still here, he'd buy her all the tarantulas she wanted.

Now Abel, so much like his mother, he'd find a comfortable spot to sit with his sketch pad and draw until his pencil was down to the nub. He'd gotten pretty good, graduating from recreating anime characters to sketching whatever was around him. He might have only been ten, but he had skills well beyond his years. If Raul had that ability when he was young, he'd probably have used his talent to spray-paint graffiti on brick walls. Not Abel. He'd been so good, so pure, Raul was sure he'd follow in his father's footsteps if teen hormones didn't come marching in and derail everything.

Raul didn't realize he was crying until he heard his tears splatting the pages of his open book.

Something slammed against the wall by the front door. The book jumped from his lap as he leaped from the swing. Bruiser flew off the windowsill and went running, disappearing into the house.

Staring at the screen door, Raul had to force himself to take hold of the handle and go inside. Dust motes danced in the bolt of sunlight that streamed into the house.

There was no blaming Bruiser for making the sound. The coon cat had been languidly taking in the rays and was just as shaken as he was by the sudden disturbance of their peace.

Raul looked around the room. The crumpled sheet and pillow were still on the couch, always there for when he passed out watching TV. Clover lay slumped over Henry on a corner of the couch.

Stepping farther into the house, his skin pricking with goose bumps, he saw it.

On the floor, beside the stairs leading to the second floor, was a broken ceramic figurine. His eyes flicked to the shadowy landing at the top of the stairs, expecting to see a dark figure standing there, admiring its handiwork. He was never so happy to be so wrong.

On closer inspection, he saw that the shattered knickknack was one of Ida's collectible pigs. She had shelves of them in her bedroom. He looked up the stairs again and could see her bedroom door. It was closed, as it always had been since he'd moved in.

Where the hell had the pig come from? And how did it end up downstairs in pieces?

It couldn't have been a person, some squatter who secretly shared the house with Raul. The wood in the old house was arthritic with age. He would have heard someone moving about upstairs. Whenever Bruiser went up there, Raul could track his whereabouts by following the pops, groans, and creaks coming from above.

Now, there was only silence.

"Ida?"

He felt ridiculous saying it aloud. Her name spilled from his lips instinctively.

Even if there were ghosts, and Ida's spirit still found comfort in her home, he couldn't see her breaking one of her prized possessions.

"B...Bella?"

If she answers, I'm going to have a heart attack.

In life, Bella had never been one to recklessly toss things around. But what did he know about death? As a priest, he'd been quick to reassure people that his faith told him there was a heaven, a place where good and just souls would be wrapped in God's warm embrace.

The truth was, no one knew what waited for them after their heart stopped beating. Even faith was a poor substitute for undeniable proof. There was a brief period when he was obsessed with accounts of near-death experiences, or NDEs, especially those that told of brilliant white lights, a reckoning of one's past life and judgment. They all fit in neatly with his belief. However, there were far too many discrepancies to suit him. The more he read, the more uneasy he felt about his faith, so he stopped.

"The simplest explanation is almost always the correct one," he said, the sound of his voice helping to soothe his nerves. The Occam's Razor theory had been used in countless books and movies, an attempt to either dispel or support the strange and paranormal.

He'd been living with voices and objects moving for the past few weeks now and had yet to come up with a viable explanation.

Could the simplest explanation in his case also be the most disturbing?

He was being haunted.

He looked down at the shattered pig.

Worst still, he was being haunted by his murdered family.

And they didn't seem happy.

Lizzy had always been the unintentionally destructive force in the family, knocking things over as she played or danced around the house with abandon. When she was angry, she would throw her toys. If there weren't any toys within reach, she'd grab the nearest object, usually a pillow, or her spoon if she threw a fit at the dinner table. That kind of behavior had been the catalyst to countless time-outs and punishments. No matter what Raul and Bella did to correct Lizzy's lashing out when she was upset, they couldn't stop her. As sweet as she could be, she was also a force of nature. Luckily, she only had her tantrums in the home, never in public, which showed a bit of intelligent calculation on her part.

Had Lizzy been mad just now, or was she simply trying to get his attention?

"I'm so sorry, Lizzy."

He was sorry for not being there to protect her. For ignoring her. For everything and anything.

Was that a child's sigh that came from the second floor?

The tiny, brief sound stopped his heart for a painful moment.

"Lizzy?"

I have to go up there.

Up into Ida's domain.

He cowered under the weight of unseen eyes watching him as he crept up the steps.

The old runner was still in the hallway, the flower print more faded than he remembered, the weave showing through in the more threadbare spots. Meager light spilled into the hall from the open door to Ida's thinking room. It was as messy as ever, shelves overflowing with used paperbacks, with a new addition of a tilting stack of hatboxes in the corner. Funny, he'd never seen Ida wear a hat. It wasn't a stretch to think Bruiser could easily bring the whole thing down, the ensuing noise giving Raul a terrifying start.

Better take them down now.

He found the chain to turn on the overhead light and tugged. The light didn't go on.

With one eye on Ida's bedroom door, he slowly made his way to Ida's thinking room. There was Bruiser, sleeping on a pile of clothes that had been tossed in a corner, a black plastic bag on the side of the mound. The cat must have been playing around with her battered paperbacks. An open copy of Anne McCaffrey's *Dragonquest* was under Bruiser's belly, as if he'd been reading it before falling asleep and rolling over.

"Reading is fundamental," Ida would say to him. "At least that's what they tell you in the commercials. I'll say this. A book is a better friend than anyone you'll ever meet. It doesn't talk back and if you don't like it, you can pitch it in the fire and the police won't come gunning for ya. Now just try that with one of your hoodlum friends back home."

It looked as if Ida had been gathering old clothes to drop at a Goodwill box. He made a mental note to finish what she'd started. The floor squeaked when Raul stepped on the threshold, waking Bruiser up.

Raul reluctantly turned his back on the hallway and set about unstacking the hatboxes, scattering them carefully around the room. It didn't surprise him that they were not full of hats, but rather the overflow of her beloved books. He scanned the covers and realized Ida read everything, from romances set in the 1800s to true crime, thrillers, and even horror. One of the boxes was full of H.P. Lovecraft paperbacks, with strange images in stark contrast to the black-and-white backgrounds. He could picture her sitting in the ratty chair thumbing through her collection. It would be nice to find a new home for her books, though Raul wasn't sure he could do it. Especially not if it would upset her and she was, by some mad twist of fate, still here with him.

That sigh, though. That hadn't been Ida.

Ida might or might not be here. But something, perhaps his daughter, was.

There was no overflow of her pig collection in here. He'd hoped to find a few stray pigs so he could tell his terrified brain to calm the hell down. Bruiser could have easily swatted a piggy down the stairs.

"You coming?" he said to Bruiser.

The cat got up, stretched, clawed the fabric for a bit, and lay back down.

"Coward."

That was easy for him to say. Ever the phony.

The floor popped with every step, spiking his heart rate along with each crack. His mouth had gone incredibly dry, even more so than on the morning of a hangover. Every part of his body hurt, crying out for the booze and pills it had come to rely upon to get through the day.

He held his breath and turned the knob to Ida's bedroom door. It stuck for a moment. He had to shoulder it open with quite a bit of effort. A cloud of stale air enveloped him like a sentient fog. Raul almost turned right around and shut the door. No one had been in the room for quite a while.

Ida had passed away in her sleep, succumbing to pneumonia, in this made bed. He wondered who had bothered to make it. Had the sheets been changed, or were these the very same ones that she had expired within? The thought brought a chill down his back.

Must have been the caretaker the lawyer sent over.

Something brushed against his leg. Raul jumped back about three feet, his heart racing.

Bruiser, squirming out from under the bed, jumped onto the mattress.

"How the fuck did you get in here?" Raul exclaimed with his hand over his chest. The door had been shut tighter than a nun's chastity belt.

The cat settled in, resting its head on her pillow.

"You want to scare the crap out of me? Okay. Get lost." Raul shooed the coon cat out of the bed. Bruiser stopped at the threshold and looked back at him, as if to give him a chance to reconsider his request.

"Go on."

Bruiser padded down the hall and, from the sound of things, down the stairs.

Raul grabbed hold of the door. "Jesus Christ."

The door might have opened in the night, and with the heat of the day a breeze could have shut it and the wood expanded. What would have happened to Bruiser if he hadn't come in here?

You would have smelled him a few days from now.

Taking a few deep breaths to settle down, he looked around Ida's room.

Nothing seemed out of place, but then again, he barely remembered what the inside of her room looked like. The top of her dresser was a minefield of perfume bottles, most of the contents either used or dried up, hairbrushes, cheap reader eyeglasses you'd buy at the drugstore, and a bowl with spare change.

What took him back were the shelves of pig figurines. Now those he remembered. Not the individual pigs, but just the collection as a whole. There had to be hundreds of them, filling every bit of wall space. He walked around the room, taking in the massive collection, careful to be as quiet as possible lest he miss out on hearing Lizzy again.

On the third shelf from the top, to the left of the window overlooking the backyard, he found an irregular circle carved from the dust. He'd bet everything he had that it was the place of pride for the shattered pig figurine downstairs. The thing was in too many pieces for him to glue it together to check for sure.

He was well past wondering how it got from here to there. It just had. Period.

Raul didn't want to be up here anymore. He wheeled around and left the room, closing the door behind him. It took great effort not to run down the stairs. He was sure someone was right behind him, knowing full well it was his imagination but unable to dispel the queasiness in his gut. He felt more exposed on that walk down the stairs than if he'd strolled naked down Fifth Avenue during the Macy's Thanksgiving Day Parade.

Keep busy. Make noise and keep busy.

Carrying the dustpan and broom from the kitchen pantry, he was about to up the volume on the TV when he heard his Lizzy's voice wafting down the stairs.

"Hi Daddy."

CHAPTER TWELVE

Raul stepped into a cloud of cherry blossom as he went to the refrigerator.

"You shmell good, Bella," he slurred, getting a fresh can of beer.

Over the past few days, he'd found a balance.

By taking a certain amount of his medication and interspersing it with just enough alcohol to keep him calm without sending him into a spiral of blackout inebriation, he could live with the sounds and smells, voices and missing objects. They were just a part of his everyday life now. And he was just numb enough to experience it without jumping or wanting to sprint for the hills or, in this case, mountains.

Problem was, he was running low on meds. He'd need to venture out to find a drugstore that could take his prescription.

"Problem for another day." He shut the door a little harder than he'd intended.

Poor Bruiser wasn't as lucky as him. The cat was flinching and scattering on a regular basis. Several times, Raul had left the back door open, giving Bruiser a chance to escape. The cat was either too dumb to realize relief was just a few steps away, or his ties to the house and Raul at this point were too strong to break.

"I'm living with ghosts. And a very nervous cat."

A nervous cat that, he had learned, liked beer. Raul had dropped an open can that had been in the refrigerator the night before. Bruiser ran to it like a man dying of thirst in the Gobi and lapped up every drop.

"You like the cheap stuff too. Runs in the family."

It was too ridiculous not to laugh.

What he'd been thinking lately was that maybe the ghosts weren't something outside of him, but rather a construct that came from within. Like a Tibetan tulpa, which was something he'd learned about yesterday while perusing the internet on his phone. To the Tibetans, a tulpa was something you could, in a sense, dream into existence. The very concept gave him some comfort in the sense that if he had created this, he could, somehow, either control it or find a way to make it all cease to exist.

Of course, he had no idea how he had brought Bella, Lizzy, and Abel into ghostly life, so it was going to be hard to reverse engineer the process to send them back to his subconscious.

Plus, there were times, especially since he'd learned the not-so-magic potion to steady his nerves, when he *wanted* them near. He'd been talking to them aloud a lot.

And sometimes, they talked back.

Right now, he needed to nurse this beer for an hour, then take his anxiety med that would last him all the way to bedtime.

Something rolled across the floor upstairs. He cast his glance upward for a moment, then looked down for Bruiser. The cat was on the couch, his ears twitching.

"No playing ball in the house," he called up the stairs as he headed out the door. Dusk would arrive in an hour, but there was still plenty of light left to read by. He'd found a leather-bound copy of the collected works of H.G. Wells in one of the hutch's drawers in the dining room. It was there mixed with tablecloths and linen napkins. Strange place to stash a book, considering Ida had a whole room set aside for them. Then again, strange was normal here now.

He'd been reading *The Food of the Gods* since yesterday, enjoying the story on a whole new level now that he was in a semi-altered state. The tale took on bizarre new meanings as he read, each epiphany lost by the time he jumped back into the book. No matter, it had become an experiential event for him.

With a slight buzzing in his ears, he sat on the porch swing and found where he'd left off, tucking the cardboard Beefeater coaster he'd also found in the hutch drawer under his thigh. It was a cumbersome bookmark but it did its job well. The grass had grown considerably; it undulated as the wind caressed the land. Each breath of air was scented with cinnamon and hints of mint. Raul felt at peace for the moment, and soon his eyelids grew heavy.

When the phone rang, his head jerked up, chin pushing off his chest. The blue sky had started to pinken, the breeze gone still.

Still in a dream daze, he struggled to get his phone out of his back pocket, swiped to answer and said, "Yeah?"

Instantly, he knew he'd made a mistake. An instinct he thought he'd tamped down for good had taken over. He'd been avoiding talking to anyone since his arrival. His initial goal had been to simply disappear, and nothing much had changed.

"Raul! I was ready to leave you a message." His mother-in-law sounded like she was on the verge of tears.

He struggled to be social. Though she didn't deserve to be shut out, it had gotten almost too easy to lose his social graces. The longer he was alone, the more content he'd been with his hermitage. Now, through his own fault, not hers, he owed it to her to be polite.

"Oh, yeah, hey, I'm sorry I haven't been getting back to you." He sounded funny, off, even to him. Sleep and his magic potion would do that. Valentina would definitely hear it.

"I understand. You need some space. But we've been worried sick about you. I can't tell you how much better I feel just hearing your voice." Yes, she was happy, but he could detect the note of concern in her voice.

"How are you and Dad?"

"We're fine. I'm more concerned about you. How have you been?"

Oh, just drinking and drugging a little too much because, well, the ghosts of your daughter and grandchildren have either come to haunt me or my own guilty conscience is trying to drive me insane. I have a cat now too!

"Just laying low. Keeping to myself. Thinking of Bella and the kids."

"You need to get out. And I'm not just talking about the house. Sometimes, the worst place to be trapped is inside your own head. It's not healthy."

"I do. For a little town, there's still plenty to do around here." He hated lying to her.

"That's good. Look, we're all living with grief. But the important word is *living*. It hurts some days more than others. I'm lucky in that I have Eduardo, and vice versa. What concerns me is that you're up there all alone with no one to lean on, especially during the worst moments."

If she tells me that Bella would want me to live my life and move on, I'm not responsible for what I say next.

"Raul? Honey? Talk to me. Please."

He sighed. "I'm not going to lie to you. Every day has been a struggle. It's a fact I'm learning to live with. For now, I need to learn it on my own."

"But—"

"I can't take anyone down with me."

"You can't think of it that way. You have to see it as someone lifting you up when you need it most. The way you did day in and day out when you were a priest. You lived in service to others. Now, it's time to let us return the favor."

"I can't."

"Yes, you can. We can come visit you. You've been alone too long."

Only Valentina and Eduardo knew where he lived now. He regretted telling them. This was no place for them. What if they heard Bella or the kids? What would it do to them? He didn't mind himself being destroyed. What he couldn't handle was the thought of his in-laws being irretrievably shattered by the strange happenings in Ida's house. Like a virus, it was best that he kept himself here, quarantined.

"Really, I'll be okay," he said, trying his best to sound upbeat. "Time heals all wounds. I just haven't had enough time yet."

She tried another tack. "We miss you."

"I know. I miss you too."

Valentina tried to talk about the goings-on at his former church, but it fell on deaf ears. He didn't care if the new priest was having a hard time connecting with his parishioners. Or that there had been a minor flood on the first floor of the house where his family had been murdered.

They eventually fell into small, meaningless talk until Valentina let him go, but not without making him promise he would call her weekly from now on.

It was a promise he wasn't entirely sure he would keep.

★ ★ ★

Lately, there had been a lot going on in the basement.

At night, Raul kept the door to his bedroom open. Since the small room was just off the kitchen, he was able to hear everything.

There were footsteps and soft bangs, as if the junk down there was being moved around or dropped. Sometimes there was muted laughter.

Right now, with the sheet pulled up to his neck, he heard the delicate ululations of Abel crying. His sobs came up through the vent in the floor. They broke Raul's heart.

"It's okay," he said, hoping it was loud enough for the ghost of his son to hear. He didn't need to see his son to know what was causing his tears. As his father, Raul had heard them all.

Abel was frightened. It was the way he'd weep when he had a nightmare or saw a large, unleashed dog.

As much as his heart ached for his child, he was terrified. Thankfully, the magic potion kept his fear to an undercurrent that merely stiffened his muscles and parched his throat.

"It will be all right," he called into the kitchen. "I'm here. Mommy's here. So is Lizzy."

In truth, he had no idea if Bella and Lizzy were down there with Abel. Where did ghosts go when they weren't vexing the living?

Bella wouldn't leave their son. Not even in death. And Lizzy was her brother's best friend, despite the occasional blowup between them.

Raul wanted to tell Abel to come upstairs, to be with his father so he could comfort him. What stopped his tongue was a vision of Abel's murdered corpse, ethereal yet pregnant with the weight of sorrow, walking through the basement door, gliding toward him in the dark. Raul would scream. No amount of magic potion would be able to quell his atavistic reaction to such a thing.

Abel was frightened enough. As his father, he could not add to his son's woes.

Again, he was failing his son. In life, in death, Raul, the great leader of his flock, preparing them for eternal life, was nothing but a weak, flimflam artist. He made himself sick.

Abel wept and Raul cowered.

"It's scary in here," Abel said.

Raul went even more rigid. It was the first coherent sentence he'd heard from his son's spirit. And it terrified him.

"Where, Abie? Where are you?"

If he was going to believe in ghosts – a rabbit hole he'd tumbled down days ago – he had to consider how things appeared in their realm. Did Abel see the basement, or something else? Did he see anything at all? Or was his son experiencing something that was beyond the senses of the living? Abel had always been afraid of the dark. What child wasn't? Was it the darkness of the basement that frightened him or the ether he was trapped within?

There was one way to eliminate a possible source of his son's discomfort.

He had to turn the cellar light on.

Raul was sure that Ida's house wasn't haunted. It was he who was haunted. Going into the basement would be no different than staying up here. At least, that's what he told himself to marshal the courage to rise from his bed. He'd taken the sloths to bed with him. Raul grabbed Henry.

His eyes never left the grate in the kitchen floor as he skirted past it, making his way in the dark to the cellar door. Abel's sobs increased, as if he could hear his father and was doing what he could to draw him to him.

I...I can't go down there. Please, let the light be enough.

Raul's legs felt weak and his hands shook.

What was behind that door?

Was Bella's spirit waiting at the top step for him, angry that he wasn't rushing to their son's side in his time of need? The thought of a furious, diaphanous Bella, her eyes burning with rage, made him take a step back.

Would that be worse than a trio of apparitions of his mutilated family, their gazes vacant, hair twisting in an otherworldly wind? Every horrid image he'd consumed in horror movies blasted him like a firehose and made his legs weak.

Anything visible behind the cellar door would obliterate him. That was the only sure thing he knew at the moment.

It was all right if they stayed *down there*, in the shadows where his eyes couldn't penetrate. Yet part of him desperately wanted them to be up here, with him, close enough to touch, to see their beautiful faces. But what if those faces blazed with hatred? Or disappointment? He wasn't sure if he could handle that.

From behind him, wafting from the cellar, came one pleading word.

"*Daddy?*"

Raul steeled himself, clutched the doorknob, and turned.

Before him was blessed, empty darkness.

He flipped the switch.

The light, as paltry as it was, came on.

Abel's crying stopped.

He squatted down and set Henry on the top step.

Raul quickly shut the door, leaning his back into it, breathing heavily. Cold sweat ran down the sides of his face as his heart whammed in his chest.

He sank to the floor, resting his head on his knees, and cried until the first rays of the morning light.

CHAPTER THIRTEEN

Raul had to get out of the house today. Not out of fear – though there was plenty of that – but because his meds and supplies were about to hit rock bottom. Morrisburgh didn't have a pharmacy, so it was back to Glens Falls. It was a beautiful day with an azure sky streaked with the occasional cotton ball cloud, warm but with a cooling breeze.

As the indestructible Subaru purred with mechanical life, Raul stared at the house, noticing for the first time how the two windows on the second floor looked like eyes peering down at him. It was ridiculous, but he felt as if he were being watched at all times. So why not the house as he drove away?

It was late morning on a Wednesday and there were very few people out and about. His first stop was the liquor store, where he bought what he thought he needed and then added to it. The man at the register didn't bat an eye or ask if he was throwing a party. In fact, he barely took his eyes from his phone. Raul saw he was scrolling through Instagram pictures of busty women in bikinis.

When he found one of those big chain store pharmacies, he made a call to his pharmacist back home (or what used to be home) and asked if they could work with the drug store here to fill his prescriptions. He got the okay and the Glens Falls pharmacist – a very pretty girl who seemed too young for the job but sounded more than competent – told him they'd be ready in half an hour.

That gave him time to go to the supermarket. He got a better variety of food and even threw in some vegetables and fruit. His magic potion, which dulled everything, was having the opposite effect on his appetite. He'd been craving oranges and rice with pigeon peas. Dropping the cans of peas in his cart, he shook his head and chuckled. Was he pregnant with magic potion? That might explain his craving.

He felt lighter being out among people, away from his inherited house of noises, voices, and tears. Was it odd that he also was afflicted with guilt? Here he was, at one with the ebb and flow of life, while his family waited for him in the dark corners of Ida's house.

Not yet ready to go back, but knowing it was where he belonged, where, perhaps, he was needed, he drove up and down Main Street. He took note of the cat hospital, just in case. He got a coffee and half a dozen donuts at Dunkin' and then stopped at Subway to grab a foot-long Italian sub. Fast food had never been his preference, though he now appreciated the convenience. No cooking needed tonight.

To his surprise there was an electronics store and they had a universal remote. If Raul still believed in an all-seeing god, he would have thanked him. He also bought a pack of batteries and a new portable radio. It was about the size of a hardcover book and had a plastic handle so he could carry it around.

His medication was ready by the time he got back to the pharmacy. He added a bottle of Tylenol for his hangovers and a six-pack of soap. Best to be prepared for the mischievous ghosts that had now taken his soap from the shower twice. Raul would be all set, unless they took the whole pack. He also loaded up on newspapers, magazines, and a couple of paperbacks.

His mood darkened the closer he got to Morrisburgh. He passed by Sully's General Store, happy he'd stocked up out of town. He suddenly wasn't in the mood to talk to or even see people. It was as if the magnetic attraction of Ida's house was altering his mind, his mood, twisting it until he was ground under the feelings of despair and anxiety. Sully's warmth and generosity seemed to Raul like garlic to a vampire.

If this were a proper horror movie, the skies would darken the moment he turned into the driveway. Real life was content to keep the contrast between the picture-perfect day and his sullen disposition.

Except there was one small kink.

A black-and-gold motorcycle was parked outside the house.

Raul slowed down. The old brakes squealed.

There wasn't anyone around. The front door was still closed, but that didn't mean some lone wolf biker hadn't helped himself inside and was lying in wait.

No, that didn't make sense. If that were someone's plan, they would have hidden the Harley.

"What the hell?"

He cut the engine and wrapped his fingers around the keys so they poked out from between them. Better to be safe than sorry.

Keeping the car door open in case he needed to duck back inside and drive for help, he scanned the yard, squinting along the sides of the house, searching for any sign of the motorcycle's owner. The wind ruffled his hair and drove a speck of grit into his right eye. It immediately watered, reducing him to a cyclops. He rubbed at his eye, careful to keep the unaffected one open and wary for the intruder.

"Man, there's nothing like a good piss outdoors."

Raul whirled and saw a man in a leather jacket emerging from behind a maple tree. He was zipping up his jeans, strolling toward him casually as if Raul regularly entertained wayward bikers. Raul had a hard time making out the man's face, both because of only having the sight of one eye to do so, and the amount of black scruff that hid the man's features.

All Raul could say was, "Huh?"

The man stopped about twenty yards shy of Raul and the Subaru. "What's the matter with you? I know I haven't changed that much." He had a slight Spanish accent. Raul stopped worrying at his eye.

"Do I know you?"

The man laughed. "You better, *abuelo*."

Abuelo? Raul hadn't been called that since, since....

"Felix?"

"Hey, the man doesn't have complete amnesia!"

Felix, his old friend he used to raise hell with when they were teens being raised by older family members who couldn't keep up with them, sauntered to Raul, his jacket creaking as he moved his arms, and pulled him into a tight hug. "It's good to see you, man."

Raul was almost too stunned to talk.

How is this happening? Raul thought. *The last time I saw Felix, I was heading off to college and he was selling hot radios from the back of his* *car. Apparently the rumors of his death were off by a country mile.*

"H-how did you find me?"

"In this white-ass place, it was easy to find the only Puerto Rican." Felix guffawed. No one amused Felix as much as himself. It appeared that hadn't changed.

They separated and Raul looked him up and down. "Seriously, how did you know I was here?"

Felix was busy looking in the Subaru's windows. "You got a lot of shit in there. Come on, I'll help you get it inside." He opened the hatch and grabbed two cases of beer. "It's like you knew I was coming." When he got to the porch, he turned around and asked, "The door open?"

Raul had to break from his paralysis. "It's...it's locked. Hold on." He loaded up his arm with several bags of groceries and, feeling as if he'd fallen into a dream, opened the door for a man he hadn't seen in over fifteen years.

"Sweet place. Just the way you used to describe it," Felix said. He brought the beer into the kitchen and opened the refrigerator. "How many shelves you want to fill with beer? You definitely have enough room."

"I've got it." Raul put his bags on the kitchen table. A can of soup escaped and hit the floor. Felix was quick to pick it up.

"Beef barley?" Felix crinkled his nose as if he smelled something terrible. "That's old people soup. Just what a grandpa would eat."

Raul headed back to the car to get the rest of the bags while Felix opened a case of beer. His old friend was drinking a warm can when Raul came back inside.

"You don't look like you're happy to see me," Felix said, wiping foam from his beard with the back of his hand.

"Huh?"

"You have someone coming over? I can leave and come back. Any cheap motels around here?"

"No, no one's coming here. That was kind of the idea," Raul said, emptying the bag that had his bread and eggs. "I'm sorry, man. I've been cooped up here alone for weeks. I'm forgetting how to talk to people."

Felix finished his beer, crushed the can, and dropped it in the garbage. "I would have called but I was told you would probably give me the brush-off."

"Who told you that?"

"Your in-laws."

"My in-laws? How do you know them? How did you even know I was married? I heard you were dead." It wasn't as if Raul had even the hint of an online presence. Going off the grid, so to speak, hadn't been difficult when he became a priest.

"A lot of people wish I was," he said with a mischievous grin. Felix grew somber. "I heard about your family. I'm so sorry. I can't believe the cops haven't caught those bastards."

Raul had to fight the hitch in his throat. "I...I feel the same."

Felix opened another beer and then one for Raul. "I saw it all on the news. I would have come sooner, but I wasn't able to get out until a week ago."

"Get out?"

"I was away at college." He draped his heavy jacket over the back of a chair.

"How long?"

"Six months. Nothing big."

College for men like Felix was a euphemism for prison. It didn't shock Raul that his friend had been 'taking classes'. He used to pray that Felix would straighten his life out and find peace. But as the years went on, he thought of him less and less and the prayers faded away.

"Man, when I saw what happened to you and your family, I actually thought of breaking out and tracking down those sons of bitches. Cops have limits. I don't. And over the years, I've become pretty good at tracking people down."

Raul allowed himself a small smile, anxious to change the subject of his family's murder. "So, you did learn a trade since we last met."

Felix chuckled. "That and a few other things. I actually came here to confess, turn my life around."

The warm beer tasted awful, but it was needed. Raul chugged the can. "Then you came to the wrong place. I'm not a priest anymore."

"Sure you are."

He shook his head. "Hard to be a priest when you don't believe in God."

Felix tapped his chest with a stubby finger. "That's the pain working its way through you now. I get it. I've seen it happen. Your faith will come back. It runs too deep in you."

"How the hell would you know?" Raul was taken aback by his sudden swell of anger. By the nature of his calling in life, he'd become taciturn over the years. Seeing his old friend was rapidly rekindling his old ways.

Holding up his hands in surrender, Felix replied, "*Tranquilo*, man. *Tranquilo*. I'm just saying, any man who becomes a priest has faith as big as a skyscraper. What happened has fucked you up now. It would fuck anyone up. Sooner or later, you'll find that faith again and that's how you'll heal."

Who the hell was this basic stranger, a man who only knew Raul the truant teen, to tell him about his pain, his faith, his healing? Raul had to clench his jaw tight to prevent himself from saying something he'd regret.

After a few calming breaths, Raul said, "Maybe I don't want to heal. Maybe I'm here, by myself, for a reason."

Felix tossed him another beer. "Maybe I'm here for a reason too."

"Yeah? What is it?"

Felix pulled a chair out and sat down. "I don't know. Why don't we chill out and see what happens?"

CHAPTER FOURTEEN

After putting everything away, Raul and Felix spent the rest of the day drinking beer and talking about the past. The booze had lightened Raul's mood enough to enjoy Felix's company. His friend's booming laughter filled the house, charging the atmosphere itself. Raul swore he could feel it, the heavy air of oppression growing lighter with each passing hour.

Throughout their unplanned reunion, Raul kept half an ear and eye out for anything strange to occur. The only problem was, Felix was so loud, it would be hard to hear anything.

He could look at it as Felix giving him peace from the ghosts that had been haunting him day after day.

He could also look at it as Felix chasing his family away. And that was upsetting him. The only way to hide his irritation was to get shit-faced. So, he did.

Night fell without either of them noticing until Felix said he needed air and they went out back. The crickets were in full swing and the air smelled sweet as honey.

"Man, this place is nice," Felix said, sipping his beer and looking out into the darkness. "It feels like we're the last two people on earth. What's that movie with the guy who thinks he's all that's left until he meets those weird white motherfuckers?"

Raul leaned against the house and closed his eyes to try to stop his head from spinning. "*The Omega Man* with Charlton Heston."

"That's it! I should have remembered, considering I stole the copy from the video store. Wonder where it is."

"If you had to remember everything you stole, you'd be in trouble." Raul could only imagine how many other things Felix had pilfered in the years since they had lost touch.

Felix walked into Raul's empty can pile, the metallic rattle upsetting the night song. "Bro, what the hell is this? You thinking of opening a garbage dump back here?"

"It's my shrine of empties."

The light coming through the window illuminated Felix's look of disgust. "Nah, that's not right." He went into the kitchen and Raul could hear him opening cabinet doors and drawers. "Where's your garbage bags?"

Good question. Raul was having a tough time getting his thoughts in coherent order. "Middle drawer to the right of the sink. I think."

A door slammed shut and Felix barreled his way out the door. "More like the bottom drawer to the left." He flapped a black plastic bag open and started filling it with the cans.

"Hey, don't do that."

"You just stand there, *abuelo*. I got this."

Felix made quick work of the garbage pile. The cans filled up three bags. He tied them up and set them against the house. "No more littering."

That made Raul laugh. "That's funny, coming from you."

"You ever see me even drop so much as a piece of paper on the ground?"

Raul had to think about it, which wasn't easy. He couldn't call anything to mind, but that wasn't saying much at the moment. "I don't know."

"Well I do, and the answer is no. I don't want to have to pick these up again, so all cans go in the garbage from now on. Okay?"

"Yeah, sure," Raul said.

"Good. You want another?"

"I wouldn't say no to that."

Felix went back through the screen door. "Enjoy it, because it's the last one. You're cut off."

"You can't cut me off in my own house."

Felix cocked an eyebrow. "Watch me." His smile lightened the brief flash of tension. "Look, I just cleaned your yard. I don't want to have to clean your puke off the floor later. I didn't come here to be a maid."

Raul wanted to protest but he didn't have enough wind in his sails.

"Come on, *Papi*, why don't we sit down before you fall down?"

Felix took his arm and led him to the picnic bench. Raul knew he was weaving but there was nothing he could do about it.

"Thanks," he said when Felix helped him to sit without falling and handed him his last beer of the night.

"You got it."

They sat in silence for a while, both just letting the night and nature envelop them in its cooling embrace. Raul cast a blurry glance at the house.

"They're in there," he said.

"Who's in where?"

"My family."

Felix looked at him quizzically. "What are you talking about?"

"Bella, Lizzy, Abel, they followed me here. I hear them walking around. Sometimes I can hear them talking to each other. Or crying." Raul put his elbows on the table and leaned forward. "They talk to me. And when I answer, they respond. You know what's the worst part? I don't know if I'm scared to death or happy they're back." The tears, the inevitable tears, came.

Felix put his hand over Raul's wrist and held it tight. "It's all right, man. It's all right. Your family will always be with you. Always."

"I'm not talking in my heart. They're actually in the house."

"Look, you've gone through hell. You miss them. You've been drinking a lot. That's not all that crazy."

Raul broke from Felix's grasp. "That's what I thought. So, I stayed sober for a few days. And guess what? They were still there. I can take the walking around. But the crying. It...it kills me. And when they call for me?" He shook his head, letting the tears really flow now.

"Let's get you to bed. We can talk more in the morning."

They stumbled inside, Raul feeling relieved that he'd told Felix but concerned that his friend would dismiss it as grief or even some kind of psychotic break.

"Where's your bedroom?" Felix asked.

Raul pointed to the small bedroom.

"Good. No stairs." Felix eased him onto the bed and took off his shoes. "Sleep it off, buddy. I'll find a place to crash upstairs."

"No!" Raul tried to sit up and collapsed back onto the pillow.

"What's wrong?"

"Just...just take the couch. Please."

Felix opened his mouth and jumped before any words could get out. "What the fuck?"

Raul's heart skipped. Had Bella or the kids, upset that Felix had come and upended their delicate balance, tried to hurt him?

"You didn't tell me you had a cat."

Raul saw Bruiser out of the corner of his eye as he ran back into the kitchen. "He adopted me. You must have scared him today. Probably been hiding." How quickly Raul had forgotten Bruiser. Just another log of guilt to add to the fire.

"I hate cats."

"Bruiser might say the same thing about Felixes." Raul felt himself slipping. Sleep was better than these bed spins.

"Bruiser? My ass."

Raul couldn't find his voice to reply.

Though, a second before he passed out, he swore he saw a faint shape move behind Felix.

★ ★ ★

Raul's hangover kicked at the back of his skull with the power of a blacksmith shaping a sword. Feeling like crap the day after had become commonplace in Ida's house, but this was a whole new level. How many beers had he knocked back? Did vodka ever come into the mix?

What was the point? Knowing wouldn't make him feel any better.

He dragged himself out of bed and shambled into the kitchen.

"I thought grandpas woke up early."

Raul's eyelids hurt as he fully opened his eyes. Felix, dressed in a t-shirt and boxers, sat at the table eating a bowl of cereal. Milk and bits of cereal were in his beard.

Funny, Raul had completely forgotten Felix was here.

"Mornin'," Raul mumbled.

"Better for me than you," Felix replied, smiling. "Go take a piss. I got something to straighten your ass out."

There was a pot on the stove and the smell of something cooking Raul couldn't place.

He went to the bathroom, dry heaved for a spell, and peed a clear stream.

When he got back to the kitchen, Felix was at the stove, the pot lid in one hand and a ladle in the other. "Sit down, bro. This is exactly what you need." He spooned what looked like stew into the bowl and set it before him. Just the smell, which would have been delightful any other time, made his insides cringe.

"I can't eat. I'll throw up."

"You can and you won't. Trust me." Felix put a spoon in Raul's hand and guided it into the bowl.

"What is it?" The steam coming off the stew cleared the pores of Raul's face. There were chunks of meat and a lot of white bits that in his present state of mind bore too close a resemblance to maggots.

"Ain't you never heard of *asopao*? My grandmother used to make it for my grandfather all the time. Got him on his feet and out the door to work. Oh, right, I forgot, your grandmother wasn't a good cook."

"Contrary to what people think, not every old ethnic lady is a master chef."

"That's why I used to tell you she was only half Boricua. Must have been some bad white blood in there. Hell, she only spoke English."

"At least in front of me. Why I never learned Spanish. Though I now wish I had. She was trying to fully embrace the American way of life. She thought it would make things easier for me, set me up for a better life."

"You always were a bad Puerto Rican, but I guess I can't blame you. Now eat."

"What's in it?"

"Jeez, you got strength to ask so many questions, you surely can eat. It's chicken and rice and sofrito with some adobo and a little hot sauce. Nothing crazy."

In theory, it sounded delicious. In fact, Raul's stomach wasn't in the mood.

"How did you have time to make stew, and where did you get all the ingredients?"

"You keep stalling, I'm gonna pour it down your throat. I went to a store. It's like two o'clock. I had plenty of time to make it and listen to your snoring and farting in there."

Raul slid his gaze from the stew to Felix and saw that there was no denying the man. The stew was hot and a little bit spicy and he almost gagged at first.

"One down," Felix announced, the way Raul used to encourage his kids to eat when they were toddlers. "Eat the whole bowl. You'll feel better before the hour is up."

When he was done, Raul put his hand over his stomach as if that were enough to keep the stew from escaping. It might have been the best stew he'd ever eaten, but he was sure he'd always associate it with this moment. Not something that would go in the regular meal rotation.

Felix took the bowl and spoon and put them in the sink. "By the way, your fat bastard of a cat kept me up half the night. When that thing moves around, the whole house shakes."

Wiping his face with a napkin, Raul leaned back in his chair and was surprised to find his headache had abated enough to blink without wanting to lop his own head off. "Where is Bruiser?"

"Upstairs. At least that's what it sounded like earlier."

Still dressed in yesterday's clothes, Raul got up and went out back. The fresh afternoon air felt good, like a shower after a day of hard manual labor.

The screen door banged shut and out came Felix with a beer. "You want one?"

"Are you serious?"

"Nah, maybe you're right. Too soon. Me, on the other hand...." He popped the top and held the can up to the sky. "To country living."

"And wide-open spaces," Raul added.

Felix giggled, which seemed weird coming from a burly biker ex-con. "You got that right. Those classrooms are pretty damn narrow." He made air quotes when he said *classrooms*. "Feeling any better?"

Raul gave a quick top to bottom check. "Actually, I do. That stuff is magic."

"*Asopao.*"

"Sure, what you said."

"So, what do you normally do up here on a nice day?"

"Stay inside and watch movies. And drink."

"Sounds boring."

"I didn't come here to have fun."

Felix found a rock and threw it into the tall grass. "I'm sorry."

"Nothing to be sorry about."

"You want to do something? Go somewhere? We can take my bike. Hell, I'll even get in your old-man car if you want."

Raul felt the effects of the alcohol and sugar spike wearing off, but the weariness of grief was sliding right in to take its place. "I don't think so."

"We can find a bar. Be a change of scenery for you. Or do priests not go into bars? At least the good ones. Or is it only when a priest *and* a rabbi go into a bar?"

Raul pinched the bridge of his nose, tamping down his frustration. "Felix, I'm not a priest. I really don't want to have to keep saying it."

"My bad. My bad."

"I need a shower." Raul opened the screen door and paused. "How long you planning on staying here? Not to be rude or anything."

Felix narrowed his eyes. Raul could see how the man had honed his look and how that flash of anger would stop most people in their tracks. "Not rude at all, *abuelo*. I don't know. I'm here for you, not me."

What Raul wanted to say was, *I never asked for you. Or anyone, for that matter. This is, in fact, the absolute farthest thing from what I want.*

Instead, he turned away, gathered some clothes from his bedroom, stripped down and stepped into the shower.

The new bar of soap he'd put in the soap dish the day before was gone.

The corners of Raul's lips curled ever so slightly.

Felix hadn't chased them away.

CHAPTER FIFTEEN

They watched movies for the rest of the day, the beer drinking at a minimum, yet enough to avoid being parched. Neither said much to the other, which was concerning to Raul. Felix was a world-class talker. The joke used to be that Felix would die and talk himself back to life, his mouth never stopping until the rest of his body took the cue that it was time to get up and go.

At one point, Felix had looked at Clover and Henry tucked into the far corner of the couch. "You're a little too old to be playing with stuffed animals, *abuelo.*"

Raul had removed Henry from the basement three days earlier, reuniting it with Clover. So far, there hadn't been a return of Abel's crying. Raul practically snarled when he snapped back, "They belonged to my children."

"Oh shit. I'm sorry. I didn't mean nothing by it."

"Can we just watch some movies and drink?"

Scratching at his beard, Felix nodded. "Dude, that works for me. You need me to chill with you and shut my mouth? I got this."

Raul wasn't sure Felix could cut the motor in his mouth, but he decided to give him the benefit of the doubt. He turned the volume up as a less-than-subtle way to let his friend know he didn't want to hear him.

A Roger Corman sci-fi movie from the Eighties by the look of it held their attention the way monster movies had when they were young and not running around the streets. It was a total rip-off of *Alien*, but so what? Corman knew how to make a fun movie on a shoestring budget. And there was always sex.

Bella had a complete aversion to nudity and racy scenes in movies. Even before they were married and just a couple of college kids in their prime. What he wouldn't give to have her come storming into the room and shut the television off, admonishing him for even thinking of watching such trash. What if the kids had walked in and seen it?

A single tear fell from his left eye and he wiped it away. Felix, sitting on Ida's old chair, watched the movie intently. Bruiser was next to Raul on the couch, waking only when a damsel in distress screamed for her life or the monster came roaring onto the scene.

Raul couldn't get into the movie because he was listening for any telltale sounds of his wife and children. The empty soap dish in the shower was both a welcome sight and slightly chilling. He thought there would be more, as there had been lately, but so far the house was quiet. Well, except for the mayhem coming through the TV screen.

When the movie ended, Felix got up, stretched, and said, "You want me to order a pizza?"

"No pizza parlors in town. Nearest one is too far to deliver."

"No shit? I thought you could get pizza delivered anywhere."

Raul gestured to the windows. "Not out in the sticks. I got some frozen dinners."

Felix shook his head. "That shit's worse than what they serve in prison. I'm in the mood for pizza."

Raul petted Bruiser. "You could take a ride to Glens Falls. Plenty to choose from there."

"Sounds good to me. Hope you don't mind riding bitch." He grabbed his leather jacket from the coat rack by the door and fished around his pocket for the keys to the Harley.

"You go. I'm not hungry. That, what did you call it, *asopao* filled me up."

"You sure?"

"Yep."

"I don't have to go."

"You also don't have to stay cooped up in here all the time. Get some air. Find a bar. School's out for summer. Your curfew is lifted."

Felix hesitated, his conundrum written all over his face.

"I'll be fine. You forget, I've been up here by myself for over a month before you arrived."

Felix looked hard into Raul's eyes. "Yeah, and from what I see, you haven't been doing well."

"Says the man who got me so drunk last night I wanted to die this morning."

Felix gave a low chuckle. "Says the man who also brought you back like Lazarus."

"You know the Bible now?"

"You can't avoid it in prison. All right, *abuelo*, I'll see you later. You on that couch petting that cat, you really are an old man."

"If my memory serves me right, you're a year older than I am."

Felix left him with, "Age is a feeling, not a number."

The door closed. Raul let out a sigh. He was glad to see him go. Would he ever be comfortable around people again? Or would his pain be a constant barrier between him and normalcy?

And to hell with anyone who talked about 'the new normal'. That just meant what you liked, or loved, was fucked or gone altogether.

"You want something to eat?" he asked the cat. Bruiser's ears perked up.

"Bad."

The tiny voice wafted from the second floor. It was clearly Lizzy.

"Daddy."

That was Abel. He'd know his son's slightly nasal voice anywhere.

Raul froze, his hand on the cat's back, his body gone so numb he couldn't feel its fur.

"Lizzy. Abel?"

The house went still again.

Bad. Daddy.

Bad Daddy.

What had he done?

Bad Daddy.

An icy shiver ran up and down his back and settled in his gut. He waited for his ghosts to speak more to him. To tell him why he was a bad daddy.

Though he knew why.

He was a bad daddy. The worst of his kind. And apparently, his children were not going to let him forget it.

★ ★ ★

"Wake up!"

The harsh command gave Raul a start. He sprang into consciousness, his heart thumping. Felix stood over him, deeply concerned.

"What? What's wrong?" Raul asked.

"I've been trying to wake your ass up for five minutes. I was about to throw water on you."

He looked around. Sun was bleeding through the windows. A flare of pain in his back and hips knocked any cobwebs free from his brain. "Why am I on the floor?"

"You just stole my question," Felix said. He reached down and helped Raul to his feet. "I came home last night around midnight and you were asleep on the couch, so I took your bed. Guess you fell off the couch in your sleep."

Raul saw that the coffee table was between where he'd been sleeping and the couch. "That means I would have had to bounce over the table."

Felix clapped him on his back and pointed at a steaming mug of coffee on the end table. "You must have moved around it. For a minute there, I thought you were dead. Especially when I saw those." He cocked a bushy eyebrow toward the amber pill bottles. "When you weren't waking up, I was trying to decide if I should drive you to the hospital myself or call an ambulance."

Raul cupped the coffee in both hands because he wasn't sure he had the strength to hold it in one. The warm jolt of caffeine was just what he needed. "I didn't overdose."

"That's easy to believe now, when you're awake. I didn't know how many pills you had started with, so there was no way for me to tell."

Raul stared at the bottles. He'd forgotten to put the tops back on. How many had he taken? He hadn't a clue. Last night was a fog, after....

After....

"Those things really knock me out."

"I can see that. I might ask you for some. I haven't had a good night's sleep in years. You take them every day?"

"No. I mean, one of them I'm supposed to, but I mostly take them when I feel I need it."

"Like when the shit just comes out the blue and hits you and you can't get out from under it?"

That told Raul that Felix knew grief, true, soul-wrecking grief. He'd always seemed so cavalier, even now, but living the life he had, he had been bound to encounter loss. He wondered who had gotten through Felix's wall of noise and gusto and seeped into his heart.

"Yeah, something like that."

Felix got his own coffee from the kitchen and sat in the living room. He had some pretty big bags under his eyes.

"You look like you need some of your grandmother's stew."

Felix waved him off. "I only had like six beers at this bar last night. I sleep too light. Force of habit. Everything wakes me up. Hell, out here, the damn bugs are enough to keep me up all night. I don't understand how people can say it's so relaxing getting back to nature."

"It does take some getting used to."

Bruiser came down from the second floor and looked at Felix. The two stared at one another until Bruiser flinched and continued on into the kitchen. "That's right, tough guy," Felix called after him with a wry smile on his face. Then he turned his attention back to Raul and asked, "Did you see them?"

Massaging a sore spot on his hip, Raul said, "See who?"

"You know."

Oh Christ. Raul had forgotten that he'd drunkenly spilled his secret to Felix the other night.

"I'm not here to judge you," Felix said. "Happens to me a lot and I don't like that shit."

Raul took in a deep breath. "I...I heard my son and daughter."

Felix leaned forward, his elbows resting on his knees. "That's a good thing. Who wouldn't want to hear their kids?"

"It's what they said that bothered me. Why I took some pills. Not to kill myself. Just to calm down."

"What did they say?"

"They just said, *bad Daddy*." Raul shivered just thinking about it, the feeling of inadequacy that had been tormenting him since the night he'd rushed home to find their bodies on the floor filling him with its venom.

"They say anything after that?"

Raul shook his head.

"You see anything? Hear anything?"

"No. Just that."

"You know your kids would never think that, right?"

"No, I don't. Hearing them say exactly that made it pretty clear."

"That wasn't them," Felix said somberly.

"I beg to differ. They were upstairs, but I heard them loud and clear."

"And you agree with them?"

Raul pulled his lips into a pale, tight line. He fought to keep the dam from bursting.

"Nothing fucks with us more than our own minds."

"I didn't make this up in my head. I heard them. Just the way I have been for weeks."

"Weeks of being up here alone, keeping everyone away, crying, drinking, and taking those things." Felix pointed at the pill bottle. "Give it enough time, you'd see talking bears sitting outside this Grizzly Adams house asking if they can come in and watch TV."

Raul shot up from the couch, his back cracking, and stormed to the bottom of the stairs, pointing. "They were up there! Clear as day. Don't tell me I'm hallucinating. You can get the hell out of my house! I never asked you to come here. Shit, I haven't even thought about you for a single moment for years! I...don't...want...you... here."

When he was done, Raul was breathless, maybe a little dizzy. He hadn't lashed out in anger like that in, well, it was so long ago he couldn't remember.

He'd said hurtful, hateful things. He backed up a step, expecting Felix to spring from his chair with his fists raised.

Only he didn't come at him, ready for a fight.

Worse, Felix's eyes were clouded with pity, and patience. "It's all right. I'm sorry. You know me, my mouth gets ahead of my brain sometimes."

"That's just it. I don't know you. I mean, I *knew* you, but that was a lifetime ago. We were kids. I'm not the same person I was. I'm sure you're not, either. What the hell are we doing here?"

Felix calmly took a sip of his coffee and said, "Can you sit down and just talk for a minute?"

Raul looked up the stairs, at the darkness waiting there, and then at Felix. After letting his emotions pour out in such atypical fashion, he found himself too tired to keep standing, to continue fighting. He sat on the couch. Bruiser came prancing in and nuzzled his ankles.

"You calm now?" Felix asked.

Raul nodded. Bruiser purred.

"When I saw what had happened to you, to your family, on the news, I made it a point to come see you when I got out. That single thought is what kept me going, kept me sane those last couple of months. When you're locked up, you need something to focus on, an important thing you plan to do when you get out. Now, I've done my share of fucked-up shit, but this time, I wanted to do something that was right."

Now it was Felix's turn to get up and pace around the room, his thick-soled boots clomping on the wood floor, chain from his wallet to his belt loop swaying.

"I rode my bike for three days to get to your church. When I got there, I saw a different priest's name on the sign outside. So, I went in. Met this old guy cleaning the place." He stopped, seeming to look inwardly, and chuckled. "I was worried the place would come down or go on fire, you know? My ass hasn't seen the inside of a church since I made Confirmation. Anyway, this old guy told me you had left. I asked him where and he gave me the brush-off. He looked like a tough son of a bitch. He stared me down the way I do your cat."

"Must have been Bill. He's a retired cop and he is a tough guy."

"I knew there was no point asking him any questions because he wasn't going to give me any answers. And neither would anyone going in and out of the church. Unlike Bill, they were scared of me, I think."

"Not shocking," Raul replied.

"I went in another direction. Found out your wife's maiden name and went to her parents' house. They were scared of me, too, until we got to talking. When I said it was important I see you, they gave me what I needed and I thanked them. I think they were grateful I turned up at their doorstep."

Raul thought they would have been, too. If anyone could rescue Raul from himself, it would be a guy who looked like Felix, a man who the world would think had never taken no for an answer.

"That's the how. But why, Felix? Why me? Why now?"

Were those tears in the big man's eyes?

"Because you were my brother. When you decided to become a priest and go to school, I was so happy for you, man, even though I knew it would take you away from me. I was proud." He wiped at his eyes and tried to lighten the mood by adding, "Your candy ass wouldn't have lasted if you stayed around me. So I lived my life and you lived yours, and in the back of my head, I always thought that when I died, things might go a little easier for me, you know, up there, because my brother was a man of God. Like holiness by association instead of guilt."

"I'm your ticket to heaven?"

"Were, until you threw it all away, you dumb shit." They grinned at one another. "The thing is, when I watched the news, I didn't know your wife and kids, but I knew you, and I could feel your pain as if it was my own. I never felt anything like it before. It just hit me like that guy on the road to Damascus in the New Testament."

"Saul." Raul was impressed Felix remembered Damascus. It wasn't an everyday place or word.

"Right. Something told me I had to be here for you. You feel pain? I want to take that from you, bro. I want you to give it all to me, because if I know anything, it's pain. I can take it."

Raul had gone from furious to touched. He recalled the day he and Felix had become actual blood brothers, cutting their palms with a pocketknife in the abandoned lot they played in when they were ten. "Pain isn't something I can give someone, even you. It's something I have to live with until I can't anymore."

Felix sat next to him on the couch.

"I can take some of it. The people who took your family from you think they got away with it."

A bubble of tension wrapped itself around Raul's heart. "They did. The police have nothing. I've given up hope that they'll find them."

"That's because they have to operate within the law. It's a system that ties their hands too much. I don't have that problem." He put his hand on Raul's shoulder and Raul could feel the steely strength of his friend. "I can find them and give you and your wife and children peace. I said I can take a lot of pain. I can give it even more."

CHAPTER SIXTEEN

Could Bella read his mind? Could the children see the darkness, the horrible thoughts that plagued his brain?

Felix's offer to find their murderers would have shocked and saddened Raul when he was a priest.

Hypocrite.

Maybe the Catholics had gotten it right by not allowing priests to marry. It lowered the stakes, gave a man less to lose, which then provided fewer reasons to abandon one's faith.

Yes, he wanted Felix to track the abominations of humanity down. Yes, he wanted Felix to be their judge, jury, and most importantly, executioner. Felix hadn't said outright that he would kill them, but the message was clear.

And on a selfish note, with Felix gone, Raul could go back to living alone with the tortured spirits of his family.

Wrestling with his thoughts that night, Raul found it impossible to sleep. His friend's heavy snores filled the house and kept Bruiser restless. The coon cat lay on the end of Raul's bed, casting annoyed glances at the living room where Felix slept.

I could take a pill. But is it too soon? Did I almost accidentally kill myself last night?

He still couldn't remember how many pills he'd ingested after hearing his children whisper he was a bad daddy. Every time he recalled their accusing voices, his stomach cramped, as if his organs were being run through a carpet wringer.

"Would it be the worst thing if I never woke up?" he asked Bruiser.

At least with Felix here, his body wouldn't be left to rot and eventually end up in the cat's belly. An image of Bruiser standing on his chest, pulling at his lips until they snapped from his face, made him shiver. Willing the grisly tableau away, his mind found it necessary to conjure up the wet sounds of Bruiser masticating his flesh.

He considered shooing the feline off the bed. Bruiser groomed himself, softly purring, the picture of contentment.

The thought of contracting a killer wasn't the only thing keeping him awake.

Here, in the dark, was when the house came alive. But tonight, it was silent – save for Felix's snoring – and empty. It was hard to describe how he felt the absence of his wife and children. It was like knowing a limb was gone, only a faint, phantom feeling of something that should still be there.

Raul missed them. He even missed the shocking tendrils of terror that would run through him when they moved around the house or spoke.

Pray on it.

That old instinct was still there, his knee-jerk reaction to everything in his previous life.

No, he would not pray on it. Prayers were a placebo that didn't work when you knew they had zero efficacy.

Instead, he said in a voice dry and cracked, "Where are you?"

He held his breath, waiting for a sign of their presence. Felix's snoring went into a heavy rattle that disturbed any sense of peace. Raul wished he would shut the hell up. The urge to storm into the living room and push a pillow over Felix's face set his teeth on edge.

Bruiser must have sensed his inner turmoil. The cat stood, stretched, sauntered to Raul's side, and rested his head on his chest.

"Raul."

His heart stopped. Raul bolted upright in the bed. Bruiser scattered, his claws ticking on the hardwood floor.

Yes. Bella was in the basement, speaking to him through the vent.

"B–Bella."

His muscles relaxed as he took a tremulous breath.

"I'm sorry. Please tell Lizzy and Abel I'm so, so sorry."

There was a soft knock on the floor under his bed. Raul pulled the sheet up to his chest. The fear, the happiness, the dread and sadness fought for control of his fight-or-flight responses.

"We…loved…you."

He was about to tell them he loved them, too, when he replayed what Bella had said.

We *loved* you.

Past tense. Did they mean they loved him when they were alive, or had his failure to protect them severed their love the moment the killers' knives had cut their lives short?

His body trembling as if he'd just stepped into a frigid night wearing summer clothes, he said, "Please, Bella. I will always love you. And Lizzy. And Abel. Nothing can change that. Nothing."

"What the fuck?"

Felix's loud protest made Raul jump. He looked out his open bedroom door and down into the living room. Felix was tangled in a blanket, pushing Bruiser off his legs.

No, no, no, you're ruining it!

"Bella."

There came two knocks on the floor. He could actually feel the vibration as it worked its way through the legs of the bed, up the box spring and mattress.

"Bella, don't go!" he shouted in desperation.

"What?" Felix called from the living room.

"Shhhh!"

Raul didn't notice Felix had gotten up until he was standing in his doorway. "You okay?"

"Please, be quiet."

"Sorry I woke you up. That cat of yours freaked me out. I don't take well to having anyone, or anything, touch me while I'm sleeping. You know?"

Raul stared at the floor, ignoring Felix.

"Hey man, what's wrong? You look, I don't know, freaked out or something."

"I was talking to Bella," Raul snapped at him.

There was a faint rap on the floor, much softer than the previous ones.

"You hear that?" Raul said.

"Hear what?"

"They're down there. That's where they talk to me often. From down there."

Felix leaned an arm on the doorway and scratched his beard. "You hear them down there a lot?"

Raul nodded. "I can hear them through the grate in the kitchen."

Felix turned around, searching for the rectangular vent close to Raul's room. "You say they're down there now?"

"Yes. And if you can just keep quiet, maybe she'll talk to me again."

To Raul's surprise, Felix got down on his hands and knees and leaned his head to the vent.

Please, Bella, speak to me. I want to hear your voice. And I want Felix to know I'm not crazy.

"I don't hear anything," Felix said.

"Just give it time."

So they waited.

And waited.

Felix eventually got up, his knees popping, and went to the bathroom. Raul barely moved a muscle.

Come back to me, Bella. Come back.

An hour passed and there was no sign of his wife or children. Felix patted Raul on the shoulder and went back to the couch.

Sleep never came. The sun rose and the birds came out with their morning song, oblivious to the gray fog roiling within Raul.

★ ★ ★

"I think I should stay a little longer."

Felix announced this while Raul cooked up spaghetti and jarred sauce for lunch.

"I'm fine," Raul said, comfortable in the lie. More than anything today, he was exhausted. Stirring the pot of simmering sauce, he felt as if he were watching himself from a numb distance.

"No, you're not," Felix said matter-of-factly. "But that's okay. You're not supposed to be."

"I'm sure you have better places to be. Places where you can have some actual fun."

Felix shook his head. He sat on a counter nursing a beer. "Not possible, *abuelo*. Not until I see you through this."

See me through this? Is he never leaving? Just kick him out.

"Not even if I told you to do the thing you asked me about?"

"In that case, I'd have to leave. But I'd be back as soon as I finished. Are you telling me to do it?" He flexed the fingers of his empty hand, the knuckles cracking.

Raul took a breath, thought about it, and said, "I'm not."

"But you are thinking about it."

"It's part of why I couldn't sleep."

"Big decisions will do that to you," Felix replied, nodding soberly. "It also shows you still have some priest left in you. And I'm not saying that as a bad thing."

Raul got a potholder and drained the pasta into the colander in the sink. Then he put it back in the pot and poured the sauce over it. Bella would never have let him use jarred sauce. She made world-class tomato sauce. Unfortunately for him, he'd always been too busy to ask or learn how she'd prepared it.

"I'd rather not talk about it."

"Fine by me. That smells good."

"If you say so."

Raul hoped that packing in some carbs would make him heavy and sluggish, maybe put him to sleep an hour or so from now. The overly spiced, almost metallic tang of the store-bought sauce did not elicit any kudos from his stomach. He filled two bowls and gave one to Felix, who ate it while still sitting on the counter.

"Do you want to talk about last night?" Felix asked after slurping up a strand of spaghetti.

"Not necessarily."

"What did your wife say to you?"

Raul almost took his first bite, but then set the loaded fork down. "It doesn't matter."

"Sure it does."

Felix had always been a blunt instrument, telling it like it is. It could seem like he was pushing your buttons, when in actuality, he was just stating the facts as he saw them. Raul had to keep reminding himself of that.

"She said...she said they loved me."

"Of course they did. They were your family."

Now his frustration was growing...again. "You don't get it. She told me they *loved* me, not that they *love* me."

Felix studied him for an uncomfortably long time. "I guess you can take it like that. Especially if that's how you think they should feel."

"I'm not making this up. It isn't in my head."

"I know. It's coming from down there." Felix pointed at the floor.

Raul felt like a fool. Why was he confiding so much in a man who didn't believe him? Everything he said just made him sound crazier to Felix.

"Not all the time. Look, just forget it. I'm fucking nuts and that's fine by me."

"You're not nuts, *abuelo*."

"Right. I can see it in your eyes when you look at me. Poor Raul. He lost his family and now his mind. He thinks he's talking to their ghosts and he takes too many pills and he wants to shut himself away from the world."

Felix hopped off the counter and set his bowl down. Raul turned away from him, determined to put something in his stomach. He'd said his piece. There was nothing more to talk about.

"You left out that he makes shitty-ass spaghetti and buys cheap beer," Felix said. A smile slowly spread from beneath Felix's beard, the grin inching its way to his eyes.

Despite himself, Raul smiled, though it might have been part grimace.

"If you say you talk to her, you talk to her," Felix said.

"I do. Bruiser hears her too."

"You talk to Bruiser too?" he said with his just-fucking-with-you tone.

"He reacts whenever they're near. It's what made me realize this is something originating from outside my own head."

Felix crushed his beer can and tossed it at the garbage. It hit the rim and clanked onto the floor. He swiped it up and flipped it into the pail. "You think they would talk to me too?"

Raul swallowed his spaghetti, the half-chewed wad nearly sticking in his throat.

"I don't know."

Shrugging, Felix said, "Nah, why would they want to talk to me? They don't know me from shit. I'd probably scare them away."

Felix might have been right. So far, the voices had only come when Felix was out of the house or asleep in the next room. It didn't help Raul's credibility that his only witness was a cat. Were Bella and the kids doing this intentionally to make him sound crazy?

"I need you to believe me," Raul said, sounding a little more desperate than he wanted to.

"I do, bro, I do."

Raul got up and dumped most of his lunch in the garbage. Felix shouted, "That's good food. Don't waste it."

Next, Raul took the beer from Felix's hand and dumped it out in the sink.

"Now I know you've lost it."

"I want us both sober tonight."

"For what?"

"To give you proof."

Felix held out his hands. "I have your word. That's all I need."

Raul shook his head. "No. This isn't about faith. It's about evidence that can't be denied. You're going to sit with me tonight, and by this time tomorrow, you'll really see."

"Sit with you? That's all we do anyway."

"Quietly."

"Quietly my ass. That's not the way I operate."

"It is tonight. For once, you're going to shut your yap and just listen. Understand?"

"Sir, yes sir. You know, you still have a little of that street punk inside you. It just came out in your eyes."

"You can take the kid out of the street."

Felix smiled. "Yeah, but never forget where you came from and what you really are. It might save your ass someday."

Raul started washing the dishes. "I don't want to be saved. Just believed."

CHAPTER SEVENTEEN

For a change, the television, that source of endless, comforting white noise, was off. Raul and Felix had eaten sandwiches outside at the picnic table, talking about old times until it started to get dark.

"Remember when I was putting stolen radios in the trunk of your car?" Felix said. He squinted into the setting sun, puffing on a dry cigar he'd found in one of the Harley's saddlebags.

"I almost got arrested that night. There I was sitting in the 7-Eleven parking lot, doing some dip and talking up this girl who had gone there to get a Big Gulp, and here come three cop cars screaming into the lot. I didn't even realize they were talking to me when they were shouting to put my hands up and get down on the ground."

Slapping the table as he laughed, Felix said, "I was just about to cross the street to put another one in your trunk. I'd swiped it out of some Toyota when I seen them lights and jumped behind a bush."

Raul picked at the wedge of crust he hadn't been able to finish, flicking bits into the grass. "Thanks for telling me what you were up to. I nearly crapped myself."

"I was protecting you. If you knew, you'd have had to lie, and they would have seen right through it. Bending the truth was never your thing. I shoulda known then you'd be a priest."

"And it's a good thing I met that girl. She was my alibi. The daughter of a cop. I wonder whatever happened to her."

"She was smart to dump your ass."

Raul snickered. "You are right about that. Not my best first date."

"Not your worst, either."

He held up his hands. "Please. Let's not go there."

"Yasmina. Man, the knockers on that girl. I gotta admit, I was jealous as hell when you told me you were taking her out."

"You and everybody else. I couldn't help it that I had game."

Felix rolled his eyes. "What game? Monopoly? You had that car and that's what she wanted."

That car. It was an eighty-eight black-and-gold Firebird he'd won in a game of dice off a suburban kid who came to their hood for the drugs, stayed to gamble, and left on his own two feet, flat broke. Raul even remembered the day he'd confessed for his actions. It was part of a long list of misdeeds he had to settle with God before he'd fully committed himself.

That muscle car was responsible for a lot of Raul's dating life that summer, at least until he wrapped it around a pole when he was racing a random guy driving a Mustang. The steady stream of interested girls magically disappeared the moment the car went to the junkyard.

"I said I don't want to talk about it."

"Did you make it to the back seat, or were you done before you could get there?"

"Please shut up." Raul put his fingers in his ears.

"Just tell me, now that we're old and it's long gone. Did you at least get those titties out of the bra before you shot your load? Please tell me you got some skin."

"You know that's insanely crude, right?"

Felix waved him off. If Bella had been alive and with them, she would have escorted Felix out the door for such talk. Raul felt the corners of his mouth start to lift.

"Come on, *abuelo*. Spill it."

Yasmina was a beautiful, dark Dominican girl with a body of soft, dangerous curves. He'd been almost breathless when they started kissing and she touched the crotch of his jeans. The rest was a vague blur, except for the embarrassing short and miserable end.

"I don't even know."

"Bullshit. I could have been kicked in the head by a horse and the last thing I'd remember would be if I touched sweet Yasmina's tits. It would be worth being called a one-pump chump."

"You say that because you weren't the one who had to endure it." God, that had been a miserable year of Raul's life. The guys had been relentless and Yasmina, he'd learned, had a mouth as big as her chest.

Suddenly, the foreign smile on his face triggered a wave of guilt and sadness that stopped him cold. How dare he talk about old flings so casually, laughing about it all as if he hadn't just buried the true love of his life? Raul felt her watching him. He cringed at how such flippant conversation could be making her feel at this moment.

He was more than a bad daddy. He was an absolutely shitty husband.

"Hey, you okay?" Felix asked him, noticing the change in his demeanor.

"It's nothing," Raul said, turning to stare into the field, a sign not to press any further. "It's time, anyway."

They collected their trash and dumped it in the metal bin in the yard.

Fun time was over.

Closing the back door behind them, Felix asked, "So, do we light candles and shit? Don't ask me to sit on the floor and hold your hand."

The way he was treating this was the proof Raul needed that his friend didn't believe him. For Felix, it was a game, like playing with a Ouija board at a sleepover. Raul bit his tongue, knowing only Bella, Lizzy, and Abel could silence Felix's doubt.

Raul looked around the house. "I think we should keep things as normal as possible."

"Oh? What passes as normal for you?"

"Since I got here, getting drunk and watching TV. We'll skip the former. I don't want there to be any doubt."

He picked up the remote and turned the television on, then clicked until he found an old black-and-white movie.

"So, we just watch TV?" Felix asked.

"For now. We'll see what happens."

Felix looked like he was about to say something but thought better of it. Raul took the couch and Felix plopped onto Ida's throne. Earlier, Raul had brought Clover and Henry into the living room and settled them onto the couch. The hope was that Lizzy and Abel would be drawn to their favorite stuffed animals and make an appearance.

Every time Felix started to say something – either a comment about how boring the movie was or a joke or basically anything to exercise his jaw muscle – Raul motioned with his index finger pressed to his lips to *silencio*.

The movie made it to the final credits and Raul had no idea what he'd just watched. It could have been a mystery or a romantic comedy for all he knew. He'd been too busy listening to the house. He muted the sound for a moment.

"That movie nearly put me to sleep," Felix said as he got up and stretched.

Raul ignored him. The house felt the same as always, but it wasn't as if there was a change in the barometric pressure within the four walls preceding the arrival of his family. He would be alone one moment, and hearing sounds and voices the next with no warning or lead-up. That meant it could happen anytime, and odds were, Felix would be talking when it did.

"They don't come on command."

"Ghosts never do."

Raul saw that Felix was being earnest and not throwing sarcasm his way. Both of their parents had come, along with *their* parents, to America from Puerto Rico just before Felix and Raul were born. They brought with them some of the superstitions from the island nation, which included a healthy respect for ghosts. As much as Raul had previously eschewed the very idea of hauntings outside of the confines of a horror movie, his grandmother had told him plenty of tales of phantoms (or as she called them, *fantasmas*) that she or her extended family had experienced back home. The only ghost story he'd believed in was the Holy Ghost.

He wished his *abuela* was here now, if not to give him comfort, so he could at least tell her she was right. She would have never doubted his story.

At least Felix was trying.

Felix whispered, "I need a beer."

"Fine. Just one."

Felix got up and said, "Besides, now with the house all quiet and shit, waiting for a ghost, I'm getting kinda creeped out."

Raul was going to ask how a tough guy like him could get the willies, but Felix left the room before he could open his mouth.

Maybe it wasn't that. They were both city people. Being out in the country could be unsettling. Silence and the pervasiveness of nature were unnatural for them. Raul had felt that way his first summer here. It definitely took some getting used to. Some nights, he wished for the sound of sirens or people talking too loud in the street.

Felix came back with two beers. He handed one to Raul. "Take the edge off. One beer won't do either of us any harm."

Raul reluctantly took it, though after one sip he wholeheartedly agreed. One day of sobriety hadn't been easy. He'd been fighting tremors in his hands, a blinding headache, and an overall pall of misery for the past few hours.

A scratching noise had them both leaping to their feet. "What was that?" Felix asked.

Raul looked around the room. It seemed to come from everywhere but nowhere. The scratching stopped as suddenly as it had begun.

"Stupid cat," Felix said. Bruiser still had his claws deep in the fabric of the back of the sofa.

"Thanks for the heart attack," Raul said to the cat.

"We should put it outside for now."

"Good luck with that. Once I brought him in, he has no desire to step even one paw out the door. I tried to carry him out with me one day and he nearly took my arm off."

"Why didn't you get a dog instead? I like dogs."

Raul let that one go.

Felix said, "You think maybe the cat was respons—"

"No."

It seemed Raul's biggest fear was true. For whatever reason, his family stayed away when Felix was near (much as they would have had they been alive).

Unless....

"You said that you've had a hard time sleeping since you got here. You blamed the noises on Bruiser. Did you ever see Bruiser moving around and making those noises?"

Felix tugged on the salt-and-pepper strands of his beard. "I didn't need to see the cat to know it was the cat."

"Not your best argument."

"Dude, it was the cat. I could hear it running around and banging into things."

"But you didn't see it."

"Because it was upstairs and you told me not to go up there!" Felix was clearly getting exasperated. As was Raul.

"That doesn't prove anything," Raul said.

"Neither does assuming any noise in the house is a ghost."

"It's not just any noise." Raul found himself balling his fists.

"So you tell me."

"Fuck you," Raul spat.

"Your ass. Fuck you."

"Why don't you leave so I can be with my family?"

"Oh, you're kicking me out?"

Raul couldn't stop his temper from flaring. And, it appeared, neither could Felix.

"Yes."

"Fine." Felix grabbed his jacket. "You talk to your ghosts. You know, I've been patient with you, taking a lot of your shit. Someone was gonna need to tell you this sooner or later, so I might as well do it now. Get your head out of your ass, man. Do the one thing your family can't do. Live. Honor them by living and doing the things they can't do. You think they're around, watching you? Then make them proud. Shit, I've spent so much of my time locked in a box. Why would you choose to do it to yourself?"

Felix turned his back on Raul as he shrugged his heavy leather jacket on. Raul, shaking with anger, barreled into Felix, wrapping his arms around his waist and driving him onto the floor. Felix tried to shake him off, but Raul, fueled by what even he knew was irrational rage, wouldn't let go.

"Don't you talk about my family," Raul said, spittle flying from his mouth. "You hear me? You don't get to talk about my family and what would make them proud!"

"Get off me before I hurt you."

Raul tightened his grip, keeping Felix pinned to the floor. A little voice in his head told him to punch Felix in the ear and make him regret messing with him. He pulled his arm back, ready to deliver one hell of a haymaker. Felix squirmed beneath him, bucking like a bull.

"Daddy?"

The faint voice could barely be heard over their struggling. But Raul's ear, so attuned to the voices of his children whenever they had needed his attention, latched on to Abel's one-word inquiry.

Felix used the moment to throw Raul off his back. He quickly turned around and backed away, breathing heavily.

Raul no longer knew Felix was in the room. Looking toward the kitchen, to where his son's voice was coming from, he said, "Abie, it's me. I'm here. Daddy can hear you."

Felix, who was now standing over him, asked, "What did you hear? Who are you talking to?"

"Come here."

"Oh shit."

Raul looked up at Felix. His mouth was open, eyes wide, face pale. Yes, he'd definitely heard it as well.

Raul got up and walked to the kitchen. He sat down by the vent in the floor.

"I'm here. Are Mommy and Lizzy with you?"

Slowly, cautiously, as if he were contemplating putting his hand to a hot stove, he lowered his fingers to the cold metal grate.

"Is that your son?" Felix's voice surprised him as he hadn't realized his friend had followed him into the kitchen.

Raul nodded.

"Mommy?"

Raul's heart fluttered and it was hard to catch his breath.

"I don't wanna."

"What's wrong, Abie? What don't you want?" He desperately wanted to hold his son.

"You have to do what Mommy says."

That was Lizzy! What were they talking about?

"Bella?" Raul spoke into the floor vent.

Felix ran his hand over his face and tugged at the end of his beard. "This is fucking crazy."

Raul didn't bother to look at him, his eyes searching the depths behind the grate for...what?...some glowing, ethereal glimpse of

Abie's or Lizzy's essence? He said, "Now do you believe me?"

His friend made the sign of the cross. Raul wanted to tell him this was no place for superstition.

"Abel? Lizzy? Bella? Talk to me." *Yes, please, talk to the bad daddy. I couldn't help you when you were alive. What can I possibly do now?*

He stayed on the floor until his knees cried out for relief and then well past that. He recoiled when Felix touched his shoulder.

"I think they're gone, man."

Raul leaned down and pressed his ear to the vent. The only sound was the old oil burner kicking in.

"It's been two hours," Felix said.

Two hours? How was that possible? Raul had just heard Abel ask for him.

"It can't have been that long," Raul said, his voice dry and cracked.

Felix showed him the time on his phone. "I don't think they're coming back. At least for now. I heard that it takes ghosts a lot of energy to appear to us. They might have used up all they had for today."

Raul's legs felt as if they had been broken. He needed help standing up. "How do you know that?" Felix helped him into a chair.

"Those ghost shows are popular in school. Motherfuckers can't get enough of them. I seen so many, I learned a lot. That's why batteries get drained and lights go out when ghosts are around. They need all that energy to, what's that word? Jesus, it starts with an *M*."

Raul had no idea. Bella would have known. Those pseudo-reality ghost shows had been her guilty pleasure.

Felix snapped his fingers. "Manifest! That's it. They need any energy they can absorb to manifest."

"Do you believe me now?" Raul felt drained. Even sitting up was a chore. His knees throbbed and his feet tingled painfully with pins and needles.

Felix couldn't take his eyes off the floor vent. "I don't know what that was."

"If you had been around my children before...before...heard them, watched them, you'd know."

"It's just…shit, I feel like I'm going crazy."

"Welcome to my world."

"Do the voices only come from down there?" Now he was pacing the kitchen.

Raul rubbed his knees. The dull ache was the only thing keeping him from falling dead asleep in the chair. "Not all the time, no. Feel free to go down there and check it out."

Felix arched an eyebrow. "Your ass I'm going down there."

A wave of relief swept over Raul. Felix looked truly scared. Which meant he thought ghosts were in the cellar.

"I'm going to bed," Raul said, using the table as leverage to get himself on his feet.

"How can you just go to sleep?"

"You forget, this isn't my first time. And this is my family. Even if they hate me and want to make me unsettled, I've decided I'd rather have that than the nothing that was in my life before." And he knew he would go to bed wondering what Abel didn't want to do. Raul's brain would be buzzing all night, unable to shut down, but what would be the point? His family were still here, but they were also *there*, and it would be madness to try to find the logic of an unknowable place. He'd heard their voices, albeit briefly. That would have to be enough.

As he walked to his room, Felix opened a beer. Raul would have bet everything he had in this world that when he woke up in the morning, the lights would still be on in the living room.

CHAPTER EIGHTEEN

The day was sunny and warm, and to his surprise Raul met it well rested and feeling optimistic. Having someone verify he wasn't insane had a surprisingly ebullient effect on his psyche. It probably wouldn't last, but he'd appreciate it while it did.

Casting a glance into the living room, he saw Felix asleep on the couch. There was quite a collection of beer cans on the coffee table. Just as he'd predicted the night before, every light was on. A pretty brunette in a smart blouse read the news from a teleprompter on the TV. A part of Raul thought Felix would have left in the night. *Fled* to be more accurate. In a way, he was glad to see he'd stayed, but that also meant Raul would have to continue sharing his family with the man.

Maybe now that Felix saw the truth, he'd feel that Raul was going to be all right, a lonely man locked away in a country house with the specters of his wife and children. Sure, it was strange, but as long as Raul was content, shouldn't that be enough?

"Bacon, egg, and cheese on a biscuit," he said to Bruiser when the cat sauntered into the kitchen. "That'll hit the spot. You can have some bacon, buddy." He stroked Bruiser between his fuzzy ears. Bruiser closed his eyes and leaned into Raul's hand, purring loudly.

A few minutes later, Raul had bacon frying in the pan and the transistor radio he'd bought tuned to a station that played classic rock. The biscuits were in the oven, now a perfect golden brown.

He gave the first crispy piece to Bruiser who devoured it. By the time he was on to frying some eggs, Felix wandered into the kitchen scratching his belly under his t-shirt.

"If you wanted to wake me up, that's the best way to do it, bro." His voice was husky, down several octaves. Felix eyed the plate of bacon, pan of eggs, and slices of cheese at the ready. "Too bad we don't have any rolls."

Raul opened the oven and took out a tray of biscuits. They were the kind that came in a cardboard tube, baking up big and flaky and buttery. "Will this do?"

Felix took a chair. "Shit, I'll have four. For starters."

They ate their sandwiches, Raul wishing he'd bought hot sauce. Neither spoke about what had happened the previous night.

Clean, late spring air wafted through the open window. It would be a perfect start to a perfect day if the bodies of Raul's family weren't decaying in their coffins. No matter what happened, he couldn't forget that. Wouldn't forget it. Yes, a part of them was in the house, with him in a sense, but not being able to touch them, to properly communicate with them, was like being in prison.

Just like Felix said, he thought.

No matter. If Bella and the kids were going to stay here, so would he. A life sentence gladly served.

As if he was reading his mind, Felix dropped his crumpled napkin on his plate and said, "What are you gonna do, *abuelo*? Lock yourself away in this house for the rest of your life?"

"There are worse ways to spend my life."

Far worse. He'd come here with the intention of a slow, empty, meaningless death. At least now there was something to look forward to. Not just their voices. But knowing there was a continuity of life, an altered existence that meant, if they forgave him, he could fully be with them again.

"I hear you. If I had my family taken away like that, and I had a chance even just to hear them once, I think I'd be the same way. Hell, what I wouldn't give just to be able to say I was sorry to my *abuela*. That would mean a lot, you know."

"I know. And I'm glad you understand."

Felix cleared the table and put everything in the sink.

"Which brings me back to what I asked you a while back."

Bruiser jumped on Raul's lap, his heavy weight knocking some of the breath from him. "What are you talking about?"

"The offer still stands. I'll find them. Believe me. I worked three years for an outfit that located people who didn't want to be found."

"You were a detective?"

"Not exactly. But I did the same kind of work."

"Wait, were you a bounty hunter or something?"

Felix winked. "Or something. Look, I'll find them and take care of them. No blood on your hands. Everybody talks about wanting to kill someone who's done them wrong, but in the end, they regret it. Because they're good people, and good people can't live with doing bad things. I'll do it to give *you* bloodless peace. And maybe peace to your family."

Before Raul could think, he heard himself say, "Do it."

Felix looked taken aback. "You serious?"

Looking at Bruiser, because it was easier than making eye contact with the man you were giving permission to commit murder, he said, "I am."

"Good. I just needed to make sure."

"When will you start?"

"No better time than now. I'll just get my shit together and be on the road." He clamped his hand on Raul's shoulder. "Even if you were still a priest, I'd tell you that you're doing the right thing. Turning the other cheek isn't for real life. Maybe when I'm done, I'll come to you to confess."

Raul nodded. "Thanks."

His friend went to the living room and started getting ready.

Only he wasn't sure he believed Felix. Bella had always been a kind woman, a woman with enough forgiveness in her heart to share. Whereas Raul, who had spent most of his adult life preaching the paramount value of forgiveness, found that he had very little. Would she approve of such a thing?

No, *did* she approve?

Tell Felix to hang on a minute. Let's think this through. What if I'm wrong?

"Hey, Felix?"

The Harley roared to life in the front yard. A cloud of dust hung in the air by the time Raul got to the door, Bruiser trailing his heels.

He didn't even have a number to call Felix.

It was done.

This was either the beginning of righteous retribution, or the moment his soul was damned.

★ ★ ★

Six beers and two pills into the day, Raul heard a loud knock on the floor above him. His body had rejected sobriety and his mind was quick to follow.

He sat up and hit the mute button on the remote. Bruiser was right beside him, so he couldn't have disturbed anything on the second floor.

"Hello?"

It seemed a ridiculous thing to say. It was probably just a pop of wood settling as the day heated up.

Rap. Rap.

That wasn't the house settling.

"Bella? Is that you?"

Did she know Felix had set out to find her killers?

The soft thumps of tiny feet running had him racing for the stairs. "Kids?" He gripped the newel post, one foot on the bottom step.

Rap. Rap.

It sounded a little like the game knock-knock-hit-bump. It was a game Lizzy and Abel had made up when they were just inseparable toddlers. They would get on different sides of the room and close their eyes. One of them was appointed the knocker. It was the knocker's job to rap their knuckles twice on the wall or a table, signaling the start. Each would then race toward the other, their tiny bellies puffed out, eyes shut tight. The idea was to see if they could bump bellies even though they couldn't see each other. Half the time they missed, two ships passing in the night (or living room) and instead crashed into the furniture.

Bella was not a fan of knock-knock-hit-bump. Sometimes, the game ended in tears when shins were banged or heads bopped. One time, Lizzy hit a side table so hard, she knocked the wind out of herself. After a few soothing minutes in Mom's arms, both were ready to go at it again. Bella pleaded with them to stop, but the laughter far exceeded the tears and she and Raul had decided it was not the hill to die on.

The kids played knock-knock-hit-bump for years. Sometimes, when Raul was working in his study, a fancy name for the guest bedroom, he'd just stop and listen to their knocking and running and giggling. Nothing in the world could fill his heart with more joy than the laughter of his children.

Rap.

Rap.

More running feet.

The funny thing was, with his hand on the newel post and his bare feet on the step, Raul thought he'd feel even a slight vibration from the commotion upstairs. Only, it was as if he were hearing the phantom playback of the game and not the game itself being played.

What could have been a giggle or a sigh or even a wisp of wind wafting through the blinds made his heart ache. He so wanted to rush up those stairs, and if not see them, at least be surrounded by their essence. Maybe, just maybe, he could feel their joy.

Bruiser made a low, growling noise. Raul looked over at the cat, who was now crouched at the foot of the stairs, his tail puffy, back arched.

"There's nothing to be scared of. It's just Lizzy and Abel playing. They would have loved you, that's for sure."

The cat wasn't reassured by his words. Bruiser backed away, his golden eyes locked on the darkness above. Raul wondered if the cat, with his heightened senses, could see something he couldn't. And if that were so, part of Raul detested the cat for his superior sight.

"You."

Raul whipped his head around so hard and fast it hurt.

Bella's voice came from the kitchen.

He inched away from the stairs.

"Bella."

Knock. Knock.

He turned back to the stairs. Bruiser yowled and ran under the coffee table.

"Let."

He spun toward the kitchen.

Feet ran overhead. Raul's eyes roamed to the ceiling. This time, there was definite laughter, faint and thin as gossamer, but most certainly the sound of his children playing their old favorite game. It would have cleansed him with love and warmth if not for the tone in Bella's voice.

"Them."

He took a few steps toward the kitchen, his gaze sliding down to the vent in the floor.

Knock. Knock.

He looked up.

Raul's head swam. He had to reach out and lay his palm on the wall to steady himself. Between the confusion of sounds, alcohol, and medication, he was having a hard time focusing.

The kids rushed headlong into each other in the space between life and afterlife above.

Any sense of bliss at hearing his children was wiped away by Bella's next spoken word.

"Die."

It was impossible not to detect the hatred in her voice.

Raul's knees gave out. He collapsed in a sobbing heap on the floor.

"Please. Please forgive me."

Knock. Knock.

Bella spoke no more.

Had she encouraged the children to play knock-knock-hit-bump? To lift his heart so it could fall from a great height when she uttered her accusation?

If she wanted to hurt him deeply, profoundly, she had succeeded.

The sounds of the children playing faded away.

No more words were spoken through the vent.

Raul remained on the floor, empty and numb, until well after darkness fell.

CHAPTER NINETEEN

That night, he slept in Ida's chair, clutching Henry and Clover. If he could call it sleep. More a series of fitful catnaps. His brain buzzed too much to get anywhere close to REM sleep. His chest hurt and his stomach was twisted in knots. Even his eyes stung from crying.

Raul got up, stretched, and opened the blinds.

The first rays of the dawn caressed the house, making it the picture of idyllic tranquility. Birds sang and a squirrel, its bushy gray tail twitching, scampered onto the porch, basking in the sun before leaping from the porch rail onto the nearest hanging branch.

Nature mocked Raul. No, that wasn't right. It was simply indifferent. The world had better things to do than concern itself with a fallen priest haunted by his family. The planet was rife with specters of those who had walked before. Who was Raul compared to over a hundred billion souls that had all called this plane of existence home?

I wish Felix was here.

Before, he'd wanted to be alone with his family. Now, he was terrified to be alone with them, or even with himself.

You. Let. Them. Die.

Each word was a spear in his body and soul. This wasn't just mental anguish. His body felt wounded to the point of death. He ached from the inside out, his nerves on fire, his blood curdled with poison.

You. Let. Them. Die.

If he could will himself to die right here, before Ida's house of restless spirits, he would.

Raul's stomach cramped and he ran out of the front door and down the porch steps, vomiting until he could feel the capillaries bursting around his eyes. It came in a torrent, a geyser of sick and guilt and grief, emptying him but not nearly enough to bring about his end.

With his hands on his wobbly knees, he spit bile for several minutes, waiting for the next wave that never came. He wiped his mouth on his sleeve and staggered to the steps.

It felt better, being out of the house, as if the spirit of his angry wife couldn't pass the threshold in reverse vampire fashion.

"I can't stay out here forever," he said to…himself?…to Bella and the kids?

Please, come in, you weak, pathetic excuse for a father and husband. We're not done with you, boyo. Not by a long shot.

He stared into the open doorway. He could see the sun lighting up the kitchen in the back of the house.

There was nowhere else to go. His wife and children were as attached to him in death as they'd been in life. He was pretty sure that even if he moved his stuff into the car, they would soon be speaking to him through the air vents, their shadows glimpsed in the corners of the rearview mirror.

The only way to face this was to come to the grim realization that he deserved it. Maybe Felix would find their killers and maybe it would set them to rest. But he doubted it. It would be yet another failure, sending someone out to do what he should be handling himself, except he'd have no idea how to even go about such a thing.

You should have gone with Felix. If he found them, you could have been there and…and….

But Raul had wanted to stay here, with his family. And now his family did not want him.

Finding Felix wasn't even an option. He was just as much a ghost as Bella and the kids.

If he calls to check in, tell him to come back. Or at least say where he is so I can find him.

But how would he call Raul? He couldn't remember ever giving Felix his phone number. Maybe his in-laws had given it to him along with his address. He could only hope.

Because hope did not spring eternal.

With his hands quivering, he opened the screen door and crept into the house.

★ ★ ★

Felix revved the Harley down I-87, squeezing between two cars driven by old ladies who barely hit the speed limit. One of them honked her horn as he passed, her cotton ball hair barely making it over the dashboard. It only made him chuckle as he opened the bike up and left them in the dust.

Damn, it felt good to be on the road. He always missed this the most when he was locked up. Many were the nights when he could only fall asleep if he closed his eyes and recalled his road trips, all of them solo. Felix didn't play well with others, even others like himself. Especially them.

Honor among thieves, my ass.

He never gave a shit about joining a gang or one of those riding clubs. His favorite company was his Harley.

But today, he was filled with worry. Raul was fucked up, big time. He couldn't blame him. It was one thing to have your whole family murdered by nameless, faceless assassins. It was another to be tormented by their ghosts.

Ghosts.

He'd always had a healthy respect for his grandmother and her beliefs. Why shouldn't there be ghosts? It was nice to think that people were more than just weak bags of skin and bone with strange thoughts and inclinations. The possibility that the next world was better than this one had always appealed to Felix. Hopefully there'd be no 'schools' on the other side. More importantly, there had better be motorcycles, or something close to them, something with power, speed, rattle, and ear-splitting noise.

Those hopes for an afterlife had been elevated from faith to certainty, thanks to Raul. He'd come wanting to be selfless for once. Maybe even forgiven, though that was dashed when he found out his friend had shunned his vows. Now, he'd gotten an answer to the greatest mystery in life.

He couldn't fail. He had to repay this debt to Raul. And he had to give justice to his family.

Ghosts better not be squeamish, because he could see this getting very ugly.

With the wind biting his face, Felix hurtled to where it had all started.

He'd find the fuckers all right, even if he had to call in every favor and turn over every rock. He'd find them and make them pay.

Being on the road had another advantage. As much as he hated to admit it, seeing that look in Raul's eyes day after day had been tearing him up and wearing him down. It was disconcerting to see his friend look so empty, his hopelessness only replaced by a feverish desperation when the spirits of his family were near. He had to save Raul from that.

Which meant Felix had to find the motive for the murders. The police might not have had a clue, but Felix had an almost supernatural ability to find the darkness in men's souls. And that's where motive for murder lay, in the foul, stygian depths (Felix's favorite word he stumbled upon reading old Conan paperbacks in his first trip to away-school), a place where most people dared not go.

He couldn't buy that their murders were random. Not a chance. It stank of premeditation. As far as the cops could detect, there was no tangible evidence left behind. Or at least they hadn't spoken about it. One thing they did know was that there had to have been at least three men in the house that night. Maybe four. Four men just happening upon a house for a quick thrill kill would have left something.

No. Raul's family had been targeted. Felix was pretty sure Raul hadn't been in their sights, either. It's why they waited until he was gone.

So, the question was, why? Why murder a suburban woman and her two children? This wasn't just any family. They were the wife and children of a priest, the center of their community.

Felix cruised past a rest stop. His bladder was pretty full and the bike was shaking things up like a pneumatic drill, but he couldn't waste time.

The answers were there, back where Raul's old life ended.

Why did someone want to kill you?

Unfortunately, he didn't know Isabella Figueroa from a hole in the wall. That was by design. When Raul had said he was going to become a priest, Felix knew he had to let his friend go and take his divergent path. It was for the best that Felix eventually faded from memory. It was either that or become the subject of a bad joke. An outlaw and a priest odd couple, fit for some Seventies sitcom.

The road had to lead to Bella. What could children possibly do to inspire murder? Kidnapping, yes. Rape, yes. But slaughtering a family? He couldn't see it. Felix had known his share of short eyes. Fucking *putas*. They wouldn't have the balls to do that.

Had it been jealousy?

Or, where he was leaning, something to do with their religion? A lot of evil, twisted motherfuckers had blood on their hands in the name of religion these past twenty years. Hell, it probably went back to the day after the first religion was started. Terrorists liked to take credit for their sick deeds. He was sure plenty of crackpots had flooded the police tip lines. They always did. A handful probably claimed they were part of some terroristic band of kooks who vowed to eradicate the scourge of Christianity.

Now, Felix couldn't recall any hate crimes like this against Episcopalians. They were like Catholic lite, harming no one. You couldn't even pin the Crusades on them.

However, they were a lot more accepting than Catholicism. Look at Raul. He was a priest, but he was also able to marry and have children. Could a fanatical Catholic priest or follower of the faith have lashed out to punish them for what was seen as a transgression?

As far as Felix was concerned, anything was possible. Everyone he knew had a dark side and was capable of very, very bad things. Even an old church lady had it in her. All a person needed was someone to push the right – or wrong – button.

Raul had it. And now, in his weakened state, it was closer to the surface than ever. Even more so than when they were running on the other side of the law back in the day. At least then it had been fun, something to do that gave them an adrenaline rush. Now, not so much for Raul, and for good reason.

Felix couldn't let that darkness take over his friend. Which is why he had to do this, and do it now before it was too late. The pain in Raul's heart and the visitations by the ghosts would break him. They *were* breaking him.

Bella.

Who were you? What did you do?

He was going to find out. Soon.

CHAPTER TWENTY

Bruiser had yet to leave his side. The company was appreciated, though the cat had almost sent him sprawling when Raul got up to get something from the kitchen or go to the bathroom.

He'd turned on every light in the house even though it was a sunny day. The radio was on in the kitchen and the TV in the living room. Raul had erected a wall of light and sound, a barrier between him and the angry whispers of the dead.

His heart raced as if he were running a marathon. There hadn't been a moment's release from the tension that was twisting him into knots. It had been six hours since he'd dared to go back in the house. Bruiser had nearly bowled him over. At first, Raul thought it was because he had forgotten to feed him the night before and he was starving. The cat didn't so much as sniff at the bowl of food he'd set for him, after Raul had nearly dropped it because his hands were so jittery.

The cat was scared.

Raul couldn't blame him.

Even Raul couldn't be sure if he was scared of his wife's ghost, or the fact that what she'd said made him feel like running a razor across his wrists.

Thinking about it made him shiver. If it was the former, the light and noise would block the sound of her voice. If it was the latter, nothing could save him from his own mind and turbulent emotions.

Several times that day, he'd thought of packing a bag and finding a motel. Lord knows, there were plenty in the area. He could drive down to Lake George and get along relatively cheap since it was a few weeks before peak season. Maybe he needed to be around other people, happy people.

In the end, it was pointless to run. Bella and the kids had never been to Ida's house, yet they'd found him. Wherever he went, so would they.

And there was no running from his guilt. Even without Bella's accusation. That would be with him forever.

Or at least as long as his heart continued beating, though at this pace, it would wear itself out in no time.

His anxiety had been in overdrive. The constant infusions of adrenaline even washed the effects of his medication away. Sure, he could double or triple the dose, but without Felix around, would he wake up this time?

Was not waking up such a bad thing?

What if Felix was right? What if he found the men who'd slain Bella, Lizzy, and Abel? Would that set Bella at ease, knowing Raul had given Felix the green light to do so? Or would she accuse him of being a coward, of not taking matters into his own hands? Or maybe none of it mattered. For all he knew, Bella and the kids could only recall their lives up until the point of their deaths. Bella's last thoughts could have been her bitter disappointment that he hadn't been there to save them, and now those thoughts would be played back to him, over and over until he no longer had ears to hear them.

There was nothing in his former faith that could even begin to answer his questions. Oh, there were plenty of ghost stories and parables, but nothing real. That was the problem. The Bible was a collection of stories written by men who transcribed oral history. Anyone who ever played the telephone game knows how that goes.

The New Testament and its account of Jesus was a testament of no one. Not a single author of the Gospels or other books was a direct witness to the man's teachings, death, or resurrection. It took seventy years for the first Gospel to even be written. If Raul had to write about a relative who had died seventy years ago, it would be nothing but hearsay. He wouldn't even trust his own narrative.

What he was beginning to realize was how thin the ice his faith had been built upon was all along.

He'd run to the priesthood as quickly as he'd run from the police when he was almost caught tagging walls or stealing cigarettes from the bodega. Maybe he ran to the farthest thing from his wayward life just to hide for a while. If there was some cosmic bookkeeper, this could be punishment for his deception.

Whump!

Even over the heavy synth musical score of an Eighties Italian movie he had on the TV, Raul heard what sounded like a bowling ball being dropped on the floor above him.

He cowered against the corner of the couch, pulling the cat closer to him. Bruiser's tail got puffy, his body stiff.

"It's just a noise and noises can't kill you."

Hadn't he read that inventors had found ways to weaponize sound waves to the point where they could kill everything within a certain radius? Or had that been in one of his horror movies?

No matter. A thump on the floor wasn't going to scramble his brain or have blood pouring out of his ears.

Whump!

"Fuck this."

After carrying Bruiser to the kitchen, which was no easy thing, he opened the freezer door, took out the bottle of vodka, set the cat down on the counter, and twisted the cap. The booze went down like icy fire. As he drank, his gaze wandered to the floor vent. He put the bottle down hard enough to force a spray of vodka to erupt from the thin bottle neck.

Squaring his shoulder into the side of the refrigerator, he pushed as hard as he could. At first, the heavy appliance was still as a mountain, impervious to his efforts. But then it felt as if something had come unstuck from the floor and it began to move. He heard the tile being ripped up as he shoved the refrigerator until it settled over the vent.

Panting from the exertion, hand to his chest, he leaned into the wall and sank to the floor. There was an alarming dull ache in the center of his chest. His vision blurred and he wiped away his silent tears.

Whump!

That was right above his head, where Ida's thinking room was at the end of the hallway. They were following him. Raul got up and grabbed the doorknob to the back door. Out back was an empty, quiet field, an oasis of nothing just waiting for him.

"Come on, Bruiser."

He opened the door.

The cat, looking around warily, turned away from him. Raul

quickly dismissed the notion of carrying the cat outside. He could tell Bruiser would only claw at him if he tried.

I can't save anyone.

Whump! Whump!

The knob rattled in his hand. His gaze darted to the ceiling, expecting to see a fresh spiderweb of cracks there, or worse, falling plaster, the lathing showing through, the space between him and his angry family growing thinner.

He jerked the door open. A blast of fresh air did nothing to quell his mounting distress.

If Bella starts speaking, I'm going to lose my mind.

He shouldn't be terrified of his wife and children, but logic had no place here. Not in a house where the dead never rested.

The screen door creaked as he took a step outside.

A breeze ruffled his hair, smelling sweet and free.

It would be so easy to go outside and just keep on walking, never looking back. He'd thrown his life away once already. He could do it again.

But they would find him. No matter where he ran, Bella and the kids would find him. His shame would find him first, though.

"Goddammit."

With the resignation of a guilty man walking down death row, Raul went back inside and closed the door. The spirits celebrated their triumph by stomping on the floor over and over, a machine-gun rattle of crashes and bangs that left him a quivering mess.

Bruiser, who had been watching him curiously from the dining room, disappeared in a flash when the cacophony began.

"Stop it, stop it, stop it!" Raul wailed to no effect. It sounded as if the second floor was being ransacked. Any second now there would be crashing glass and furniture tossed down the stairs.

When he'd come here, he avoided the second floor out of respect to his aunt. Now, he was terrified of the thought of even looking up those stairs.

There was only one way to remain in the house and shut it all out.

He swiped the vodka bottle off the counter and tipped it back, ignoring his gag reflex as he sucked in heavy gulps. Half the bottle was gone by the time he pulled it away from his lips, clear liquid spilling down his shirt.

If they wanted to persecute him, he would let them. Let them exorcise their hate. On the other end of that, perhaps they could find the love they once had for him. The only way to get to that point was by numbing himself senseless.

"I'm not leaving," he said. "Do you hear me? I'm not leaving. I love you. Please remember, I love you. We loved each other."

The vodka penetrated his brain. He was so tired, more exhausted than he remembered ever feeling. He lay on the cold kitchen floor, cradling the bottle to his chest. His gauzy stare focused on the front door two rooms away.

The pounding stopped.

He felt a change in the air itself, a thinning of the atmosphere after the passing of a storm.

"We...loved...each...other," he said, slurring his words.

Bruiser, who had been hiding somewhere in the living room, padded into the dining room and stopped when he spotted Raul on the floor. He knew it wasn't possible, but Raul swore there was pity in the cat's eyes.

"Come here," Raul said, motioning with his free hand, desperate to hold on to another living thing.

The cat, like all cats, ignored him.

Behind the cat, a shadow floated from the bottom of the staircase and passed from one side to the other in the living room. Raul wiped his eyes. His hand came away wet. His vision cleared for a moment.

The shadow came back.

Only it wasn't a shadow.

A pair of legs, tan and toned and bare, stood before the front door.

Swallowing hard enough to hurt, Raul dared himself to look up. The legs ended at the thighs.

"Dear God."

The bodiless legs walked toward him slowly, deliberately, one steady step after another.

They were in the dining room now.

The cat didn't react. It didn't turn so much as cock an ear or try to face the ghastly apparition.

Raul felt the weight of each footstep through the floor.

"No. Please," he whimpered.

One leg stepped right over the cat. Now they were stopped at the threshold of the kitchen. Was it possible for a pair of disembodied legs to exude menace?

Yes.

All Raul could do was curl himself into a ball, shutting his eyes tight, willing the vodka to knock him out.

CHAPTER TWENTY-ONE

Felix parked his Harley across the street from Christ Church. The modest house where Raul's family had been butchered was separated from the church by a dark, narrow alley.

Perfect place for someone to hide.

It was a Thursday, so he didn't have to worry about frightening any churchgoers. He walked up the five steps to the wooden double doors and pulled.

Locked.

That made sense.

This didn't look like the most affluent church, but he was sure there were things in there worth something, if not monetarily, at least spiritually and emotionally to the people who came there.

A light was on in an upstairs room in the parish house. Or was it a rectory? Felix wasn't sure. Church stuff had never been his thing. The last time he'd been inside one was at his forced Confirmation when he was twelve. His grandmother had been so happy that day. He was almost as happy, knowing that days wasted with religion class and even going to church were over. Deep down, he didn't care whether it was called a parish house or a rectory. It was a house, plain and simple. And one that came as a perk with the job. Until it became a murder house.

Raul's replacement would be useless in terms of information. The man hadn't been in the parish when the murders occurred. But Felix did want to get inside and look around.

What were the odds a priest would let him waltz right into his house under the pretense that he was looking for the people who'd murdered the family that had lived there before him? Slim to none. Especially not with the way he looked. The guy would probably take one glance through the peephole and double-lock the door. Of course, Felix could always wait for the priest to leave and force his way inside.

What about that old guy who cleaned the church? Bill Samson.

Raul said the man spent more time in and around the church than even he had. He was a retired cop with, Felix figured, a guilty conscience. Spending all his time volunteering at a church screamed atonement for some bad shit he'd done.

Probably a dirty cop, Felix thought. *Plenty of them to go around.*

Felix had spent two months in a county jail down in Georgia after a crackhead thief turned him in for breaking into a Target. Felix had come out empty-handed that night — which in the end helped save him from a much longer stint in school — because the safe code the squirmy bastard had given him had been wrong. Turned out that crackhead had been a cop who thought it would be funny to fuck Felix over because he'd simply looked at his girl, a meth-head who resembled nine shades of hell, one night when they were hanging out at some dive bar in the sticks.

So, yeah, Felix knew all about guys like that.

One thing Samson wouldn't be was afraid of him. Wary, sure. He could work with wary.

What were the odds the handyman was around on a late Thursday afternoon?

Felix tried the doors again. Then he knocked and waited, stopping himself from pressing his ear to the door. Anyone passing by would surely get suspicious and call the cops.

No dice.

He looked around, saw the coast was clear, and walked down the alley. It was dark as night in there and smelled like mildew. It led to a small fenced-in yard in back of the church. There were two long picnic tables in the center of the lawn and a big kettle charcoal grill. Felix could picture the Sunday picnics, charity yard sales, and fundraisers held out here. The grass was lush and a color green that almost didn't seem natural. He could smell that it had been recently cut. The wooden fence was gleaming white, most likely the recipient of its annual spring coat of paint.

"Can I help you?"

The voice sounded anything but helpful. Felix flinched, slowly turning toward the man who had gotten the jump on him.

Samson had come up from the cellar, the double doors open, a heavy steel shovel in his hands.

"I hope so. Remember me?" Felix quickly regained his composure. He could chastise himself for letting an old man sneak up on him later.

Samson kept him locked in place with his hard gaze. This was a man who had perfected the art of the move-and-I'll-kill-you stare. In defiance, Felix walked over to the picnic tables, turning his back on him.

"I know who you are. Or who you said you are."

"I wasn't lying."

"You look as honest as the day is long," Samson replied sarcastically, fully emerging from the cellar. He still wielded the shovel like a weapon.

Felix chuckled. "They say I got a face made for radio. I blame my parents."

"Why are you back here?"

No niceties here. That was fine. Felix was used to that.

"I just came back from Raul's place. I was staying with him for the past week."

Samson narrowed his gaze, plainly not believing him. "Uh-huh."

"He's in a bad way, man. Real bad."

"I suspect he would be."

Felix eyed the shovel. "You think you could put that down so we can talk like regular people?"

"Nothing about you screams regular people."

"True that. True that. But aren't we all unique snowflakes?" He took off his leather jacket as a way to show Samson he wasn't armed. It seemed to work because the man lowered the shovel a bit, color returning to his knuckles.

"So, what brings you back?"

"I'm here to help my friend."

"And how do you plan to do that?"

Felix sat down and scratched a fingernail into the wood table. "Find the men who murdered his family, for one."

"And what makes you think you can do what an entire police force can't?" Samson said with a sneer.

"Because they're cops and I ain't. You want to find a bad guy, you send a bad guy." He scratched at his beard and made sure to look Samson in the eye. "I bet you found your share of bad guys."

Samson visibly stiffened. This was the point where he either came at Felix with the shovel, told him to get the fuck off the property, or settled down and listened to what he had to say. It could go any way and Felix was ready.

"You trying to say something?" Samson said.

"Every time we talk, we're saying something," he responded casually. "What I also will try to say is that I don't give a shit what you did when you were a cop. I'm just thinking you understand what I'm saying better than most."

There was a long moment of tense silence. Samson's face clouded with fury, but his breathing was slow and regular. A man at war with himself. Felix sat back and took it all in, refusing to break first. He could wait all day if needed.

"How do I know you are who you say you are? You could be one of the very people the authorities are looking for. You damn sure look the part."

"If I killed Raul's family, this is the last place I'd be."

"A lot of killers smarter than you have hidden in plain sight."

Felix took a cigar out of his pocket and lit it, drawing in a mouthful of bitter smoke. "Look, I'm going to let your little insult on my intelligence pass. I just came from his Aunt Ida's place and I don't have a lot of time. I'm afraid if I don't get this done soon enough, something might happen to Raul."

Samson's entire posture changed. He shoved the point of the shovel into the perfect lawn and sauntered to the picnic table, taking the bench opposite Felix. "I heard him mention Ida. Not a name you hear much anymore. How is he?"

"Pretty fucked up." Felix cast a nervous look at the back of the church and made a quick sign of the cross. Samson smiled for the first time and then a pall of sadness fell over his face.

"I know a lot of good men who have been looking for the cretins that did this to them. Highly decorated veterans who know what they're doing and they can't make any headway. Speaks to a highly organized, thoroughly planned crime. I'm supposed to think a thug in a biker jacket is going to do what they can't?"

Pointing his cigar at him, Felix said, "That's right. See, you get it."

Samson shook his head. "You think this is some kind of game?"

That irritated Felix. He sneered at the groundskeeper. "This ain't no fucking game. I'm trying to be nice. I just want to ask some questions, and then I'm gone. First, can I go inside the house?"

"I highly doubt you're going to dust for fingerprints."

"I just need to see. To get a feel."

"Took three coats of paint to cover the blood. I even pulled up the floor and put in new boards. Nothing in there to see." Samson paled, his eyes looking somewhere else.

"Please. It's important."

"Next question."

Felix bit his lip and took a breath. At least he had Samson talking. He didn't want to jeopardize the ground he'd made. "Tell me about Bella."

Samson's jaw flexed and he took a long while to respond. "She was a good woman. Loved her kids. Never complained about them. So many mothers seem to take it for granted. To her, they were a gift. Raul doted on her and she gave back what he put in. It was like...like one of those families on an old TV show. Sure, there were times when I could see tension between them, but not often. I envied what they had."

"A man of faith blessed with the perfect wife, the perfect family. Sounds almost too good to be true."

"Sounds it. But it wasn't. I saw it every day. Kids used to call me Uncle Bill on account of my being around so much." His eyes clouded with tears but he didn't make a move to wipe them away. He just let them tumble down his cheeks. "I know they say God has a plan, but I've been having a real hard time trying to figure out what that plan might be."

From Raul and Samson, Bella sounded like a saint. Felix wished he'd at least met her once, just to get his own read. When people died, their history was rewritten by the survivors. His own father had been an abusive prick, but after he died, you'd think he was father of the year, listening to how people remembered him.

Felix remembered. He kept his mouth shut and he didn't let the past get erased from his mind.

He'd lay some pretty big odds that Samson would say Raul was the nicest, straightest-edged guy he'd ever met. He didn't know Raul's past.

Someone would know Bella's past.

It was important not to just fixate on Bella, though. Someone from Raul's former life could have done this to hurt him in the worst possible way. Felix had been there with Raul during the bad old days, and he couldn't come up with anyone they might have double-crossed that would wait out for such horrible vengeance. But it was still possible.

"How about I make you a deal?" Felix said.

Samson eyed him warily.

"You get me inside that house and I'll tell you where Raul is staying. He'd be pissed at me if he found out, but I don't think a man should be alone like that, especially when he's hurting." *And being haunted by ghosts.*

"I wouldn't want to upset him. He respectfully asked me to let him go."

"He doesn't know his ass from a hole in the wall anymore."

"Jesus, it's that bad?" Samson sounded deflated.

"It's why I have to do this."

"I don't suppose there's any chance you'd call the police if you found the bastards, is there?"

Felix puffed on his cigar and shrugged. "Who knows? I've done stranger shit." He went to make the sign of the cross again and thought, *What's the point?*

Samson put his palms flat on the picnic table and stood. "I'm not sure how Father Gilmore will feel about this. Might as well give it a try."

Felix followed the slightly limping Samson back down the alley.

CHAPTER TWENTY-TWO

The night had been warm enough for Raul to sleep in the backyard. He didn't remember coming out there, or dragging his mattress and setting it in the grass. But he did recall with frightening clarity Bella's dismembered legs coming at him. He must have passed out, and then drunkenly set up a place to sleep outside. It was a good thing it hadn't rained or the temperature hadn't taken a dip. Maybe the only bit of good luck he'd had since moving in.

The Other Raul was busy last night.

Shielding his eyes from the sun, he sat up too fast, making the world spin and his head hurt. Squinting, he eyed the back door, the screen keeping out any bugs. The interior of the house was lit by sunlight because he'd never gotten around to closing the blinds the day before. He'd been too busy cowering in terror.

Poor Bruiser had been trapped in there all night, yet again. It pained him to get up and his bare feet were assaulted by tiny pricks as he walked over dry dirt and grass to get to the door.

"Bruiser," he called through the screen.

He dared to step inside. The empty vodka bottle was on the floor. A clean square showed on the floor where the refrigerator used to sit, the edges marked by dust and a thin black stain.

Raul shivered and hugged his arms.

"Bruiser?"

Now's not the time to play games, you stray.

The house was bright and quiet, but most importantly, it felt empty. He relaxed just enough to breathe without holding every other breath. That didn't stop him from flinching every time the floorboards creaked under his feet.

Bruiser was asleep on the couch. Raul wished he could enter the oblivion of an animal. There was no fearing the past or the future. There was only the moment, and when it passed, even if it had been petrifying, it simply ceased to be. The cat's ears flicked back and forth when Raul walked past the couch. He turned on the television, grateful for the grating noise of some tape-delayed drag race.

He was about to go back to the kitchen to get some water when his flesh rippled.

Did I turn the TV off last night?

Or the radio?

Now that he realized it, the lights had been turned off too.

I was blackout drunk. I must have turned them all off before stupidly setting up my bed outside.

What made that thought less than convincing was the fact that if, even in his inebriated state last night, he'd been so afraid he had to sleep outside, wouldn't he have left everything on rather than plunge himself into darkness?

The tiny hairs on the back of his neck started to rise.

Bella and the kids may be quiet now, but they're here, watching me. Waiting.

And then there was the niggling part of him that believed the vision of disembodied legs had all been in his imagination. What was worse? Being terrorized by your murdered wife or rapidly going insane? That was a coin flip at best.

"I'll just stay outside," he said to Bella, causing Bruiser to stir. "You win. I'll keep away from you when all I really want is to be with you again."

He paused, waiting for…what? A bang from upstairs? The soft, pleading voice of his children whispering, *"Please don't go, Daddy."* Or Bella telling him, *"I forgive you,"* before bathing him in an ethereal warmth?

Oh, how he would pray for such a thing if prayer was the answer.

When silence was his only reply, it was easier to lean toward him having had a slight mental break. It didn't make him feel better.

He set about getting things ready. First, he had to feed Bruiser. As soon as he put the can opener to the can, the cat came rushing into the kitchen, wide awake and hungry. His head dove into the bowl and he didn't come up for air until the bowl was empty.

"At least someone's hungry."

Raul couldn't remember when he'd last eaten. His stomach felt sour, too bound up to allow for even the merest morsel of food.

That was not the case with the cat. Raul poured some dry food into the bowl, watching zen-like as Bruiser went in for seconds. This time, he left a handful of the fish-shaped treats behind.

Next was a much-needed pit stop in the bathroom. While he sat on the toilet, he peered into the shower. Once again, the soap was gone. He wondered where the hell the soap and other small items were going. Were they being hidden somewhere in the house, or taken as booty to the great beyond? What was the point of it all?

To let me know they can take whatever they want from me. Take it and never give it back.

Soap. Keys. His sanity. It was all there, waiting to be snatched.

When he went to his bedroom, the sheets strewn all over the floor from last night, he saw that the sky had darkened considerably. He pulled the blinds apart and saw dark gray storm clouds rolling in.

"No. No."

The rumble of thunder, the kind of thunder you never heard in the city, shook the house, preceding the rain by a minute at most. The rain started as a light, intermittent tapping. Raul ran outside to save the mattress. By the time he'd gotten his hands on it, the trickle became a downpour, soaking him to the skin in seconds.

"Damn you!"

Coming down in sheets, the rain hurt his face and shoulders as he struggled with the mattress, the fabric feeling as if it were absorbing every fat drop until it was heavier than stone. Mud caked up along the bottom as he dragged it to the door. It snagged on a corner of the concrete patio. He tugged and tugged to no avail.

An eye-searing flash of lightning struck much too close.

He dropped the mattress, an offering to the god of thunder and misery, and ran inside, chased by what seemed like a never-ending rumble of country thunder. The storm raged with the fury Raul was sure Bella felt for him, so much so that he wondered if he'd stumbled into some warp in time and space, a place where spirits could manipulate nature itself as easily as they could his bar of soap.

Rain hammered the house like marbles tossed at high velocity. Lightning lit up the sky in zigzags and pulses with very little break between strikes. Each clap of thunder was an atom bomb detonating high up in the atmosphere.

He stood in the doorway, watching his mattress get destroyed, shielding his eyes from the barrage of cobalt lightning.

Bruiser came over and licked the rainwater from his bare feet.

"Stop that." He shooed the cat away.

He was trapped. The house creaked and groaned, making his balls shrivel to raisins.

The car.

He still had the Subaru.

Running to the front door was a mistake. His feet were soaked and the hardwood floor unforgiving. Raul slid from the dining room into the living room, pinwheeled his arms to keep his balance, and lost the fight. He went down hard enough to jar a glass candy tray from the nearby bookshelf. A shard of glass pierced his ear. It felt like getting stung by a bee. He clamped his hand over his ear and struggled to catch his breath, all while experiencing a spreading pool of pain in his upper back that reached around to his chest.

Sparks of light flickered on and off through the living room windows. There were noises everywhere. It sounded as if the house was about to collapse on him. It was like falling in a funhouse and he couldn't get his bearings.

Managing to roll over, he pulled his hand back and saw the smear of blood in his palm.

Laughter came from the kitchen. It came from the cellar. It was all around him, fading in and out between bursts of thunder that made his ears pop.

Energy, he thought. Felix talked about ghosts needing a source of energy to manifest. What better generator of energy than a fierce storm with dozens of bolts of lightning?

Bella's throaty laugh and the high-pitched chuckling of Lizzy and Abel mocked him, reveled in his pained helplessness. They were enjoying his suffering.

There was no point in asking them to stop, in once again pleading for forgiveness. He had to get the hell out.

Raul shifted to his hands and knees and slowly stood up. Something felt sharp and biting and funny in his back and his vision went sideways for a moment. Taking a deep breath was pure agony.

With the floor vibrating from the latest thump of thunder, he cautiously approached the door, looking for his car keys on the hook on the wall.

They were gone.

Where the hell did I leave the keys? he thought frantically.

If the Other Raul could move the heavy mattress outside in the dead of night, he could have easily misplaced the keys. The problem was, Raul had no way of getting into the head and memories of Other Raul.

Bella's laughter echoed up from the cellar.

Raul scanned the living room. The keys had to be close by.

Or shit, they could be with the bars of soap, lost forever.

A flare of lightning barely preceded the *whump* of thunder. Bruiser came tearing ass from behind the couch. Raul watched the cat dart up the stairs.

"Come back here!"

His keys were in the cat's mouth.

Raul raced after him.

"Bruiser! Stop!"

Not that the cat would listen to him.

He saw Bruiser's back as the cat slipped into Ida's thinking room.

Something fell downstairs. He looked down the staircase just as the lights went out.

Six red, glowing orbs hovered in the darkness at the bottom of the stairs.

Raul screamed and hurried to Ida's thinking room, slammed the door and pushed his back against it. He fumbled for his cell phone and turned on the flashlight app. Bruiser was in Ida's reading chair, the Subaru's keys between his massive paws. Raul cursed the cat and the fact that he was trapped in the room.

Eyes. Raul knew those red lights had been eyes.

They had been the eyes of his family, red with hate, hate for him, hate for the people who had taken their lives, maybe hate for the world. Raul was sure of it. His teeth chattered. Every quiver of his body made the pain in his ribs worse. He craved a drink and his pills, the craving building into a physical need.

"You fucked me, Bruiser! You really fucked me!"

The cat didn't seem to care a lick. But its eyes were wide and fixed on the door.

There were heavy footsteps downstairs. And more of Bella's laughter. Raul went to lock the door but saw with dread that there was no lock.

What the hell good is a lock going to do against ghosts?

Keeping one foot on the door, he grabbed the chair. Bruiser yowled and leaped off. Raul tilted it so it was wedged under the doorknob. He backed up until his back came into contact with the bookshelves. Bruiser nudged his shin with his head.

Knock-knock.

Raul's blood froze.

Tiny feet thumped down the hallway.

Laughter came, as it always had, but this laughter was warped, demented-sounding. The cackling of a lunatic.

Raul shivered. Some paperbacks were rattled from their precarious spot on the shelf and clattered to the floor. He yelped and jumped at the same time as Bruiser.

Knock-knock.

Thump-thump-thump-thump.

Ahahahahahahahahahahaha!

The abominable simulation of his children's favorite game played over and over, just inches from where Raul cowered. The storm raged and thunder shook the glass in the lone windowpane. In between the cloudburst and knock-knock-hit-bump, Bella howled with insane laughter.

The doorknob slowly turned.

Raul pitched forward to grab it with both hands.

You can't get in. You can't get in! YOU CAN'T GET IN!

Sweat slicked his hand, making it difficult to keep his grip. The doorknob fought against him.

Two raps on the door sent him reeling so hard, he crashed into the shelves, raining books down on him.

The doorknob turned all the way.

The door opened just a sliver. Raul held his breath.

The chair shifted, but it didn't fall.

Knock-knock sounded on the wall outside.

The footsteps retreated.

Abel and Lizzy, or something pretending to be them, laughed their monstrous laughs as they faded away.

CHAPTER TWENTY-THREE

Felix woke up in his motel room, showered, and walked across the street to a greasy spoon that served only two things – bacon, egg and cheese on a hard roll, or sausage, egg and cheese on a hard roll. He went all in and got one of each, took them back to his room, and ate them over the small table beside the window. A light storm had passed the night before, leaving the mostly empty parking lot clean and glassy.

While he ate, he thought back to his visit to the parish house the day before. Samson obviously didn't hold the same place of trust with Father Gilmore as he had with Raul.

Kids used to call me Uncle Bill.

Gilmore was young and birdlike, with a pointed noise and busy eyes. The second he saw Felix, he physically recoiled as if Felix had just brought a golden calf to his door to worship. In that moment, Felix renamed him Father Chickenshit. The priest let him and Samson in reluctantly, sticking close, Felix assumed, to make sure he didn't steal anything.

The house still smelled of fresh paint and the furniture all looked new, cheap stuff from Ikea. Samson, slipping easily into cop mode, talked Felix through what had happened that night. How the door had been broken, which must have made a hell of a racket, and pointing out where and how Bella and the children had been murdered. His voice faltered when he came to the part about the kids, but he'd pressed on.

Samson had been right. There was nothing to see. All traces of that night had been extinguished. In the back of his mind, Felix had been hoping to catch some kind of vibe, not necessarily a psychic impression, just something that would connect with his criminal sense. No such luck. Though he did enjoy the nauseated look on Father Chickenshit's face as he listened in on the details, knowing this was the house where he was living now and probably having glossed over the details when he'd moved in to make his stay more palatable.

No one liked to live in a slaughterhouse.

At least no one sane.

"Nobody saw nothin'?" Felix asked Samson when they left the house and Father Chickenshit. "Just breaking that door down should have gotten the attention of some of the neighbors."

Samson rubbed the back of his neck as he limped back to the alley and Felix followed him to the yard. "There was a storm that night and it was on the cold side. People had their windows closed. They might have thought it was thunder. Who knows?"

"But someone had to hear something. Raul told me the cops were in the house by the time he got here."

"Anonymous call. The timing of it is hard to pinpoint, but there's a chance it was made either during the break-in or possibly before."

"Before?"

"An off chance, but yes."

Felix had chewed on that and was still gnawing on it along with his breakfast sandwich. There was no doubt in his mind that the call had been made by someone in connection with the murders. That further cemented the case for it being premeditated.

Who could want Bella dead? Were the children targets as well?

It was time to poke around the dark places.

Felix didn't know this city all that well, but people like him had a kind of sixth sense when it came to finding each other. After breakfast, he lay back on his narrow bed, the mattress in need of replacing years ago, and watched some TV. It was nice to be able to control what he watched.

The shit people take for granted, he thought, switching channels until he found a morning show with a pretty redhead with a killer body interviewing some celebrity he'd never heard of. That program ended and rolled into a game show. He hated game shows. It seemed like half the other channels played court shows. No way was he going to watch that. He'd had his fair share of real courtroom drama and couldn't see why anyone would want to bring that shit into their home.

Boredom put him to sleep and he awoke in time for lunch.

He got up, feeling like there were cockroaches crawling under his skin. As much as he wanted to get moving, to make some progress, he had to wait. Criminals were not morning people. Or day people, for that matter.

Riding around town, he scoped out the good parts from the bad, making note of seedy bars and derelict-looking clubs that he'd visit later that night. There was going to be a risk to this. Not so much to his life. He was a survivor and thrived in his element. That element attracted the police, and he could find himself caught up in a bust that came out of the blue like a storm that had lain low under the weatherman's watchful eye. Then it would be back to his own courtroom drama and another semester of school.

Some guys, when they got out, they realized life was better on the inside, so they did what they needed to get back where they belonged. It was easier to wheel and deal in the joint than hustle for your next meal or fix or piece of pussy in the real world.

Not Felix. He preferred his freedom, thank you.

Rarely, and this was one of those times, risking his freedom was worth the task. He and Raul had parted ways over fifteen years ago, but a brother was always a brother. And his brother was in a bad way. Besides, Felix wasn't getting any younger. It was time to do something in the positive column.

Just thinking about Raul made his guts twist. It was better not to dwell on the ghosts. That was a problem that might be beyond his ability to fix, though he would try with all he had.

He stopped at a food truck and ordered a pulled pork sandwich on a fresh-made brioche bun. Felix had no fucking idea what a brioche bun was, but it tasted pretty damn good. His whiskers were stained with barbecue sauce. He'd suck on them later, savoring the spicy sweet flavor.

The Harley took him where it wanted to, or at least that's how it always felt when he spent a day cruising. His job was to sit back and enjoy the view, or in this case, spot potential locations for wayward souls. The sun went from searing yellow to a dusty orange and shadows crept out from between the buildings and houses.

It was time.

Gus's Place, though the second *s* and the *p* in *Place* had burned out and it read 'Gus' lace', was his first stop. He stepped into a haze of smoke and stale beer and vomit-soaked wood. Lynyrd Skynyrd played on a jukebox. There was a pool table, there always was in dive bars, its felt worn in spots, leather pockets frayed. Two older guys, both bikers according to the emblems on their jackets, shot nine-ball. They made a big show out of not paying him any mind while actually sizing him up with weathered, calculating eyes. Four old-timers sat at the bar, harmless gray-hairs who Felix bet had parked their asses on those stools every day for decades.

The bartender was another geezer, but he had the crooked nose and wiry arms of a man who could still scrap if pushed too hard. Felix ponied up to the bar.

"You lost?" the bartender asked.

"Gimme a bourbon, neat."

The bartender eyed him suspiciously for several beats before pouring his drink. The booze looked a little too clear. Probably fifty per cent tap water. Felix downed it like a shot.

"That'll be five bucks."

It tasted more like a buck at best, but Felix wasn't going to push it...yet. He slapped a ten on the bar and knocked for another.

Now all eyes were on him, even the bikers.

At least I have their attention.

"You need directions to a taco joint?" one of the bikers asked, smiling as if he'd told the world's funniest joke. His partner chimed in with, "Hey Walt, you didn't tell me you were getting a new cleaning guy."

The old men at the bar chuckled.

Walt, the bartender, replied, "Why the fuck would I clean this place? You guys'll just make a mess of it. Though I bet this guy will make the shitter *spic* and span." He drew out the word *spic* as if Felix were too dumb to catch his drift.

Now everyone was having a good laugh.

Felix shocked them into silence when he laughed the hardest of them all. "You guys are funny. I didn't know this was a comedy club."

"Why don't you get the hell outta here, beaner?" Walt less-than-kindly asked.

Felix tapped his chest with his fingers. "Beaner? You think I'm a fucking Mexican? I'm insulted."

One of the bikers slipped his hand in his jacket pocket. Felix knew what that meant. So much for subtlety at Gus's Place. He said, "Look man, I'm not here for trouble. I'm just looking for someone."

"Ain't nobody here," one of the drunk geezers said.

"You know about the Parish House murders?" Sometimes it was best to just come out with it.

"Yeah? So?" Walt replied curtly.

"I'm looking for the guys that did it."

"Good luck with that," Walt said.

Felix studied the bikers' faces. If anyone would have their ear to the ground, it would be them. Sure, they reacted, but more in the way of being sickened by the mere mention of the massacre. Most people didn't realize that even criminals had their boundaries.

Walt, on the other hand, looked like he couldn't give a rat's ass. He just wanted Felix gone.

Felix slid off the barstool. "All right. Just asking. You all can go back to rotting in here."

"*Adios, muchacha,*" Walt called after him.

The weight of their gazes pushed hard on his back as he left. He straddled his Harley and waited a few minutes before firing her up. Most times, a guy had information, he liked to give it in private.

Not this time.

He tried three more bars, one even less welcoming than Gus's, played a lot of pool (he'd have to get more quarters for tomorrow night), scored some weed off a guy standing outside a bodega, which earned him a couple of questions, shot dice behind an abandoned store and, to cap things off, managed to get himself into a cockfight in the basement of a seedy apartment.

He'd realized the bull in a china shop might not be the best approach. If this were his hometown, he'd know exactly where to go and who to ask. Out here, he was an outsider, marginally accepted because people could immediately see he was a criminal lifer.

By sunup, he was exhausted. All he wanted to do was grab a bag of McDonald's egg McMuffins and go back to his room to smoke that weed and pass out. Grease from the hash browns stained the bottom of the brown takeout bag. He parked his bike outside his door and searched for the motel key. The place was that old that it still used keys instead of cards.

Fumbling with the lock, he accidentally dropped the bag of McDonald's. Bending down to pick it up, with the key still in the lock, he heard the rushing scuffle of footsteps. Felix shot back up and turned around.

A man wearing a black tracksuit and matching black ski mask came at him with a knife. Felix brought his arm up to fend off the attack. The leather of his jacket was thick and might just be enough to ward off the stabbing.

His attacker changed tactics, dropping the knife to his side and ramming his shoulder into Felix's chest. Felix smashed into the door. Every breath of air in his lungs exploded out of him and he dropped to the ground. Christ, this guy was made out of cinder blocks.

As Felix slid down the door, he lashed out with his boot, hoping to get the guy right in the balls. His steel-tipped boot grazed the man's inner thigh instead.

The man in black spun like Jackie-goddamn-Chan and kicked Felix in the face. His head whipped to the side and something crunched deep inside him. Everything went gray and gauzy. Felix just about registered the fact that another man, this one slighter and shorter, was now straddling his chest, pointing the dangerous end of the knife at his face.

Something hot and wet bloomed on his forehead. He wanted to grab the man's arm, but his own arms were dead weight.

The man brought his knee to Felix's windpipe as he worked on his forehead. In his mind, Felix hurled every curse and threat he knew at this motherfucker.

At least until everything went dark and silent and numb.

CHAPTER TWENTY-FOUR

It rained all day and into the night and next morning. Raul rolled the window down a crack to get some fresh air, filling the car with the aroma of damp earth and ozone. The windows had fogged up and he could no longer see the house. Not that he wanted to.

This is ridiculous. How much longer am I going to sit here?

Being separated from the ingredients of his magic potion had left him feeling as if he had the flu. Several times he'd been ready to sprint into the house to grab a six-pack, but his uncorralled terror kept him in the car.

His back and shoulders ached. When he took a deep breath, his ribs let him know it, but they felt a little better than the night before. His knuckles were swollen and bruised from punching the dashboard. It didn't feel as if anything were broken. If he'd caught thirty minutes of sleep, not even in a row, he'd be surprised. His eyes hurt when he blinked, dried out after crying a bucket of tears.

They can't hurt me. They're ghosts, for Christ's sake. That's Bella, Lizzy, and Abel. My family. I can't be afraid of my family.

Another part of him begged to differ. But today was a new day and he wasn't going to give that cowering corner of his mind room to move.

Maybe if I just think of them as still living with me. I wasn't afraid of Bella when she was mad at me. Not that she got mad often, but when she did, it would last a while. Abel and especially Lizzy would stomp and hurl the occasional "I hate you!" when I punished them, but I never thought they could and would hurt me.

Yes, but the legs! The things Bella said!

Bella's legs. For all I know, that was all she could manage to show. Shit, I used to look forward to seeing her legs.

When the rest of her was attached to them.

Stop it!

Yes, stop it. I probably made that shit up in my head anyway. Bruiser didn't seem to see them. But the other stuff....

He was breathing heavily, clenching the steering wheel to ground himself and not spiral completely into his own head.

That's my wife in there. Those are my children. I am not afraid of them.

Something clicked in his brain and it sparked a flowing sense of calm that set his taut muscles at ease. With clarity came conviction.

I'm afraid of myself. It's my own self-loathing that I'm running from. Bella is only here to help me see the truth.

With that came a cold knot of dread that settled in the pit of his stomach. Bella was confirming the worst things he'd thought of himself. Instead of asking for forgiveness, he would plead for redemption. Bella had always been the calm in the storm, able to think and see clearly when things were at their most turbulent. She'd been trying to break through his inner tempest the only way she could.

Raul opened the car door. His arm became coated in a fine mist as the rain tapered off. It felt as if every bone popped when he stretched. He yawned and rolled his neck, trying to work the kinks out.

He was going into the house where he would remain. No more running. No more hiding from his family. From himself.

Trudging up the front steps, he cast a glance at the porch swing. He'd left one of his books on the seat. It had swollen up like a fat toad from the rain. A moth flittered past the door, erratically making its way along the covered porch and disappearing behind the house. Somewhere in the cold gray morning, a dog barked. Maybe it had spotted a squirrel and was telling it to get off its lawn.

The world went on, uncaring about Raul and his ghosts or troubles. Storms roiled and passed. Every day brought new hope, fresh heartbreak, surprises, and disappointments.

Today will not bring fear.

He pushed the door open. The squealing hinge echoed in the empty – not empty – house. Ida's vacant throne sat in its usual spot. Maybe Ida settled into it when he was asleep. All things were now possible. If Ida could speak to him, would she shush his fears in her plain folk way as she had when he was a child, or would she side with Bella and the kids?

It didn't matter.

Raul had to learn to live with himself if he was going to coexist with the restless souls of his family. Even Ida couldn't fix that.

"I'm back," he announced, his thready voice calling Bruiser from his perch on the dining room windowsill. "I understand now."

He walked to his bedroom where he stripped out of his clothes, taking extra care when he removed his shirt, his aching muscles and bones unhappy with the awkward movement. A tiny mule kicked at the sides of his head and he had to stop a moment, close his eyes, and take a deep breath. He made a stack out of a pair of clean jeans, a white t-shirt, underwear, and socks. Passing through the kitchen, he stopped and put his clothes on the table.

The refrigerator.

He'd have to move it back. It was cowardice that made him cover the vent in the floor. Pushing it back was almost as hard as the first time, but it eventually settled into its groove. Bottles clinked inside and he knew some items had fallen over. That was a mess for later.

Confirmation that he was doing the right thing stared him in the face when he went into the bathroom.

A green bar of soap was in the soap dish in the shower.

Was this a peace offering?

With the water as hot as he could stand it, Raul lathered up and let it burn the previous night off his skin. He soaked in the uncomfortable spray until it seeped into his pores and cleaned him from the inside out. It loosened some of the knots in his back and neck. He found he could breathe just fine without feeling as if a lung were going to be punctured as long as he kept it slow and steady. Only when the hot water ran out did he turn the faucets off and step out to dry.

Bruiser sat on the closed toilet lid, looking like a fur-covered gargoyle. He watched Raul shave, brush his teeth, and comb his hair. A new man stared back at him in the mirror, though there was no denying the glimmers of permanent anguish in his eyes.

"Hungry?" Raul asked the cat after he'd gotten dressed.

Bruiser jumped off the lid and rubbed against Raul's legs. "I bet you are. For food and company." He picked up the coon cat, a feat that required two hands. "Let's hang for a while."

A bowl of dry cat food for Bruiser and cereal for himself. He even let the cat eat on the table, the two species sharing a moment while they ate, occasionally catching one staring at the other.

Spots of sunshine flashed between the clouds, and if Raul had just walked in on this scene in the kitchen, he would not have been able to imagine the horror from the night before.

Thirsty. He guzzled a liter of bottled water and had to catch his breath. His dehydrated body needed more. With only beer and half a carton of milk in the fridge, he decided it was time to go to the store.

On the way out of the house, he turned on the television, preferring not to come home to a silent house. He stopped on a channel airing cooking shows. Bella had loved those cooking shows. So had Lizzy. Abel just liked the food his mother was inspired by them to make. Lizzy always begged to help in the kitchen.

The Figueroa home was often filled with the sounds of food sizzling in pans, vegetables being chopped, and a celebrity chef walking their viewers through the process of making chicken thighs with creamy mustard sauce or sweet potato casserole. That was the sound of his family in their comfort zone. When they were happy. When they were alive.

"You like this one," Raul said. The smiling woman specialized in Spanish dishes and had become a kind of hero to Lizzy. She wanted to grow up and have her own cooking show just like the TV chef from Chile. Raul remembered buying her one of those toy kitchens with a colorful plastic stove and prep table, complete with pots, pans, utensils, and a wild array of fake food. Lizzy would play with that kitchen all day, blabbing to her imagined viewers while she whisked away in her tiny bowls and set the timer on the oven.

Feeling tears coming on, Raul locked the door and got in the car. It smelled like his body odor, that extra-sour adrenaline sweat that had come in waves last night. He rolled down all the windows and drove well over the speed limit to get some solid airflow.

Hurry home.

He nearly slammed on the brakes, unsure if the voice had been in his head or whispered close to his ear. The car shuddered and his ribs clenched. Fighting a tremor that bloomed in his gut, he continued on, concentrating on the task at hand.

There was something in the voice's tone (and for the life of him, he couldn't tell if it was Bella, Lizzy, Abel, a conglomeration of the three, or something entirely different) that said he better not drive all the way to Glens Falls.

No, better to obey the voice, no matter who it belonged to or where it came from. Fighting and running were no longer the answers.

Sully's General Store was just up ahead. He pulled in front, flicking a quick glance at the car before he walked inside, expecting to see...he wasn't entirely sure.

"Hey there, son, where ya been hidin'?"

Old man Sully was stacking cans of tuna fish on a shelf. He wore slacks up past his navel, held in place with suspenders.

Raul nearly jumped at the man's voice because he'd been preoccupied thinking about the command to hurry home. Sully smiled and Raul saw he was missing two of his front bottom teeth.

A friendly voice was like a lifeline to the real world. Raul desperately wanted to grab hold and not let go.

Hurry home.

"Just laying low," Raul replied, plucking a basket and searching for essentials.

"Must be a lot to do at your aunt's. Ida wasn't very handy and she didn't like strangers in her house."

He thinks I'm spending my days wrapped up in DIY projects, Raul thought. *If he only knew that I've only even stepped onto the second floor once.*

He answered with a breathy, "Yeah." His eyes were focused on the aisles. He was afraid that if he got pulled into Sully's warm gaze, he'd give in to the urge to connect with another person over all things banal and simple. To do so would delay getting back to a house listening intently to a cooking show, waiting for him.

"That was some storm. Did your power go out?" Sully took the empty tuna box and set it down behind the counter.

Raul had no idea if the house had lost power. Ida hadn't left behind anything with a digital display, so nothing was blinking twelve o'clock, the default setting for most, when he willed himself to go back inside.

He put four cans of soup in his basket. "No, I got through it all right."

"That's good. That's good. You need more beer? I just got a delivery the other day."

More beer would be nice. It would also dull everything. He was tired of that. It was time to feel everything with all its sharp, dangerous edges, no matter the consequences.

"No, I'm good," he said, his gaze locked on the nutrition label on a box of cereal.

As he shopped, his basket getting almost too heavy to carry, Sully spoke and he replied with short answers. Raul made it clear he wasn't in the mood to talk, but Sully was either thicker than a pyramid or didn't care.

When Raul put the basket on the old, scarred counter, Sully set to working his pencil on a paper bag, tallying his haul.

"You been having company?" Sully asked as he added another row of numbers.

Raul was looking out the window at the Subaru. "Huh?"

"Passed by your aunt's place yesterday. Saw you had someone parked outside the house. That's good. Young man like you shouldn't be alone all the time."

Yesterday? Felix hadn't been there, nor his bike. The old man must have had his days mixed up.

"An...an old friend came to visit," was all Raul said.

"Old friends are the best." Sully tucked his pencil behind his ear and told Raul what he owed. Raul was sure he'd intentionally not added some items to his calculation. He paid Sully in cash and thanked him.

As he was scooping his bags into his arms, Sully asked, "You mind me asking you something?"

Yes, he very much did. Raul said, "No."

"You feeling okay? You look a little pale."

Raul made up a quick lie. "All that work in the house. Guess I'm not getting enough sun."

A little of the worry lifted from Sully's face. "All work and no play. Take your breaks out back. Nice plot of land Ida has there. A little vitamin D will fix you right up."

"Thanks."

He hustled out of the store, the bell over the door chiming at his back. He spotted Sully out of the corner of his eye, staring at him through the big plate glass window as he loaded up the Subaru.

I'm watched everywhere I go.

Gravel spit from his tires and he hit the gas a little too hard.

Hurry home.

Sweat broke out on his forehead and trickled down the back of his neck as he sped down the pitted country road. He made a hard turn into his driveway and skidded to a stop. The sight of the house set his heart racing. Raul turned the engine off and sat in the still car, waiting to see if the voice would say anything else.

"I did what you said. See?"

Inside the house, the television was still on but muted. The Chilean chef had been replaced by a woman with hair like a cockatoo. Bruiser was asleep on the couch. A floorboard creaked above him. Raul's flesh prickled. The air itself was heavy, pregnant with the pressure of too many souls packed into one place. They had waited for him, limited his time away from them.

Raul's body wanted to turn heel, drop the bag, and go back to the car.

"I'm not leaving," he said through clenched teeth. And then, louder, so they could hear him from every corner of the house, "I'm...not...leaving. Do what you want to me. I'm never leaving you again."

He expected the intense banging to commence like the clapping of a crowd at a ballgame. A window rattled in its frame as a stray wind gust blew over the house. He held his breath for several beats.

"Silent treatment," he muttered, taking his groceries to the kitchen. The small hairs on the back of his neck perpetually stood on end when he was in the house.

As he stepped into the kitchen, he staggered and dropped the bags. The bottoms burst and his cans and boxes flooded onto the floor.

Ida's butcher knife, the one he'd watched her wield when she would carve the chickens she bought from the farmer's market, was buried into the wooden chopping block on the counter. He spun around. There was no one behind him. Raul backed into the kitchen, his eyes on the hallway, protecting himself from someone overtaking him from behind.

Which was silly, because a living person hadn't done this.

He was never more sure of that than when his eyes glanced at the cutting board.

On it, written in crayon, were two words that set his head spinning and his gorge rising.

JOIN US.

CHAPTER TWENTY-FIVE

Felix examined the ragged cross that had been carved in his forehead. He applied a dab of bacitracin on the wound, muttering, "You fucking *puta*," under his breath the entire time. Aside from the flesh wound, the rest of his face was mottled with bruises. His head hurt and his eyes kept tearing up. Wiping them from his cheeks only reignited the pain.

When the motel manager had found him unconscious outside his room, he'd helped him up and promptly asked him to leave. At that moment, Felix's brain wasn't firing on all cylinders.

"Huh? I just got jumped. Did you see the assholes?" he'd said, holding his head with both hands to keep it from exploding.

"I'll give you your money back," said the manager, an Indian guy with a thick accent, wearing a white dress shirt with deep, dark pit stains. If the man had any sympathy for Felix's plight, his fuzzy vision was unable to read it on his pinched face. "I don't want any trouble here."

"Me neither, dickhead." Felix leaned his back into his room door to keep from falling. Blood pooled in his left eye and his face throbbed. "You can't kick me out."

The manager folded his arms over his chest. "If you don't leave, I'll call the cops."

He'd said the magic words. Any man that ran a seedy piece-of-shit place like that knew people like Felix. Bringing in the cops was not an option. And though Felix knew the jerk would rather eat his own shit-streaked underwear than have to answer a bunch of questions from the five-oh, it was easier to take his money and go.

"Go get my money." As the manager turned to head to the office, Felix said, "And throw in another twenty."

The manager cast a calculating eye at him.

Felix shot back with, "I may be hurt but I got enough in me to ruin your day. Your call. And bring me a towel."

Minutes later, he had a handful of cash and a stained hand towel. Felix pressed it to his forehead and made it a uniform red.

Another fleabag motel was just a mile away. This manager, a kid who couldn't be more than twenty, sat behind bulletproof glass reading a graphic novel. He barely looked up at Felix as he checked him in.

A bag of ice for his face and a restless sleep later, Felix was not pleased by what he saw in the mirror. It had been a long time since someone had thrown him a beating like that.

"Getting old, Grandpa," he said to himself. He wondered what color his skin was under his beard. Good thing he had the face fuzz to hide some of the damage.

It did prove one thing. He'd either talked to someone associated with the murders, or word had gotten around. The crimson cross on his head was all the proof he needed.

The upside-down cross was a clear signal that he wasn't dealing with people who filled the pews on Sundays.

Felix had met plenty of guys in prison who sported upside-down cross tattoos and brands. None of them were Satan worshippers. Just hard-asses who thought the image made them look even scarier. Or wannabes who listened to that death metal shit that sounded like a buzz saw in a deli slicer gone mad.

Or maybe these were people who really did think they were doing the Devil's work on earth. There was just so much information he could get from a throbbing wound on his forehead.

He loaded up a bath towel with ice from the ice machine a few doors down. It helped dull the throbbing pain in his right cheek especially.

He might not have been the brightest bulb that ever came from the Rodriguez pack, but he knew all about motivation when it came to crime. It had been months since Bella and the kids had been put in the ground. It had resulted in costing the parish their priest, and that man a part of his sanity. There were easier ways to get rid of a priest.

These were people who lived with hate. Who cared as much about God as Felix did about politicians.

And they weren't regular people. Normal citizens would not

have been plugged into the crowd Felix had infiltrated the night before. This was no random crazy motherfucker who hears voices and one day decides it's best to heed them.

A man can learn a lot from a beating.

He'd riled up the hornet's nest last night and gotten a permanent reminder why he should keep his nose out of it.

Well, that only encouraged him.

Again, he couldn't shake the feeling that it all came down to Bella.

Time to pay her parents a visit. If they were reticent to let him in their home the last time, his face might send them bolting the door now. No matter. He had to try.

As he rode his Harley to their house, the wind felt like it was laced with tiny pins and his face was a cushion. He stopped at a drugstore to get some ibuprofen, washing four pills down with bottled water in the parking lot. Hopefully, they would start to kick in by the time he got to the Diaz house. His head hurt like blue blazes and his helmet irritated the top part of his cross wound.

Irritable and tired, he pulled up in front of their suburban ranch house twenty minutes later. His bike's exhaust, which could resurrect the dead, caught the attention of a woman walking her dog and a neighbor peeking through her blinds. They didn't get many bikers out here, especially the same one twice in a month.

Felix rang the bell and waited, gingerly touching the cross. Was it getting puffier?

The door opened and Valentina Diaz went from pleasant to mildly concerned in a flash. "Oh my. Is that you, Felix?"

"Yes ma'am. I'm having a bad face day."

"Come in, come in." She whisked him through the door. Whether it was out of concern for him or keeping him from prying eyes of the neighbors was a toss-up. "Eduardo!" she called out as she led Felix to the living room and nearly pushed him into a comfortable chair. "What can I get you? Something to drink? You really need a bandage on that. Do you need some ice?"

Her brow furrowed as she stared at his new body art. She made a quick sign of the cross. "*Dios mio.*"

"I'll be fine."

"You look pretty far from fine," Eduardo said as he entered the room. He had a rag in his hands and was using it to wipe grease from his fingers. He looked at Felix's forehead and his eyes darkened. "Who did that to you?"

"I wish I knew. Guy jumped me last night."

"And then you came here?" Raul's father-in-law said suspiciously. "I thought you were going to stay with Raul?"

The pair stood over him, making him feel at a disadvantage. Valentina looked like a worried mother while Eduardo was the father who knew his son could be full of shit at times.

"I *was* with Raul. I came back here to help him."

"Oh my, how is he? He hasn't called for the longest time," Valentina said.

Felix shrugged. "Not so good." He didn't think that would be shocking news. They didn't need to know their daughter's ghost was driving him mad. "He's not taking things well, as you can imagine."

Eduardo said, "So how can you help him down here?"

Felix eyeballed the couch across from him, hoping the couple would take the hint. They didn't. *Guess I have to spell it out.* "You might want to take a seat."

He was thankful when Valentina quietly urged Eduardo to sit beside her.

After taking a deep breath, Felix said, "I thought it wasn't a good idea for Raul to be alone. I thought I could help him in some way, you know. Problem is, there's too much going on up here with him." Felix tapped the side of his head carefully. "And here." He patted his chest. "He could be surrounded by ten people and he'll be alone with the things that are weighing him down."

Valentina looked like she was going to cry.

"I could keep my ass in that house with him until we're both gray and it wouldn't change a thing. There are too many questions that he can't answer. I don't know if he'll ever be the same person again. But I have to try to give him some, what do you call it...."

Eduardo leaned forward. "Closure?"

Felix snapped his fingers. "Yes, that's it. Closure. The same for both of you. You've all been through the same hell."

"What do you propose to do, then?" Eduardo asked. He made it pretty obvious he wasn't buying all Felix was selling.

"I'm going to find the people who killed them. And I know I must be close, because this is what I got for trying."

"You should call the police," Valentina said.

"What will they do? Guy like me, they'll just assume I earned it. At best, they'll laugh it off. At worst, they'll add to my list of problems."

"But if you can give them some description of the person who attacked you, there's a chance they could finally have their first lead." She looked so hopeful. Felix didn't want to let her down, but there was no way around it.

"I didn't get a good look at the guy. I was too busy being used as a punching bag, and then a tree trunk. Besides, most cops couldn't find their assholes if you gave them a mirror and a flashlight."

"Bet you're usually on the other side of something like that," Eduardo said coolly. Felix thought he was being sarcastic, but the man's slight grin said otherwise.

"I've never hit someone that didn't deserve it. And I sure as hell never did some sick shit like this to no one."

"Language," Eduardo warned him.

"I'm sorry. I'm not used to watching my mouth."

"It's okay," Valentina said, though she looked a little paler. Felix had that effect on women on a good day, and this wasn't a very good day at all.

"Look," Felix began. He could sense his welcome wearing out quickly. "Did Bella have any enemies? Someone who had a grudge or something against her?"

"Why on earth would you ask such a thing?" Valentina said, wringing her hands.

"I'm sure the cops asked you back when it happened, but it's hard to think straight when you're numb. I'm asking because I think your daughter was targeted. I don't know about the kids. But someone out there wanted her gone. Can you think of anyone?"

Their immediate, tandem answer was, "No."

He pressed on. "Maybe someone from school she didn't get along with."

"School?" Valentina said. "That was ages ago."

"I know. I also know that hate dies hard."

She shook her head. "No. My daughter wasn't a bully or a backstabber. Why, in school, she barely talked. She was so shy then. Painfully so. She didn't even go to her prom. It broke our hearts. Bella told us she never wanted to go, but we knew it was really because no one had asked her. College was a little better, but she was there to study. I guess in college, where most kids spend all that money to party, that would have made her an outcast. Again."

An outcast. They were usually the ones to watch out for.

"What about ex-boyfriends?"

Eduardo shifted and put his hand on his wife's knee. "There were none."

Felix couldn't believe it. Everyone had an ex. He cast a quick glance at a small, round table cluttered with framed pictures. They showed a smiling pretty little girl with a high ponytail grow into a very attractive woman with high cheekbones and a dazzling smile. A woman like that would have men stumbling over each other to ask her out. He could see why Raul had married her. His old homeboy had snagged a woman way out of his league.

"Not even in college?"

"None that we were ever made aware of."

"And Bella told me everything," Valentina said. "No, if she'd had a boyfriend before Raul, she would have said something."

He doubted it. Everyone had their secrets, especially from their parents. But could Bella have hidden a boy – or man – from her mother long enough to form a bond with him strong enough to eventually make him want to kill her? It seemed unlikely.

Valentina's eyes glazed over and when she spoke, it was as if she were watching the past play out before her. "We were so happy when she told us about Raul. I prayed for her every night, prayed she would find someone to share the love I knew she had inside her. You should have seen her whenever she talked about him. Oh, he was the one. And that he was studying to be a priest? It was almost as if the hand of God had guided them toward each other. He was everything she needed and wanted, and watching them together over the years, it was mutual. A priest and a husband were exactly what she needed to...to keep her safe. To fill her life with love."

Felix noticed Eduardo give her knee a squeeze and she was suddenly back in the present, her eyes darting around the room as if she were trying to get her bearings.

"Why did Raul being a priest mean so much? Usually those Holy Rollers are some pretty big sinners before they become saints." And if they only knew how true that was.

Valentina was about to answer when Eduardo said, "My daughter needed a good man. She was...fragile." He pinched his eyes shut and gently shook his head. "Maybe not fragile. Just, delicate. The wrong person could have broken her. But Raul was the right one. He brought her out of her shell, made her grow. He did it by feeding her with love and trust. Do you have any kids?"

"Not that I know of." Felix suspected there were a few bastard bandits running around out there.

"Then you can't know what it's like to want everything for a child and spend years worrying it will never happen. And when it finally does, it changes you. It changes everything."

"And she'd been through so, so much," Valentina added. A sharp look from Eduardo kept her from expanding on this.

They're hiding something.

Eduardo wasn't going to tolerate his questions much longer.

"What had she been through that you felt it was best for her to marry a religious man?"

The silence that followed was thick enough to displace all the air in the room. Eduardo shot Felix an intimidating glare. The old man was tough, Felix would give him that, but he'd faced down far worse. Valentina looked ready to cry.

"I think I explained myself quite clearly," Eduardo said, barely able to open his mouth while he spoke.

Felix could press, but Eduardo was on high alert. Maybe without him there, he could get Valentina to talk, but this wasn't the time.

He got up and winced as the bruises on his body filed a complaint against getting out of the chair. "Look, I didn't mean to upset you. These are ugly people who did what they did. It means I have to ask ugly questions. I mean no disrespect to your daughter. Trust me. I only want to make these fuc— people pay."

Eduardo got up but Valentina remained on the couch, again lost in her thoughts. He escorted Felix to the door. "Thank you for the offer, but nothing you can do will make things better. There's no closure in vengeance."

"The whole criminal justice system is built on that," Felix said.

"I want them found and punished more than you could ever imagine. But I want it done the right way. Enough evil has already been done. And when I look at you, I see a great capacity for evil."

Yeah, just like when you looked at Raul you saw a dude who was white as snow. We all see what we want to see, buddy.

"I'm sorry I upset your wife." *But not so much you.* "You take care."

The door didn't slam at his back, but it was pretty close.

Standing in the sun, Felix just wanted to find a patch of grass and lie down and rest. Maybe the heat and some vitamin D would help his head wound. But he was close to something. He needed to get Valentina alone. But how?

A man wearing jean shorts and a Jimmy Buffett t-shirt kept a sharp eye on Felix as he mowed his lawn. Felix smiled and waved. The guy nearly twisted his head off from looking away so fast.

Felix looked to the house on the other side of the Diaz home. There went the blinds again.

I'll bet there's some nosy old biddy in there. Every neighborhood has them. One thing about window-peeking biddies, they see everything. All the gossip flows through the old lady mouths.

He took a deep breath, walked onto the porch, and rang the bell. The name 'RANDALL' was in hand-drawn block letters on her mailbox. He could feel her looking at him through the peephole, assessing him. Hopefully knowing he had just come from her neighbors' house would earn him at least the door opening a crack.

"Who are you?" the frail voice said from behind the locked door. "You don't look like those Jehovah's Witnesses. They at least dress nice before they pester you. Mind you, I've already dialed nine-one-one."

"Just a friend of the Diazes," he replied, though hearing the words was even hard for him to believe, much less the distrustful old lady.

"I've lived next to them going on thirty years. You're not the type of people they associate with."

She had a point. He decided to count on her all-seeing endeavors. "Surely you must have seen me here before." There was a slight pause. He jogged her memory. "I was just here a few weeks ago. You must have heard my motorcycle."

He took a step back when a lock turned and the door opened a sliver. He could see the chain dangling above a head of cottony hair and wrinkled brow. "How do you know them?"

"I was their son-in-law's best friend." Might as well be honest.

"The preacher? I highly doubt it."

Her pale blue eyes were clouded with distrust. She looked ready to shut the door.

"Growing up. We were best friends growing up. We lost touch but I came back when I heard what happened."

She looked away. When the part of her face he could see returned, it was pained by sadness. "That poor girl and her babies. I remember when she was just a baby herself. No one should have to bury their children. And no one should die in such a way."

"On that we both agree." Now here came a lie and he had to do a little praying of his own to make sure it came off right. "You see, I used to be a cop. Worked undercover for years until I got hurt on the job, had to take early retirement. I'm just trying to see if I can find something the local PD can't. I didn't know Bella, so I'm trying to get some background on her."

One thing he knew about biddies was that as much as they liked to gather intel, they also chomped at the bit to show off what they knew.

"Oh, what she'd been through."

Again with something that had happened to Bella.

Whatever reticence she might have had about his backstory was overtaken by the need to tell. Felix knew all about these neighborhood watch ladies. Mrs. Marcone, his neighbor growing up, had taught him all he needed to know about this particular breed. She'd gotten him in more hot water with his grandmother because of her snooping and fat mouth.

The door closed and the chain slid from the lock. When she

opened it fully, he saw that Mrs. Randall was all of five feet and bent over like a question mark. She gripped a walker to keep on her feet.

"I hope you're not insulted if I don't invite you inside," she said in her papery falsetto. "My cats are taking their afternoon naps and I'd rather not get them all riled up."

And a cat lady to boot. Felix detected the musty, ammonia odor of a place that housed way too many felines.

"That's fine. If I could just ask a few questions."

"What happened to your head, son?" She squinted at the cross.

"I had an accident."

"You should get that looked at."

"Yes ma'am. I plan to do just that later today. Before I do, can you tell me what Bella had been through? Valentina and Eduardo, I think it's just too painful for them to talk about right now, all things considered."

She pulled a tissue from her pocket and wiped at her eyes. He didn't think it was from crying. She looked like the kind of person who had perpetually wet eyes. One thing he never wanted to be was old. Living the way he did was a safeguard against ending up like Mrs. Randall.

"It was just awful," she said. "I thought there was no way to ever recover from such a thing. But she did. It was a blessing. And Lord knew, she'd earned her share of blessings."

Felix wanted to shake her and just tell her to spill it, but he had to take a deep breath and stay cool. It was coming, albeit at a glacial pace.

"Did it happen when she was young?"

She nodded. "Oh yes, I think she was eleven. Or was it twelve? No, it was eleven."

Eleven? This could be a dead end. She'd probably gotten sick, maybe so sick she'd almost died. That wouldn't lead to her murder decades later.

He was about to thank her for her time when she said, "I mean, how many people do you know that have gone through an exorcism? I didn't even think it was a real thing. Just something from the movies. But no, it's real, and it happened next door."

CHAPTER TWENTY-SIX

It would have been too easy to lose himself in the bottom of his bottles of pills or vodka. Raul saw the words *JOIN US* everywhere. Not physically, as they had been on the carving block. They were imprinted on his eyes like an afterburn. No matter where he looked, there was their faint outline, grower thinner with each blink, but ready to return the second he adjusted his sight line.

Raul was on the cold hard floor of the kitchen. His cheek was only inches from the vent. He'd been like that for hours now, waiting for Bella or the kids to return. They were down there. When he closed his bedeviled eyes, he saw them floating near the basement ceiling, ears hovering close to the vent, waiting for him to make a sound.

Those words – *JOIN US* – meant he could no longer ask for forgiveness. They had given him his path to absolution.

Perhaps now, their silence, their utter absence, was further punishment. A solution had been offered. For the time being, they'd turned their backs on him.

Ball's in your court, honey, he could hear Bella say.

Here he was, his hips, knees, and shoulders going from agony to numb in this uncomfortable position for so long, keeping as still and quiet as he could, wanting to call out for Bella, Lizzy, and Abel, yet afraid of both their silence or what they would say.

They've said what they're going to say.

If he doubted it, he could pick himself up off the floor and read the words again.

Or just look at the wall and see the ghosts of the words on his retinas.

His heart picked up its pace when he felt slight taps on the floor. His anxiety was quickly quelled when he spotted Bruiser making his way to the kitchen. It must have been getting close to his dinner time. The cat rarely went to the kitchen other than to feed. Raul had wondered about that. Was it because the back door that led to the great outside was so close? What had Bruiser seen that had made him too afraid to go back out there? It wasn't like the inside of Ida's house was a bed of roses.

He closed his eyes in the vain hope that he wouldn't catch Bruiser's attention and the coon cat would sniff around and go back to whatever comfortable spot he'd been hiding in. The cat was too smart for that. He meowed as he approached him and licked Raul's nose with his sandpaper tongue.

Please just go away.

Bruiser's engine got going and he purred up a storm, circling around Raul and even walking gingerly across his back. His meows got louder and he pawed Raul's face. It became clear he wasn't going to be ignored.

"Fine."

Raul tried to move and found that his muscles and bones refused to co-operate. The sharp pains in his joints were staggering. It felt as if his entire body was on fire with pins and needles.

"Fuckmefuckmefuckme," he muttered, grabbing hold of his aching hip and ribs and trying to work the kinks out and the blood flow in. Raul was barely able to stay on his feet, and Bruiser decided to complicate things by doing figure eights around his legs.

Once Raul felt he could move without collapsing, he eyed the cupboard where he kept the cat food.

It was directly over the cutting board.

Keeping his gaze forward, for looking down would be akin to peeking at bubbling lava as you walked a tightrope over an active volcano, he opened the door and swiped the first can he saw, then turned his back on the message before its cold reality could take another bite out of him.

He dumped the pungent contents in a bowl and set it down. Bruiser made a beeline for it, smacking his lips loudly as he devoured the mess.

Raul leaned against the counter and stared at the vent.

JOIN US.

What pained him most was his cowardice. He'd thrown away his faith when he lost his family, and that was a kind of conviction, a faith unto itself. A belief that there was nothing to believe in.

Seeing those words, the first thing he thought was, *Suicide is the greatest of the sins.*

And that drove home the fact that he had no foundation upon which to stand. He couldn't be a man of God, yet he couldn't fully be a man without God.

He was as lost as a man could be, and there was no compass to guide him anymore. Too terrified to live, yet too frightened to die, at least in the way his family demanded.

"I wish I'd been there instead of you," he said aloud for the first time. He'd thought it a million times, for sure. This was the first time he'd said it to Bella and the kids. "They should have taken my life. Maybe I should have stayed at the church. Waited for them to come back. There's always a chance they would have come for me too."

A sharp clang, like the sound of a hammer whacking against a steel drum, rang out from somewhere in the dark cellar. Raul jumped as if bee-stung. Bruiser sprinted out of the kitchen and up the stairs.

"Is that you?"

Silence resumed beneath him.

I can't keep doing this.

When he swallowed, it felt as if he were trying to force down an entire hardboiled egg. He took a few deep breaths, gripped the knob to the basement door, and slowly pulled it open. Before he went down, he yanked open drawer after drawer until he found one of Ida's flashlights. She kept them all around the house in case the power went out, which was a common occurrence out here, at least when Raul was young.

"Bella?" he called out, taking the first two steps and pausing.

"Lizzy? Abel?" Two more steps. Then stop.

He listened hard, the dull hum that came with stillness increasing in volume.

Sweat dripped into his eyes. He felt as if his flesh was on fire. Panic, fear, expectation, uncertainty, longing, desperation; they were just a few of the roiling emotions vying for control. He was either suddenly feverish from an illness that had been secretly brewing, withdrawal, or this was just a physical manifestation of the war going on within his brain. A chill rippled up his back. When he shivered, the dull agony in his ribs sparked and he had to stop to collect himself.

Somehow, he made it all the way down to the cellar without passing out or running up the stairs and out of the house again.

A soft, silent, familiar prayer began in the back of his tormented brain. Raul had to will that tiny voice to shut up. Prayers would not be answered here.

The flashlight's beam swept across the cluttered basement. There was an old steel can filled with long wooden sticks, the ones Ida used to tie her tomato plants to, just under the window that had been blacked out with spray paint. He couldn't find anything next to it that would have hit the can to cause the loud noise.

"I'm here," he said almost too softly to be heard. Even his hands were slick with perspiration. Going against his better judgment, he dragged the stool out from under the workbench, took one more look around, and flipped the flashlight off. He was instantly wrapped in absolute darkness.

The gut punch of terror that nearly knocked him off the stool was unlike anything he'd ever felt before. That included two times when he was sure he was going to die at the hands of a fellow thug, both with him staring down the barrel of a gun, and the night Lizzy had stopped breathing from a lung infection when she was seven months old as they were rushing her to the hospital.

As much as he wanted to get the hell out of there, he also didn't want anything to come between him and his family, not even the meager glow from a flashlight. If they wanted to scare him to death to bring him to the other side, so be it.

It could have been his imagination, but he felt a displacement in the air, as if someone had just entered the cellar. He couldn't see, hear, or even catch a scent, but they were there.

Or perhaps not.

A man on the brink as he was could conjure all sorts of things in this quasi-sensory deprivation chamber of horrors.

No! They're here! I know it.

"Just speak to me," he said, his voice shaky, sounding as if he were sitting on a vibrating chair.

The salt of his sweat invaded his mouth. He wiped his upper lip with his sleeve.

As he stared hard into the dark, specks of infinitesimally small lights flashed on and off like dust motes dancing in a warm column of sunlight. Raul tried hard to convince himself they were artifacts of his brain or floaters in his eyes. Man craved the light and would fill the black emptiness with whatever he could to stay sane.

He rubbed his eyes, but that only made it worse. His teeth chattered as he fought to keep his body from shaking.

"Raaauuul."

It was impossible to tell if his yelp was expressed vocally or just in his head.

She was here.

Her voice seemed to come from everywhere.

"Y-y-yes, B-Bella."

Was that a whisper of wind that kissed his ear? He cupped his ear and cringed.

"Kill."

His heart pounded hard enough to break whatever undamaged ribs he had left.

"No, please."

"Yourself. Join us."

The bitter irony was that he had come to Ida's to do just that, albeit it slowly and in a dull fog. Somewhere along the way, he'd realized he was too weak-willed to follow through with his plan. Now here was his wife, asking him to man up, and the best he could do was cower on the floor and beg her to change her mind.

Struck by a sledgehammer of disorientation, Raul slid off the stool and barked his elbow on the concrete floor. Whimpering and vacillating between hot and cold, he said, "Please, Bella. You can't mean that. Just take me now. I want to be with you and the children. But I can't do it that way. If you love me, kill me."

With his blood rushing in his ears like rattling subway cars at rush hour, he had to strain to hear her reply. And when he did, he wished he hadn't.

"Only...way."

He reached for the stool, his wet finger slipping off the cool, smooth seat.

"There has to be another way."

"Pay for your sin."

This time, Raul did scream, loud and long enough until he tasted copper.

The center of his chest felt as if someone had kicked it with the heel of their boot. When he shifted on the floor, he felt dampness through his pants and realized he'd wet himself.

Raul wept, his sobs like the barking of a seal through his damaged throat.

"Please, Bella. Please."

Then, in a clear voice that offered no chance for mercy, Bella said, *"Kill yourself, Raul. There is no heaven. There is no hell. Be with us. Be with us."*

He couldn't take it any longer.

Raul somehow made it to his feet and tripped his way up the stairs. At his back, Bella said, *"Join us. Join us now."*

His toes caught the top step and he spilled into the kitchen. Scrambling madly, he kicked the door closed.

Pacing the kitchen in circles, he pulled at his hair as he hyperventilated.

There is no heaven. There is no hell.

Bella had never lied to him.

Many times, he had wondered if her faith was even stronger than his own. She could quote the Bible far better than he ever could, and was much stricter with the children when it came to their religious studies and the way they conducted themselves both in public and in the home.

If his heart hadn't given out now, when would it? When he was an old man?

She knew.

It was why she wanted him to take his own life.

But wait.

Aware of the conflict suicide would cause him, she gave him all the reassurance he needed.

Without heaven or hell, what was there?

Did it matter? All that mattered was that he would be reunited with his family.

He stopped his pacing and glared at the cutting board.

The knife was still there.

JOIN US.

Raul touched the handle with the barest graze of his fingertips.

All he had to do was wrap his hand around it and make a vertical cut or two down his wrist. They said bleeding out was peaceful.

JOIN US.

The board came up as he tugged on the knife. He had to hold it down with his other hand to get it free, like extracting the sword in the stone.

"I will," he said between hitching breaths. "I will, Bella."

He jumped when Bruiser leaped onto the countertop. The knife slipped from his tenuous grasp and clattered on the linoleum. The coon cat peered into his watery eyes as if he were admonishing Raul for even thinking of doing such a thing. Bruiser went so far as to sit on the board, covering up Bella's scrawled words.

"Get the hell off there," Raul said. He wanted to swipe the cat away, but his balance was off and he ended up backpedaling until his ass bumped the kitchen table.

Bruiser remained where he was, now taking in Raul's desperate state with pity.

The knife was right at Raul's feet.

Why did he feel that the cat would pounce on it the second he tried to pick it up? He was anthropomorphizing the cat too much. Bruiser was just a cat who heard him thrashing around and couldn't resist his natural curiosity.

Keeping his wary stare on the cat, he quickly bent down and plucked the knife off the floor.

The blade jittered as he pointed the tip into what he hoped was a vein in his wrist.

Shouldn't I start higher?

He'd counseled several families that had been devastated by suicide. Now, he wished he'd asked them how their beloved had done it.

"Ahhh."

He pushed the blade in. The skin broke with a miniscule *pop*. A drop of blood welled around the triangular tip.

I can't do this!

"Yes. Yes you can and you will!"

He should drink some vodka, take his pills, and do it in the bathroom. But in that time, he might have second thoughts. Raul couldn't afford second thoughts.

JOIN US.

There is no heaven. There is no hell.

Unable to control his weeping, every pore in his body leaking foul-smelling sweat, he applied more pressure, sinking the blade deeper.

The phone buzzing in his pocket almost sent him crashing into the ceiling. Again, he dropped the knife. A lazy creek of blood wound down his wrist and into his palm.

He reached into his pocket and grabbed the phone, prepared to toss it against the wall. His shaking thumb accidentally swiped to answer. Felix's voice thundered from the other end of the line.

"Raul! Oh, holy shit, Raul. I have something very important to tell you. Raul? Come on, I know you're there. It's about your wife. Talk to me, *abuelo*. You need to hear this. Now."

It was about Bella?

What in the world would Felix have to tell him that he didn't already know?

"Dude, I can hear you breathing. Are you okay? Look, this is some serious stuff. Hell, you don't wanna talk? Don't talk. Just listen."

Raul stared at the phone, *MOM* glowing on the display. Felix was with Bella's parents. But why?

He tried to speak, but his throat had suddenly closed up.

Felix's voice dropped, as if he didn't want to be overheard. "I'm not sure if she told you this, man. When I found out, your father-in-law looked like he was going to kill me. Your mother-in-law, I think she's been waiting to tell someone for a long time. She gave me her phone to call you."

Licking his lips, Raul croaked, "What about...Bella?"

"I hope you're sitting, man. When she was twelve, she was...this is weird to say. They thought she was possessed. I guess the church did too, because after a shit ton of tests, they sent a priest to perform an exorcism. It took three weeks, dude. Three weeks of some very scary shit. Did she ever tell you about it?"

Raul let the phone slip from his fingers. He just managed to pull a chair out and fall onto it.

Bella had been possessed.

Had gone through a three-week exorcism.

No, his wife had never told him these things.

What else hadn't she told him, then?

And what was she not telling him now?

CHAPTER TWENTY-SEVEN

"Raul, are you okay?"

His friend's silence made Felix nervous. The guy was in a fragile state. This news could have caused him to pass out where he could hit his head and be really hurt.

Felix walked to the back of Valentina and Eduardo's yard and leaned on a tree growing in the corner. There was a beautiful gazebo just big enough for two a dozen yards to his right. Eduardo looked like the kind of man who would have built it himself. All Felix knew about gazebos was setting one on fire by accident during a very drunken night in Wildwood.

"*Abuelo*? You still there?"

"Yeah. Yeah."

A wave of relief washed over Felix. He flicked a quick glance at the patio door and saw Valentina watching him with her hands clasped close to her chest. When Felix had returned to their house and just spit out the news he'd gleaned from their nosy neighbor, Valentina had started to cry while Eduardo's face got so crimson, Felix thought the man was going to have a stroke. The pair had exchanged a look that was an all-out war and then Valentina had said, "Yes, it's true," followed by Eduardo storming past Felix and into his car.

Once Valentina had started talking, it was like a dam breaking down. At one point, he asked her if he could call Raul. It would be better if she told her son-in-law directly. What she had revealed gave Felix goose bumps (and he was sure nightmares would come later) and he'd started to feel that he was the wrong person she should be sharing this hidden part of her family's life with.

"I think it's better if your mother-in-law tells you everything," Felix said, nodding to Valentina. She slid the door open and took a tentative step onto the brick patio.

"I...Felix...I can't wrap my head around this."

Raul's voice sounded strange – hoarse and weak.

"Now, I don't know if this has anything to do with...you know...but I think it's important for you, you know?" He walked over to Valentina and put the phone on speaker.

"Maybe we should sit," Valentina said. Her eyes were red and puffy and her upper lip quivered. Felix pulled out a chair and sat next to her, setting the phone down on the glass table between them. She leaned closer to the phone and said, "Raul? Honey? I'm so, so sorry."

"It's true?" Raul said.

Valentina dabbed at her eyes with her sleeve and replied in a shaky voice, "Yes. Bella never wanted to talk about it when it was... when it was over. She made us promise to leave it where it was, in the past. I had hoped one day she would have told you, but some things are too painful to even think about, much less share. My poor baby went through so much pain. I never brought it up because I didn't want to see her relive those months."

"H-how did it happen?"

"We don't know. She was playing with her friend Gisela, just riding their bikes around the neighborhood. They went to the bike path in the woods by Carlin Park. Gisela told us that Bella challenged her to a race. Bella was tall for her age, such long, strong legs. Gisela couldn't keep up. She called out for Bella to slow down but eventually lost her. When she finally made it to the end of the trail, Bella wasn't there. The path stops at the woods where the ground is too uneven to ride a bike. The only way out was back the way they came. Gisela pedaled home as fast as she could and told her mother that Bella was missing. She called me and I called the police."

Valentina had to pause to collect herself. Felix put a reassuring hand on her arm.

Raul said, "What happened to her? How long was she gone? Dear God, was she abducted?"

A secret within a secret, Felix thought. *What the hell's next?* There was a moment when Valentina had started telling him about Bella's ordeal that he'd considered keeping it from Raul, at least for now.

He wasn't sure it was a good thing for Raul to be alone when he learned about his wife's past. But maybe knowing about this would help Raul deal with her restless spirit. Could this be why she was still here instead of moving on? As for the children, what mother would let her young children stray too far? Where Bella went, so did the kids.

Hearing Raul's strained voice made Felix wish he'd kept him in the dark, at least until he was with him.

Shaking her head, Valentina said, "The entire neighborhood turned out to search for her. Because she was a minor, the police didn't need to wait twenty-four hours to mobilize. It was the longest day of my life. I don't remember breathing. I just remember the fear. Eduardo was out with the search team. I stayed home in case she showed up. I was just about insane with worry when she walked in the back door just after ten o'clock at night. She...she looked like she was sleepwalking. Her eyes, they were so empty. She didn't respond to me when I called her name, not even when I held her. We didn't have a cell phone then, so I called the police to let them know she had come home. Ten minutes later, the house was full. Poor Bella, she was in shock. She never said a word that night. They wanted to take her to the hospital, but I said no, she had been through enough that day. I slept beside her. She just closed her eyes and didn't wake up until eleven the next morning. Eduardo and I took her to the hospital and though she seemed a little better, she barely spoke. When the doctors and police asked her where she'd been, she got a faraway look in her eyes. She never did remember. Or perhaps she did and pushed it away. The doctors concluded she had not been physically...harmed. But whatever happened to her in those woods damaged her mentally. And soon after, we learned, spiritually."

Her head drooped and her shoulders shook as she wept silent tears.

A flaming red cardinal landed on the fence post and started to sing. The bird's clueless chirping made Felix's cross wound throb. He wanted to throw something at it and send it on its way. Instead, he said to Valentina, "I think that's enough for now. Raul, you two should talk later. Give yourself time to digest this."

"No," Raul said, surprising Felix with his conviction. "I want to hear it now."

Valentina raised her head and sniffled, wiping away her tears. She patted Felix's hand. "It's okay."

On the other end of the line, Raul sighed. "I'm sorry, Mom. I know this hurts. I just wish you or Bella would have told me before."

"Please understand, I couldn't. She made me promise not to."

"But I was a priest. Surely if anyone could understand...."

"Your being a priest is the one thing that brought comfort to Bella, and to me and Eduardo. With you, she would be safe from the demon that took her over. Her future mattered so much more than her past. And with you, she finally had a future to look forward to."

This was the part that was going to give Felix nightmares. His *abuelita* once caught him and his friend watching *The Exorcist* when they were ten years old. After pulling the plug on the VCR and shooing Raphael out the door, she proceeded to tell Felix how the story was true, but even more horrible than what was depicted in the movie. Even watching such a thing could invite the evil into his soul. She told him about her friend who had been possessed when she was in high school and how it had permanently destroyed her family. The exorcism hadn't worked and the girl had slashed her wrists open in front of her mother and father while, according to them, levitating two feet from the floor.

Now, even at ten, Felix was already streetwise enough to think his grandmother was just trying to scare him from watching adult movies. But there had been a conviction in her eyes that put him on unsteady ground. He'd never tried to watch *The Exorcist* again.

"What made you think she was possessed?" Raul asked.

Valentina took a deep breath. "We didn't think that at first. Eduardo and I worried that she had some sort of post-traumatic stress disorder. We even took her to see a psychiatrist. She'd become quiet, sullen, and avoided her friends. No matter what we did, she wouldn't say more than ten words to us a day. I could see something was troubling her."

She sat back in the chair and looked to the heavens as if asking for strength. Valentina leaned over the phone and continued. "Then, one night, I heard someone talking. It was late and Eduardo was asleep. I went downstairs to make sure he hadn't forgotten to turn off the television. In the dark living room, I realized the voice was actually two voices and they were coming from Bella's room. I was so scared, I woke Eduardo up. I thought someone had broken into the house and if they were talking that loud, something must have happened to Bella. Eduardo grabbed the baseball bat he kept next to the bed and ran into her room. All of her lights were on and the voices continued as if we hadn't just practically torn the door down. Bella was sitting on the bed with her eyes rolled up, so we only saw the whites. She was the one who had been speaking, only it wasn't her voice. It sounded like two men, old men. They were mumbling in a language we'd never heard before. Later, when it happened again and we recorded it, we found out it was Akkadian."

Felix's brow furrowed. "Akkadian? What the heck is that?"

"It's an ancient language spoken in Mesopotamia well before Christ," Raul said. "You'd be hard-pressed to find anyone in the world that can understand it today other than a handful of scholars. Mom, were they sure about this?"

A fresh tear splattered on the glass top. "Yes. Eduardo took the recording to the university to confirm it. Bella's therapist did some research on his own and yes, it was Akkadian. After that first night, she stopped eating. Her hair started falling out in clumps. Her skin, I can't begin to describe it. It was almost gray. She broke out in sores and boils. We rushed her to the emergency room. She spent four days in the hospital undergoing every test imaginable. They couldn't find anything wrong with her. Her doctor suggested this was a psychosomatic response to whatever had happened to her when she went missing. We knew he was partially right. We called Father McCammon. He was our priest at St. Andrews at the time. He's since passed on. I always wonder if his ordeal with our Bella hadn't quickened his death. He came to us a strong, young man, and not soon after, he grew tired and weak and old. Father McCammon died in his sleep a year after Bella's exorcism."

"Did he perform the exorcism?" Raul asked.

"No. After visiting with her, he took her case to the bishop, who sent Father Abruzese to perform the exorcism. He was older and said he'd performed the rite two other times, with success. Father

McCammon stayed to help, both the exorcist and us. Many nights he held our hands and prayed while the exorcist was in Bella's room, trying to cast the demon out of our child." Valentina looked to Felix and he could see the agony of those weeks in her eyes. He saw great fear there, too. It was obvious she was afraid to talk about it even now. Not afraid of failing her daughter's wish to keep her past a secret. No, this was a palpable terror, the kind that knew dark things were lurking, waiting to be released through the mere act of speaking of their deeds, giving life to that which was dead and buried.

"I'm so sorry," Felix said. He didn't know what else to say. He was also worried about her.

Raul must have sensed it even all the way from the Adirondacks. "Mom, you don't have to say any more. It's all right."

She steeled herself and sat up straighter. "It wasn't like you see in movies. She just wasn't Bella. She was sick in body, mind, and soul. Most times, as the exorcist prayed over her, she just slept. When she was awake, she spoke in that other voice exclusively. We didn't think she would survive much longer. She'd stopped even drinking and when I changed her clothes, I could count every rib, every bone in her body. Three weeks to the day the exorcism started, I was in the living room on my knees, praying to Jesus, when I heard her call for me. For a moment, I thought I had imagined it. I hadn't heard her actual voice in so long. It took Father Abruzese coming to look for me to make me realize my daughter had come back. He had to practically carry me to her room. Oh, I can't express the joy I felt at that moment. Joy and fear, because I worried the demon had taken more from her than she could ever recover from. Thank God I was wrong."

She recovered, all right, Felix thought. From possessed pre-teen to a preacher's wife. But maybe the event had marked her, somehow. That black cloud was always there, and she would never have a happy ending.

Raul was crying now as well, and Felix stepped away while they spoke.

Could a demonic force control the living and exact revenge for casting it out of Bella? Felix was still on the fence about possession being a real thing. It made for a terrifying story, and if you think something is real long enough, it becomes real to you. If it was a product of all their imaginations, had Bella somehow invited this and her murder into her life by thinking it into being?

It sounded crazy, but so did everything else he'd heard today.

Or if it was real, was this a revenge killing through a paranormal force?

Where had she been in those woods, and with whom? Could that person, these many years later, have been lying in wait to finish what he or she had started?

Then there was the fourth option. It was simply an unfortunate period in Bella's life and had nothing to do with her murder. What had happened to her in the woods that day? Whatever it was, it fucked her up real bad.

Her spirit was definitely up there in that house with Raul. Why were the souls of Bella and the kids torturing Raul? And what lay beyond death?

This whole thing was overwhelming. It was making him question the very fabric of existence, when all he wanted to do was find a tangible person and make them pay.

Felix gave Valentina's shoulder a gentle squeeze as he passed by, leaving without saying goodbye.

Someone real, not a demon, had cut him up last night. He'd have to start there and try to forget about the supernatural stuff. He wasn't equipped to help Raul with that. Time to do what he did best. Find those who didn't want to be found and deal with them the only way he knew how.

CHAPTER TWENTY-EIGHT

Raul sat on the front porch, drinking straight from the vodka bottle. There hadn't been much left, but the little there was had been enough to cut some of the buzzing in his brain and nerves. Bruiser watched him from the window. Raul had brought Clover and Henry outside and set them on the little table beside the porch swing. Every now and then he'd pick them up and bring the tops of their fuzzy heads to his nose. Hints of his children were still there. He cried a bit and smiled at other times, remembering the sloth puppet show Lizzy and Abel used to put on, Clover teaching Henry how to sing, or Henry chasing Clover around the couch for stealing his food. Bella would sit on Raul's lap while they watched their children play with their sloths, and always give a round of applause when the improv play was done. They were some of the sweetest moments of Raul's life.

"Every time I try to sober up, something happens that changes my mind," he said to the cat.

Drink himself to death. Scare himself to death. Cut his wrists. There was a running theme here that he couldn't escape.

It was easy to want to die when he had nothing to live for. More so when he had something to die for.

Now, he didn't know up from down.

Bella had gone missing as a young girl and couldn't recall where she'd been. Something beyond terrible had to have happened for her to either end up believing she had been taken over by a demon, or worse, having been truly possessed. Was it PTSD or supernatural? Or both?

Even when he was a priest, Raul had been skeptical about possession. The science of psychology had illuminated much of the darkness surrounding the workings of the mad mind. Yesterday's cohabitating with the Devil was today's psychosis, many times corrected with the right cocktail of pharmaceuticals and talk therapy.

She spoke Akkadian.

That wasn't the kind of thing one could easily find and learn. She certainly hadn't picked it up in passing.

If he was going to believe she had been possessed, it all hinged on that one fact. It was too big to easily dismiss.

And now, as he sat in the setting sun, surrounded by picturesque beauty, his mind wandered to uncharted places.

Could the demon have hijacked her soul as well? Is that what's haunting me?

It was a stretch, for sure, but nothing was outside the realm of possibility anymore.

Bella, the Bella of now, an incorporeal voice, wanted him to kill himself. If Felix hadn't called, he'd be dead right now.

He had believed her. He was so desperate to see her and Lizzy and Abel again, he was willing to do the unthinkable.

Now he no longer knew who was speaking to him. Was it Bella, the woman he'd married, loved, and lost? Was it the same demon that had sunk its claws into her soul twenty-plus years ago? Or was it a Bella he never knew, a woman who appeared whole and holy and healthy, but had a sinister undercurrent whose fetid waters had been fed by her past? And what about Lizzy and Abel? Were they somehow attached to their mother? Or was it a form of demonic mimicking? The questions were dizzying.

Belief was something that had been getting harder to come by for Raul.

"What the fuck am I supposed to do now?" he asked Bruiser. The cat regarded him with the kind of absolute indifference that was in the DNA of their species. "It scares you too. I've seen you run and hide."

It was a nice enough night to just pass out on the porch swing. Let Bella, or what might have been passing for Bella, have the house for now.

Wonder what notes I'll wake up to.

This was not living. It was barely existing. Felix was on his goose chase, seeking justice for Raul's family that he'd never even met. Raul was here, vexed and comforted by whatever was in his house.

Suicide had seemed so logical before.

At least it was an answer. An end to the constant questions.

A blue jay fluttered past and alighted on an old empty bird feeder Ida used to refill several times a week. It cocked its head at Raul and flew away, free and unfettered by uncertainty and fear.

Felix's call had saved Raul from taking his life.

But was it just delaying the inevitable?

★ ★ ★

There were times in the night when Raul wanted to go inside and get his pills to help him sleep, but the thought of stepping over the threshold made his skin crawl. He'd have to pass the kitchen to get to his room. In the kitchen was the cutting board with *the message* and the knife that had been left for him to fulfill the message's request.

The number of nights he slept outside was beginning to creep up to the number he'd spent inside. It was bordering on insane, but so was Raul.

A porch swing was not made for sleeping. The occasional nap, maybe. He kept waking up every fifteen minutes or so to shift his position because the unforgiving wood didn't care a whit about his comfort. It had gotten chilly as the night went on, and a few times he woke up shivering. Bruiser stayed in that window as if he were keeping an eye on Raul. He hadn't even complained when dinner time came and went. The cat food was in the kitchen too.

So, neither of them ate and it appeared neither slept as well. He wished his keys weren't in the bedroom. The seat in the Subaru would feel like a downy bed in a five-star hotel compared to this. And it would be warmer.

And quieter. The normal white noise of the crickets was an overwhelming wall of sound when you slept outside.

This wasn't making his ribs feel any better either.

Misery was his only company.

Somehow, he managed to nod off curled up on his side, the slight breeze rocking the swing just enough to put him at ease.

It lasted long enough for the sound of furniture being tossed around to wake him up with such a start, he fell off the swing.

Clover and Henry were shaken off their perch on the nearby table. Raul's shoulder and hip slammed onto the porch, and for a moment he couldn't remember where he was and why his body felt as if it had been tossed ass over heels down a steep, rocky hill.

Whump! Crash!

Bruiser was scratching at the door to get out. As soon as Raul opened it, the coon cat dashed outside and zipped down the steps and into the night, never once pausing or looking back. It was the first time the cat had willfully gone outside since Raul had let him in.

Raul didn't blame him. It sounded as if the house was being ransacked.

His blood froze.

What if there was a thief in the house? Or vandals? Everything didn't have to be paranormal in origin. Ida's place had stood empty for a while. This could be some teens, pissed off that Raul had encroached on their hangout spot.

What sounded like the clatter of the utensil drawer being dumped on the floor had him closing the door softly so no one would realize he was there. Stepping away from the door, he leaned over so he could peer inside. It was pitch black inside, but he hoped if he looked long enough, his eyes would adjust so he could see something, anything.

A sliver of moonlight came through the kitchen window. He saw a wisp of a shadow pass quickly through the light and heard the thump of what could have been a chair whacking the wall.

The rager was happening in the kitchen only. In the place where Bella primarily spoke to him.

No, this wasn't the work of a thief or vandal.

Raul clamped his hands over his ears and shouted, "Stop it! Stop it! That's enough goddammit!"

To his utter surprise, it worked.

Silence settled back into the empty house.

Raul turned and sat on the step, crossed his arms over his knees, and rested his head on his arms. He spotted the sloths and pulled them to him.

He was emotionally and physically drained, so much so that he wanted to cry until he couldn't cry anymore. If Aunt Ida were here, she'd tell him, "Crying ain't for boys. A busy mind ain't got time to cry. Now go mow the lawn, and if you still feel sniffly, I have some other chores that'll keep you preoccupied."

Thanks to Ida, he hadn't cried until the night he lost his family.

After shedding so many tears for Bella, Lizzy, and Abel, crying no longer felt like something to be ashamed of. He didn't need or want to be preoccupied. It was fine to wallow. More than fine, it was natural.

He just wished he had someone to wallow with.

Even the cat had left him.

But not Bella. Or the thing pretending to be Bella and the kids.

No, that was right here with him. Most likely watching him at this very minute. Probably thinking, *What a sorry, broken-down excuse for a man.*

There was one way to stop it all.

JOIN US.

CHAPTER TWENTY-NINE

Even Felix couldn't believe he was back at the church, though this time the door had been open and he was inside. In a pew. Praying. The lights were very low and it was eerily quiet. Yet it still gave him a small modicum of comfort. He recalled coming to church during the off hours with his *abuela*, lighting candles for deceased family members, and for his mom and dad, wherever they were. Maybe a flickering candle would guide them home.

It never happened.

The whole exorcism story had creeped him out. Thugs and guns and cheats and fights were commonplace to him, something he could, if not always control, at least handle.

This shit, no way.

He couldn't blame Bella for choosing Raul. Those scars must have run deep. She probably lived in fear all her life, wondering if the demon was ever going to come back. Having a priest by her side must have brought her great comfort.

"Didn't think I'd find you in here."

The voice startled him. Felix unclasped his hands and whipped his head around. Bill Samson was there, holding a bucket.

"Where the hell did you come from?" Felix asked. He hadn't heard the guy walk in.

"Not from there, I'll tell you that much." He set the bucket down. "Sorry, I didn't mean to interrupt your prayers. Don't mind me."

Felix was going to go the bluster route and insist he wasn't praying, but decided against it. Samson would see through his lie without even squinting.

"I spoke to Bella's mother today," he said.

"Oh."

"Yeah. Oh. She had some real crazy shit to tell." He flicked an apologetic glance at the altar.

"Mrs. Diaz? She doesn't seem like the kind of lady with crazy you-know-what on her mind."

"It was about her daughter."

"What about her?"

Samson walked to the pew opposite Felix and took a seat. He'd slipped into cop mode. Felix suddenly felt like he was in a small room at the station, ready to confess his crime (which he never did – it was better to shut up and wait for your lawyer).

Felix looked up at the crucifix and swallowed hard. He shouldn't even be telling Samson this.

"Bella went missing when she was a child."

Samson's eyebrows knit together. "Missing? For how long?"

"The better part of a day. It was long enough to get the town up looking for her. She came back on her own and never spoke about where she'd been or what had happened to her."

"Not even her parents?"

Felix shook his head.

"I can't imagine it had been anything good. That poor, poor girl." The old man scratched at his chin.

"That's not the worst part. Not long after that, she started to change. It got bad. Real strange. They thought she was possessed. They even brought in an exorcist. Said it took weeks to free her from a demon that had taken over her body."

Samson took this information in stride. He looked at Felix, waiting for more.

"You look like you hear stories about people being possessed every day," Felix said.

"I've seen a lot. Enough to let me know I don't know half of what's possible in the world. The church believes in possession, and I believe in the church. I can't imagine what that must have been like for her and her family."

Felix shook his head. "It wasn't good. Bella made her parents swear never to talk about it. Seems to me it's been something that's festered under the surface in that family for twenty years."

Samson leaned out of the pew, staring at Felix. "What happened to your head? If you want to come back to Christ, you don't need to go that far."

Felix tapped the wound. "It was a gift from a masked stranger."

"I don't suppose you filed a police report?"

"What do you think?"

Settling back into the pew, Samson cast his eyes to the ceiling and said, "So, Bella as a young girl goes missing and ends up being possessed. She has an exorcism and keeps it quiet even when she meets a priest. I'm assuming Father Figueroa didn't know about this?"

"No. Valentina just told him. I don't think he took it too well."

"I don't suppose he would. She marries a man of faith, as close as you can get to God on this planet. Then, one night, she's murdered by assailants for no apparent reason. Father Figueroa loses his faith and leaves the church. And when you try to find the people who slaughtered his family, you end up with a giant cross carved in your forehead." He paused a moment, chewing at his bottom lip.

"Thanks for the recap," Felix said.

"You don't think that's too much of a coincidence?"

"I don't know what the fuck to call it. Oh, sorry." He made a quick sign of the cross.

"Where you going to be a couple of hours from now?"

Hidden within that question was a clear, *not in here.*

"I don't know."

"There's a coffee shop a couple of blocks down the road. Scratch that. You'd stick out like a sore thumb. The neighborhood is still skittish after what happened. Meet me at Sid's Saloon over on Maple."

"Why?" What Felix wanted to do was get out there and track down the son of a bitch who'd done the artwork on his forehead.

"You're a pretty dense guy. Miracle you've made it this far."

Felix's hands balled into fists. He didn't take kindly to insults, especially from cops who no longer had a badge to hide behind. Beating an old man in a church would be, when he thought about it, one of his lesser offenses. He could live with that.

Samson saw his fists and smiled. "Don't get yourself all twisted. I'm just having a little fun with you. I need to talk to some people and see if anything shakes out." He got up and his knees cracked loud enough to echo in the church. "Sid's in two hours."

★ ★ ★

Felix could see why Samson had chosen Sid's. It was a true dive bar, but at least the regulars here were just old drunks and not miscreants. They gave him a quick look when he walked in but then went back to their drinks and conversations. The tube TV to the right of the bar played some black-and-white detective show Felix had never heard of.

Sitting on a stool by a high-top table at the back of the bar, Felix downed a shot of tequila and mellowed it out with a sip from a cold beer.

"Damn." It was the coldest beer he'd ever had and even though the beer itself was commonplace and cheap, it tasted amazing.

A couple of paper plates tacked to the wall had a handwritten menu. Hot dogs were a dollar each, and twenty-five cents extra if you wanted cheese or chili. That explained the strange smell when he'd walked in. He bet there were grade D beef hot dogs sitting in a stew of dirty water in the back. He was hungry but not that hungry. Sid's also served pizza by the slice. The bartender, a pudgy guy with a black-and-gray broom mustache dropped a plate with a slice on the bar for one of the patrons, some geezer with no teeth. The pizza was a gooey rectangle, which must have made for easy eating for old toothless.

Half an hour and three beers later, Samson walked in. He nodded to the bartender, spied Felix in the back, and limped over to him. The stool scraped against the floor as he dragged it to the table. No sooner had he sat down than the bartender waddled over and set a cold beer down.

"Thanks, Clance."

"Just let me know when you need a refill."

Samson looked older, pale. The long sip of beer added a little color to his face.

"So, Mr. Church Guy is a regular at a shitty bar," Felix joked.

"Jesus loved wine. Nothing wrong with a drink." He finished his beer in two gulps. Clance the bartender saw Samson lift an arthritic finger and had another one ready in seconds. "I'll have two hot dogs with mustard when you get a chance."

Felix's nose crinkled. "Nasty."

"Iron gut. So, I talked to the lead detective on the case, guy named Zelinski. I used to work with his father. Zelinski tells me he's been losing sleep over this one. Been trying to call Raul but he doesn't answer or return his calls. I wanted to run through the records of people calling in to claim credit for the murders. Anytime there's a crime, you get enough crazies looking for attention to fill a stadium."

"I think I know how that shit works," Felix said.

Samson arched an eyebrow. "Oh, so you're a cop *and* a criminal now. Good to know."

Felix let it roll over him. His forehead itched and he wanted to get out of there before he had to witness the old man eating one of those foul-smelling hot dogs. "And?"

Samson took a drink. "I think you may be on to something."

Felix's heartbeat quickened. "What is it?"

"Back when it first happened, they got dozens of calls at the station. Some with tips that never panned out, others saying they did it, and others either trying to pin it on someone they had a beef with or claiming it was committed by monsters, ghosts, Muslim crusaders, you name it. About a week after the funerals and the trail was colder than an Eskimo's balls, some guy calls and says they were..." He pulled out a small notepad and flipped through the pages. Felix wondered if all retired cops carried around similar notebooks, unable to fully part with their past. "...Satan's Appetizer."

"What the fuck does that mean?"

"He said they were preparing the way for the Devil's feast. Said he wasn't there that night but he was part of a cult that called itself the Children of Behemoth."

"Sounds like a bad movie title."

"Sounds insane, which is why they didn't dig too deep. Anyway, the caller said to remember the Children of Behemoth when the skies rained blood and death walked the earth. Like I said, insane. No way to trace the call. He ended it by laughing his fool head off. Cop who took the call hung up on him. He did do a little follow-up, but was unable to find any Children of Behemoth."

"If you're a Satanic cult, you probably don't advertise."

"These days, I'm surprised they don't have a website and take selfies inside a pentagram," Samson grumbled, downing his beer. The hot dogs, quivering gray tubes wedged in soft rolls, came along with a fresh beer.

"So, that's it?" Felix said.

"It's more than the case has had from the jump." He took a bite and Felix almost hurled.

Felix slid off the stool. "Wait, are your cop buddies coming to talk to me?"

"Calm down. Zelinski said he'd look a little deeper, but I think more out of placating me because of my ties with his dad than thinking it's got legs. But that doesn't mean you and I can't run this down too."

"There is no you and I."

"I beg to differ." He ate the first hot dog as if he were in the Nathan's Eating Contest at Coney Island. "We just need to find these lost children and ask them a few simple questions. Like, did they know about Bella's past? Now that we know she was supposedly possessed at one time, I find it hard to dismiss the idea that there's a strong tie between that and this Satanic group."

"True. The question is, where do we start to go about finding an underground Satanic cult? It's a little out of my area of expertise. I'm sure yours too," Felix said.

Felix thought about it, trying not to watch Samson eat the second hot dog. "It don't matter who they worship. They're murderers. That's right in my wheelhouse. And I know for a fact they're watching me." He pointed at the cross on his forehead. "You got any juice left in that hot dog body for a sting?"

Samson dabbed the corners of his mouth with a napkin. "Just a couple more and let's hit the road."

CHAPTER THIRTY

Bruiser hadn't come back.

Raul couldn't blame him. Even a cat would realize it had walked into a world of unbearable strangeness. When furniture in empty rooms got tossed around, there was no safe place to take a nap.

He hoped Bruiser wasn't out there, starving. The coon cat had lived just fine on his own before. It wasn't as if a few weeks of domestication could eradicate its survival skills. In fact, the cat was more than likely doing better than Raul.

When day finally broke, Raul went inside the house and surveyed the carnage in the kitchen. Everything had been turned upside down.

Except the cutting board.

Of course not.

He went to his bedroom, grabbed a change of clothes, car keys, and pills, and slipped out back. As he was putting on his shirt, he realized he'd forgotten deodorant and his toothbrush. No matter. Today was going to be a bad hygiene day.

Leaving his old clothes in a pile by the back door, he went around the house, swatting away gnats, and got in the car. Time to drive. Just get the hell away.

Everything was in bloom, from the trees to the wildflowers, the grass green as the fields of Ireland. Morrisburgh was a pretty place, always had been. Farmers rode their tractors, cows lazed about in the sun, grazing, and hawks circled overhead like helicopters over a highway wreck.

Raul was big on family drives. Nice days like this, they'd pile into the car and just hit the road, the windows rolled down so they could get fresh air. They had a radio rule. Each person got to pick a song that Bella controlled with her MP3 player, and they would rotate. This way, everyone had their chance to hear their music and Raul and Bella got to expose the kids to musicians like Carlos

Santana, No Doubt, the Red Hot Chili Peppers, Alejandro Sanz, and so many more. They would drive for hours, stopping whenever they came across something interesting or a little out-of-the-way place to eat.

Those days were pure joy, bordering on magic. Raul and Bella knew a day would come when the kids wouldn't want to be cramped in a car being driven Lord knows where. Moments like that were fleeting and they needed to hold on to them as best they could.

He never thought Lizzy and Abel wouldn't make it to the age where they thought it would be boring or corny.

Driving around town, what little there was of it, he grasped for that magic. All he could touch were memories made painful by the absence of his family in the Subaru.

Morrisburgh faded in the rearview mirror and he found himself heading toward Lake George. He and Bella had been meaning to book a vacation there some day. Back when they thought they had time, it was easy to say, 'definitely next year'.

It was early in the season, but the roads were still full of cars and pedestrians, especially in the center of town. He pulled over and got out, walking in the sun by Fort William Henry. Back when he was a kid, his aunt had taken him to the museum to learn all about the history of the fort. As an adult, he remembered watching one of Bella's ghost shows, the old fort bathed in green night vision as they hunted for the spirits of soldiers past.

He grabbed a slice of pizza and ate while he walked.

So many happy families here. So many giggling children. It hurt to look at them. To see their smiles. This kind of easy happiness was once his world. He could slip into it at will, just by looking at his wife and children.

JOIN US.

Surrounded by so much...normalcy...he knew there was no way he could ever return to this.

He walked along the lake, watching the rented boats sail by. A wave of vertigo had him grasping for the back of a park bench. Unfortunately, his hand roughly brushed against a man wearing a bucket hat scowling at his phone.

"Watch it," the man said, barely looking up at him. Then he muttered, "Asshole."

Exhausted. I need sleep.

There was a small strip of sand just over the observation wall. It was tempting to just lie there and sleep until the sun went down. He was pretty sure the cops would have something to say about that.

Driving back to the house was out of the question. He'd nod off at the wheel for sure. His concern about crashing wasn't so much about himself as it was hurting someone else on the road.

He found the nearest motel (and there were plenty to choose from), checked in, locked the door to his room, and pulled the curtains closed.

Sitting on the edge of the bed, Raul stared at the unfamiliar image of himself in the mirror over the narrow work desk. What looked back at him was a haunted, broken man. Pale, hollow eyes, his skin pulled tight over his cheekbones, he was a grinning skull. A man who had died but forgotten to fall.

"Are you Other Raul?" he asked his reflection.

No.

He wouldn't wish this on Other Raul.

This was him in his purest, bare-naked form.

"They said I'd come to nothing and die young. I fucking ran as hard as I could from that life and I still lost. I lost it all and more than I ever thought I'd have."

JOIN US.

He pictured the day he, Bella, Abel, and Lizzy had gone to the beach and a pop-up storm had driven everyone running for shelter in droves. Instead of packing their things and rushing the kids to the car, Bella had sat back in her beach chair, smiled and said, "Hey, we came here to get wet anyway."

The kids had been shocked. Raul had to admit, even he was taken aback. Warm rain ran down Bella's face. The kids smiled and cheered, doubling their efforts to make sand castles with dampening sand. When the storm blew through just ten minutes later, the sun popping back out from behind a dark gray cloud that resembled a dragon breathing vaporous fire, they looked around and realized they were the only ones left. People trickled back in over the next couple of hours, but for a while there, they had the beach to themselves. All they needed in the world was each other. As long as they had that, even Mother Nature couldn't rob them of their joy.

Something broke inside him. He could almost hear it, a slow tearing of tendons, the crack of a dry branch, the lonely sound of a mind falling to pieces.

The Raul in the mirror smiled an awful smile, a grin that never reached his bedeviled eyes. He smiled without blinking until his eyes had run dry and his jaws hurt.

And then he simply closed his eyes, shut his mouth, lay back on the bed and spiraled into a deep, dreamless sleep.

* * *

He woke up physically refreshed for the first time in ages. When he recalled his smiling reflection from the night before, he shivered down to his troubled soul. Raul was pretty sure he hadn't even moved during the night, which accounted for a deep ache in his bones, but it didn't matter. His brain felt clear. It had been a few days since he'd stopped taking his pills and some of the fog had lifted. There was still a bit of a tremor in his hands as his body craved a drink. It would pass.

That moment last night, that strange sound he'd heard in his head, had been terrifying, but it had also brought clarity.

He could picture Ida beside him, munching on something she'd baked, saying, "Good to see you got your head out of your keister. If it stayed in there any longer, I was gonna make a call to search and rescue."

There was a text message from Detective Zelinski. Raul was tempted to delete it sight unseen. What news could he possibly have? Probably another check-in to see how he was faring.

"I'm losing my mind, thank you. And I feel much better than before."

His thumb accidentally opened the text.

Had Bill Samson at the station asking about cults. I know he worked at the church. Not sure if he's been in touch with you about it. Just wanted to give a heads-up and let you know we believe that's a dead end. So sorry.

A dead end. Pun intended?

"What the fuck is Bill doing asking about cults?"

None of it mattered. Raul tossed the phone on the bed and stripped out of his clothes.

He took a long hot shower. The soap, encased in its wrapper, was right where it was supposed to be. Changing back into yesterday's clothes chipped away at his fresh feeling. A stop at a small diner was necessary. Biscuits and sausage gravy with wheat toast, home fries, a fried egg, coffee, and orange juice was maybe a little overboard for breakfast. By the time he got to his car, his stomach was bloated and he felt like he needed a nap.

Walk it off.

Ida's house could wait.

Mingling amongst the early-bird tourists, he eyed the various shops in town, many of them selling beachwear and water toys, artsy candles and soaps and souvenirs. He stopped to look at the window of an old-time toy shop. In the display was a Lego set for a lighthouse. Abel loved Legos. Truth was, so did Raul. His grandmother couldn't afford them when he was a kid, so he had to find other kids who had them.

Abel had so many Legos, they'd had to buy two plastic bins to hold them all. Raul and his son would sit on the living room floor and build planes and buildings, superhero cars and battleships. For a change, he didn't feel like crying when he thought about his family. He even saw the beginnings of a smile in his reflection in the window.

His family was still here.

JOIN US.

Were there Legos in the place where they existed now?

He would find out.

The question was, would it be sooner rather than later?

It was getting on noon and the sidewalks were starting to jam up. Little kids cried because they were hungry or tired of shopping.

Time to go back.

Raul took one last look at the main strip before getting in his car.

They would have loved it here.

He took his time driving back to Morrisburgh. For the first time in months, he felt like he had his sea legs. It had been a while since he could think clearly. If this is what came from being driven to the brink of desperation, he was sorry it hadn't happened sooner.

If Bella or the children had visited him in his hotel, they would have had to drop a chair on his head to wake him. He wondered if they had tried to contact him as he slept. Lizzy used to love sneaking into their bedroom and holding her hand over his face as close as possible without touching him, waiting for him to sense her presence and wake up. He'd sweep her into his arms and she'd giggle as he kissed her all over.

What he'd been experiencing at the house had not been demonic. If Bella had been possessed as a child, she certainly hadn't been as an adult. Not once had he ever had an inkling that she was not all that she had appeared to be. Bella was beautiful, shy, devout, silly, adoring, devoted, loving, intelligent, inquisitive. She wasn't perfect. No one was. But he was sure it would take him a long time to find someone that encompassed all of her wonderful qualities.

Evil had not resided in his wife. Nor his children. Quite the opposite. Her brush with evil in its purest form had baptized her by fire and brimstone, driving her farther into goodness and light where she could never be harmed again. It had driven her into Raul's arms and he finally understood how he could have found such an amazing woman to take a flawed man like himself for her husband.

It no longer mattered if she was furious with him on the other side. Just as when they were alive and she was mad at him, he would come to her, embrace her, and they would work it out.

Knowing he would never have a day with his family like he'd had at the lake yesterday, there was no point in delaying the inevitable.

He and Bella would work it out and he would hold Lizzy and Abel once again.

Raul went well past the speed limit, anxious to get to Ida's. Anxious to finally go home.

CHAPTER THIRTY-ONE

Last night, Felix had left Sid's Saloon two hours before Samson so if there was someone watching him, they wouldn't put two and two together. Samson had assured him that everyone in the bar itself had been former cops, so there was no need to suspect them.

The old man also said he was an expert at tailing people without being spotted. He had an advantage now that he hadn't when he was a cop. No one suspected old guys of doing much of anything, much less keeping an eye out for a Satanist.

Felix had to trust him, which wasn't an easy thing to do. Cops and Felix were like oil and water. But there was something in Samson's clear eyes that said he would live up to his word.

It was obvious Felix had struck a nerve the night before his head carving. So, the best thing to do was to revisit every place he'd gone to. This time around, he was looking for the fuck who had sliced him up and he promised anyone within earshot that he wasn't leaving town until he found them and chiseled his initials on their dick before shoving it up their ass.

It was some real old Western movie stuff, for sure, but he meant it.

At Gus's Place, the same ass-sniffers were stinking up the place, including the bikers at the pool table. Walt the bartender took one look at Felix, grinned, and said, "You get some of that plastic surgery, Julio? I gotta say, it's an improvement."

That gave everyone a laugh.

"You like it?" Felix said.

Long, gray hairs peeked out from under Walt's armpits, his stained wifebeater holding in his saggy man boobs. "Better you than me, *amigo*. Unfortunately for you, we don't serve churchgoers in here, so you should maybe do an about-face and walk the fuck outta my bar."

222 • HUNTER SHEA

Felix wedged himself between two old drunks and leaned on the bar, getting so close to Walt he could smell the stale beer on his breath. He shot a quick glance at the bikers to make sure they weren't going to jump him. Yet.

"You know someone who likes to draw crosses on people?"

Walt's rheumy eyes locked onto Felix's forehead. "Not draw 'em. Maybe light one or two on a wetback's lawn."

Holding back his urgent desire to knock out whatever teeth Walt had left in his gummy maw, Felix looked over at the bikers. "How about you two?"

They turned away from him and resumed their game.

"You come across any...artists...you tell them they can find me at the Dew Drop Inn. Unless they're too chickenshit." To seal it, he added, "Like most white people."

That would turn up the heat. Even if Walt or the bikers weren't behind his attack, lowlifes like them would spread the word just to make sure a guy like Felix got what he deserved.

He did pretty much the same thing everywhere he went, stirring up hornets' nests and hoping the right ones would come for him later. The question now was, how bad would they sting? Felix touched the wound on his forehead and grimaced.

It was exhausting work, even more so because he desperately wanted a drink. He needed to be sober for this, though. Self-restraint was a bitch.

The early morning sun announced it was time to head back to his motel. The Dew Drop Inn was on the outskirts of the city and the very definition of a shithole. There was blood on the sheets, lightened to a dull brown after several washings, enough pubic hair in the tub drain to make a very curly wig, and a floating turd in the toilet. Classy. What did he expect for fifty bucks a day?

Shit, prison was way better than this.

A lot of guys, the long-termers, they got out and could only afford hovels like this. It was no wonder they got themselves thrown back in so quick.

Felix parked his Harley right outside his door, keeping his eye on the window so he could catch the reflection of anyone coming up at his back. He was alone. Dammit. That meant he'd have to go inside.

He was really hoping there'd be people waiting for him outside so he could avoid the blood/turd opulence of the Dew Drop Inn.

The room was hot and stuffy and smelled like skunk weed and mildew. He plopped himself onto the secondhand chair by the window and turned the relic of a TV on. He clicked the remote, and put it down on the round table by the chair once he hit on a station showing three blond MILFs doing yoga by a sea cliff.

He'd had three prostitutes in his first week of freedom. Since then, he was as celibate as a eunuch. When this was done, he was going to Atlantic City and treating himself. The money he'd stashed away before his arrest would keep him in hos and slots for the summer if things fell his way.

It would be nice to think Raul would be by his side like in the old days.

Nah. He wished for better for his friend. If all of this didn't break Raul for good, hopefully he could get his life back, maybe even return to the church. Felix needed someone holy in his corner.

Felix's eyelids grew exceedingly heavy as he watched the spandex-clad women get into ungodly positions. He was so tired, even little Felix wasn't rising to the scene on the television.

Wonder where Samson's hiding out? he thought.

They'd agreed it was best for Samson to find a place near the motel and wait, rather than trail behind Felix all night. That didn't mean Samson hadn't followed him. And if he had, he was as good as he'd said. Felix never once spotted the man.

It looked like today was a bust. The sun was high in the sky and the sound of morning traffic whizzed by outside.

Might as well take a nap. Get an early lunch or late breakfast later.

Sleeping in the chair was just fine with him. He'd passed out in far more uncomfortable places.

As he closed his eyes, he felt the weight of time working against him. Leaving Raul up in the boondocks with his ghosts for too long wasn't good. If and when Felix got to the bottom of things, what kind of man would he be giving the news to?

"I'm trying, bro," he muttered, his chin dropping to his chest.

The door smashed in, hitting the wall hard enough for the knob to punch through and stick.

Felix snapped awake with such a start. He fell backward off the chair, leaving him in a very vulnerable position. Two men wearing black ski masks came rushing in. The one in the lead spotted Felix on the floor scrabbling to get up. They pounced on him, pushing his face into the stained carpet.

Felix had a fleeting thought – *If I survive these two goons, the infection I'm getting from this goddamn rug is gonna kill me!*

"You want another reminder why you need to keep your fucking mouth shut?" one of them said, spittle flying from his red, moist lips. He punched Felix in his forehead. Felix felt the bit of scab that had formed break, fresh blood seeping from the wound.

The other one delivered a series of rabbit punches to Felix's side, knocking the wind from him.

I'll be pissing blood for a while.

He heard the distinctive *snick* of a switchblade right by his ear, then felt the cold kiss of metal on the edge of his ear.

"Unfortunately for you, we don't give second chances."

Felix brought his elbow up and connected with the guy's hand. The blade went flying over the bed.

"You little shit!" the guy who wanted to Van Gogh him exclaimed. The idiot forfeited his superior position over Felix to fetch the switchblade.

That was all Felix needed. He kicked the other guy off him, turned around and got to his feet, fists up and panting, not from exhaustion, but excitement. He loved to brawl, especially when there weren't prison guards to break it up.

"Come on, *pendejo*," Felix said to the one who had been punishing his kidneys. "You got your free shots. My turn."

Felix rushed him, ramming him into the open door. The wood cracked and a jagged split raced down the center. There was no such thing as fair play when you were outnumbered. Felix grabbed the man by the balls and squeezed hard enough to make sure there would be no future generations of Satanists. As the guy screamed for mercy, Felix broke his nose with a sharp chop of his hand. The Satanist fell to the floor, wheezing and gasping while clutching his crotch.

It only took seconds to disable him, but it was enough for Mr. Switchblade to reunite with his weapon.

"You're gonna pay for that," the guy said after taking a glance at his blubbering friend.

"I don't think so, *maricon*," Felix growled. He reached into his leather jacket and extracted a knife that would have made Rambo envious. One side was serrated and looked like it could saw through a whale. The other was smooth and sharp enough to filet a rhino. "You steal that fucking knife from a little girl?" he said, looking at the man's puny blade.

The sight of the knife had the man's head on a swivel, looking for a way out.

The room was bathed in shades of red. Felix wanted to hurt these two in ways that would make a serial killer blush. He was about to jump over the bed and tackle the chickenshit Satanist when a voice boomed behind them.

"Drop it, asshole!"

At first, Felix thought someone had called the cops and they'd set a land speed record to the motel.

Then he saw in the mirror on the far wall that it was Samson, his gun trained on the Satanist.

"Where the fuck were you, man?" Felix said without taking his eyes off his attacker.

"Running is no longer my specialty," Samson said. Then to the Satanist, "You don't drop that knife, I'm going to shoot you in the throat. The last thing you'll feel before you die is pain that'll make hell seem like a day at the circus."

The man dropped the blade. Felix rushed over and punched him in the face. The mask gave too much cushion, so Felix ripped it off and hit him again. This time, the smack of flesh on flesh was much more satisfying. In fact, it was so good, Felix just had to repeat the process a few times before he felt a tug on his arm.

"We need him to talk, yet you keep hitting him in his mouth," Samson said. He was breathing heavy and sweat trickled down the sides of his balding head.

Felix stepped away and inspected his knuckles. A piece of a tooth was embedded under the skin of his middle knuckle. He plucked it out and tossed it at the Satanist.

"We better get them out of here before the cops come," he said to Samson. "I'm sure the manager at least heard that door getting smashed in. Your car close?"

"Close enough. Promise me you won't hit this turd. At least in the face."

Felix grinned at the bloody man. He looked ready to piss himself. Judging by the smell, he already had. "I'll try."

"Oh shit."

Felix turned. "What?"

"The fella who looked like he couldn't move is gone."

"Oh shit is right. Get the car."

He bent closer to the wounded man. "Guess your butt buddy is running home to tell Mommy what happened. Which means, I don't have a lot of time to play around with your stupid ass." Felix pointed the knife at the man's eyes. "You tell me what I need to know, I let you keep your eyes. You don't...."

It was best to let the unsaid part linger.

By the time Samson pulled up outside, the Satanist was crying.

Felix gave him credit for one thing. At least he wasn't asking for God to help him. Nothing worse than a hypocrite Satanist.

CHAPTER THIRTY-TWO

Raul pulled up to Ida's house and didn't stop to take a breath or linger on his fear. This was his life, for now, and he was not going to run from his family again. His head had been twisted every which way the past few weeks. Doubt, ever-present, life-wrecking doubt, had clouded his thoughts (along with pharmaceuticals and alcohol), and added to his fear.

A life of faith, he now saw, was far simpler. This inability to cling to any belief long enough to get a foothold was hell on earth.

He should have never doubted Bella.

What she was doing in the house was her only way to get his attention.

What she asked of him, he was sure she asked in desperation. She and the children had been ripped away from this world, from his life. People liked to think that time was immaterial to the soul. Perhaps they were wrong. Waiting for Raul to pass on might seem to them to be far too long, an interminable interval.

He stepped into the house.

JOIN US.

Nothing else had been disturbed since the day before. The kitchen was still a mess, but the rest of the downstairs remained untouched. Bruiser was still AWOL. That was for the best. He needed to reacclimate himself to living on his own.

Raul walked to the kitchen, slowly lowered himself to the ground and whispered to the vent in the floor, "I'm so sorry I left you. Please forgive me."

It was just another in a litany of apologies and he was sure Bella was tired of hearing them.

"I won't run from you again. I want you here, with me, you and Lizzy and Abel. Please."

All was silent in the cellar as well as the gap between life and death that existed in the house.

The tears came as they always did, without warning and flowing freely. Salty drops of his sorrow fell in between the metal grates.

Thump, thump, thump, thump.

The laughter of his son and daughter overhead as they played.

From below, a whispered, *"Raul."*

He laughed as he wept.

"Yes, honey. I'm here." He looked toward the ceiling. "Lizzy. Abel. I hear you. Daddy's home. Please keep playing."

God how he loved that sound. How had he ever been afraid of it?

Raul lay on his back, letting the sounds of his family wash over him, seep into him. He was not going to run tonight. Not from them. Never again.

What he needed to do was run *to* them.

"I miss you."

Every hair rose on Raul's body, only this time, it was in a good way. Bella knew he was no longer afraid. She knew he wanted to be with her and the kids now. There would be no temper tantrums in the house tonight.

"I miss you too. You can't ever know how much I've missed you."

Upstairs, Lizzy cried out, *"Got you!"*

Abel giggled and said, *"No you didn't."*

Frantic footsteps pounded overhead as his children played knock-knock-hit-bump. What he wanted to do was rush up the stairs and join them as he had when they were alive. Oh, how he used to chase them around the house, the high-pitched squeals of his running children filling his heart. When he caught them, he'd scoop them up and tickle them, smothering them with kisses as they squirmed, telling him to stop and when he did, begging him to do it again.

If he ran up there now, would they disappear? Could he hold a ghost?

No, it was better to lie here and bask in their presence.

Raul had made a ritual of playing with the children when Bella prepared dinner. It gave her the space she needed to do one of the things she loved most, enjoy her glass of wine and cook their meals that Raul would bless when they were laid out on the table. Closing his eyes, he could almost smell Bella's chicken and rice, see her smile as he ran past the kitchen in hot pursuit of a cackling Lizzy.

"Be with me," Bella implored.

Raul tried to respond but a lump in his throat took his words away.

"Raul, be with me. Be with us.*"*

Getting his voice back, he said, "I will. I *need* to be with you."

Something that sounded like a sigh whispered through the vent.

He had made her happy. That was all that mattered now.

He just needed one more day to get things in order.

One more day.

Then he would once again be with his family.

CHAPTER THIRTY-THREE

"This seems wrong, even for me." Felix stared at the man tied to the chair in the dingy basement.

"No one will hear him down here," Samson said, tightening the knot around the man's wrists. The Satanist's head lolled. He'd struggled when they were tying him up and Felix hit him with a haymaker. "Besides, I like irony."

Felix had to admit, the basement of Christ Church did seem like the perfect spot to interrogate a person without fearing prying eyes or ears were going to ruin everything. Plus, it was kind of dingy and cluttered with all kinds of religious stuff. If this prick was one of the Children of Behemoth, the setting alone was going to put him on unsteady ground.

"I maybe shouldn't have hit him so hard," Felix said. The guy was actually snoring now.

"I think that goes without saying." Samson reached into his pocket and pulled out a small white capsule. He broke it open under the guy's nose. His eyelids fluttered and he shook his head, groaning at the sudden realization he was in pain and tied up. Samson looked at Felix. "Ammonia capsule."

"You're like a Boy Scout."

"One of us has to be prepared."

The man in the chair looked to be in his mid-forties. He had a lean build but had the start of love handles. His brown hair had flecks of gray, but far more streaks of red from his and Felix's blood. To Felix, he looked like the kind of guy who managed a Best Buy or thought accounting was fun.

"If you let me go, I'll make sure you live," he said, the words sounding strange as they passed through his busted lips and cracked teeth.

"That's mighty white of you," Felix said. "How about this. You answer my questions and I won't feed you your intestines. That sound good? I ain't got time to play around with you. How much this hurts all depends on you. I'm sure your little butt buddy is already running his mouth."

The man spat at him, the crimson wad of blood and mucous landing inches from Felix's boots. Felix eyed the mess. Then he glanced at Samson. "You might want to leave now."

The retired cop looked like he was struggling with whether he should go or stay and witness the interrogation. He was a good man, and Felix was about to do some very un-good man stuff.

Samson turned to the stairs, then back at the man, and finally to Felix. "I'll be upstairs to help take out the body." He gave Felix a wink that the man couldn't see.

Samson tromped up the stairs, each footfall making the Satanist's eyes grow wider and wider.

Felix pulled up a chair and sat across from him. "Ah, now it's just me and you. So, what should we talk about?" He tapped his temple, then his cheek, moving to the bridge of his nose and finally the puffy cross on his forehead. "Oh yeah. Which one of you dickheads did this to me?"

The man shook his head. "It wasn't me. I swear."

Felix chuckled. "Every guy I've ever been in the joint with has said the same thing. And most of them look and sound like they mean it. Well, even if it wasn't you, I'm pretty sure you knew it was going to happen."

In a flash, Felix was on his feet and grasping the man by his jaw. He pulled out his giant knife and pushed the tip deep into the guy's forehead. The man tried to scream. Felix squeezed his jaw tight while he worked. It only took a few seconds to make a matching cross, only this one was a little deeper. Blood seeped into the Satanist's eyes while he blubbered.

"That shit hurts, right?" Felix stormed over to a table and grabbed the salt he'd brought with him. He poured a liberal amount in the open wound, the man's eyes when they flashed open, and even in his mouth. He flopped in the chair, straining against his bindings, until the chair was at the tipping point. Felix steadied it by burying the heel of his boot in the man's crotch.

Feeling their time running out, Felix had decided he had to go for broke. Pain was a great motivator to talk.

"Who the fuck are the Children of Behemoth and why did you jump me?"

At the mention of the cult's name, the man clammed up and went still.

Leaning close, Felix grinned. "That's right, asshole, I know who you're with."

"You won't get away with this."

Felix looked around the gloomy room. "It kinda looks like I am."

"Hail—"

Felix punched him in the center of his chest.

"Satan, yeah, I know. I've seen the movies. Look, if you want to go to hell, I can send you there right now." He dragged the blade across the man's throat. A line of tiny blood droplets marched across his flesh. The man whimpered. "Or, I could cut off your balls and watch you bleed to death. You'll scream like a little girl."

The man resumed his struggling.

"I'll ask again, and then I start cutting. Why did you jump me?"

His eyes darted all around the room.

"Ain't no one coming to save your sorry ass. Only people here are me, the old man, and Jesus. And I don't think he wants anything to do with you. And vice versa."

The man opened his mouth, then thought better and closed it.

Sighing, Felix said, "Okay." With two quick slashes, he sliced off the Satanist's ears. When the man screamed, Felix shoved them in his mouth, pushing them deep into the Satanist's open maw until he puked all over himself.

Felix stepped back to avoid the mess. "Now that's disgusting. I thought Devil worshippers are supposed to be all evil and tough and shit." He spit in the soupy puddle at the man's crotch, right into the ridges of one of his severed ears.

"Why did you jump me?" he shouted.

The man flinched, his face pale as cream. He struggled to speak.

"You're not deaf...yet. Why...the...fuck...did...you...jump...me?"

"B...because you're getting in the way," he sputtered. "The door is opening. We can't...we won't let you stop it."

Scratching his beard with his bloody knife, Felix said, "Door? What door? What the hell does a door have to do with me?"

The man closed his eyes and turned away.

Felix couldn't lose him now. He ripped the man's shirt open. His eyes opened wide. This time around, Felix cut off his nipples, opting to flick them into the dark recesses of the basement instead of in his mouth. Feeling that wasn't going to be enough to get the message through, he pried the man's mouth open and went to work making deep gouges in his gums between his top front teeth. It didn't take long for the blood to nearly choke the fucker to death. Felix let him go and pushed his head down to his chest so the blood could dribble out.

"I'm going to jam my knife under every one of your nails next, and then I have a real big surprise waiting for you," Felix growled. His heart was racing and he had to fight the urge to finish the piece of garbage.

Felix jammed his thumb into the raw, bleeding hole where one of his nipples had been.

"No! No! Nononononononono! Please!"

"Then talk, dammit!"

"I will! I will! Please, just don't hurt me."

This time, between the blubbering and choking, he answered every question Felix asked.

Felix's stomach turned sour midway through. His head throbbed. He'd heard things he couldn't un-hear. Ever. Terrible things. Much worse than he could have ever imagined.

When it was done, Felix went upstairs toting leaden legs. Samson was sitting in a pew, his head back and staring at the ceiling.

"You get what we need?" Samson asked, his voice echoing throughout the dark and deserted church.

Felix had to lean against a pew to keep from falling.

"Hey, what happened?" Samson asked, rising.

"We...we need a plastic baggie, and then...then we gotta dump him." He glimpsed the big hanging crucifix. "After that, I have to haul ass back to Raul."

"What did he say?"

Felix felt something inside him break. His eyes blurred with tears. "I don't wanna say. Not yet."

Samson rubbed his jaw, took a moment, and nodded. "All right. You tell me on the way to Raul's." He looked over Felix's shoulder to the door that led to the back of the church. "Can you tell me why we need a baggie?"

Felix walked down the aisle as if he were in a trance. "For his ears. In case he ever wants to wear glasses."

CHAPTER THIRTY-FOUR

Raul sat out back and watched his kids playing tag in the field of tall grass. His vision was hazy from tears and sun and he might have been hallucinating the entire thing. No matter. He wasn't going to move from that spot until the vision dissipated.

Lizzy and Abel ran round and round silently, trying to catch one another.

Their stuffed sloths were on the table. Raul had turned their heads so they could look into the field as well. He hoped his children would see them and come closer.

To his back, inside the house, he listened to the hurried thumping of their feet. He was surrounded by his children and for the first time in months, he was happy.

Bella had allowed this to happen.

His beautiful Bella, who was waiting for him with open arms.

She hadn't spoken a word for the past several hours, though letting Raul enjoy their children said volumes.

He might have cracked up, but so what? He was happy. If insanity was the price to pay to smile once again, he would let his mind break into a million pieces without a second thought.

Two shadows flitted against the harsh backdrop of the afternoon sun. He so wanted to run and join them. The fear that his doing so would frighten them away or shatter this wonderful dream kept him glued to his chair.

When he'd first started coming here, his Aunt Ida used to force him to turn off the TV and go outside. Yes, the countryside was beautiful, but who cared about aesthetics when you had no one to hang out with? Raul used to dread sitting around outside, bored to tears. It took him the better part of a month to learn how to explore and find his own adventures. By the end of that first summer, it took a scolding from his aunt to get him back inside the house.

"Why didn't I bring you kids here?" He wiped another wave of tears from his eyes, and for a moment he lost the images of his children. When new tears brimmed, they were back again. "You would have loved Ida. And she would have loved you. At least you had each other. You would have had so much fun. I got too wrapped up in myself, in my work, in making sure I did everything right for you both, that I forgot about Ida. About this."

His arm swept across his field of vision, stopping at the massive weeping willow at the edge of the grassy meadow. He used to take early afternoon breaks under the shade of that tree, reading paperbacks Aunt Ida let him pick out at the free book swap outside the general store. Back then, two folding tables were set outside Sully's, and on them were produce boxes filled with used books Sully had gotten from the Glens Falls library whenever they had too many books on hand and needed to disperse them rather than throw them out.

Raul discovered a love for science fiction, devouring tales by Asimov, Clarke, Bradbury, and Card. He used to wonder if you had to be a white dude to write sci-fi. He'd long harbored a dream of being the first bestselling Puerto Rican science fiction author.

It would be nice if there was time to pursue that dream.

As the sunlight began to wane, Raul realized his children were no longer there. All had grown silent in the house as well.

He patted the picnic table, picked up Clover and Henry, stretched, and went back inside.

It took some searching in his bedroom to find his little pad that doubled as an address book and a place to store computer passwords and email addresses.

He knew for a fact that Valentina only checked her email once a week, on Sundays. That was her day to look through her inbox and respond to the few emails that weren't spam. She often talked about making tea in the afternoon and firing up her tablet, seeing if there was anything worthy of her attention.

That meant it would be four days before she got to what he was about to write. Four days was a little longer than he would have liked, but it would have to do.

Raul plugged his phone in so he wouldn't lose power while he composed the email.

Dear Mom and Dad,

I want you both to know that I love you as if you were my mother and father. You embraced me into your family from the first moment we met and made me feel welcome and loved. Please know that what I've done is in no way due to a lack of your love and support. I have discovered that life beyond death is real, and there is no longer a need for faith when faced with absolute certainty. Bella, Lizzy, and Abel have been with me ever since I moved to my aunt's house. There are things I've seen and heard that are world-changing. At least for my world.

Please know that I'm not crazy. I could have easily come to that conclusion if my friend Felix hadn't experienced it for himself. That was a pivotal moment for me, and I thank you for sending him to check on me. He's been gone for days now to search for the people who took them away from us. I think he feels it will bring me closure, maybe some kind of comfort. He may be right.

But it doesn't matter anymore. The only thing that will bring me comfort is Bella and the children. And they're right here, waiting for me. I'm not ending my life. I'm just continuing the one I built with my family. They've asked me to join them and for once, I'm filled with joy. I have no fear, because I know they will be waiting for me. Just as we'll be waiting for you, when your time comes. Please know that we will be with you both until that day. And know that we are happy and bathed with love.

There's no need to mourn for me. Be happy for me. For my family. For our family.

Love,

Your son, Raul

* * *

It took Raul an hour to edit and rewrite the letter. No matter what he did, he knew they would think he'd had a breakdown and taken his life. It was impossible to convey in a book, much less an email, what he'd experienced and how it had changed him, opened his eyes. He'd walked through the valley of darkness and he did not fear death because now he knew there was no such thing. He didn't need to cower behind his old faith to give him solace.

Because he knew.

After he pressed send, he went about tidying up the house. When the police came to find him, he didn't want them to misconstrue what they saw and think there had been some kind of break-in or struggle. The house had to be in order.

He put everything in the kitchen back where it belonged and took a shower, cleaning himself until the hot water ran out. Naked and dripping, he packed his belongings in his bedroom and set his bags on the floor against the box spring. The ruined mattress was out back where it would remain.

Four days would be a long time before his body was found. He knew that rationally, there wasn't a shower invented that could stay the steady march of putrefaction. He hoped his odor wouldn't seep into the fibers of the house and make it an unlivable place for the next owner. This was a house meant to be treasured and loved in and lived in.

Raul locked the doors so Bruiser wouldn't get inside. It was best he stay outside now, for many reasons.

The sky was filled with streaks of light and darkening purple.

He sat on his made bed, staring into the kitchen.

"I love you."

Picking up the glass of water he'd set on his night table, Raul swallowed his pills two by two until there were none left.

★ ★ ★

In the darkness, there came a rumbling sound. Not quite a sound. More like a deep tremor in the air. As if something were rushing toward him.

Raul tried to open his eyes. Perhaps he had, but the coal-black depths prevailed.

Where was he?

He felt as if he were floating in a big emptiness. His body didn't exist. He was simply an untethered consciousness.

Was this death?

Or a waiting place between his old life and the next?

Fear didn't exist here. But confusion did.

Did I do something wrong?

Bella!

Lizzy! Abel!

They could be right next to him for all he knew.

He couldn't see them because he had no eyes.

He couldn't hear them because he had no ears.

He couldn't feel them because he had no body.

He wanted to shout their names like a beacon, but it was very hard to do without a mouth.

Wait, he could hear.

What was that pounding? Was it his heart, beating its last?

Bella, please come for me!

Raul didn't like this place, this endless nothing, thrumming with the *whump* of a dying heart.

Had Bella and the kids gone through this as well? They must have. The thought broke his heart, or what constituted a heart in this new reality/unreality.

They must have been so frightened. Had their pain and fear from the moments before their deaths followed them here, increasing tenfold? My babies. My poor, terrified babies. Oh, Bella, I wish for a world where you would never have to experience this.

Bump-bump-bump-bump-bump!

If that was his heart, still trapped in his mortal body, it sounded as if it were about to break through his ribcage. A heart desperately clinging to life, to its function, its purpose.

You can stop now. I need you to stop so I can move on.

Raul was convinced that as long as his heart functioned, he would be trapped in this between space, denied the thing he so desperately desired. And what if four days had passed and his mother-in-law had read the email and alerted the local police? What if they found him unconscious and whisked him to a hospital where he would be trapped in a coma, unable to live in any world?

Please don't let that happen to me. Haven't I been through enough?

He felt no remorse for his self-pity. Nor was he beseeching the aid of a fickle god. He was pleading with his own heart, that organ of muscle and blood. The very thing that seemed to swell whenever he looked at his family. Now, it was depriving him of seeing them again.

Betrayed by his own heart. The very idea infuriated him.

Stop! Just stop now! There's nothing to hold on for. I'm telling you to stop, goddammit!

Bump-bump-bump-bump-bump!

Crash!

What was that?

The pounding had stopped.

His heart had listened, after so many years of *him* obeying the whims of that vital organ.

He felt dizzy, as if he were spinning in space, though this sensory deprivation chamber of half existence refused to allow him perspective.

Was he being drawn to Bella? To his children?

Were those New Age people correct in saying he would be whisked into a winding tunnel, a vortex of blinding light and emotion?

Raul was ready. He let himself go, clearing his mind as best he could and allowing for the moment.

"Flip him over!"

What was that?

There was a major shift in the void.

What's happening? Who's out there?

His vision came back to him in a rush. The light was blinding after so much darkness. He felt hands grappling with his body.

Something was jammed down his throat and he felt his stomach lurch. Lava bubbled in his gut and raced up his throat. He heard the roar of a waterfall, tasted the bitterness of failure.

"We have to get him up."

The scene before him went all tilt-a-whirl. The floor, awash with his vomit, swung away and now he was facing the wall. He caught a brief glimpse of a man's profile.

"Who are you?" he said. The reply was something thick and unintelligible.

"I'll get the shower running." A voice, so familiar, the source of it moving quickly out of the room.

"How many did you take?"

Raul heard the question but couldn't understand what it meant. He was so tired. Why were these people not letting him sleep? He'd been having a weird dream. Now what was it? How did it fall from his grasp so quickly? If they'd just let him be, there was a chance he could catch it by its tail.

"Raul!" The man's voice was harsh, blustering with authority. "Do you remember how many you took?"

Raul turned and found himself inches from the man's mouth. It was hard to focus, but he did see gray stubble.

"Wuh? Leave me alone."

"Bring him in!" the other voice called out.

Raul was half carried, half dragged out of his bedroom. He heard water running. Why were they taking him outside into the rain?

His eyes rolled to the ceiling as his body was jostled and jerked.

"Wake up, *abuelo!*"

The cold water pelted his face and encased his body in ice. Raul was jolted out of his fog. He fought to get away from the icy spray.

"Not yet, old man."

Hands like vises gripped his shoulders and kept him in place under the showerhead.

"Why are you doing this to me?" Raul cried, close to tears.

"To save your ugly ass, that's why. What the hell is wrong with you, man? You don't do this kinda shit."

Felix. It was Felix who was keeping him under the shower.

Suddenly, the water turned off, and Felix helped him out of the tub and dried him, wrapping the towel around Raul's waist.

"You with me?"

Raul's head still felt like it was full of helium, but he was able to think a little straighter. "Yeah. I'm with you."

Felix clapped him on the back. "Good. Now time to walk."

"I'm fine now. I just want to lie down."

He tried to move toward his bedroom, but Felix pulled him back. "Nice try. We're gonna walk your ass around this house until I say so. Samson, that coffee almost ready?"

Samson? Did he mean Bill Samson?

"Just another minute. Want to make sure it's nice and strong." Sure enough, there was Christ Church's caretaker. What the hell was he doing here?

Felix put Raul's arm over his shoulder and held him by his wrist as he walked him to the front door and back to the kitchen. Bill Samson was pouring a cup of coffee.

"Bill?"

The old cop smiled. "Good to see we got here in the nick of time. You feeling any better?"

Before they'd arrived, Raul was pretty sure he'd felt nothing. Now he was dizzy and nauseous and weak, so no, he wasn't feeling better at all. He waved the coffee away. "Too hot." The tendrils of steam rising from the mug were thick and dense.

"It won't be for long. You just make sure you drink it all. There'll be more where that came from."

Felix turned him around and they headed back to the living room.

"Why is Bill here?" Raul asked, not sure if he could fully comprehend the answer.

"Because I couldn't ditch him. Besides, we might need him."

"Need him for what?"

When they got to the living room, Felix looked furtively out the windows, searching for something.

"We'll get to that later. For now, just keep walking."

Raul swayed and bumped into the coffee table.

"Hey, where's that dumb cat of yours?"

His shin ached and his stomach turned.

"He ran away."

Raul doubled over and threw up again. He thought he heard Felix say, "Fuck this shit. I'm not cleaning the floor."

CHAPTER THIRTY-FIVE

After an hour of walking and three cups of coffee, Raul was finally allowed to sit in Ida's throne. Felix had wrapped a blanket over his shoulders and was drinking something from a black coffee mug that Raul was pretty sure wasn't coffee. Bill Samson was finishing up cleaning the floor, tossing paper towels in a bucket.

"You done puking?" Felix asked. He couldn't take his eyes off the windows and front door. Part of the frame had been reduced to splinters. He was making Raul nervous.

Raul had his hand on his stomach. All that was in there was coffee. "I think I'm good." Now that his head was clear, he noticed the huge upside-down cross on Felix's forehead. "Who did that to you?" A tremor went down his spine as he studied the pink, raised wound.

"The fuckers who we have to get you away from."

"That...you're not making any sense."

"Right now, I ain't got time to explain everything to you. I'm packing your stuff and we're getting out of here."

He could hear Bill dumping filthy mop water into the kitchen sink.

"Wait. What? Where are we going?"

Felix opened the door and peered outside. It was night and with no streetlights around, there wasn't much he was going to be able to see.

"Anyplace but here. Samson has a fishing cabin in Pennsylvania. That might be the best place for you for a while."

Raul's head started to throb. What was going on? Why was he being railroaded out of his house?

At least they're not taking me to a hospital and letting a psych ward get their hands on me for the next week.

Raul remembered taking the pills. And the message from Bella. And why it was so important that he convince Felix and Samson to leave so he could do what he had to do, although now without the pills since they were all gone.

"I'm not going anywhere," he said, sounding more like a recalcitrant child than a man drawing a line in the sand.

Felix spun around and winked at him. "Oh yes you are. In fact, we should already be gone."

"Why are you acting all crazy? What the hell is going on?"

"I got as much as I could." Bill Samson came into the room carrying Raul's suitcase and a full black plastic bag. "I'll put these in the car."

Raul stood up and had to give his head a moment to gain some equilibrium. "Now, wait a second."

"I got your back," Felix said. To Raul's horror, he took a gun out of his waistband, opened the door and stepped onto the porch, squinting into the darkness as Bill hustled with his gimpy leg to his car and tossed Raul's things in the trunk.

Samson came back inside and handed Raul a shirt and jeans. "Get dressed, Father."

Raul stared at the clothes in his hand. "I'm definitely missing something. Felix, what did you do? What kind of trouble are you in? And how did you rope Bill into it?"

Felix's stare hardened. "It ain't me that started this. Put your clothes on and I'll tell you in the car."

Raul turned to Bill for help. The retired cop looked as serious as an incoming tornado.

"We saved your life once tonight. Now it's up to you to save it again," Felix said.

Raul bristled. "Saved my life? You fucked everything up! I didn't ask you to come breaking into my home. You didn't save me. You stopped me from being with my family. I'm not leaving them."

Bill and Felix exchanged a worried look. "Okay, you can get dressed in the car," Felix said and grabbed his arm. Bill grabbed the other and they lifted him off the floor, carried him to the porch and down the steps. Raul feebly tried to twist out of their grasp, but he was still weak. He gazed back at the house. "Bella!"

Why hadn't she spoken while they were all in the house? Just one incorporeal word from her would have stopped them dead in their tracks. If she wanted Raul to be with her, why had she let them take him away?

"Bella's not there," Felix said, shoving him into the back seat. He climbed in next to Raul.

"You heard her! You know she is. Don't lie, Felix."

Bill started the car. Raul reached for the handle to get out of the car. Felix pounced on top of him. Bill looked back as they struggled.

"Just go," Felix barked. "I can handle him."

"Why are you lying?" Raul blurted "You can't take me away from my family. You have no right! You have no right!"

Again, Raul felt the all-too-familiar heat of tears. He was so tired of crying. All he wanted to do was get back to Bella and the kids and end his days of sorrow. Why were Felix and Bill so hellbent on denying him some peace?

Felix kept a tight hold on his arm. "Look, man, I hear you and I know why you're upset. But you're going to have to trust me on this."

"Fuck you."

Felix kept his eyes on the windows. "I've been told worse. You want to put some clothes on or not?"

"I want you to stop the goddamn car and let me the fuck out."

Raul went for Bill's shoulders, but Felix was quicker than he looked, blocking Raul with his arm and shoving him back into his seat.

"Listen to Felix," Bill said. "He's telling—"

A wall of flame erupted at the end of the driveway. Bill stomped on the brakes and the car fishtailed, the back end bouncing off a tree trunk. The engine sputtered, a moment away from dying.

"What the fuck?" Felix exclaimed. The gun was back in his hand.

Raul went rigid. The initial blaze pulled back, started to coalesce into a distinct form.

It was a cross. A great, burning cross at least ten feet high.

Except it was upside down.

"Dammit, they were waiting for us this whole time," Bill grumbled. He tapped the accelerator to keep the car from stalling. "Is there another way out to the main road?"

Raul's eyes hurt from staring at the flaming inverted cross. Who would do such a thing? Was this some sort of rebuke for his leaving the priesthood? His mind burned as hot as the cross with questions.

"Raul!" Felix nudged his side. "Is there another way to get to the road?"

Feeling as if he were moving through a sea of cold honey, Raul leaned forward and stuck his head between the two front seats. "No. This...this is the only way."

"Well, shit." Bill put the car in reverse, turned in his seat and drove back toward the house.

"They're probably waiting for us at the house, man," Felix said.

"They're definitely waiting for us up there," Bill said.

Felix and Bill knew something Raul didn't and even though he wanted to demand they tell him, now was not the time. He'd have to do what they had asked of him.

Trust them.

The car skidded to a halt inches from the front steps. Bill Samson jumped out of the car. Raul saw he now had a gun as well.

"Come on," Bill said after looking about the front yard.

Felix practically kicked his door open and dragged Raul out.

"Go inside, I'll cover you," Bill said, sidestepping up the porch steps.

Felix and Raul dashed into the house, Felix at the lead with his gun. "Did you lock your back door before you...you know?"

Raul stumbled to Ida's chair, fighting the impulse to sink into the soft cushions.

"I locked everything," he replied dreamily. Unfortunately, Felix and Bill had had to break the front door in to save him. If people were coming after them, they could just waltz right in. Bill came hustling inside and slammed the door, pushing his back against it.

"Swing that couch over here," Bill said.

Felix looked as if he were waiting for Raul to get up. Raul was too numb to register that Bill needed his help.

"I got it," Felix said, pushing the couch until it wedged against the door. Bill made sure the windows were locked and closed the blinds while Felix double-checked the back door and kitchen windows. The house was filled with the hurried stomping of their feet instead of Raul's children playing knock-knock-hit-bump.

When Bill was done, he leaned against the wall and tried to catch his breath. His face was beaded with sweat. He took his cell phone out and dialed. "It's dead."

"What?" Felix said.

"Try yours."

"I don't have a phone, man. Raul, what about yours?"

Raul tapped his pockets with deadened hands. He somehow pulled his phone from his back jeans pocket and handed it to Felix.

Felix tapped out the three numbers and put the phone to his ear. "Nothing. Not even a dial tone."

"They must have a jammer," Bill said. "Any chance there's a landline phone in here?"

Raul shook his head, staring at the wall.

"Looks like we're trapped in here. Too many goddamn windows," Felix griped.

"Or maybe just enough if they set fire to the house and we have to get out," Bill said.

Set fire to the house?

"I need you both to tell me exactly what's going on here," Raul said calmly, even though he wanted to shout at the top of his lungs.

Felix ignored him and peeked out from between the blinds. "The fire is out."

"Makes you wonder what they're up to now," Bill said, wiping the sweat from his forehead. "But I'll bet my departed mother's ass they'll light it right up again the moment we get back in that car."

In fact, the smell of burning wood and some kind of chemical accelerant filled the air in the house.

"It sure as shit got our attention."

Raul shot up from the chair. "Tell me what the fuck is happening! Now!" The effort made his head spin, but he forced himself to stand his ground.

Bill and Felix glanced at one another. Raul knew that look. It was the one he'd seen in hospitals when someone had died, the staff silently hoping someone, anyone, would break the news to a family member or friend who had come to visit.

In that gap of silence, Raul noticed the pulpy red cross on Felix's forehead. It was upside down, just like the one at the end of the driveway. Even in his hazy state, how had he missed it this entire time?

Felix noticed him staring and exhaled loudly. "It's bad, bro. I'm not sure how you're gonna take it."

"I've been living in hell. Try me."

Rubbing the back of his neck, Felix paced the room, buying time to collect his thoughts.

"It's about your wife."

Raul's gaze instantly went to the kitchen, to the vent in the floor, wondering if Bella were listening to them now.

"What about her?" he said in a tone that he hoped conveyed his need to tell Felix to tread lightly.

"She wasn't who you thought she was."

Raul clenched his fists. "What do you mean?"

"That exorcism she had when she was a kid. It either didn't take, or it opened something up inside her."

A wave of vertigo set Raul on his ass and onto Ida's chair. Bill took a step toward him to see if he was okay. He waved him off.

"I don't know what you're talking about."

"Those people out there, the ones who burned that cross, they're part of a Satanic cult called the Children of Behemoth." Felix jabbed his gun at the window. The wound on his head paled along with the rest of his face. He looked like he was in pain just talking about it. "Bella wasn't just a part of the cult. She was their leader."

CHAPTER THIRTY-SIX

Raul had difficulty drawing in a full breath. "Take that back. That's... that's bullshit."

"I wish I could, man. I'd give anything to be wrong."

"You never even met Bella. How the hell could you know anything?"

Bill put a calloused hand on Raul's shoulder. "Calm down. I know this isn't easy. Just hear him out." It was a practiced tone, one Raul was sure he'd used on victims of crime countless times. Raul shrugged away from his touch.

Felix grabbed a dining room chair and sat a few feet from Raul. He looked sick to his stomach. "I asked around a lot of bad places, trying to find anything out about who murdered your family. The next day, I was jumped and got this." He tapped the upside-down cross on his head. "That's how I knew I was getting the attention of the people I was looking for. Samson here gave me a hand snatching the bastards who did this to me. One got away, and I'm sure told the people in his cult their fucking game was over. The other I got to talking and we came as fast as we could."

Raul put his hands on his thighs so they couldn't see how much he was shaking. "Who are the Children of Behemoth and how would my wife have anything to do with them?"

"I don't know how it all started. I didn't have time to get everything. I just know that in their fucked-up cult, she was the one who called all the shots. She'd been with them for a long time, I think. Like probably before you were even married."

"No. No. I don't believe you."

"This is the bad part," Felix said, his tone softening, face in his hands. When he looked back up at Raul, he said, "Your family wasn't attacked by random lunatics. It was all part of her plan. She had the Children of Behemoth break into the house. She...she offered herself and the kids as a...as a sacrifice."

Raul thought he was going to puke. His ears rang and his vision grew fuzzy at the periphery. "A sacrifice?" was all he could muster.

Felix took several deep breaths. "She offered them up to Satan."

"No. She would never have done that! Have our kids murdered? For Satan? She knew the Bible better than I did!"

There was no way anything Felix was saying could be true. This Satanic cult had deceived Felix. Bella wouldn't give a Satanist a second glance, much less lead a cult. Impossible!

As much as it clearly pained him, Felix continued. "Their sacrifice was only the first part. It's all been about you."

"I think I saw movement out there," Bill said. He pulled the blinds aside with his index finger and stared into the darkness.

Felix grabbed hold of Raul's hands. "This shit is crazy but we don't have a lot of time. I just need you to hear me. Okay?"

Raul gave an almost imperceptible nod.

"This whole thing was designed to drive you insane. Your wife and kids, they were killed so you would want to give up on life. It's all so you would commit suicide. You would be the ultimate sacrifice. A priest taking his own life. And they would be there to make sure it happened."

"But you're wrong," Raul said. "Bella, the kids, they talk to me. I hear them all the time. You heard her too."

Felix shook his head. "They rigged this place. They've been watching you ever since that night. They probably had the parish house bugged, too. Apparently, according to the bastard I caught, you talked a lot to yourself when you were drunk. They knew you were coming here and got everything in place before you moved in."

"But...Bella...."

"Recordings she made. Like I said, she set this whole thing up down to every last detail. Well, except one. She didn't know I was going to find you and fuck everything up."

Raul felt untethered from his body. "Recordings?"

"In the basement and upstairs," Felix said.

"But, things have moved around."

"It's them, coming in here and screwing with you. They've been out there this entire time. You haven't been talking to your family. It's just what they've wanted you to think."

JOIN US.

Bella *had* wanted him to kill himself. Not to join her and the children.

As an offering to the Devil.

How was he supposed to accept this?

"I...I...."

"You okay up here for a minute?" Felix asked Bill.

"Trust me, I'll let you know if I need you."

Felix pulled Raul by the arms and got him standing. "Come on."

Raul shuffled after him, though it felt more like floating. Felix led him to the cellar door and opened it. He took a penlight out of his jacket pocket and turned it on, the narrow beam emitting a powerful white light.

"Why are we going to the cellar?"

"To show you what you need to see."

They went down the stairs and into the gloom. Felix swung the light across the ceiling. "You said Bella talks to you through the floor vent, right?"

"Most times, yes."

"Where would it be down here?"

That was a good question. It wasn't as if Raul spent much time in the cellar, and when he did, he was unsettled and anxious to get out. Just like now. "I don't know."

Felix walked around the cellar, eyes to the ceiling, knocking things over in his rush to find the vent. He'd gone around a corner and out of sight when he called out, "Found it."

Raul followed the sound of his friend's labored breathing. The light was trained on a rectangular grate set in the ceiling.

Bella?

"Hold the flashlight."

Raul did as he was told, transfixed by the now-silent vent. Felix grabbed a couple of wood crates and set one atop the other. He climbed up and said, "Point it right there." Raul swung the light so it shined on the corner of the vent and Felix's prying fingers. "You can tell these old screws were messed with recently. They didn't even tighten them all the way."

Grunting and huffing, Felix worked his fingers under the small wedge of space between the metal vent and ceiling. He tugged hard, over and over, until the vent was ripped from its mooring in a shower of dust. Some got in Raul's eye and temporarily blinded him. He rubbed his eyes to get it out.

"Hand me the light," Felix said. He reached his arm into the vent. It sounded like something ripped, and when he pulled it out, he held an oblong speaker. "That's your wife and kids. I'll bet there are bugs throughout the house but we ain't got time to look for them."

He handed the speaker to a dazed Raul. For a moment, Raul thought it was going to burn his hand the way a crucifix singed a vampire's flesh. It felt as if he were holding something evil, malignant.

"I can't believe this." He turned to Felix. "But what about the children. I've seen them…and other things. How could they fake that?"

Felix took the speaker, threw it on the ground and crushed it with the heel of his boot. "They got the ball rolling and all those pills and shit you were taking did the rest. You're not well, *abuelo*." He tapped the side of his head. "And don't get me wrong, I'm not blaming you. Grief is stronger than anything, especially the kind you've been carrying. You throw in what these fuckers have been doing, drugs and booze. You saw what you wanted to see, and what they wanted you to see."

"It can't be all in my mind. What about you? And Bruiser?"

"I didn't *see* shit. But I *heard* plenty. Did the cat react to things you saw, or what you heard?"

Raul stared off into the distance. "I don't know. I'm not sure of anything at this point."

"Your kids are always with you, just in a different way," Felix said, gripping Raul's shoulders. "It's natural to see them…to want to see them…from time to time. But all this other craziness? It's all about driving you crazy, which wasn't hard to do."

Bella, Lizzy, and Abel were well and truly gone, not visiting him, living with him, waiting for him to join them.

He'd never really known who his wife was. The woman he'd poured every ounce of his love into had betrayed him, spit in the face of her parents.

Worst of all, she had willfully allowed their children to be slaughtered. All for the sake of a misguided need to please Satan.

The woman who cringed at any movie rated more than PG, could recite scripture with practiced ease, had lovingly cared for not just Raul and the kids, but an entire parish, was in actuality a demonic killer.

Raul thought he could live for a hundred more years and not be able to fully reconcile himself to the horrid truth.

He brought his gaze from the speaker to Felix. "But I didn't kill myself. They...she failed. Thanks to you. Why won't they let us leave?"

"Because they're a cult of freaks. They need to get rid of us because of what we know now."

Glass shattered upstairs. Bill's footsteps raced down the hall.

"Get up here!"

Felix ran past Raul, stomping up the steps. He heard him mutter, "Oh shit."

Raul let the evil speaker fall from his hands and drifted up the stairs. Pebbles of glass littered the living room floor. Bill and Felix stared at the ground, at something between their feet. Raul followed their gaze and bit on his lower lip hard enough to draw blood.

Lying on the floor was a great ball of crimson-stained fur.

Raul knelt to get a closer look.

"Bruiser."

★ ★ ★

Bill Samson had turned out all the lights and asked Felix to watch the back door. Raul sat with Bill in the living room. Bruiser lay under a sheet on the floor.

Raul wouldn't say he'd loved the cat, but it had grown on him, and when the cat left, there'd been a definite void. So why was he so choked up?

"These people are sick," Raul said.

This cult of lunatics Raul had never met, never even knew existed, had taken everything away from him, all in the name of a sacrifice to a deity that was a figment of man's warped imagination.

If Raul was given the chance to choke the life out of each and every one of them, he would take it. Seeing the life bleed from their eyes would be a pleasure beyond compare.

"Do you have an extra gun?" he asked Bill.

It was hard to see Bill's expression in the dark, but he heard the concern in the man's voice. "Have you ever even held a gun, Father? I mean, Raul?"

Old habits died hard.

"I've done more than that," Raul said coolly.

"How much more?"

"I never shot anyone, if that's what you're thinking." *But I will now*, he thought.

Fabric rustled and Bill tapped his arm, handing him a lump of cold steel.

"I'm actually not surprised," Bill said. "You don't come to know a fella like Felix without having spent some time on the dark side."

Raul hefted the gun, making sure not to touch the trigger. The last thing he needed was to accidentally shoot Bill. "You could call it that."

The drugs had completely worn off and Raul was getting antsy. Cowering in the dark didn't seem like the best tactic. Why give the Children of Behemoth a chance to gather their forces outside? What they should do was take them by surprise.

The Children of Behemoth. Who were they? He'd never heard of them. He guessed that was the point. If you were so dedicated to Satan, keeping a low profile would seem the prudent thing to do.

How many times had Bella slipped away to see the Children of Behemoth, *to lead them*, without his knowing? When she said she was visiting the elderly in the parish to check on them, was she actually sneaking off to conduct Satanic rituals with these barbarians? If Raul had anything left to throw up, he'd be heaving over the sink now.

She killed Lizzy and Abel.

Bella had been a monster in an angel's clothing all along.

Was it some form of PTSD from whatever had happened to her in the woods that day and the ensuing exorcism?

Or had the possession never really ended?

No, possession isn't real. It's a mental disorder. And Bella had been truly mentally disturbed. A sociopath of the highest order who had learned to build a mask of human emotion that was impossible to see behind.

He got up and looked outside the window. He saw nothing but trees half bathed in shadow and moonlight. Nothing stirred except his churning gut.

But they were out there. Raul didn't need to see them to know that. His ears told him everything. It was dead quiet outside. Not a single cricket. Not the patter of night critters scampering through the brush.

Nature knew the unnatural had come.

Were there enough Children of Behemoth to surround the entire house and block all their means of escape? He couldn't imagine a secret cult capable of a large membership. Behind the house was woods and what seemed like endless stretches of farmland, some of it having once belonged to his family. There was no way they could cover all that ground. Raul, Bill, and Felix could make a run for it and spread out in different directions. Maybe not run, on account of Bill's gimpy leg. Sooner or later, they would come upon a farmhouse and ask the owner to call the police.

What would they say?

"Officer, there's a cult of Satanists after us and they mean to sacrifice us to the Devil."

How many seconds would pass before they hung up the phone?

After that, if they were found, Raul's arrival at someone's doorstep would only put them in danger. He couldn't allow that to happen. His life was not worth any more than another's.

"Think we can wait them out until daylight?" Felix asked from the kitchen.

Bill quietly peered out all of the windows in the living room. "Doubtful. Whatever they plan to do, they need the cover of night." He'd shoved a chair under the knob of the front door to keep it closed. It wouldn't keep anyone out for long, but it would delay their getting inside.

Raul thought back to all the action and horror movies he'd ever watched, montages of characters making homemade arsenals flashing through his memory. If only it were that easy. The most they could come up with in here was tossing the detritus from the cellar at the cultists if and when they attacked. Raul was pretty sure neither Bill nor Felix knew how to make bombs out of everyday cleaners.

At least they had guns. The trick was to only shoot when they had someone dead to rights. Wasting ammo was not an option.

Just a few months ago, he'd been a happy priest with a family that was more than he ever could have asked for.

Now he was calculating shooting his way out of this mess, his heart leaden with the new realization that he'd loved a monster.

If his shattered heart didn't kill him, the waiting would.

Raul walked into the kitchen and stood beside Felix, who was leaning against the back doorframe. Stray shafts of moonlight lit Felix's wounded, anxious face. When he saw Raul, he put his finger to his lips.

"What?" Raul mouthed.

Felix pointed out the window.

Shadows ran back and forth beyond the picnic table but before the high grass. Raul counted at least five, though it was hard to distinguish one from another as they scooted in a tight cluster.

"If those fuckers can just stand still for a moment," Felix hissed between his teeth. The muzzle of his gun was pressed against the glass.

"They're too far away," Raul said.

When they were seventeen, Felix had bought a hot .38 from some addict who needed a fix. The boys had spent months practicing shooting it in abandoned buildings and the grounds of the old paper towel factory that had seen its last roll come off the assembly line a few years before they were born. Raul had been the better shot. Felix was reckless and prone to letting his anger get the best of him, shooting wildly if he missed his first target. Then he'd proceed to spray the area with bullets.

Raul had pilfered a few issues of *Guns & Ammo* from the bodega shelves that fall, to indulge his brief fascination with firearms. He had big dreams of buying all kinds of different handguns, both as a collection and a means of protection. But once they ran out of bullets and money to buy more, Felix tossed the .38 in the sewer.

Now, Raul wished he'd kept up with it and had more than Bill's handgun.

"What are they doing out there?" Raul whispered.

"I don't know, but they're really busy at whatever it is."

"What if we fire one shot in their direction, see if they scatter? Make them aware that we're armed. Maybe it'll be enough incentive to get them to back off."

Felix slid his gaze to Raul with a smirk on his face. "I like the way you think, cowboy. Good to see all those Hail Marys didn't make you lose your edge. Okay, you open the door and I'll take the shot. Maybe, with any luck, I'll hit one of them."

"On three." Raul took the doorknob in his hand and counted on his other fingers. The second his third finger went up, he swung the door open.

Felix stepped into the open doorway, shouted, "What's up, *putas*?" and fired straight ahead. He stepped back into the kitchen and Raul shut the door and locked it. They looked out the window, scanning the ground for any writhing shadows.

Bill came racing across the house. "What happened?"

"Just sending them a message. We hope," Raul said.

"You see anything?" Felix asked.

Raul narrowed his eyes, wishing he had night vision. "No." It looked like Felix's shot had, at most, hurt some grass. "However, I also don't see them running around anymore."

They waited a minute for the cultists to return.

And another.

Darkness and silence ruled the night once more.

"That was too easy," Felix grumbled.

"I think you're right. Next time you try something like that, give me a goddamn heads-up," Bill said, slinking back to the front of the house.

"I really want to go out there and see what they were doing," Raul said.

"Yeah, well I wanna grab a stripper's titties when she shakes them in my face at the club. Doesn't mean I should."

"Can't remember the last time I was in a strip club." Raul had willfully forgotten a lot of the things he used to do.

"Same shit. All just costs more than back in the day. We get out of this, I'll take you to a good one. I'll even pay for your lap dances."

"We'll see about that." The last thing Raul wanted to think

about at the moment was going to a strip club. What was keeping him focused was his newfound hatred for his wife and what she'd done to their children.

"They're coming," Bill called over to them.

"Where?" Felix said.

"Four, headed for the front yard."

Raul's body tensed.

"They're splitting up. Now there's more."

"How many?" Raul asked.

Bill paused for a beat. "Eight. No, more. They're going toward the sides of the house. You see any out back?"

Felix peeked out the window. "Not yet."

Raul's mouth had gone dry. His nerves tingled with anticipation. Was he moments away from shooting people when they broke into his house?

As Felix would say, *Turn the other cheek, my ass.*

The banging erupted on both sides of the house simultaneously. It sounded as if the Children of Behemoth were pounding on the exterior with hammers. The noise inside was deafening and set Raul's teeth on edge.

The barrage of heavy banging got worse and worse until Raul was sure they were going to hammer their way through the walls.

CHAPTER THIRTY-SEVEN

"Shut the fuck up!" Felix shouted. Not that he could be heard above the din. It sounded like the whole house was about to come down around them.

Raul turned this way and that, ready to pull the trigger any moment. Felix barked, "Stop pointing that gun at me, man!"

"Sorry. Sorry."

If the Children of Behemoth wanted to rattle them, it was working.

Felix took a quick peek out back. The shadows had returned to that same spot. All that banging on the house was probably supposed to distract them so the cult could continue doing whatever it was without fear of being shot at.

Guess you were wrong, Felix thought. He opened the door.

"What the hell are you doing?" Raul screeched.

Felix fired into the shadows. He rattled off three shots before Raul yanked him back and kicked the door shut.

"What'd you do that for?" Felix said.

"They're all around us and you had the door open. What if they rushed you and stormed inside?"

"Then fucking shoot them."

"One's on the porch now," Bill said. The front windows rattled in their frames.

A window broke upstairs.

Then another in the cellar.

The Children of Behemoth could bust in at any time and they wanted Raul and Felix and Samson to know it.

In an instant, all of the pounding stopped.

"The one on the porch is gone," Bill announced. "Ran to the side of the house."

Felix's chest heaved. He tried to settle himself down, but it was damn near impossible. He wished one of them would come through a window or something so Felix could give him a proper beating. It would feel so good to smash one of their faces in, even though his knuckles were sore as hell.

Whup!

Felix knew exactly what that sound was. He'd attended enough biker parties in the sticks to recognize the sound of a bonfire erupting.

Orange flames crackled and writhed in the yard.

"Oh shit, here they go again."

Raul nudged him aside so he could look out the window. "What is it?"

"Another fire, except I don't know what the fuck it's for. It's too far away to touch the house, though."

"Yet," Raul said.

It wasn't exactly a bonfire. The flames didn't go high enough. It illuminated some of the shadows flitting about the yard and Felix didn't like what he saw.

People dressed in black and white robes milled about, getting close to the flame and then stepping away. He couldn't make out any faces because they were hidden in the shrouds of their hoods. People in hoods and robes ignited an atavistic fear in him. Nothing good ever came from hoods and robes and fire. It felt as if an old-time lynch mob had come for them.

"Are these Satanists or KKK assholes?" Felix said.

"Maybe both," Raul replied.

There was a tremendous crash from the front of the house. Felix turned around in time to see a large stone bouncing along the living room floor, just missing the cat's corpse. Bill skittered away from his post by the broken window.

It wasn't just a stone.

It was on fire.

"Keep an eye out back," Felix told Raul. He ran to Raul's bedroom and grabbed the sheets that were in a pile by the door. Running through the living room, he just missed being brained by a rock that shattered the dining room window. He ducked and leaped, tossing the linens on top of the burning stone. The flames were extinguished a few seconds later.

Another window broke.

Samson fired into the empty window frame.

Something slammed against the front door. The chair wedged under the knob shifted a few agonizing inches. More windows blew out upstairs. Felix stayed crouched on the ground in case the cultists had guns and decided to open fire. Samson must have been thinking the same thing because he squatted behind the chair Raul's aunt used to sit in.

You picked a great time to get back into Raul's life. See what happens when you try to do something good? There's no justice. You just get fucked. Sometimes, like now, you get your ass killed. Felix cursed himself for even thinking that way.

If Raul ever needed him, it was now.

They'd scrapped their way out of some dicey situations when they were kids. Nothing like this, but Felix always felt they had a lucky streak that would protect them from the worst.

He hoped that streak hadn't left them in the intervening years between dustups.

When the door shook again Felix shot into its center. He thought he heard a thump outside and hoped it was a dead Child of Behemoth.

The window behind Samson exploded, peppering him with glass shards. The old man was pretty quick. He spun around on his heels and blasted away. If someone was in the process of climbing in, they were now on the ground, checking out for good.

"You forgot to read them their rights," Felix said.

"Doesn't matter when you're not a cop." Samson grunted and got up to check on the front windows. "Looks like the coast is clear."

"For the moment." Felix checked in on Raul. "What's going on back there, *abuelo*?"

"Just a lot of people gathering around that fire."

A lot of people? Felix didn't like the sound of that. Nor did he like the breeze blowing through all the broken windows. From what he could see, there wasn't an intact window in either room. Here on the ground floor, they were sitting ducks.

Felix got to his feet, went to the nearest window, and pulled the trigger. He went to the next and did the same. When he tried again, the hammer hit an empty chamber.

Samson came up beside him. "Were they trying to come in?"

Felix rummaged through his pocket gathering loose bullets in his hand. "I'm making sure they don't try."

"Remember, I didn't give you an endless supply," Samson said, watching Felix reload the gun.

"I'm not saving them for a rainy day." Felix snapped the cylinder shut.

He was about to discourage any Satanists from approaching that side of the house when the front door was reduced to splinters.

Men clad in black came streaming in behind two people holding a battering ram.

"Fuck!" Felix exclaimed, firing wildly into the crowd. One person grabbed their upper arm and fell to the floor. Samson went to shoot but someone tackled him, pinning him to the floor. The old man put up such a struggle, three more bodies were needed to subdue him. Samson unleashed a torrent of expletives and threats that were the antithesis of a man who spent his every waking day in service to the church.

Felix dove at one of the men, attempting to peel him off of Samson.

Ripping pain lanced Felix's shoulder and back as his arm was wrenched behind him with no mercy. He felt and heard tendons and ligaments ripping.

"You goddamn *pendejo!*" he shouted, seething at the fact he'd been overpowered. His jaw was unhinged by a sucker punch that came from his left. Arms wrapped around his legs and dropped him, slamming his face off the hardwood floor, shattering his nose.

Things started to fade to black real fast. Copper flooded his mouth. He fought against his attackers, raising his head from the dining room floor. "Raul!"

He hoped his friend had found a way to get the hell out while these bastards were focusing on Felix and Samson. Hoped but doubted it was even possible.

They were overrun by human-sized rats.

Felix's skull was smashed so hard, his vision filled with millions of bright white dots before he slipped away.

* ★ *

Raul saw the men charging into the house but didn't dare shoot for fear of hitting Bill or Felix. The two men who he knew were tougher than ten pounds of gristle were far too easily overwhelmed. Bill Samson disappeared under a pile of bodies.

A light burst on and Raul saw the spade of a shovel crash down on the back of Felix's head. The sharp twang it made on contact rang over the tremendous din.

"You fucking sons of bitches!" Raul screamed. He fought the impulse to jump into the fray with his fists and try to take out as many as he could. Back in the day, he loved a fight, fair or not.

But this wasn't back in the day and he'd last about two punches before getting taken down hard.

Almost a dozen men were crammed in the house and heading for him.

Raul backed against the door. The windowpane in the door burst. A strong hand shot through and grabbed Raul by the forehead, snapping his head back. Before he could react, a wet cloth was clamped over his mouth and nose. Raul tried to raise the gun at the advancing figures, pulling the trigger. His shots went into the kitchen floor. He smelled something sweet and his vision wavered, his mind separating from his body in a horrid instant.

CHAPTER THIRTY-EIGHT

When Raul woke up, he felt as if his flesh was on fire.

Painfully turning his head to the side, all he saw was a wall of flickering flames. He tried to get up, to get away from the fire, but his limbs wouldn't obey him. His legs and arms were spread apart. His shoulder and hips crackled with sharp pains.

His first thought was, *They're burning me alive!*

He screamed until he thought he would black out again.

Panting, panicked, and in blazing agony, he was able to lift his head from the earthen floor and look down at his body. His chest was a bloody mess. Turning to his left and right, he saw his wrists were bound by leather straps tied to stakes driven deep into the ground. The same for his ankles. Try as he might, there was no give in his bindings. Every inch of his flesh was smeared with foul-smelling blood. It couldn't all be his. He wouldn't be alive now if that were the case.

"Help me! Somebody help me!"

It was still night and as far as his limited vision would allow, he was alone. He realized he was in the backyard, and the flames were the same ones he'd watched the cult light earlier.

Where were they? Was the idea to leave him here to die, waiting for the wind to fan the flames his way and roast him like a pig? Raul could think of very few ways to die that were worse than being burned alive. He twisted his arms and legs, hoping to at least loosen the straps. Anything to give him hope.

"Felix! Bill! Are you there?"

They could be right behind him and he'd never know it, especially if they were unconscious as he had been just a few moments ago.

What if they'd been killed? Raul couldn't help but feel responsible for their deaths.

He remembered how unhappy he'd been to see Felix when he'd

arrived on his doorstep. At the time, Raul just wanted to be left alone so he could watch his life unravel, thread by thread.

All Felix had wanted to do was help him.

Even if Raul died tonight, Felix had done something incredible for him. He'd found out the truth, no matter how terrible, and possibly paid for it with his life.

Bella had set this wheel in motion. It was still hard to think of her as a despicable subhuman, because how else could you describe a woman who worshipped Satan and had her own children butchered just so she could drive her husband to suicide? The Bella he knew wasn't even capable of thinking such a thing.

I didn't know Bella at all.

Perhaps no one had.

The fire crackled. A cloud of woodsmoke wafted over him, filling in his lungs until he started hacking.

He felt the footsteps before he heard them.

A heavy foot stomped dangerously close to the side of his head.

Another landed on the other side.

Raul looked up at a crimson nightmare.

A bare-chested man wearing boots made to resemble cloven hooves towered over him. His entire body was painted a brilliant red. Or was it blood? His head was shaved, and it appeared he was wearing contacts, unless it was possible to have sparkling yellow eyes. All he wore was some kind of tight-fitting underwear or bathing suit, that too the maroon of freshly spilled blood.

When their eyes met, the red man smiled, his too-white teeth augmented by pairs of fangs protruding from his upper and lower jaws.

He's the Devil, Raul thought. *Or at least what the small human mind fancies the Devil to look like.*

The absurdity of it distracted Raul from his pain and fear.

Out loud he said, "If you think you frighten me, you're wrong. Did you forget this isn't Halloween?"

The red man's smile evaporated like water on baking asphalt. Raul had gotten to him. He bet this jerk-off wanted to make a grand entrance and frighten Raul half to death. All it did was make Raul realize how pathetic these people were. Wearing costumes did not impress him. The only thing that did worry him was the dancing flames. He was fine with dying. Just not that way.

"He's awake," a woman's voice from beyond his field of vision said.

An elderly woman as frail as an autumn leaf stepped close to the red man. She had to use a cane and wore a black robe that looked heavy enough to drag her to her knees. Her long white hair was in a braid that snaked down her chest. The fire danced in her wide dark eyes.

"Where are my friends?"

She looked at the red man. "Seems an odd first question, doesn't it?"

The red man stared impassively at Raul, his fingers flexing, knuckles popping.

"You wanted me. You got me. Let them go."

The old woman shook her head as if silently pitying a dimwitted child.

"I can do this for you, *priest*," she said, holding on to the red man's muscular arms to bend a little closer to Raul. "I will untie one of your arms if you agree to kill yourself. Don't you want to make your wife proud?"

Proud? Was this woman out of her mind?

Raul closed his eyes to shut out the insanity. Of course she was crazy. They all were.

Make Bella proud.

He thought of his children, the very picture of innocence.

He opened his eyes, stared at the old woman and snarled, "I hope she spends an eternity in misery."

The old woman shrugged. "You won't like it if we have to…do things to convince you that suicide is far better than living in pain and misery your Christ never even conceived."

"Go fuck yourself." He spit at her, but it fell far short, instead landing within the red miasma on his chest.

She looked at the red man. "Wash him down."

Suddenly Raul recalled the day back at Sully's General Store when he'd spotted the old woman being carried away by what he thought was her caretaker. They had been watching him all along.

Someone wearing a black robe with their face hidden under a hood came over with a bucket. The old woman smiled. "Lemon water with salt. You'll beg me to make you that offer again."

The robed figure dipped a mop in the bucket. It came out dripping. The mop smeared over his torso, igniting an intense explosion of white-hot torment. Every muscle and tendon in his body went as taut as piano wire as he nearly levitated off the ground.

Raul looked down his body and saw the blood sluice away with the stinging mixture. What he saw horrified him.

Strange symbols were carved deep into his chest and stomach. There were triangles with crosses beneath them. A circle with eight arrows pointing outward. A pentagram. And a series of closed and open triangles that went down to his groin. The lemon and salt water settled into the red and pink folds of those wounds. Raul wouldn't have been surprised to see wisps of smoke writhing from the carvings, they burned so much.

The extreme pain robbed him of his breath, stifling the scream in his throat.

His eyes filled with tears. The flames looked like they danced behind a rippling waterfall.

More people gathered around him. All wore robes, most black, but some white. They had their hoods up, their faces hidden in shadow.

There were so many.

The Children of Behemoth was far bigger than he ever could have imagined.

And Bella had led them.

He tried to picture her in one of these robes, standing next to the Satanic cosplayer, chanting while surrounded by burning black candles. It was absurd, but it was real.

There was no way he was going to take his own life. No matter how painful the next few moments looked to be. He wouldn't give the Children of Behemoth the satisfaction.

The ring of robed cultists stood in silence. The old woman donned her hood and stepped back and out of Raul's view. The red man stayed where he was, glaring at Raul.

The carvings on Raul's body pulsed, the pain taking root in his bones. Raul ground his teeth to keep from crying. His jaws felt as if they were at breaking point.

He looked up at the red man. "You...look like a...fucking fool."

Seeing that flash of anger in the red man's twisted face gave Raul a moment of grim satisfaction. Bella might have bought into this nonsense, but that didn't mean he would. They weren't the lost siblings of Satan. They were twisted murderers, plain and simple. And they were going to do to him what they had to his children. Raul was ready. If Lizzy and Abel had had to endure this senseless agony, so would he.

"Raise it," the old woman shouted.

Raul tensed, waiting for the next wave of torture.

Instead, six robed people, three on either side, pulled on a long, thick rope.

Something came rising from the ground, backlit by the flames.

This time, Raul did scream.

CHAPTER THIRTY-NINE

The inverted cross was pulled to its full height. It wasn't empty.

Bill Samson's arms and legs were lashed to the wood beams, hanging upside down. He was either unconscious or dead. It was impossible to tell. What Raul could see was that his face had turned purple, swollen beyond measure. The Satanic savages had brutalized the man.

"You sick fucks," Raul said between gritted teeth. He almost told them he wished they'd burn in hell but stopped himself, realizing that was perhaps their primary goal.

"Watch your mouth, priest," the old woman scolded.

The robed cultists started to speak, a low babble of nonsense words.

"*Ensensior, bakthud, egat, lanathem. Ensensior, bakthud, egat, lanathem.*"

Raul screamed as loud as he could to drown out their idiocy.

"Our lord Behemoth will rise, fallen one," the old woman said, slowly walking toward the cross and Bill. She scowled at Raul. "Your blood and the blood of your entire family will fill his veins." She raised her hands to the sky. "Oh great Behemoth, hear your children!"

"*Ensensior, bakthud, egat, lanathem!*"

The chanting grew louder, more urgent. The red man stepped over Raul and approached the inverted cross.

A soft breeze blew across the field, carrying a noxious smell that made Raul's nose cringe.

"No."

The cultists, several dozen of them, a mix of men and woman if Raul could judge them by their voices, joined the old lady in lifting their arms.

The red man picked a stick off the ground. The end of it was rounded, bulky.

He dipped it into the fire and it caught with a loud *whoosh*.

"No!" Raul roared.

The red man paused to look at Raul and smile with those ridiculous teeth. He touched the flame to the top of the cross. It only took seconds for the fire to race down Bill Samson's body.

"*Ensensior, bakthud, egat, lanathem!*"

Raul's heart clamped at the sound of Bill's agonizing cries.

He hadn't been dead.

Through the licks of orange and yellow, Raul saw Bill's eyes were wide open, taking in the horror of his demise. He struggled to get free, to find a way to douse the flames. The inverted cross teetered, but the cultists holding the ropes kept it from tipping over.

"Help me!" Bill shouted from behind the shroud of fire. "Help meeeeee!"

All Raul could do was fight against his restraints and shout Bill's name over and over again. He struggled to get free, to run to Bill and douse the flames. The leather straps bit into his flesh, drawing fresh rivulets of blood.

Raul felt as helpless as he had the night his family had been murdered. It stoked his rage. His left wrist felt as if it were dislocating, yet the bindings held fast.

Bill's voice rose in pitch and then suddenly stopped. As did his wriggling to get off the cross.

Raul was overcome with the smell of kerosene and burning wood, hair, and meat. He watched his friend burn, refusing to look away. He at least owed Bill that. There were no more tears left in him to shed. He could only whisper an apology to Bill's smoldering corpse.

The red man disappeared for a moment and came back brandishing a sword. He looked Bill's blackened body up and down, the flames starting to sputter but refusing to die. The tip of the sword was raised so it was level with Bill's side.

"Get the hell away from him!"

The red man drew the sword away.

And then drove it deep into Bill's side. Bits of ash, blood, and purple organs rained out of the wound.

"Hail Behemoth!" the old woman cried.

"Hail Behemoth!" the others repeated in zealous unison.

"Murderers! You're nothing but murderers! The Devil can't hear you because he doesn't exist." Raul felt something break inside him.

He started to laugh.

His laughter brought a halt to the chanting and hailing.

"You ignorant, misguided fucks. Do you realize how ridiculous you look? How asinine you sound? Did you cobble your cult together from a series of B horror movies?" Raul couldn't control himself. He tittered like a madman. "Hail Behemoth! Hail Behemoth! You goddamn fucking dumb pieces of shit."

The red man licked the end of the sword, glaring at Raul.

"Untie him," the old woman said.

At first, Raul thought the red man was going to take Bill off the inverted cross. Instead, four robed cultists darted forward and undid the bindings on Raul's wrists and ankles by cutting through the leather with box cutters. He prepared himself to jump up and run.

He hadn't counted on his limbs being numbed to the point of uselessness. Someone pushed him into a sitting position. As the carvings on his body shifted, the pain hit another level of intensity, though not enough to quell the dark chuckling that had Raul in its grip.

"You call us misguided," the old woman said.

He squinted at her, fighting the pain and maniacal laughter. "You left out *fucks*. Among other things."

"Ye of no faith. Your wife is powerful beyond measure. She has seen the fiery forever and it has seen her. She learned at the feet of the Great Deceiver and even deceived you, holy man. Would you like to see what your wife and true belief in the one powerful god has wrought?"

Raul noted how she spoke of Bella in the present tense. "All I see is death and pageantry. I see evil. True evil. It's the evil that lives in everyone. You're not special. None of you. Least of all my wife. She *was* a sick woman who deceived all of you into going along with her sick delusions."

His arms and legs tingled with excruciating pins and needles. He looked for a way past the circle of Children of Behemoth. They had tightened their ranks. If he tried to get away and managed to break through, he didn't think he would get very far before one of them overtook him or his pained and depleted body betrayed him.

Where would he run to?

And where was Felix? He couldn't leave without knowing what they had done to Felix. It surely looked as if they had killed him earlier in the house. Considering what they had just done to Bill, it would be a mercy. But if there was a chance Felix was alive, Raul had to find him.

Raul was no longer laughing. In silence, he calculated.

The old woman saw through him. "You won't make it. Some fates you can't escape."

She motioned with her head at the red man. He clomped over to Raul with his cloven hoof boots and got behind him, locked his arms, and lifted him up as if he weighed as little as a newborn baby. The red man might have been silly to look at, but there was no denying his strength. He demonstrated it by flexing hard enough to bring Raul's joints to breaking point.

Raul smelled garlic on the man's breath.

He was carried to the fire the Children of Behemoth had set while Raul, Felix, and Bill had been trapped in the house. Now that he stood above it, the fire made sense.

A pentagram had been etched by flame, enclosed within a burning circle. Four large red candles were set into the ground just outside the circle. Raul had seen enough bad horror movies to know that each candle most likely represented one of the four elementals — earth, air, fire, and water, all aligned with the four points on a compass.

The cultists gathered behind the red man and Raul, picking up their chanting. Raul detected bits of Latin, but the conjugations were off. Any Latin word he understood was sandwiched between languages he'd never heard before. He suspected they were mostly made up.

The old woman handed the red man a knife. Raul cringed. "No!"

He didn't feel the blade carve a diagonal slash across his stomach. But he did see his skin begin to part and the trickle of blood that seeped along the gash. The red man scraped the blood from his nerve-frayed stomach into a black pot.

He gave the black pot to the old woman.

"There is such power in blood," she said to Raul. "You and your sheep drink the wine, never knowing what true blood can deliver. Special blood. The ultimate lamb, betrayed by his shepherd."

She reached into the pot and flicked her hand over the fire. He spied tiny, crimson flecks take to the air. When they hit the burning pentagram, the flames jumped ten feet high. Being so close, Raul felt his eyelashes singe and curl. The sudden burst of heat felt as if it were cauterizing the wounds on his torso.

"Do you see?" the woman said.

Raul's feet were lifted off the ground and he was brought half a foot closer to the inferno. He turned away because it felt as if his eyeballs were going to melt.

"See!" the Children of Behemoth said. "See! See! See! See!"

Only the red man stayed silent, obviously taking great joy in hurting Raul.

"See, priest. Look into the flames and see!" the old woman commanded.

He refused to open his eyes. What would be the point? Satisfying their demands was not his priority.

Fingers pried his eyelids open. The old woman hissed in his ear, "She waits for you, priest. Are you afraid of your wife? Oh, how your blood calls to her!"

The old woman hobbled around the flaming circle. Standing above a candle, she slipped a large knife from out of a pocket in her robe and sliced the blade down her left palm. She squeezed her hand over the candle. When her blood spattered into the candle's flame, it turned white and crackled like fireworks. She repeated this with each of the candles. When she was done, she thrust her wounded hand into the writhing flame of the circle around the pentagram until it was encased in an undulating white brilliance. Smiling instead of screaming, she lifted her hand to her face and puffed on it as if she were blowing out the candles on a birthday cake. Winking at Raul, she turned her palm so Raul could see.

The wound was gone, her flesh unmarred by the fire.

Then, she turned to the center of the pentagram and pointed.

If Raul thought his mind had irrevocably broken moments earlier, it had gone past the point of no return now.

There, standing within the conflagration, stood his wife. But not the Bella who had been his wife. This Bella was made entirely of white flame, all of her curves and edges flickering and losing form, only to regroup.

Her eyes burned blue and her lips were the crimson of a poison apple. Her hair, which she'd always kept long but tied in a ponytail, fanned around her head like a hellish halo. She was Bella and she was terrifying to behold.

Raul felt every bit of strength bleed from his body.

Bella opened her mouth, but words didn't follow. She spread her arms, as if waiting for him to embrace her.

This couldn't be! It had to be a trick of the light. Or maybe whatever had been in the black pot had contained some hallucinogenic that got into Raul's lungs and now was messing with his brain.

The Children of Behemoth resumed their chant of, "See. See. See." Followed by, "*Ensensior, bakthud, egat, lanathem.*"

"I can't…I can't believe my eyes," he said dejectedly. He wanted to collapse into a pile of nothing.

"*Raul.*"

"Dear God, no!"

Bella's voice sounded as if it were made of static and the crackling of a roaring fire.

"*Burning feels so wonderful.*"

"Please. Stop! Stop!"

"*Burn with me. Forever.*"

Bella smiled as she beckoned him.

"What did you do? What did you do?"

Bella's smile widened and widened until the corners of her mouth went to the top of her fiery skull.

Raul stared at the monstrosity and was gripped by a primal fear that threatened to shatter him into billions of particles.

Her hand reached out of the circle, coming for him. Raul tried to squirm out of the red man's iron grasp. She was going to set him on fire, burn him alive just as they'd done to Bill. Only *her* flame came from the bowels of hell where she lived and belonged. "Noooooo!"

It was real.

All of it.

His wife had led this cult in league with the Devil, and the Devil was real. His dead wife lashed out and laid her burning palm on the pentagram carved into his chest. Raul expected to be wrapped in flames, the hand melting through his chest, not stopping until his heart was roasted.

But her touch was like ice. A chill mushroomed from his heart to his extremities. Raul started to convulse. By the look on Bella's flickering face, his agony pleased her very much. A level of pain he didn't know could exist went deep into his marrow. It felt as if he were being frozen from the inside out, and when it was complete, his bones would pop and break, bursting from his flesh like tiny erupting volcanoes.

An animal growl ripped through his throat as he shook uncontrollably under his evil wife's baleful gaze.

"You can make it stop."

Raul barely registered the old woman's words.

"Look down. Your salvation is at your feet."

It was hard to focus as he spasmed uncontrollably. Raul shakily dipped his head and saw a bone-white skull with two great curving horns resting on the ground. The ram's skull leered at him with its black, empty eye sockets.

"Impale yourself on its horns," the old woman whispered in his ear. Her voice echoed in his head, rising above the wailing of agony. "Only Behemoth is real. Be his vessel."

The chanting around him grew louder. The red man let Raul go. He sank to the ground as if he were made of soft rubber. Barely able to hold himself up off the ground with his arms, Raul loomed over the ram's skull. The horns were thicker than his forearm. Their tips were sharp and jagged, perfect for puncturing and tearing. He was frightfully aware that if he didn't find the strength to back away, gravity alone would drive him into one of the horns.

"Fuck your vessel." He spat a thick wad of blood on the skull.

"*You belong with me,*" Bella intoned from deep in the fiery pentagram.

He lifted his head to look at her shimmering image. "I belong with Lizzy and Abel. Not you. Never you."

Her face pinched and a lick of flame leaped from the circle and singed off most of the hair on the side of his head. He clapped his hand over his burned ear, the fresh jolt of pain animating his body enough to jump away from the ram's skull.

"*Come to me, Raul. Now!*"

Raul knelt on the hard earth, clasped his hands together, and did what used to come so naturally, what had been so difficult to deny, no matter what he'd been telling himself.

He prayed.

He spoke the Lord's Prayer aloud. His voice building in strength with each repetition. He shouted, "For thine is the kingdom, and the power, and the glory. Amen!"

The Children of Behemoth whipped into a frenzy, shouting, "Hail Behemoth!" louder and louder, drowning him out. They then also broke into the Lord's Prayer, only saying it backward.

"*Ever and ever for, glory and the, power and the, kingdom the is thine for.*"

No matter. They couldn't come between him and the Lord he had turned away from. He trusted that God would take him back, forgive him his transgressions, his loss of faith. If he was going to die here at the hands of a demon, or worse, he wanted God to save his soul from the place of torment and madness his wife existed within. And, if he was deemed worthy, reunite him with the souls of his children.

"Please forgive me, Father! For I have sinned! Mother Mary, pray for me. Pray for my children who were taken by these monsters. Hail Mary, full of grace, the Lord is with thee. Blessed art thou among women, and blessed is the fruit of your womb, Jesus!"

"*Shut your fucking mouth!*" Bella roared.

A lightning bolt of flame struck his face. His lips were seared. The smell of roasted flesh just under his nose made him gag. His teeth felt too hot for his gums. Any second now, they would drip from their sockets as his gums melted.

Bella turned to the red man. "*Bring them!*"

He clomped off in his clumsy boots, then bent down to pick up something in a cloth sack outside the ring of fire, beyond the reach of its light. When he came back, he held Clover and Henry in his hand, their long stuffed arms and legs dangling.

"*There*," Bella said. Her blazing finger pointed to a spot on the ground beside Raul. The red man, flashing a look of evil delight at Raul, dropped the stuffed sloths unceremoniously onto the grass. He lifted his leg and stepped on them for good measure, grinding them into the earth as if he were putting out a cigarette. Raul lunged for him but was easily kicked back.

"Don't you dare touch them. Don't you dare!"

"*Or what?*" Bella said. "*You couldn't keep your children safe. What makes you think you can even take care of a couple of worthless toys?*"

Raul attempted to grab the sloths but Bella, the demon bitch, was far quicker. With a flick of her hand, a beam of blue fiery light reduced the stuffed animals to cinders.

"You bitch!" Raul wailed.

Bella reared her head back and laughed. The Children of Behemoth, gutless sycophants all, roared with laughter, anxious to please their resurrected leader.

Tendrils of smoke wafted from the ground. All that was left were the charred glass eyes.

He recited the Lord's Prayer and the Hail Mary over and over despite the agony and stench. The words came out near-incomprehensible as he barely took a breath between each prayer. What mattered was his intention, and his absolute conviction that good and evil, God and the Devil, did exist.

For a moment in his prayers, he wondered if this was God's punishment for Raul's turning his back on him. Even now, his faith was a false thing. Now that he had seen proof of the everlasting evil, he no longer needed faith to believe. Again, he had failed, embodying man's impulse to glean more from the bad than the good. What worse way to fully embrace God than by knowing there was a Devil?

No matter. Prayer was all he had now. He was wounded, bound, burned, and outnumbered.

No matter what they did to him, he would not take his life for them. For Bella. If this was just the beginning of the agonies he would have to endure, so be it. It wouldn't last forever. At one point, all of his human suffering would end.

"Lizzy. Abel." He sobbed.

"*Nothing but dead pawns,*" Bella said to him.

Black, terrible anger flared within Raul. He glared at the fiery demon that had pretended to be his wife. If she weren't already dead, he would have jumped into the flames to kill her, extinguish her forever.

"*You should have heard their pathetic cries. Mewling like worthless cats. Like the worthless sacks of disappointment that slithered from between my legs. They deserved to die.*"

"Fuck you, you monster!"

Raul trembled with rage.

"*You did. Many times. And you loved it.*"

Raul grabbed the ram's skull and threw it into the fire, into the center of Bella's shimmering form. The fire that was her body flashed a blinding yellow. The skull was propelled back at Raul. He spun away, the tip of a horn grazing his throat.

It hit the ground and rolled under its own power until it was once again in front of Raul.

"Punish him!" the old woman shouted.

The cultists echoed her words.

The red man stepped away and returned carrying a long, thick whip. He seized the back of Raul's shirt and ripped it down the middle. When Raul tried to turn around, a beefy backhand caromed off his cheek. Raul ended up on his hands and knees, hovering over the ram's skull, blood pouring from his mouth.

The first kiss of the whip on his bare back nearly dropped him on top of the horns. He tried to sweep the skull away, but it wouldn't move. It felt as if it had been screwed into the ground.

"Again!" the old woman roared.

"*Again!*" Bella shouted gleefully.

"Again!" the Children of Behemoth bellowed.

The second blow landed on the same spot as the first. Raul thought he was going to pass out. He felt his skin split and wouldn't be surprised if the back of his ribs were exposed to the night air.

"Please, God, help me!"

Bella mocked him. "*Too late to cry for Daddy! He gave up listening to you.*"

"Our Father, who art in heaven!"

Crack!

"Hallowed be thy name!"

Crack!

"Thy...thy kingdom come...thy...."

Crack!

"Thy...thy."

Crack!

He was faltering, sinking toward the horns.

The red man paused in his flagellation and yanked Raul by the hair, lifting him up.

Bella said, "*Do you wish to stop your torment?*"

He didn't have the breath to answer her. He felt his blood running down the sides of his body.

"*Throw yourself on the skull, Raul! Throw yourself now!*"

Raul mustered what little strength he had to mutter, "No."

"Continue!" the old woman yelled.

Bella writhed in the pentagram of flame, watching Raul and slipping her hand between her legs. "*Your suffering is the sweetest nectar. It only makes Behemoth stronger. Pray, little man. Pray and die knowing your worthless god has abandoned you.*"

He turned his head just enough to see the red man rearing back for another lashing.

A high, warbling screech sounded to Raul's right. He saw a flash of something moving quickly across the grass.

"Gaaahhh!"

The red man dropped the whip. The handle landed on the back of Raul's leg. Raul spun around and saw the Satanic cosplayer was struggling to remove something from his face. As the red man flailed and staggered toward the burning pentagram, Raul saw a massive ball of fur, most of it sticky with blood.

Bruiser!

The coon cat clawed at the red man's eye, its back legs scraping at the man's red-painted chest, carving ragged gashes everywhere they touched.

"Help him!" the old woman shouted.

Several robed people ran to pull Bruiser from the red man's face.

A shot rang out and one of them grabbed their side and collapsed.

Raul whipped his head around and couldn't believe what he saw.

Felix walked unsteadily toward them. His face was covered in blood, looking like a true demon. He pulled the trigger again, dropping another cultist. Their eyes met and Felix actually smiled.

"I got this!"

Raul didn't share his confidence, but he was overjoyed that his friend was still alive and doing his best to take out the Children of Behemoth.

"*Noooo!*" Bella yowled. "*Kill him!*"

The Children of Behemoth ran to Felix. He kept coming, picking them off as fast as he could, but it wouldn't be enough.

Bruiser squealed as he clung to the red man. Raul forced himself to get up. He threw himself at the red man's legs, wrapping his arms around his thighs. The red man fell forward. Bruiser leaped off his face a second before he crashed right into the circle of fire.

Raul jumped to his feet, and stomped on the small of the red man's back, ensuring he couldn't extricate himself from the flames. His body went up like kindling. Raul backpedaled to avoid being set ablaze as well.

Whatever paint the twisted man had used must have been highly flammable. Raul watched with pleasure as the red man rolled farther into the flame in a mad attempt to get away. When he landed at Bella's feet, he burned blue, his body reducing to ash in seconds.

Bella glared at Bruiser as he sat and watched the spectacle, his bushy tail flicking with agitation.

"*You!*"

Raul threw himself onto the cat and used his momentum to roll them away. A bolt of flame scorched the ground where the cat had been. He and the cat exchanged a look as Bruiser untangled himself from Raul's grasp. "Thank you," Raul said.

The cat looked at him and Raul saw something in his eyes that sent a chill down his spine. It was almost as if the feline was imbued with a humanness that defied logic and nature.

Bruiser set off after the cultists who were attacking Felix.

"*Muere, malditos monstrous!*" Felix howled. Two more robed people dropped. Several stopped or ran in other directions.

His gun clicked and the remaining three attackers jumped him.

Raul ran to him, though he had no idea how he could even stand at this point. Bruiser was ahead of him, latching on to a robe. He pulled the hood back, revealing a shock of blond hair. It was a woman. If Raul had seen her on the street, he would have thought she was just another soccer mom going about her daily to-do list. She swung at Bruiser and missed. When she saw Raul, she screeched, "Why couldn't you just kill yourself?"

He shut her up with an elbow under her jaw. Her eyes rolled up and she went slack.

Felix used the butt of the pistol to pound on the side of a person's head. Raul reached down to pull the person off. The hood came off and Raul staggered.

"Eduardo?"

Bella's father turned back and snarled at Felix. "You worthless piece of shit!" He left Felix to tackle Raul. Raul hit the ground hard. The wind was knocked out of him. Eduardo had always been stronger than him. After all he'd been through, Raul was no match for him now.

Felix grunted.

"You got him?" Eduardo said.

"Yeah. He's out," a man answered.

"Good. Let's get this over with."

Raul saw Bruiser running away into the tall grass while Eduardo dragged him back to the pentagram.

CHAPTER FORTY

Raul was dropped between two dead Children of Behemoth like a sack of garbage. Some of the fleeing cultists had returned. They no longer bothered to raise their hoods. They were men and woman of all different races and ages. Some look frightened, especially when they saw their fallen members. Others had the glazed expression of someone in a trance, which is how Raul assumed they lived most of their pathetic lives.

Felix was dragged and left next to him. The wound in his skull from earlier was bad. Raul had no idea how Felix had managed to get up and fight back as well as he had. He touched the side of his neck and was relieved to feel a pulse.

"Let me kill him," Eduardo said.

The man Raul had considered a father looked down at him with pure hatred in his eyes. Raul was past wondering how Eduardo could have been mixed up in the madness. This night had shown him that nothing and no one was as they appeared. Not even himself.

The old woman shook her head.

"Behemoth demands that the priest do it himself."

"He's too much of a coward."

"He's human, and he can and will be broken. There's no one left to save him now."

"*Bring him to me!*" Bella shouted.

Eduardo roughly grabbed him and pulled him back to the pentagram and waiting ram's skull.

"Why?" Raul sputtered, looking back at his father-in-law.

"Because my daughter was chosen that day. She wasn't lost in those woods. She was *found*. Satan walks the earth and sows his seeds. Bella was young and fertile and ripe for him. He gave her a gift, and she shared it with me. The fire of her newfound life in Satan cleansed me! He has given her power to change the world."

Raul's head swam.

"You've known all along. You allowed Bella to murder your grandchildren."

"It was all part of a greater plan. You didn't meet her by chance years ago. She chose you. For that, you should thank her. Bella came back from those woods with a power you can't begin to imagine. For those she allowed to see it, our lives were changed forever. We bowed before her. To Satan. For decades we've waited. And in turn grown stronger. While you grew fragile. Soft. Bound to the weakness that love and compassion bring. Your fixation on the children only demonstrates your decrepitude in the face of the almighty."

Raul trembled inside. He wanted to gouge Eduardo's eyes out. Piss in the wounds. Set fire to his body and listen to his agonized cries.

"Where's Mom?"

Raul wondered if Valentina was one of the faceless robed corpses in the yard.

Eduardo scowled. "That dried-up old bitch isn't worthy to receive Behemoth."

Sighing heavily, Raul whispered, "Thank God." At least there was someone pure in Bella's family, someone who had not been masquerading all these years. He hoped she was still alive but had severe doubts. This was an endgame and it appeared Valentina was a playing piece that was no longer needed.

"Fuck your god," Eduardo spat. "You're going to kill yourself now, or I'm going to throw your friend to Bella."

They had demonstrated how easy it was to murder those closest to Raul. Bill's corpse still gave off wisps of smoke.

Felix murmured something unintelligible. One eye opened. It rolled around for a moment and then settled on Raul. "You okay, *abuelo*?"

"Not really?"

"Yeah. Me neither." Felix's eye closed and he was out again.

Raul stared down at the ram's skull.

"*He'll burn so well,*" Bella said, her cobalt eyes fixed on Felix.

Could Raul be responsible for another death?

But if he did as Bella wanted, what would become of so many

others with Behemoth called from the depths of hell? How many more lives would that cost?

As much as it pained his soul to say it, Raul looked to Eduardo and said, "Then take him."

That visibly jolted the man he'd called *Father.*

"He'll suffer like no man has ever suffered. Even your precious Jesus," Eduardo said.

"I'm not going to help you. If Behemoth, Satan, whatever you want to call him, is so strong, why need me?"

Eduardo spat in Raul's face.

Raul wiped it off, flicking the mucous into the flames. "Sounds like he's the weak one. Not me. You want to kill my friend? Do it. It won't make me change my mind."

Raul wondered if he'd carry his guilt into the afterlife. He looked at Felix and wanted to throw up.

"So be it," the old woman said. She nodded at Felix's prone form. Eduardo recovered and grabbed the collar of Felix's leather jacket, walking backward as he dragged him to the fire. Bella's flames pulsed brighter and brighter, anxious for the offering.

"Please God, take his soul now," Raul pleaded.

"Feed him to her!" the old woman bellowed.

Eduardo got his hands around Felix's waist and lifted him up. Felix's eyes opened, his gaze unfocused.

"Give him to me!"

Bella reached out with blazing hands.

I can't, Raul thought.

He sprang up and raced toward Eduardo and Felix. Squaring his shoulder, he barreled into Eduardo, catching him in the center of his back. It was like battering into a brick wall. The older man's grip on Felix faltered. Felix's dead weight and gravity did the rest, breaking him free from the maniac.

Felix rolled toward the fire.

Raul jumped over Eduardo so he could grab on to Felix. His friend was only inches from the ring of fire. The flames acted as if they were sentient, reaching for him like hungry fingers.

His momentum was about to bring Felix's bearded face right into the maelstrom.

Raul took to the air, leaping over his spinning friend. He somehow managed to land in the miniscule strip of ground between Felix and the fiery circle. Felix hit into Raul's leg and stopped.

There was very little chance to celebrate. Raul felt his balance falter. His body was too weak to compensate and right himself.

Bella's face split in half with a growing, evil grin.

The old woman yowled behind him, "Prepare for Behemoth! The priest has thrown himself into the fire!"

Raul realized his mistake. Whatever the sick rules were with the Children of Behemoth, his sacrificing himself to save Felix must qualify as a sacrifice for Behemoth. He had no way of knowing what he was about to unleash upon the world, but he knew in his depths it would be awful beyond measure.

"*Yessss, Raul,*" Bella hissed hungrily.

The flames shot into the sky and the heat started to cook him before he'd even touched the fire. It felt as if a hot iron was being pressed into the side of his face. The ends of his shirtsleeves curled and smoked. The stench of his own searing flesh was overpowering.

He fell. Slowly, inexorably, into his demon wife's open, blazing arms. He looked up into the starry night and wondered what would become of the world in the ensuing moments, days, months, and years. Maybe they were right and he was weak. So weak, he'd damned the entire planet.

The flames licked his body as he plummeted into the pentagram. Bella howled with wicked delight.

A gleaming ball of white light burst into existence between him and Bella. Raul didn't even have time to pray before falling into the stoked flames of Bella's murderous lust.

He collapsed into the sparkling brilliance, ready to be reduced to ash. Raul closed his eyes and offered himself to God.

Bella screamed.

Raul landed on his back, smack in the middle of the pentagram. His eyes fluttered open. Bella hovered inches over his head.

How was he still alive?

Why wasn't he on fire?

The white light encapsulated him, protecting him from the flames.

The Children of Behemoth standing outside the pentagram cowered in terror.

Raul followed their horrified gaze.

Two pale figures stood between the Children of Behemoth and the pentagram.

Eduardo's eyes bulged and he shook, backing away. "No!"

"Hello," the tiny figures said in a singsong voice. "Grandfather."

They reached for his hands. The moment they touched him, Eduardo convulsed and was consumed by a shroud of undulating colors. It was like watching the Aurora Borealis descend on the man, wrapping him in their unearthly, wavering light. His face began to melt and his eyes bulged from their seeping sockets.

Eduardo turned toward the flaming effigy of his daughter. "Bella, save me!"

Just as quickly as the colors came, they disappeared.

And so had Eduardo.

When the figures turned around, Raul could see the beautiful faces of his son and daughter. They looked as alive as they had the day when he'd last hugged them before Bella had taken them to school.

Raul felt something swell within him, a rising pressure that he thought would force its way out through his pores.

"Lizzy? Abel?"

His children gave him a brief glance, their angelic faces stony with determination.

The Children of Behemoth panicked and started to run.

Lizzy and Abel sent forth jets of kaleidoscopic colors from their eyes, trapping each of the robed figures before they could get away. They disappeared into the maelstrom of light and color, leaving empty spaces in their wake. Their final, tormented cries echoed into the night.

A man and a woman holding hands ran for the house. The man clipped his hip on the picnic table and fell, dragging his wife with him. Lizzy made a quick turn toward them and shot twin beams of swirling light onto them. The woman shrieked as if her flesh were being penetrated by thousands of knives. The man made an inhuman howl. Seconds later, they were gone.

One by one they fell, any proof of their existence evaporating like smoke on a windy day.

Raul watched the eradication of the Children of Behemoth from within the safety of the protective bubble. He looked up and saw his demonic wife take in the destruction of her cult with shocked incomprehension.

Abel's deadly gaze found a man shedding his robe and trying to climb into a tree, as if he could hide until everything was over. The tree became a prismatic portal into another world. The man hollered, "Gaaaahhhhh, it hurts!" Man and tree blinked out of existence.

Silence settled onto the field.

The only one left was the old woman.

Raul watched his children slowly approach her. She shivered like a frightened puppy, imploring them to leave her alone. Any second now, Raul expected to see her devoured by their touch.

But they stopped several feet away from her.

The old woman looked to Bella. The fiery being that had been Raul's wife thrust her arms out and sent jagged ropes of fire at the children. Raul screamed, his voice trapped by the protective bubble.

The flames passed through Lizzy's and Abel's bodies and set fire to the grass.

They shook their heads at the abomination that was their mother.

"No," Lizzy said.

"More," Abel said.

Bruiser scampered between them and leaped for the old woman. She feebly raised her quivering arms. The cat knocked her to the ground. The old woman wailed and cried as Bruiser dug into the soft flesh of her throat. Blood and torn skin were tossed aside as Bruiser tunneled into her. Her legs and arms shook, and then went still. The cat sat on her chest, looked back at Raul and licked its red lips.

Lizzy and Abel approached the pentagram. Raul noticed the flames had started to die out.

"*Get away from me!*" Bella shouted.

"You're a," Abel said.

"Bad mommy," Lizzy finished.

Their tiny feet touched the burning circle and extinguished the flame. All that was left was Bella and the pentagram.

Bella unleashed a shriek that nearly shattered Raul's eardrums. He slapped his hands over his ears but it did no good. His heart fluttered in his chest, becoming unmoored by the high keening.

"*We killed you! How dare you disobey your mother! Get back from me!*"

Lizzy and Abel kept coming, unaffected by her cries.

The second they touched one of the points of the pentagram's star, the fire died.

"Come," Lizzy said.

"Here," Abel said.

Bella flinched but not enough to avoid their touch.

"*Noooooooooo!*"

Raul's children stepped around him and embraced their mother. The fire that comprised her body went from blue to orange, to white and violet and every color the human eye could perceive. She writhed like a bucking bull, desperate to break free of them. Lizzy and Abel locked hands and hugged her close, their bodies as immovable as twin mountains. Their heads tilted up and they watched Bella's desperation with cold indifference.

The temperature inside the bubble that had been shielding Raul rose. It felt as if the air were being sucked out. Every breath burned and hurt. He looked over at Felix. If the heat was getting too much for Raul, what was it doing to Felix, who lay unprotected?

His friend must have felt it before he had, because it appeared to have jolted him from unconsciousness. Felix was on his feet and staggering from the spectacle within the center of the doused pentagram. He made the sign of the cross, his eyes reflecting the light show.

Bella let out a cry that sent a colony of bats streaking across the sky, anxious to be away from the hellish bellowing. She cast her hate-filled eyes at Raul. "*Damn you and your fucking children!*"

Sweat dripped down Raul's face and stung his eyes. "We're not the ones that are damned," he replied.

He watched Bella shatter into what looked like a million twitching fireflies. They fluttered out of Lizzy and Abel's embrace for just a moment, and then winked out of existence.

And so did the bubble that had protected Raul. He took a desperate breath of air, laced with burned grass and blood.

Lizzy and Abel released their hold on one another and turned to Raul. Standing before him were his babies as they had been before their own mother had betrayed them all.

Raul wept. "I've missed you."

"We love you, Daddy," Abel said.

"We always will," Lizzy said.

He rolled to his hands and knees, crawling toward them. All he wanted to do was hold them in his arms and never let go.

"I'm so sorry I wasn't there to protect you."

"We're happy," Lizzy said. He saw the tiny freckles on the bridge of her nose. He remembered kissing them when he tucked her in at night.

"It's not your fault," Abel said. He smiled and Raul felt an overpowering surge of love that lifted him to his feet.

Bruiser, finished with the old woman, bounced to Lizzy and Abel. The coon cat sat between them, its tail swishing back and forth.

Tears blurred Raul's vision. When he wiped them away, Bruiser had disappeared.

Instead, standing over his children, was his Aunt Ida.

"Ida?"

"Someone had to keep an eye on you. You always were one for trouble." She winked at him and patted the tops of his children's heads. "I'd stay, but since I can't enjoy a beer anymore, what's the point? You take care of yourself. And my pigs."

Ida stepped back into the darkness and dissolved.

Raul staggered.

His children rushed forward. He felt the weight of them press against his body and he put his arms around them, sobbing uncontrollably. He kissed the tops of their heads.

"I love you. I love you. I've been so lonely without you."

Lizzy looked up at him. "We'll always be with you, Daddy."

Abel said, "Always."

Lizzy's spirit walked to a pile of ash, bent, and lay her hands atop it. "Clover. Henry."

The ashes began to swirl under her tiny hands. Her eyes glowed as she watched the charred remains of Henry and Clover take shape. It didn't take long until they were once again a pair of stuffed sloth toys, their marble eyes reflecting Lizzy's brilliance.

"How did you do that?" Raul asked.

Lizzy smiled. "We can't take them."

"With us," Abel finished. They looked to Raul. "You keep."

"Them," Lizzy said. "We have to go now."

Raul's precious children walked away from him, to where Ida had disappeared.

"Wait!"

Lizzy and Abel turned around.

"Take me with you. Please. I can't go on without you."

Lizzy smiled. "You will. And we'll be together. You'll see."

He watched his children walk away. They stopped before Bill's crucified body and touched it. He was encased in white sparks. An instant later, he was gone. Raul knew Bill was in a far better place, back with his wife, his limp long forgotten.

No, no, no, no! Even a week was an eternity to Raul. He couldn't lose his children a second time.

Raul ran to Felix and grabbed the pistol that was stuffed in his waistband. He cocked the hammer and put the gun to the side of his head.

"What the fuck are you doing, man?" Felix snapped. He reached out for the gun but Raul easily stepped away.

Abel and Lizzy stopped, turned, and stared at their father.

"Take me with you," Raul said. "I can't live without you."

"You," Abel said.

"Can," Lizzy said.

Raul shook his head, keeping a step from Felix, who was too weak to catch him. "No. I don't *want* to live without you. Not anymore."

His children moved toward him. "Not that way," Lizzy said.

"You could never see us," Abel said.

"That way," Lizzy said.

Raul's legs turned to stone.

Of course. How could he think suicide was the right thing to do when he'd just fought Bella's twisted plan from the depths of hell to do the very same thing?

Black despair flowed through his veins. There was no way he could continue on like this. How much suffering could one man endure?

Felix slapped a hand on his shoulder and plucked the gun from his hand. "Listen to them, Raul."

Raul looked into Lizzy's and Abel's eyes.

Every minute he was separated from that sight would be an eternity.

"Kill me," he said to Felix.

"What? Fuck. No."

"Please. I'm already dead. More dead than you can imagine. Don't let them leave without me."

Felix backed away. "You're not thinking straight. You can't ask me to do that. It's wrong and it isn't fair."

Raul grabbed Felix by the collar of his jacket. "You came here to help me. Right?"

"Helping you isn't killing you, *abuelo*. It's the fucking exact opposite."

Raul flicked a glance at his children. They hadn't moved, hadn't disappeared. He felt time racing by.

"I belong with them," he said. "I have nothing here."

Felix scratched at his beard. His fingers came away wet with blood. They stared at one another for a long while. Raul thought he saw Felix's resolve begin to soften. Felix broke first and addressed Lizzy and Abel. "I'll go to hell for this. Tell him."

"Not," Abel said.

"For this," Lizzy said.

Raul sank to his knees and clasped his hands together. "I'm begging you. Please, Felix."

Lizzy and Abel stepped closer to Raul.

Felix looked at the gun in his hands as if it had magically appeared in his grip. He took several deep breaths and tapped the gun against the side of his leg. "Of all the things you could have asked me. This sucks. You suck."

Raul smiled. "What do you always say?"

Felix shook his head. "I got this."

Raul nodded. "That's right. You always do."

Sirens sounded in the distance. Time had just about run out.

Felix sniffled. "I can't do this with you looking at me."

Raul closed his eyes and felt his spirits rise. "I understand." He turned around on his knees and opened his eyes so he could see Lizzy and Abel. "I love you."

The gun tapped the back of his head.

"Thank you, F—"

★ ★ ★

Felix roared when he pulled the trigger. Raul's head shot forward hard enough for his chin to bounce off his chest. Bits of skull and brain matter flew in the direction of his children. His body went limp as a wet dishrag and collapsed forward.

Hot tears stung his eyes. Felix wiped them with his jacket sleeve. He shoved the gun into his pocket. The heat from the barrel singed his belly.

What had he done?

The kids looked down at Raul without expression. Felix was afraid they would turn their eyes to him and he wouldn't like what he saw.

Fire engines blurted their horns, their sirens screeching like banshees.

Between the fire, gunshots, and screaming, it was a miracle they hadn't come sooner. Felix contemplated his next move. If he stayed, he was going to jail. Maybe that wasn't such a bad thing. He'd just murdered his friend. Even though Raul had pleaded for it, that didn't make it the right thing to do. Felix deserved prison.

"Thank you."

Raul, or the spirit of Raul, because his dead body was still facedown in the grass, held the hands of his children. Lizzy and Abel were smiling as they looked up at their father.

"Now go," Raul said. "They won't connect you to any of this."

Felix blinked back tears.

"Oh yeah? How do you know?"

Raul smiled. "I just do. And if a cat comes waltzing into your life, be nice to it."

Felix chuckled. "Nice to a cat? My ass."

Raul went to a knee to bring his children into a hug before they dissolved. "And please, take good care of them." The spirit of Felix's friend looked at the limp bodies of the stuffed sloths.

Felix saw strobing red lights in the front of the house.

He picked up Clover and Henry.

It was a long way back to the city and his Harley. Using Bill's car was out of the question now. He was beaten and bloody and exhausted beyond measure. How he was going to get out of this was anyone's guess.

Felix walked into the tall grass.

"You better be right, *abuelo*."

By the time the first responders made it to the yard, he was gone.

CHAPTER FORTY-ONE

Felix pulled up to the gas pump. His Harley's engine called everyone's attention to him. He got off and removed his helmet. The red bandana he wore on his forehead to hide the cross scar was damp with sweat.

As he got off the Harley, he stretched his back and stared at the blue, cloudless sky. It filled him with both joy and dread, knowing there was more up there than the eye could see. Poor, bedeviled Raul had proven that to him. When Felix had come to him, Raul had one step on insanity from his grief and the other on addiction. The combination would have been enough to make Raul see and hear the things he did. Anyone would crack under that pressure.

Now, having nothing but time to think about what had happened, Felix knew it was more than that. Yes, Raul had been haunted, but by more than the tortured memory of his family. More than the tricks and traps set by that crazed cult.

Ghosts were real. Lizzy and Abel had been in that house with him. And his aunt.

What vexed Felix the most was why they hadn't intervened earlier to save him. Maybe the ghost shows were right and there hadn't been enough energy to draw from at the time.

Or, perhaps it all needed to go down that way, as horribly as it did. He had come to believe that personal choice determined everything. There was no such thing as predetermined fate.

Bella had been corrupted as a child by a sinister force. But she had chosen to have her children murdered to appease the Devil. From what Felix had seen, the Devil could just as easily have taken the children himself.

So, Raul had had to suffer in ways no person should have to suffer, pushed to the brink to make his ultimate decision. The power within him had more to do than just being a priest who no longer believed.

The forces of good and evil, God and the Devil, required lowly humans to choose their destiny.

Which meant every living person had an incredible amount of power within them. The power to choose their eternity. Felix would take that over any superhero ability any day.

Now, he just had to hope that all his choices going forward had him going up instead of down. He'd seen what hell could be, and it gave him nightmares.

He'd started to pump the gas when an attractive blonde wearing short shorts and a tank top eyed his bike.

"Sweet," she said.

He gave her a nod and picked a bug out of his teeth.

She walked to the front of the Harley. "Oh, they're so cute." She lifted Clover's arms. The sloths were carefully strapped to the handlebars.

The blonde smiled at Felix and sucked on her bottom lip. "I love sloths. Can I have one?"

Felix topped off the tank and put the pump back on its cradle.

There was a time he'd let a woman like that have whatever she wanted. She was definitely the kind of girl who rarely heard the word no.

He got back onto his Harley and kicked it to life, turning the handlebars away from the hot chick.

He said, "Up yours," and headed back onto the highway.

Clover and Henry rode with him as they had the past year, the trio enjoying the open road and freedom.

FLAME TREE PRESS
FICTION WITHOUT FRONTIERS
Award-Winning Authors & Original Voices

Flame Tree Press is the trade fiction imprint of Flame Tree Publishing, focusing on excellent writing in horror and the supernatural, crime and mystery, science fiction and fantasy. Our aim is to explore beyond the boundaries of the everyday, with tales from both award-winning authors and original voices.

•

Other titles available by Hunter Shea:
Creature
Slash
Ghost Mine
Misfits

Other horror and suspense titles available include:
Snowball by Gregory Bastianelli
Thirteen Days by Sunset Beach by Ramsey Campbell
Think Yourself Lucky by Ramsey Campbell
The Hungry Moon by Ramsey Campbell
The Influence by Ramsey Campbell
The Wise Friend by Ramsey Campbell
Somebody's Voice by Ramsey Campbell
The Haunting of Henderson Close by Catherine Cavendish
The Garden of Bewitchment by Catherine Cavendish
The House by the Cemetery by John Everson
The Devil's Equinox by John Everson
Hellrider by JG Faherty
The Toy Thief by D.W. Gillespie
One By One by D.W. Gillespie
Black Wings by Megan Hart
The Playing Card Killer by Russell James
The Sorrows by Jonathan Janz
Will Haunt You by Brian Kirk
We Are Monsters by Brian Kirk
Hearthstone Cottage by Frazer Lee
Those Who Came Before by J.H. Moncrieff
Stoker's Wilde by Steven Hopstaken & Melissa Prusi

•

Join our mailing list for free short stories, new release details, news about our authors and special promotions:

flametreepress.com